MW01105844

The Battle for Harpatia

Book 1
Daniel Neves

To: Richard Blosser
Glad to have finally
met a kid my own age
to play with! Thx for
being a super cool boss and
good friend!   Enjoy

M.V.M. Mech vs. Magic Books

Copyright © 2010 by Daniel Neves
Edited by Nathan Janota

ISBN 978-0-9848055-0-1
LCCN: 201196042

Your Friend and Servant!
Daniel Neves

Dedication:

Thank you to my wife Kelly and two kids Alex and Troy, without you there would be no M.V.M. Thank you Al Neves for being the best Dad a guy could ever wish for. Thank you to my mother, Diane Howard for all of your help and support through this process, I love you all very much.

Acknowledgements

Thank you to Josef Faber at nun2small.ca for the awesome web design and great friendship, Joe you are awesome. Thank you to Concrete Shooter A.K.A. Paul Venables for being a great friend and offering support where few else would. Special thanks to Fred Beasley for your awesome friendship, advice, and support. Thank you to Hunter Matlock for your true friendship.

I want to thank Nick and Naomi Boulland for being there creatively when no one else was. Thank you to all the people that supported me along the way, for real friends are hard to find. Now let's make history!

Introduction

"Bean me up Scotty" lol

A thin haze of blue vapor trailed King Leinad Seven of Harpatia as he teleported rapidly away from the massive steel lance that was about to impale him. As he reappeared behind the RS-777 mech, the tall King stared deeply at it. Leinad's bright turquoise eyes glowed as he examined this large humanoid robotic war machine that had just attacked him. The King unsheathed his golden broadsword and, in one fluid movement, slashed off its right leg. In the next instant, Leinad felt a sharp pain in his ribcage as he was pummeled from the side by another mech.

As he stumbled to the ground, Leinad saw an oversized sword blazing downwards toward his head. The impending blow was miraculously blocked by the fierce warrior Cassion, the King's best friend, and General of the Harpatian Elite Guard. Leinad watched as the slightly shorter Elven-Bracelian hybrid warrior parried away the mech's sword. The warrior reached out with his left hand and grasped the mech in a telekinetic hold; as though it were an extension of his arm, he slammed the mech into the nearby castle wall. The mech hit the nearly indestructible bluestone wall, and fell to the ground. Cassion quickly jumped on top of the downed war machine and thrust the blade of his magical Katana through the vulnerable chest plate of the mech, impaling the operator.

Leinad scrambled back to his feet and briefly studied the mech lying on the ground. It must have been eight feet tall and made from some nearly invincible metal. The mech was humanoid-shaped, with a stylish head piece. It was equipped with alien weapons Leinad had never before seen, and its hull glowed with a bright metallic silver hue.

"What *are* these things?" Leinad asked the sweating Cassion.

"They are a hostile abomination, and a threat to our people. We must destroy them all," shouted the warrior.

Although Leinad was sure he had never seen these mechs before, he could not help but feel a strong sense of familiarity with them. As the two friends rushed toward the next group of RS-777s, Leinad severed the machine gun turret off the first mech he encountered, and followed the attack with a blast of level ten ice magic, which froze the mech in place. Leinad then shattered the frozen war machine into chilled dust with a combat arts-aided kick to its chest.

Leinad landed, glancing up at a fierce stream of high-caliber machine gun fire headed straight for him. He closed his eyes and instantly teleported, reappearing behind the mech. He then extended his left arm, as a mastery level blast of lightning magic streamed out from his hand and poured into the mech. A shower of sparks burst from the mech as it collapsed. Cassion quickly impaled the operator within the downed machine.

With the use of their jet packs, a small group of ten mechs then flew into the battle, quickly surrounding Leinad and Cassion.

"*I must summon Monte*," King Leinad Seven thought, as he quickly sheathed his sword and closed his eyes.

Leinad folded his hands and called out to his friend Monte telekinetically. Almost instantaneously, an impossibly large crimson colored dragon appeared in the skies above. The massive dragon swooped down to the ground, his sweeping long tail sending the mechs flying up into the air. Leinad and Cassion quickly mounted the dragon Monte, climbing high into the sky, before stalling and sailing back down toward the mechs. The crimson beast unleashed a blast of fire upon the mechs on the ground… The mechs began to glow red hot as they found themselves engulfed in the dragon's breath. Monte continued to blast the mechs until they were rendered inoperable.

Leinad and Cassion flew Monte away from the battlefield. While heading toward Dakineah, they noticed two missiles advancing rapidly for them. The missiles had been launched from a capital size air ship, and it was most certainly not a Harpatian craft. Before they had time to fully assess the situation, one missile struck Monte on his right flank and ricocheted off the dragon's crimson scales. The impact launched Leinad off the dragon, and he began to tumble into the murky darkness below. Leinad felt himself losing his grip on consciousness as he plummeted toward the ground, but he quickly regained his senses. When he was nearly to the treetops, he teleported, a cloud of vapor the only mark of his descent. If he had not teleported at just that moment, the King of Harpatia would surely have perished.

When he reappeared safely on the forest floor, Leinad was confused. He had to return to Dakineah and warn his people. However, the colossal warship that had fired upon him moments earlier was now hovering just above him. Hundreds of small portholes opened on the ship's hull, and just as many missiles were launched, likely at him. Leinad prepared to meet his death as the missiles grew closer. The King's bright blonde hair stood on edge as he braced for impact...

* * *

King Leinad Seven awoke in a cold sweat. To his surprise, he was lying in his own bed, somewhere deep within the Castle Dakineah. He rose quickly, stumbling over to his mirror, where he saw the sweat dripping down his face like a waterfall. Leinad wondered if what he had just experienced was a nightmare, or perhaps a vision from the Life Source. He was fairly certain that it had been a vision, but he would not... no, could not... mention this to anyone yet. The King did not want to make such absurd claims that an alien species, with never before seen technology, was coming to invade Harpatia. He vowed to inform his people and make his armies ready if the visions appeared again.

* * *

King Leinad Seven is the King of Harpatia, and a Level 10 Wizard and dragon tamer. His is the power to manipulate all the elements: Earth, wind, water, and fire. He also possesses telekinetic capabilities. Of Elvin descent, he stands about 6ft 5in tall with a muscular build. He has blond hair and blue/green eyes, and would like to think of himself as handsome.

Quite large by Earth standards, Harpatia is separated into different territories. Dakineah, the capital territory, and a land of castles and villages, is Leinad's home country. The civilization is very much unlike that of Earth. Harpatia possesses a mystical source of power known as the Life Source. Through this Life Source the Harpatian's are able to supply power to their planet wirelessly through the use of magic. It is believed that some Harpatians, such as Leinad, have a natural link to the Life Source that enables them to use their magic.

Thousands of wizards and their apprentices live in Harpatia. Of those thousands, only three possess level ten abilities: Leinad; his brother Gressit (who has not yet mastered them, but has the potential), and their childhood friend, The Warrior Cassion, who uses his abilities in hand-to-hand combat. Gressit is the high Chieftain of the Harpatian Armies, and King Leinad's General and best friend.

The intelligent beings of Harpatia include Elves, Bracelians (similar to humans), Dragons (that can speak), and Nowries (an insanely strong and highly intelligent ogre-like creature).

Dakineah, a lush region, is full of waterfalls, canyons, and untold beauty, and is the ancient home of the royal Elven families. The other territories include Nowah, home to the Nowries, and Aurora, the dragon territory, a mountainous area with a great many caves. Once trained, these Auroran dragons become the elite protectors of Harpatia. Harpatia also has the Blue Forest territory, which is largely populated with Bracelians, a peaceful people who work in various trades: carpentry, source flow energy for homes, general labor, and other less significant trades. Very few Bracelians are wizards. For some mysterious reason, the use of magic does not interest them; therefore, most of them have never tried to tap into the Life Source.

Harpatia has been a planet at peace for several hundred years. The Wars of Segregation are over, and for the most part they all have lived together in peace and harmony. That is, they did until the humans from Earth arrived.

Chapter 1: The End of an Era

It is the year 3000. Earth as we know it no longer exists. Worldwide anarchy has arisen. America has maintained a semblance of law and order, but it is nowhere near where it needs to be to maintain a peaceful, civilized society.

In the year 2080, the nations of the world exhausted the supplies of petroleum; and overnight, panic set in. Gas prices soared, and electric bills quadrupled. Only a few decades of reserve resources remained, if that. During this volatile period, the U.S. was the dominant world power. This power was due to their M.V.F., a mechanized robotic vehicle force composed of vehicles called mechs. Twenty different models of these mechs were manufactured.

The most common, the RS -777, is a robotic suit which envelops the operator in a solid steel, platinum, and titanium exoskeleton. The robo-suit stands nearly fifteen feet tall and is the core for the design of all other mechs. The RS-777 is equipped with an M-100 Gatling gun mounted on each shoulder, and a rocket launcher on either the wrist or shoulder. The turret has been heavily modified to prevent both jamming and overheating. The RS-777 also has a jet pack capable of flying at speeds of over 500 MPH, and it can operate in the vacuum of space for only short periods of time before recharging.

The US government has devoted most of its time and resources to defending the nation from would-be invaders. It has also been forced into keeping the peace locally despite the increased crime rate that is the result of insane electricity prices and massive food shortages.

Meanwhile, in Egypt, archaeologist Kelly Styles is hard at work uncovering the meaning of the Hieroglyphics that she discovered with her team a few days ago.

"Hey Jake, I've got it!" Kelly shouted as she rocketed to her feet in excitement.

"Are you sure?" Jake questioned with a dubious glance.

"Of course I'm sure. I've been working on this for 72 hours. The code says there is an everlasting source of energy able to supply an entire galaxy with electric power—a self-sustaining Life Source that can be tapped into. According to these writings, there is a distant planet deep out in the cosmos, where this power source exists. There seems to be some sort of star map here that gives directions to this planet. It says you must travel through a worm hole, which will take you to a land of absolute mystery. The Hieroglyphics clearly state to use extreme caution, for this power that we seek is unpredictable; and very few know the inner workings of how to use it safely," Kelly whispered excitedly.

"We've got to reach the Pentagon," Jake said with a strong sense of urgency.

Jake Baker, a special liaison officer from the Department of Defense, was assigned to watch over this expedition and to keep an eye on Dr. Kelly Styles, if only to ensure that any findings remained classified. He had to ensure her safety, as well.

Within the bowels of the Pentagon, the atmosphere was among the commanders was electric. General Hezekai, along with the Joint Chiefs of Staff, assembled a meeting in the Pentagon conference room to discuss their options for the exploration and possible invasion of this previously unknown planet. The President had given full control of this expedition to the mysterious planet to General Ram Hezekai. Hezekai a 20-year veteran of the armed services with a flawless military record was known for his savage nature and brutal tactics. This assignment of power made many of the U.S. leaders fearful of the mission to come.

"I want to thank everyone for coming today," announced General Hezekai. "We need to assemble a task force for this mission to the unknown planet. We will need five scientists, a biologist, a few archaeologists, and an anthropologist. We will also need two capital ships capable of carrying a total of 2,000 people and 1,500 mechs. The capital ships must be outfitted with a full battle package before departure," explained the General.

A full battle package consisted of twenty or more fully automatic fission lasers, a wide range of missiles and bombs, and heavy caliber machine gun turrets. Within the huge ships were living quarters, exercise facilities, a restaurant, and charging bays for the mechs.

"We are going to need half of the M.V.F. fleet to ensure this mission's success, in the unlikely event we meet resistance," Hezekai stated curtly.

"Half the fleet?" asked Joint Chief Colonel Smith, incredulous at Hezekai's demands. "How can we give you half the fleet? That will leave us with a major disadvantage if China or Russia decide to attack us while you are gone."

Hezekai stood. "Don't worry, Colonel. Only those with the highest security clearance codes will know of this expedition. I am aware China is building its own mech force, but I highly doubt they will build up the nerve to invade any time soon."

"I hope you are right, Sir," Smith replied, in a half mocking tone.

"I hope *you* do not doubt *me*, Colonel." Hezekai glared at the Colonel with a fierce look that would have paralyzed most men.

"Moving on, we need 2,500 M.V.F. units— 1,500 of the RS-777 models which are best suited for ground and limited air combat should suffice. I also require 500 jetfighter mechs to retain air superiority should there be any air defenses in place on this alien planet. Intelligent life exists on this planet, and we don't know what their reaction will be once we have made contact," declared Hezekai.

"It sounds like you are preparing for war, General Hezekai," Smith stated bluntly.

"I am *always* prepared for war, Colonel. But if you are implying that I want to start one, then you are out of line." Hezekai paused, then continued. "Now, let's get back to business. In addition to the M.V.F, I will need 3,000 infantry and about thirty good officers to command them. The mission departs in two weeks, so you have exactly fourteen days to assemble this task force. I'll see you on the launching pad two weeks from today at 0500 hours. Do not let me down. This meeting is hereby concluded. You are all dismissed," ordered Hezekai.

"Yes, Sir," shouted the hundred or so on the task force committee.

Meanwhile, somewhere in Texas, Kelly Styles was finishing her packing while she waited for her assistant and private security liaison officer, Jake Baker. She and Jake were going to be on the top-secret mission to the mysterious planet. Kelly, a short young woman with a beautiful face, blond hair, blue eyes, and an attractive athletic build, was a welcome addition to the expedition.

When they arrived at the mission's launching pad, they were well received by General Hezekai. "Make yourselves at home. I will have my staff show you to your rooms," said Hezekai.

Kelly thought to herself, *what a fearsome looking man the General is,* and instinctively yet inexplicably felt sorry for him.

Hezekai was a tall, dark-skinned man with brown hair. He had a very large and muscular build, and he was dressed in his military blues, with more decorations for valor and military accomplishments than Kelly had ever seen. He had an intimidating scar that started at the corner of his right eye and continued down to his throat.

When Kelly and Jake arrived at their rooms, they parted ways. "I am always right across the hall if you need me," Jake said.

"Thanks, Jake. I'll buzz you on the two-way radio on channel five if I need you. I think I'm going to get some rest now," Kelly smiled.

When Kelly woke up a few hours later, she found a message in her government-issued laptop's email inbox. The message said take-off had been delayed a couple of hours, and her presence was required in meeting room A for a briefing. Kelly left her room to find Jake waiting for her in the hallway.

"Are you ready?" Jake said.

"Yes. Let's go," replied Kelly.

The pair made their way down the well-lit hallway of the Destroyer Class space ship until they reached an elevator. When the elevator chimed, a display lit up with the words "please slide identity card." Kelly swiped her card, and the elevator began a descent to floor 35. Kelly and Jake exited the elevator and followed the signs to meeting room A. The guard, dressed in a black M.V.F. uniform, checked their IDs and allowed them entry into the meeting room.

"Ah, welcome Miss Styles. Nice to see you again, you look lovely as always," remarked General Hezekai.

"Thank you sir, I try," Kelly replied, blushing.

"You do not have to call me "sir," young lady," smiled Hezekai. "The purpose of today's meeting is to merely give you a list of our expectations for you in this mission, and to answer all of your questions regarding the mission. I will start by saying that, since you were able to decode the star map and decipher the message, you are of great use to us as a linguist... and a mediator. I will rely on you to set up a peaceful contact with the leaders of this new world. I have assigned a member of the M.V.F. Elite Guard to protect you. You probably know this man as Jake. I know him as Lt. Colonel Baker. LTC Baker is ex-Special Forces, and a master operator of the RS-777 mech. He will be held personally responsible for your safety and your protection. His career depends on it, so I am certain he will do a great job," mocked Hezekai.

"Thank you, sir," Jake retorted defiantly.

"No problem. Now that we have gotten the formalities out of the way, do you have any questions for me or any of my staff?" asked Hezekai.

Kelly looked around the spacious, sparsely furnished meeting room. The titanium walls were made with blast doors at the entrance, designed to close in the event of an atmospheric leak. Two silver support pillars stood in the middle of the room, and in between them was a throne-like chair where Hezekai sat. The room was dimly lit in blue light, but it was sufficient to see everything in surprisingly clear detail. "How long will it take us to reach the planet once we enter the worm hole?" Kelly asked.

"Our quantum physicists estimate the trip will take about two weeks once we launch," Hezekai explained. "In the meantime, feel free to relax and enjoy all the amenities of the *Lancer I*. If you want to meet the ship's Captain, he will be in the dining hall tonight at 2000 hours," said Hezekai.

"Thank you General. I'll be sure to do that," said Kelly.

"If there are no further questions, you are both free to leave," remarked Hezekai.

Kelly and Jake proceeded to the recreation room, which was full of modern exercise equipment and TVs. About an hour into Kelly's invigorating workout, a message came over the communications speaker.

"All personnel: strap into the nearest takeoff safety seat. Launch will commence in five minutes," the voice announced.

Jake and Kelly strapped themselves into their safety restraint seats in the recreation room and stared out of the reinforced windows.

"Launch in five, four, three, two, and one. Blast off!" announced the Captain.

Chapter 2: Harpatia

It had been a typical day for King Leinad Seven, the most powerful wizard in all of Harpatia. Leinad woke up on Monday around sunrise. Feeling refreshed from a good night's sleep, Leinad made his way out of his royal chambers in the Castle Dakineah. The chambers were constructed from a blue steel known as Jezelite. This raw material was as strong as platinum, as light as graphite, and far superior to anything Earth had to offer. Looking in the mirror, the King studied his image. His statuesque height, combined with blonde hair and blue-green eyes, reflected back to him as a very handsome man. Yet Leinad remained unmarried. He claimed to be waiting for the chosen one, and that he would "know her when he saw her."

As he made his way to the royal dining hall, he was joined by his brother Gressit, and the warrior. Cassion was dropped off at the Castle Dakineah as a baby and was raised with Leinad and Gressit.

Gressit was a few years younger than his elder brother, and next in line for the throne should anything happen to Leinad. These three men were the very best of friends, and did almost everything together in this time of peace. Gressit was an apprentice dragon tamer and a level nine water and fire magic user, with some telekinetic abilities. The full scope of Gressit's abilities was undetermined and had yet to be tested in battle.

The Warrior Cassion had been tested his whole life, as he was a member of the Harpatian Elite Guard. He carried a ten-foot Katana-like blade, with a beyond surgical, razor-sharp edge. No one knows where he had obtained his weapon, but he had possessed it for many years now. When people asked him about his blade, he just told them he had found it. The Katana was light blue, indicating some Jezelite properties. It can alter size and shape upon being willed to do so, and is held at his side by a magic spell of some kind. He can leave his weapon miles away, and it will come to him instantly upon being summoned. Cassion has very strong telekinetic magic and lightning reflexes which make him Harpatia's most fearsome warrior. The Warrior Cassion possesses level ten combat arts.

As they were eating breakfast, Leinad suggested, "Let us go practice our magic and battle techniques today after breakfast."

"Ok. Sounds like fun, brother," Gressit replied.

"Let us do it, my King. I promise I will go easy on you," mocked Cassion.

"I hear you, my good friend. And I will try not to kill you," Leinad bantered playfully.

When they were done eating, they sauntered over to the training area, a lush field of grass that stretches for miles. The walk to the fields was rather lengthy for the three friends, but they enjoyed the exercise. When they arrived at the fields, they had their servants set up various archery and magic targets, as well as obstacles, for them. The first target stood about 60 feet tall, a stone slab in the form of a huge warrior. The second target was about 100 feet long and was shaped in the form of a dragon. The attendants also placed an obstacle similar to a huge building, made from Jezelite, in their way. Hundreds of humanoid dummies filled the building and the fields.

As they entered the fields, the Warrior Cassion said, "I am going to practice on the stone warrior with my sword today."

Gressit replied, "That's good. I think I will practice my ice magic on the dragon statue."

"And I will practice with all of my magic on the rest of the obstacles on the field," said Leinad.

The three men split their separate ways. Cassion dashed towards the oversized stone warrior with a magical burst of speed and leaped about fifty feet into the air. As he approached the neck of the target, he slashed at it using a technique that Leinad had taught him. He then landed on the chest of the stone warrior, before flipping backwards to the ground, thus falling with the decapitated head of the statue. Once on the ground, Cassion thrust his magic katana into the soft ground and sprinted to the rear of the next statue.

"Come to me," Cassion said as he summoned the sword with his magic. Instantly, the sword sprang from the ground and flew cleanly through the statue, severing it into pieces as it came to a rest at Cassion's side. The only way Cassion was able to wield this sword was through an ancient spell. Held at his hip as if sheathed by magic, the sword could only be moved by Cassion's own hand. It followed his every command.

"Very impressive, Cassion," commented the approaching Gressit.

"Thanks," replied Cassion, sweat dotting his handsome brow.

"Watch this, my friend. I will not disappoint you," Gressit exclaimed.

It was now Gressit's turn to train. Knowing that his friend and his brother were watching him closely, he prepared himself mentally. Intent to put on a show, Gressit approached the dragon statue, and with his hands summoned up a massive blast of ice magic. The ice beams shot towards the dragon, instantly sheathing it in a cover of ice. Gressit then soared into the air and summoned a cushion of wind magic, which enabled him to hover nearly motionless. He summoned a fiery staff and hurled it into the dragon target, decimating its tail into pieces. Using telekinesis, Gressit then hurled a cloud of large stones at what remained of the target. Upon impact, the stones crushed the dragon into thousands of pieces. With the sound of thunder, the dragon settled into dust.

"Your sword trick is nothing compared to my ice magic," Gressit boasted to Cassion.

"If you thought that was impressive, then you are going to *love* this," Leinad smirked as he summoned up a blast of level ten ice magic which instantly froze the multitude of targets on the field. Bolts of lightning streamed through his hands, obliterating the frozen targets upon impact. King Leinad rose through the air using telekinetic and wind magic simultaneously. He burst through the door of one of the large buildings on the field, and brought out his dual-bladed staff, pointing it at the humanoid targets inside. Lightning, fire, and ice leapt from his sword. He dashed forward, slicing the statues into pieces with the dual blade of his magical staff. Leinad dropped down to the base of the building and summoned his dragon, Monte, using his manifest magic. The dragon dove from the sky with a clap of thunder, took in a deep breath and exhaled, instantly engulfing the building in flames. He then whipped his giant tail into the burning building's foundation, and it settled to the ground with a reaming crash.

Monte was the oldest and best trained of the entire dragon legion, and he had been the King's personal guard since Leinad was born. The dragon's skin was scaled with unknown biological armor that seemed virtually impenetrable. The only known weak spot on the dragon was near the throat and eyes. The magic of the dragon and that of Leinad had been linked by the Council of the Elders at the time the King was born through an ancient dragon-taming spell. The Council of the Elders was a secret society of wizards and mages who, throughout the years, served in an advisory role for the royal family. Very little is known about the council- their very existence is unknown to the civilizations of Harpatia.

The territory of Aurora boasts nearly 1,000 fully mature dragons. The exact population of their offspring is unknown. The dragons feed only once per year, as their lives are largely sustained through the Life Source. The actual location of the mysterious Life Source was known only by King Leinad Seven, and a select few of his most trusted friends. They visited the Life Source periodically to derive knowledge from it, and communicate telepathically with it.

"Good job, Monte. Thank you for your assistance with this training session. You may return home now. I will summon you when I need you again," said Leinad proudly.

"Yes my master," replied Monte. The dragon Monte rose majestically into the air, and, within a minute, the handsome crimson dragon vanished.

After the morning's battle practice, Leinad, Cassion, and Gressit traveled to the Blue Forest territory. They had a few important business matters which they needed to attend to there. Although it would take a couple of hours to walk, and though they could teleport or fly to the Blue Forest, they enjoyed the exercise and social conversation they shared during these small journeys.

"I am glad we decided to walk to the Blue Forest today," said King Leinad. "I grow weary of teleportation and dragon flight."

"Yeah, you are right. It is always good to stay in shape," said Cassion.

"I much prefer to fly," countered Gressit, with a shrug.

Upon their arrival to the Blue Forest territory later that day, they were greeted by Santei, the King of the Blue Forest people, and a master archer.

The Blue Forest people were the predominant archers of their time. The skills of archery were passed down from one generation to the next. The Blue Forest was appropriately named- intense light and dark blue multi-hued foliage covered the landscape. It was a breathtaking landscape with waterfalls, ponds, and lush blue ferns everywhere. Leinad considered the Blue Forest to be his personal paradise.

"What brings you to the Blue Forest today, my King?" asked the polite Santei.

"The Life Source has been sending me some very disturbing signals lately. I can't quite decipher their exact meaning yet, but I sense danger, somehow. I will be visiting the Life Source later on today, but I wanted to inform you of these feelings so that you can alert your people to the possible danger," whispered Leinad. His voice rose to normal volume. "Other than that, we are just taking a stroll and enjoying the landscape today, taking in all of its beauty."

"Very well, my King. If there is anything you need, please let me know. I will have my servants on call," responded Santei, with a bow.

"Thank you, my good sir. I don't think servants will be needed today... feel free to give them the rest of the day off, and enjoy your day as well. If I need you, I will summon you," stated Leinad.

"Yes, my King." Santei bowed once more.

"Santei is a good man, is he not?" said Gressit, as they became free of Santei's presence.

"He is a gentleman... and a reliable warrior," said Cassion.

"Now, my friends let us not over-analyze this situation. The man is merely trying to win favor with the King," Leinad chuckled with a spark in his eye. "Why don't we go down to the Ponds of Rejuvenation?" asked Leinad.

Deep in the heart of the Blue Forest territory lie the Ponds of Rejuvenation, which are not easy to find. The King, however, knew exactly how to get there- for he had been there many times. The Ponds of Rejuvenation were known to cure the mortally wounded after only a few hours immersed in the crystal waters. Those without injury who swam in the ponds would be endowed with a crisp, energetic feeling of rejuvenation. In ancient times, if those who were wounded in battle could make it to the ponds before they died, they were often healed within a short time. These mystical ponds of Rejuvenation were truly a gift... for those who knew how to find them.

King Leinad, Cassion, and Gressit arrived at the ponds after walking through the Blue Forest for nearly an hour in the warm afternoon. They stripped themselves of their clothing except for their undergarments, and dove from a towering cliff into the sparkling still waters.

"Man, it is very cold in here," spoke Gressit through shivers.

"Oh, quit being such a weakling," Leinad mocked.

"It is not cold in here...it feels great! I think both of you are going soft on me. Why don't you dive down to the bottom with me?" asked Cassion. "Maybe we will find some Bluestone."

Bluestone was one of the hardest known compounds in all of Harpatia, and it was used for manufacturing weapons, as well as construction of castles. A very rare element, bluestone was also used for jewelry. Due to its solid nature, and virtual impenetrability, bluestone was extremely valuable, and it could be traded for gold coins or other goods and services throughout the land. Gold was the primary currency in the lands of Harpatia.

"I think I am done swimming for now. We have some business to attend to in Nowah," said Leinad.

Nowah, the land of the Nowries, was a significant distance from the Blue Forest. The Nowries were a strong race of ogre-like people with green skin, and purple spikes on their backs. They were raised for battle, but they were a very intelligent race as well. In times of peace, ironically, the Nowries were primarily farmers. They spent their free time with their families and simply enjoyed life. The Nowries had become great allies and neighbors to the people of Harpatia. They were often part of the Harpatian police force and were scattered in various groups across the lands.

"We must visit the Nowries at once," Leinad declared. "I must tell them of my visions."

"Very well my King. Let's go," affirmed Cassion, drying off.

"Can we fly this time?" whined Gressit.

Chapter 3: Nowah

Sitting with his legs crossed and arms extended, Leinad summoned the dragon Monte and told him to depart and bring back two other dragons with him. Within a few minutes, the dragons appeared, Monte leading.

"How may we be of service, master?" Monte asked.

"We need to go to Nowah." stated Leinad.

"We will take you there at once, my lord," replied Monte obediently.

The two other Dragons with Monte were somewhat smaller than their leader. The dragon Nieko was Cassion's personal dragon, with red skin, and a black tail. The dragon Twinkles was a female dragon and, like Monte, was crimson in color. Twinkles was the smallest of the three dragons, only about half the size of Monte, with a blue tail. Though not as strong as the other dragons, she was twice as fast in flight and she possessed a lethal breath of fire.

As the three men strapped themselves firmly into their harnesses, Leinad commanded the dragons to take them to Nowah.

"Yes, my lord," answered the dragons in perfect unison.

They gracefully beat their wings against the air, rising high into the sky before summoning a spell of wind magic and speeding away at an astonishing speed.

Gressit truly loved flying with the dragons. No matter how many times he had experienced dragon flight, it always felt like the first time- breath-taking. When he was strapped on the dragon high above the land, he felt invincible. Seeing the world from so high up was an amazing experience for Gressit. Flying with the dragons made him feel like he was a kid again and he loved that.

Cassion, on the other hand, did not care much for dragon flight because he could not always control his dragon. That made him very anxious, even though he trusted his dragon, Nieko, with his life.

Leinad, a master dragon tamer, had linked his magic to that of the dragon Monte. Therefore, he could evoke a spell and then take total control of the dragon's every move. This was made possible by the powerful skill of telekinesis that Leinad possessed. Monte trusted the King entirely, so he did not mind when the King took control over his mind. Leinad absolutely loved *everything* about the dragons. He enjoyed every moment of flight, and every second of time he spent taming them. He loved being a part of their lives, and they loved him for it.

Over the course of the hour-long flight to Nowah, Leinad thought about how he would reveal his findings to the Nowries. They were a peaceful people now, but for many centuries, they had been a barbaric species of war. Leinad felt strongly that something terrible was looming, and he did not know how Roiden, King of the Nowries, would respond.

Roiden, a muscular giant with light green skin, and purple spikes on his back, was a very intimidating creature. He was a brilliantly trained and seasoned battle veteran. The average lifespan on Harpatia was about 7,000 years. Roiden was quite old compared to the young, few-hundred-year-old Leinad, but that was of no concern to the King.

The dragons slowed their glaring speed after passing over the ocean. As the trio descended, the King and his entourage could see the beautiful expanse of Nowah. Taking up about nearly a quarter of Harpatia's land mass, Nowah was incredibly expansive. Although the population of Nowah was primarily made up of Nowries in the greater cities, there were also many Elven and Bracelian settlements in the outer regions. Split between incredibly large farm plots and bustling industrial blocks, Nowah had much to offer to its people. The Nowries were builders, industrialists, and farmers during peacetime; and that was how they preferred to remain.

Upon landing in Hapunah, the capital of Nowah, the men tied their dragons to a large metal pole and prepared to stroll into the city.

"Wait here, my friends," Leinad instructed the dragons. "We will be back tomorrow for the return trip home."

"Yes, my lord," the dragon Monte replied in a deep, gargled tone of obedience.

As Leinad walked through the city of Hapunah, he was pleasantly greeted by all he encountered. He decided they would stop for lunch at the Hapunah Tavern, one of the most popular eateries in the land. The three men enjoyed a filling meal of mixed greens, as well as lahi and other fish steaks. Lahi was much like tuna, and was used as a main ingredient in many Harpatian dishes.

"Boy, the food sure is incredible in Nowah," mumbled Gressit as he inhaled a bite of his sandwich.

"Yep, the Nowries sure do know how to cook it up," Cassion chimed in as he slurped his beverage.

"I agree with you both, my friends. And now we must head to Roiden's Castle," Leinad said, "to discuss our options for battle should one arise."

The Castle of Roiden seemed to span for miles. But in reality, it stretched only a couple of hundred yards across, and was ten stories high. Having various floors for quarters, a dining hall, meeting rooms, and more, the castle had stood for centuries upon centuries. It was made of the impenetrable bluestone and was shiny and very sturdy in appearance. King Leinad was immediately greeted by King Roiden's guards and ushered into Roiden's chambers.

"Have a seat, my friends. Are you hungry?" asked the giant, yet amiable Nowrie.

"No thank you, my friend. We just ate at the tavern," Leinad replied as he rubbed his stomach.

"Ah, that's my favorite place to eat and have a few pints. I have quite a few fond memories of that place," murmured King Roiden pleasantly.

Roiden was very well-spoken and mannered. He made Cassion, Gressit, and Leinad feel right at home. "So what brings you all the way to Nowah today?"

"Well, my friend, unfortunately, I feel that I have some disturbing news for you," Leinad lamented.

"Please tell me of this news," replied Roiden, the comfortable atmosphere at once tense and electric.

"I have been receiving some very perplexing and disquieting visions from the Life Source lately, and I can't quite make them out. The details are not clear, but I feel as though… war is coming. I'm not sure from where; I just know that it is coming, and I want you to make your armies ready and prepare for such a possible war. Set up secure zones for your people to reside in to ensure their safety," Leinad said in a serious tone.

"You worry too much about all these bizarre dreams that you are having, my King," Roiden said teasingly and dismissively.

"I do not believe that these are *just* dreams, King Roiden. I believe these are messages from the future: received directly from the Life Source itself. I will be visiting the Life Source when I return home to Dakineah to further explore these strange feelings." Leinad stated.

"Very well, my King; I will make all the necessary preparations. I will assemble my council in the morning and inform them of your visions. We will make all the necessary preparations. We will be ready, should we be forced to act," stated the muscular Nowrie resolutely.

"Thank you for your cooperation, King Roiden," Leinad bowed.

"Gressit, I have not seen you in a couple hundred years," rumbled Roiden nostalgically.

"I've just been living in the shadow of my brother. It is hard work being the brother of a King."

"Do not be such a victim," said the warrior Cassion. "You love being the brother of the King. It affords you all the comforts and luxuries in the world."

"Yeah, I guess you're right," Gressit replied as he tossed his hands in the air and shrugged.

"Well my friends, feel free to enjoy what Nowah has to offer, as much as you like. You will be granted anything you wish as long as you're in my land. I will send one of my servants with you to attend to your every want and need," Roiden offered kindly.

"Thank you for the offer, but I do not think it would be necessary. We're just going to walk around and see how things are going. I appreciate your hospitality, King Roiden," Leinad politely refused as he extended his hand to shake with Roiden. Roiden shrugged good-naturedly.

"Have a wonderful day, and do not worry. I will prepare our people for battle. Enjoy your stay here while you can," said Roiden as he bowed to King Leinad.

The three men exited the chamber. Upon leaving the castle, they were approached by a senior member of the Elite Guard of Nowah.

"Good day, King Leinad, gentlemen. Lord Roiden wanted me to give you these three fine horses," said the guard. "Please come to the royal guest quarters and enjoy a night's stay with us."

The large horses, which stood nearly nine feet tall, were similar to Clydesdales on Earth. These horses were capable of reaching some impressive speeds when spurred on.

King Leinad, Gressit, and the warrior Cassion rode on horseback to King Roiden's royal guest house. The house, a miniature castle, was rather large and looked like a very comfortable place to spend the night. This beautiful red brick castle was capable of accommodating far more than just the three men. Upon reaching the guest house, the King and his entourage were greeted by the royal guest house servants. A Nowrie, shorter than his King, informed Leinad and his men that dinner would be served in about an hour.

"Please let us show you to your quarters, my sirs," said the servant, bowing hospitably. "I am the head servant. My name is Alex."

"Cassion, Gressit, meet me in the chambers to discuss our different options for the upcoming battle," ordered Leinad.

"Yes, my King. We will meet you there at once," affirmed Cassion.

"Let me set my things down in my room, and I will be right there," said Gressit.

After settling into their rooms, Leinad, Gressit, and Cassion met together in the central meeting chambers of the castle.

"Alright, my friends, I will try not to keep you too long. I know you both must be hungry *and* tired after our journey. We all need some good rest, for we will return home tomorrow to Dakineah to visit the Life Source. I am sure tomorrow will be a very grueling day," Leinad said as he paced the halls of the elegant meeting chamber.

"As you both know, I've been having some disturbing visions lately of an impending battle here on Harpatia. Cassion, as General, I need you to prepare your armies and get them ready for battle," ordered Leinad quietly.

"Yes, my King. I will start training them on their battle formations. They will be ready if the time comes, my lord," Cassion said.

"*When* the time comes, Cassion." Leinad turned to his brother. "Gressit, as High Chieftain, I need you to appoint new leaders and prepare them for command. Both of you do *whatever* you must to prepare yourselves mentally and physically for this. I want you both to be more than ready," Leinad commanded fervently.

"Yes brother, I will be ready. I will make sure we have strong and competent leaders. I will take all the necessary steps," nodded Gressit.

Cassion unsheathed his magical katana and pointed it in the air, standing to his feet. "Not to worry, my King. I will ready the armies for battle. This will be our first dance on the battlefield together, and we shall look forward to it." Cassion said excitedly.

Cassion was a mysterious soul; one who had never known who his parents were, and who always had a sense of anxiety about him. He had some inner anger issues that needed to be explored, and it seemed he may get the chance to explore them soon. The following day they bid farewell to Roiden, King of the Nowries. The three men returned to their dragons in thoughtful silence. "Take us home, Monte," Leinad commanded firmly yet quietly.

The three dragons then rocketed into the air took flight. Once airborne, Monte evoked a spell of wind magic, and they were off. Through the use of the Life Source, they were able to attain speeds that would seem impossible for any dragon to fly.

Soaring over the ocean, and then over the Blue Forest area, they soon reached the outlying lands of the Dakineah region.

Chapter 4: The Life Source

Upon their arrival in Dakineah, King Leinad, Gressit, and Cassion were greeted by a welcoming party and ushered back to the castle. King Leinad requested that the other two meet him in his quarters after they had gotten settled. Leinad settled himself quietly and waited.

Gressit and Cassion met up with the King as requested, just under an hour later. They walked to the far wall of the King's chambers together, and Leinad slid his bulky wooden dresser noisily away from the wall, revealing a recessed door. He recited a spell, placed his hand on the door, and sent a small electric charge into the door's engraved seal. It opened to reveal a long series of tunnels that were about six feet high and four feet wide, carved out of bluestone, stretching into the dark depths.

Leinad, Cassion, and Gressit began their journey to the Life Source. This would be Cassion's first visit to the Life Source, as the location had always been kept in absolute secrecy by the royal family. Giving outsiders the opportunity to be close to the Life Source could be very dangerous for them, if they were not ready. Few could handle the intensity of the energy that the Life Source emitted.

"Well, Leinad," Cassion gushed excitedly, "I cannot wait to see the Life Source today."

"There is a first time for everything," replied Gressit, chuckling.

"This should be a very interesting experience," Cassion replied, in a slightly more nervous tone.

"We will need to draw as much information and foresight from the Life Source today as possible," instructed the King gravely. "It is very important that we move forward in the right direction."

After traveling for what seemed an eternity, the tunnel opened into the cave, where Leinad picked up a large gourd holding about three gallons of liquid. At the top of the cave there was a small trench which led all the way to the end of the cave system. Leinad emptied the fluid from the large gourd into the narrow pipeline and chanted a spell. A flicker of flame spurted from his fingertips, and the fluid exploded in flame, the caves instantly lit up with bright light. Cassion admired the light system in the caves, and he marveled at the simplicity of it.

As they traveled deeper through the tunnels, Cassion stared deeply at the beauty of it all while Gressit admired the fine craftsmanship. On the walls were etchings of ancient wizards chanting spells as well as pictures of dragons chiseled out of bluestone with amazing skill. They also spotted carvings of Elves, Bracelians, and Nowries in battle.

"They must have commissioned the finest artists in Harpatia to do these drawings," Cassion said.

"As a matter of fact, that is exactly what they did, my friend," Leinad replied, smiling, as he made his way down the corridor.

This truly was an ancient place, and they could feel the power emanating from within the Life Source as they got closer. A few hours later, they reached the end of the tunnel. There was a massive chamber at the end, and a bright blue light pierced through. "*This...* is the Life Source, Cassion," Leinad announced triumphantly.

With eyes wide open and a large smile stretching across his face, Cassion whispered, "It is beautiful, absolutely beautiful, my King." A giant, glowing, blue sphere of energy, the Life Source spanned nearly a thousand feet across.

The path they had traveled was the only way in or out from the Life Source, as far as Gressit and Cassion knew. This would explain why the tunnels were carved out of bluestone, for it would be almost impossible for these tunnels to ever collapse. However, Leinad knew of an alternate route to and from the Life Source in the case of an emergency.

"What do we do now, my Lord?" said Cassion.

"Well, my good friend, there is only one thing to do. We must sit down in a circle in the meditation area," said Leinad as he led the two men to the meditation area.

The meditation area was a large flat area of bluestone with the royal seal engraved in the middle: a large number seven with two swords crossing through the middle wrapped by a blue dragon. This was the place where the ancients would come to draw power and wisdom from the Life Source.

"Follow me, men," Leinad said as he slowly walked over to the meditation area and sat down with his legs crossed. He put his arms out, and turned his hands upright with his knuckles resting on his knees. With his index finger touching his thumbs on both sides, he began taking deep breaths and chanting. The other two men followed suit. Almost instantly, they became engulfed in the bright blue light. It felt as if they were being sucked out of their seats and brought into the Life Source, but they remained seated in the same spot. Their spirits were merged with the Life Source at that point, and now they could truly communicate with it.

"Oh, my God, what is happening? I have never felt it so intense before."

"Remain calm, Gressit," said Leinad. "The Life Source is melding with us. We will soon share a collective conscious with it, and then we must draw as much insight from it as possible."

"Thank you for receiving us today, my great Life Source. We seek knowledge and insight into the visions you have been sending me. I must know about this impending danger. Please, oh great Life Source, tell me what I must do," Leinad said.

"A war is coming, great King. You must prepare your people, and you must prepare yourself," said the Life Source.

The Life Source, which spoke telepathically through the use of its own magic, made the men feel as if they had a voice in their heads. This type of communication would probably drive the average man insane, for speaking to the Life Source was like seeing a ghost. Fortunately, these men were very well trained in the use of magic, telepathy, and telekinesis.

"King Leinad, a great alien force is coming—humans from Earth— and they will not be diplomatic. We have the power source they need. We could give it to them quite easily; but we must first learn of their intentions before we agree to help them, for misuse of our power could be devastating to the entire Galaxy as a whole. They will have soldiers of metal, and leaders with very poor moral standards. They will do horrible things, and there will be casualties. Harpatia's survival or destruction will be entirely up to you, great King Leinad," said the Life Source. It then continued, "I am only an observer. I am only here to feed life... and observe. I cannot intervene directly. However, with the proper use of the energy I give you, and the ability to hone your skills, you can win the battle; but you must be prepared for the tragedy that is to come. You must find a way to minimize your losses, and make this enemy force see the light," said the deep, thundering voice in Leinad's head.

Instantly, floating images of giant metallic War Machines appeared in the minds of the three men. Visions of war flooded their thoughts as intense battle scenes raged in their minds. They saw, in meticulous detail, the lethal force that was inevitably coming for them.

"You must come back when the humans arrive. I will be able to offer you greater advice then. In the meantime, I advise you to go to the mountains of Harpinia, and speak to the Council of the Elders. The Elders know much about the humans, and should be of great help to you," the Life Source said.

"Thank you, Great Life Source, for all of the knowledge and insight you have imparted to us today. We will return to you when the situation escalates," said Leinad as he grasped the hands of Gressit and Cassion and led their life forces back to their bodies.

After the three men had recovered and made their way out of the tunnels, they discussed at length their experience with the Life Source. Cassion was absolutely overjoyed, and enlightened, by all he had seen and heard on that day. Gressit was a bit more nervous and subdued, and Leinad was already gravely drawing up a battle plan. Upon their return to Dakineah, the men departed for the Castle of Harpatia. Once there, Leinad ordered Cassion to return to the land of the Nowries and help them make ready for battle.

"Have a safe journey, my friend." Leinad gave the warrior a pat on the back, as he departed.

"Same to you, my King," replied Cassion with a smile on his face.

Leinad then ordered Gressit to help assemble the armies of Bracelia, and the Royal armies of Harpatia as well. "Appoint the officers, and prepare them thoroughly. I must go to the Council of the Elders alone. I will return soon. Be ready, my brother... and Godspeed," Leinad spoke somberly, as he gave his brother a hug.

Chapter 5: Aboard the *Lancer I*

A message was sent out over the communication board of the capital ship ordering all support staff, commanding personnel, and scientific crew members to report to briefing room "A" immediately. As they were only a few days out from the planet Harpatia, General Hezekai needed to set up the initial plans for the mission— and possible invasion. He wanted to go over *all* of the details at length, before their arrival. As Kelly Styles and Jake Baker entered, they saw a number of faces they did not recognize.

Kelly peered around at the impressive collection of grim-faced, medal-sporting, uniformed officers. *This is* really *happening*, she thought. It was all starting to become reality for her, and the thrill was making her anxious.

"Welcome everyone. As you all should already know, I am General Hezekai. I will be leading this expedition to our mystery planet. We do not know whether or not we should expect resistance, but we need the great power source they possess. We are going to politely try to negotiate with them for it. If they do not negotiate, we will take it by force. But before we can take it, we must determine its location. That is why our scientific staff is so essential to us. We need them to determine how to harness this power once we locate it. This is our greatest concern— and our top priority for the saving of our planet," said Hezekai.

My God, he is already talking about invasion. Kelly had the feeling this could only end poorly for the U.S.

"Sir, we do not even know what to expect when we get there. How can we possibly be already thinking of an invasion?" Jake Baker replied in a dubious tone, his hands twitching nervously.

"Are you questioning me, *Lieutenant Colonel*?" spat Hezekai while looking the young man dead in the eye.

"No, *Sir*, I am not questioning you. I just think we should use the utmost *caution* when going to new places," Baker countered, not backing down. Hezekai continued without skipping a beat.

"I will deploy a reconnaissance team the moment we land," Hezekai stated plainly. "We will give the team a couple of weeks to scope out the planet and gather intelligence. Meanwhile, if we make contact with the power source, we must be ready to deal with it accordingly. Colonel Baker, you will lead the recon team; and we will send Doctor Styles to accompany you, and assist the team with translation, or any scientific needs that you may encounter. You will be responsible for her safety."

"Yes, Sir," Jake replied firmly. He hesitated, and then added, "We will execute the mission in a peaceful manner. The less blood spilled, the better."

"Get it done any way you can, soldier. We have a mission to complete. I am not worried about the details as long as the mission is a success," replied the intimidating General. "I will order all of the M.V.F. soldiers to engage only upon my command. Hopefully, it will not be necessary. I must now visit the hangar bay to ensure all of our mechs are in working order for the upcoming mission."

"Attention on deck!" shouted Lieutenant Attune as General Hezekai walked into the Hangar Bay to get a view of his mechanized fleet.

"At ease, everyone. Lieutenant, I am here to make sure that all of our mechs are ready for battle," Hezekai stated.

"Yes sir, General!" The lieutenant snapped a crisp salute and motioned to the armored suits filling the bay. "The mechs are fully charged, with their weapons loaded, awaiting your command to arm. For this mission, each unit is outfitted with rocket launchers and a shoulder-mounted, military-modified Gatling gun. I took the liberty of equipping your personal unit with the shoulder-mounted, high-power laser cannons instead. You also have flame throwers, and, for maximum maneuverability, the command-grade jet pack. Would you like anything else, sir?"

"Excellent Lieutenant, you've chosen well. I believe that will be all for now." General Hezekai activated the communication device on his wrist, addressing the soldiers and commanders on both capital ships. "Attention expeditionary forces. We will be making landfall on this foreign planet soon. A reconnaissance team will deploy first to explore and gather intelligence before we launch our mission. No one is to engage the enemy unless you are ordered by me, and me alone. If a battle should ensue, everyone must be ready. We do not know what to expect other than the unexpected. I want everyone to perform an equipment check, no matter whether you have an RS-777, Battalion Tank, or Jet Fighter mech. Make sure you are good to go. This concludes my announcement. As you were, men. Have a good day, that is all for now," concluded Hezekai as he dismissed the group with a wave of his hand.

Chapter 6: Harpinia

Accompanied by his dragon, Monte, King Leinad began the 1,500 mile journey to Harpinia. Although the journey was an incredibly lengthy one, it did not take long thanks to Leinad's teleportation magic.

Upon landing in Harpinia, Leinad flew Monte to the base of the Harpinian mountain range, and instructed him to wait for his return. Since teleportation was extremely exhausting and could sometimes lead to extended fatigue, the King walked the remainder of the way to the Council of Elders. He was saving all of his magic energy for the upcoming battle.

The Mountains of Harpinia, shimmering in brilliant hues of green and blue, were covered in ice and snow. The range spanned for hundreds of miles. Leinad starred with amazement at the beautiful snow-capped peaks as he began his journey. Even with his magical powers, the journey took him several grueling days. Whenever necessary, Leinad made an igloo to sleep in; which, with his elemental magic, was a relatively easy task. On the fourth day, Leinad reached the entrance to the Council of the Elders. The Jezelite door was massive: a towering twenty feet high and mammoth thirty feet wide, with the seal of the royal family engraved elegantly in the center of it. Leinad depressed a small button on the door. A chime sounded, followed by a voice. "Welcome, King Leinad. What brings you to our humble order?"

"I have recently visited the Life Source, and it has guided me here to seek council with you... in a certain matter regarding humans from Earth," mumbled Leinad as he shivered from the cold.

"I always knew this day would come. I am Elder Traf, one of the leaders of the Council. I will be happy to enlighten you, my King. Please step inside." The door opened with a groan and Earth-shaking rumble, and an Elven man greeted the King.

"Welcome. King Leinad. I am Elder Tone. I will take you to High Elder Rom and the other High Elders of the Council."

"Thank you very much, Elder Tone. I appreciate your assistance." Leinad followed the portly elder through the expansive hallways of intimidatingly tall temple, and into the much narrower underground tunnels. The hallways, like much of the rest of the kingdom, were made primarily of bluestone, and were painted in various shades of red, yellow, and green. Their route was enhanced by intriguing works of art, ranging from sculptures of ancient kings to paintings of Harpatian landscape.

"Your temple is very beautiful. As a child, I had the privilege of visiting once or twice; I have never seen this area of it before, though" Leinad marveled, as he took it all in.

"That is entirely understandable, my King, for the Council of the Elders has always been one of Harpatia's most... secluded places. The information we keep here is very sensitive. Should any of it fall into the wrong hands, the results could be devastating."

"I understand your point completely, Elder Tone. I only wish to know about the humans from Earth," said the King, not pausing.

"Elder Traf is the most knowledgeable in that area; and with the aid of the other senior Elders, he will be able to tell you all you need to know of these humans. At the end of this hallway, you will find a red door. Knock on the door three times, and announce yourself. They will let you in."

"Thank you very much, Elder Tone. I am sure we will meet again soon."

The smaller man bent over nearly double, in a formal bow. "You are very welcome, my King; and a good day to you, my Lord."

The sound echoed off the walls when Leinad knocked on the door. "This is King Leinad Seven, of Harpatia. I wish to speak to Elder Traf."

"Enter, King Leinad Seven, of Harpatia." The door slid open noiselessly, and a black-robed Elven man nearly his own size greeted Leinad.

"Welcome, great King. I am Elder Traf. Please... have a seat," he intoned, motioning with a sweeping gesture of his hand toward the great blue-green round table where all the Elders sat.

Leinad took a seat, and Traf pointed to each Elder in succession. "These are Elders Tone, Revy, and Rom. On behalf of the entire Council of the Elders, we would like to welcome you to our humble order."

Elder Tone had come in through a passageway in the rear of the chamber a couple of minutes earlier. He nodded politely to Leinad. "It will be my honor to assist you, my lord."

"Excellent! I want to thank all the high Elders of the Council for giving me an audience today. I seek knowledge of the humans from Earth. I believe these humans are coming to visit us with hostile intentions. I feel a war is coming, and I know very little of this enemy," said Leinad.

"What exactly did the Life Source tell you, my King?" Traf inquired.

"The Life Source showed me visions of these humans, and of their armies, and said that they are coming here to seek our power... for unknown reasons. I wish to know more of these humans," said Leinad, as he ran his hand through his hair, thoughtfully.

"My King, this may take quite a while," cautioned Elder Traf.

"Take all the time you need," replied the King nonchalantly.

"Bracelians and Elves visited the planet Earth many thousands of years ago," Traf began. "They made contact with this species and found the people of Earth to be quite inferior to their race. They were selfish, and hate-driven. Throughout human history, the only thing that remained constant was war. Humans kill and take what they want with little desire for diplomacy. Although they claim to be a "civilized" race, they are a savage group of egotistical fanatics. At least, this is the opinion of the Council," intoned Traf.

Elder Revy nodded quietly throughout this conversation and spoke up quickly once Traf had finished. "We have some ancient spacecraft which we use for intergalactic space travel. There is also a worm hole that can take us to Earth in a short period of time. We have used this frequently to observe their culture," he added.

"You used to travel there frequently? Why was I never made aware of this?" Leinad demanded hotly.

"We felt it would be best to keep this a secret, for the intermingling of two different worlds could have deadly effects. Earth is a very dangerous place, and we did not want to encourage anyone to even *think* about visiting there," Revy stated, his head bowed slightly. He took a breath, then continued, "A long time ago, a small population of Bracelians, and even some Elves, lived on the planet Earth to observe, and collect data. We learned much about the humans while we were there. Every few years, our astronomers would return and submit their notes and video recordings to us, from which we made many discoveries about the humans. While Earth has many who love peace, there are even more who love war. Their actions are destroying them— and their planet. It is no surprise to the Council that some humans may have found our location and learned of the Life Source. It is obvious they want what we have, for they have been depleting their own resources for quite some time."

Leinad did not like what he was hearing, but remained silent as Elder Revy continued with his revelation, his eyebrows knitted in concern.

"Humans are a destructive species. They care little for one another and seem to be concerned only about their own selfish gains. Their family values are almost nonexistent, and they have people living homeless and hungry on their streets. The fortunate humans walk past the unfortunate, and look at them as though they are bugs on the floor. Some family members will not even step in to assist their so-called loved ones. The humans care only for material wealth, and care nothing about family. This is appalling to even consider," the Bracelian Elder shook his head.

Elder Traf clasped his hands behind his back, a pose that accentuated his muscular build, and began to pace the floor. "The humans are a self-serving population only concerned with wealth and power. They have had more wars since the beginning of their existence than any other planet in our universe. Worse, they are a self-destructive people with little to no moral code. I wish I could be more positive about them, but, at this time, I cannot." He stopped his pacing and looked Leinad in the eye. "I do not know what else to tell you, my King, except that they possess weapons of great technology, and that they will leave a path of destruction in their wake wherever they may go."

"Do not misunderstand us," chimed in Elder Rom. "Some of the humans are very caring and loving individuals with strong family values, but they are of the minority, and they are usually poorer than the rest. The humans currently in power are a savage bunch who put selfish gain and social status above everything else," Rom fumed.

"We have some holographic videos of Earth, its people, and their culture. We would like you to watch them- and learn what you can."

"It would be my pleasure," Leinad replied, his head swimming.

"Then, without further delay," finished Rom, as he set up the hologram display.

Chapter 7: Revelations

As Leinad sat patiently, watching the holographic videos, he was stunned by the history of the humans from Earth. Leinad watched videos of wars dating back to the earliest times in the planet's history. He observed horrific acts of cannibalism, where humans actually *ate* one another to stay alive, as opposed to hunting, trapping, or growing their own food.

He swept through the history of the Aztecs, Mayans, and early American Indian races. He witnessed the bustling days of the Old West, and its absolute lawlessness. He watched in horror as the people of the Middle East slaughtered each other in acts of vicious genocide. Leinad watched holographic videos of World War One, and Two.

After the war scenes were over, scenes of love and human compassion began to play: families on outings who truly loved one another, and friends who were genuinely having fun together. Although what he had previously watched horrified him, these scenes of people playing games and getting along made Leinad feel that the humans *were* capable of being good.

In stark contrast to Earth, every citizen of Harpatia had the basic right to live in comfort, with food, shelter, and love. The King could hardly imagine why the humans cared so little for one another. In Harpatia, criminals were dealt with swiftly and severely. The punishment for heinous crimes was almost always death. They did not bother to incarcerate their murderers, rapists, or serial killers. They would simply kill them on the spot, by hanging them in the public square for all to see. And this type of punishment served as a very harsh reminder to all those who might commit these types of atrocities, thus reducing the Harpatian crime rate to nearly zero.

In Harpatia, the level of peace and compliance among the people was astonishing. As the video of Earth continued, Leinad kept thinking to himself, "My God! These poor people have never been shown love. They are all caught up in a desperate battle for survival consumed by the fear of not having the food, shelter, and medical attention they need. Their souls are tainted, and their governments are to blame. By not providing for the basic needs of their people, the Rulers of Earth had created the very thing they hated most: their own society."

The video of Earth began to show that the humans were indeed running out of their natural resources on Earth. The fact that their homes did not run on free energy was mind blowing for Leinad. In Harpatia, power was provided wirelessly, free to all dwellings through the Life Source. All homes, buildings, and businesses were powered at no cost. This was another of the basic rights of each Harpatian citizen.

Harpatia was an extremely advanced planet. Yet, they kept their lives simple, and did not yearn for technology the way the humans did. The hologram entertainment systems were probably the most used technology on Harpatia, but, other than that, the Harpatians preferred to live by the old ways. Leinad believed that if you did not starve your people, they would not steal food; and if everyone had entertainment, then no one would feel deprived. By providing for the most basic needs of his people, Leinad was able to cultivate a rather pleasant society.

Everyone worked in some way on Harpatia, and gold was the primary currency exchanged for goods and services. The barter system could also provide all of these things. There were some exceptions to the rules of equality when it came to certain possessions such as private teleportation devices, hover cars, large yachts, and fully-grown Dragons. These items were only available to the royal families, and a few opulent industrialists.

In Harpatian cities, teleportation hubs were provided, free of charge. Though the technology Harpatia possessed was great, the people preferred to live without relying too much on it. They found such a way of living to be less stressful.

The Life Source was the provider for all in Harpatia, and it did not need to be rewarded. Leinad understood the humans were in poor shape, and he was very sure that they were coming to Harpatia to attempt to harness the Life Source's energy. He knew Harpatia could spare a portion of the Life Source's energy; but, as discussed with the Life Source, the misuse of this energy could be catastrophic. Therefore, he could not justify giving any of the Life Source energy to such a barbaric people as the humans.

Leinad used the next hour to reflect on what he had just seen. Elder Traf, accompanied by Elder Rom, Revy, and Tone, entered the screening room. As they sat down, Elder Revy queried, "So, what do you think, great King?"

"The humans seem to be very... barbaric," Leinad shook his head. "I fear their military strength will be a force to reckon with."

"Indeed it will," replied Tone. "Their military is a lethal force, but there are a few things you do not know, my King. As the Council of the Elders, we have held onto a few secrets that we think you should now be aware of, my Lord.

"We have a fleet of ancient spacecraft, which would be considered "technologically advanced" to the human race. These craft are fully equipped with powerful weaponry, and are ready for atmospheric or space battle if necessary. We will train you in the use of the spacecraft, and we will find a solid hundred men to pilot the rest," stated Elder Tone.

"Well, gentleman, I am slightly put off, that such news has been kept from me for so long. That being said, immediate training in these crafts would be greatly appreciated," said Leinad.

"My King, we must first discuss weaponry," Elder Rom began, ignoring the King's mild rebuke.

"While you and your Royal Guard are well-versed in the combat and magic arts, the townsmen and common folk are not. We have an armory filled with energy rifles and machine guns. We also have grenades and other projectile weaponry available to us, and we shall train the townsmen in the use of these weapons.

"We have developed a plasma type of energy from the Life Source for use in our rifles," Elder Tone explained. "We have several thousand of these rifles, and a thousand or more bombs and grenades that can be used to defeat the mechanized armies of Earth.

"Unfortunately, we do not currently have enough weaponry to defeat them as a whole, but we will begin a mass production of these weapons immediately," said Traf.

"Between our Magic, and these weapons, we should be able to stave off the enemy," Leinad said. "I have my brother, Gressit, assembling the commanders of the Harpatian Armies, and coordinating with the Bracelians. The Warrior Cassion is assisting the Nowries. I do believe we will be ready for war- when the time comes. In the meantime, I would like to take a look at the weaponry and the spacecraft, if possible," said Leinad.

Elder Tone stood and said, "The hangar lies deep within the mountains of Harpinia."

Arriving at the hangar, Leinad noticed the stones had changed color, from blue to red. The red stone was not as strong as the bluestone, but it was strong enough to support the underground hangar. The Elders led the King to a large metallic door, and it slid open mechanically. Once completely open, Leinad could see a huge warehouse.

Bracelian technicians were hard at work on an assembly line building rifles, when Leinad arrived. Leinad had never before seen such weapons, though he had heard of them being used in the Ancient Wars of Segregation. There was little use for such weapons in times of peace. The Harpatians primarily used traditional weaponry such as swords, staffs, bows, and some catapults and cannons in Royal Guard training. However, magic was the primary weapon in the Royal Guard.

Leinad looked to Elder Tone and said, "How long has this been going on?"

"We have had this secret team of engineers down here for many years, my King. They develop all of the experimental and prototype weaponry that we have learned about throughout the years we have been observing Earth," replied the portly Nowrie.

Rom walked up to a technician and said, "Excuse me, sir. Do you have a rifle that we could use for test purposes?"

"Absolutely, Elder Rom. One moment, please." The technician retrieved a DX-66. The rifle was a black, short stock, long barreled weapon with a color-coded clip from green to yellow to red.

"What does the clip hold? Munitions?" asked Leinad.

"No my King. It holds a charge of energy. The clip contains miniature crystals that allow the rifle to deploy an energetic pulse composed of neutrons, protons, and Life Source energy," said the technician.

"Life Source energy, neutrons, protons...very impressive. What is the purpose of this energy gun?" asked Leinad.

"Well, sir, the DX-66 is a high powered energy rifle used to disrupt mechanical vehicles that rely on electricity for power. Upon impact to the appropriate areas, the energy beam can disable an electric vehicle. The intensity level of the rifle can be set from low to high depending on the type of target you wish to disrupt. Keep in mind: when the power meter goes to red, you will need a new energy magazine," said the technician.

"Fascinating!" said King Leinad. "How does this thing work?"

"It is quite simple, my King. You see the red button here? That is the safety. When you push it in the color next to the trigger turns green. That lets you know that the weapon is ready to fire. At the top of the gun are your sights. You simply depress the switch and the weapon will sight on its target automatically. The rifle will also adjust itself to varying ranges. Any bowman or rifleman will be able to master this weapon very quickly," stated the technician confidently.

"Would you instruct me in its use?"

"Yes, my King, you simply point the rifle at your target, aim down your sights, and pull the trigger. The intensity of the pulses that you fire will depend on the power level that you set the gun to prior to firing. The dial down here by the stock goes from zero to ten. A couple of shots with the level five setting will kill a healthy man. A level ten shot will destroy a vehicle, even a Harpatian one. Although we have never used these weapons in battle, we have developed them just in case we ever need to defend against a large mechanical force," said the technician."

"Do you have a range down here?" asked the King in a tone of excitement.

"Yes my King. It is just down the hallway over there to your left."

"Excellent! Come Elders; we must go shoot."

The range operator was a very large green skinned Nowrie with very pronounced purple spikes on his back. The operator welcomed the King and gave him a hot range and told him to fire at will. Leinad thanked the man and took his shooting stance, with one knee on the bench in front of him and his left elbow on the table. With the push of a button, he activated the hover car target down range. He dialed the rifle's intensity meter to seven, took careful aim and pulled the trigger. The shot hit dead center and sent an electrical pulse through the car. The target exploded like a newly blown volcano.

"Impressive," Leinad murmured as he slowly lowered the weapon.

He continued testing the weapon on various targets, dropping them one after another, for about the next hour or so before returning it to the range operator. "Impressive, indeed." He nodded with approval and added, "Let us go to the hangar bay and examine the spacecraft.

The Elders escorted King Leinad away from the range and down the hall to a door marked "Lift," and entered. After a rapid ascent, the lift came to a gentle rest. In only a minute, the lift had risen nearly two miles under the mountain.

As they exited, Leinad found himself in a huge warehouse area surrounded by gaping, wide tunnels which he assumed led to the top of the mountain.

"I cannot believe the King of Harpatia was left unaware of all of this," said Leinad as he gave the Elders an intense stare.

"I humbly apologize. My Lord, at the time we felt you did not need to know. Please forgive our poor judgment," said Elder Tone.

"I understand, Elder. I will not disturb myself with the details right now. What is important now is that I receive full disclosure from this point on," said Leinad.

"Yes my King, let us show you around," said Elder Revy.

The hangar was at least a mile long and a half mile wide deep beneath Harpatia. Made of Jezelite Steel walls and doors, Blue Stone pillars supported the structure throughout the complex. Able to resist any blast or Earthquake, the hangar could also serve as a hideaway for the people in the event of a major disaster. Leinad had been mostly unaware of the existence of the fleet. Now that he must prepare his people for invasion, however, it was critical he know everything about the equipment available for defense. The Elders took Leinad further into the hangar bay and opened a large steel door to reveal several hundred cylindrical shaped space craft.

These are the space craft?" asked Leinad.

"Yes, my King, the ancient spacecraft of Harpatia used to travel the galaxy. In the olden days, the Harpatians were explorers. I am sure you have read of these craft in the Hall of Secrets within your castle. The history of these craft remains largely a mystery, as only a chosen few were ever granted access to this world of ours," Rom said.

"We as the Elders are not only a council which possesses a vast knowledge of Harpatia. We are also astronomers and pilots. We have taken the spacecraft to various regions of the galaxy, and we have also visited some of the neighboring planets of Harpatia. While you and others of the magic arts can teleport to these nearby planets with ease, such travel would be impossible for a person incapable of magic, without these craft," said Elder Rom.

"Can we go inside of one?" asked Leinad.

"Absolutely my King," replied the muscular elven Elder Traf.

The Elder tapped in a sequence on the keypad and the door opened with a soft hiss followed by the extension of a ramp from the ship to the floor. When Leinad entered the craft he was surprised to find about a thousand square feet of space. There was a sleeping berth that could hold four people comfortably with separate beds, a well-equipped bathing area and the bridge. The huge black captain's chair in front of the control panel looked like it was fit for a King.

Armament included cannon emplacements in the rear of the craft and turrets above and to the side of the bridge. "This spacecraft appears fully equipped for war," Leinad said. "Elders, can we take one of these for a spin?"

"My King we must wait until twilight. We do not want to alert anyone to the existence of this place or these things," said Rom.

"These tunnels lead to the highest peak of the Mountains of Harpinia. We will leave through these tunnels and launch undetected. It would be our honor to show you how to fly the spacecraft," said Elder Tone.

"We only possess about two hundred of these craft and it takes months just to build the frame of one of these great craft. We will only use these spacecraft in combat as a last resort," said Elder Revy.

"I understand Elder Revy. We would not want to lose a valuable piece of our history," Leinad stated thoughtfully.

In all honesty, the King did not want to use the technology at all. *He was at peace with himself and his people living life the old way, the good way,* he thought. He had complete confidence in his dragon-mounted warriors, but they had not seen battle in recent history, and as King, he responsible for the welfare of all the people. He must ask the Elders to select citizens to be trained as pilots of the spacecraft.

The blue-colored cylindrical spacecraft was beautiful, Leinad thought. He decided to call it *The Equalizer*. In fact, he would come to refer to all of the spacecraft as *The Equalizers*. Leinad felt that, if, for some reason, he was ever in the horrible situation to need one of these things, the ship would serve as the equalizer against his foe. Leinad was familiar with the operation of the turrets and gun emplacements; however there were many things about this beautiful ship he had yet to learn. A sense of purpose he had not experienced in years filled him; the Life Source was flowing within him.

Leinad and the four Elders took their places in the cockpit and prepared for take-off. Elders Traf and Rom each manned a cannon emplacement. Elders Revy and Tone sat in the bridge and began to show Leinad the controls.

"This lever makes you go up and down," said Revy, indicating the control yoke in front of Leinad's right hand.

"Left, right, diagonal, and so forth and this is the thrust lever. Push it up increase speed, pull the lever back to the middle to slow down and stop and pull the lever all the way back to reverse the drives," instructed Revy.

"Be careful of reversing my King," warned Elder Tone. "If you put it into reverse while flying at high speeds you will slow instantly and could destroy your propulsion drives and possibly the ship."

"Thank you for the warning. I will apply my entire attention and dragon riding experiences in learning the ins and outs of *the Equalizer*," said Leinad.

"This one idles the throttle," pointed Elder Tone, showing him all of the controls.

"You see this joystick over here? This one is used for firing this ship's weapons. The first trigger is for firing your laser turrets. The second is for the energy missiles. Energy missiles have ten times the explosive power of any known missile on planet Earth, and could wipe out dozens of ships simultaneously, if used correctly," stated Revy confidently as he grasped the targeting controls.

"This is rather fascinating, my friends," wondered Leinad aloud.

"Now that you are familiar with the basic controls, we will prepare to launch," stated Elder Tone triumphantly. "Launching in ten... nine... eight... seven... six... five... four... three... two... one... **launch!**" shouted Elder Tone. The ship blasted off down the tunnel at speeds Leinad had never felt before. It was an exhilarating ride down the tunnel as Elder Revy guided the ship through the twists and turns at extraordinary speeds. Less than a minute later the tunnel shot straight up. The ship rocketed out from the mountain with a loud whoosh sound of compressed energy as they exited the tunnel system.

At that point Leinad was informed they were about fifteen thousand feet in the air. They flew over the mountains of Harpinia, then over Dakineah down to Bracelia then over the lands of Nowah. They then journeyed to all of the outer lands and continents of Harpatia. Leinad had experienced flight hundreds of times before by way of dragon riding, but even with magic the flight on the ship was faster and more fluid in motion.

In the outlands there were a few secluded colonies that wished to live a more technologically advanced style and Leinad marveled at all of the lights shining brightly from them. Next Elder Revy bucked and turned the spaceship straight up at full speed and within seconds Leinad noticed a strange energy enveloping the craft. They were about to exit the planet's atmosphere and enter space.

Today they were flying at speeds unknown to Leinad and he was having the time of his life. "This is incredible!"

Elder Revy glanced over at him and smiled. "Would you like to take over?"

Revy did not need to ask twice. "What do I do?"

"Pull back on the yoke a little, and keep us going straight."

"Will do," replied Leinad. About a minute later they had entered the wide expanse of space. The Elders then instructed Leinad to improvise- and have fun.

Leinad turned, bucked, rolled, and looped the ship wildly like a kid playing with a new toy. He tried every possible maneuver he could think of, and the Elders helped him along the way- teaching him the protocols necessary in the pre- and post-flight checklists. He put the ship through its paces, evaluating its combat capabilities.

Elder Revy depressed a button marked "Evasive Maneuvers," and chaffe poured out of the rear of the ship. The chaffe was designed for defense during air combat, though there was no air combat to be had today. The purpose of chaffe was to interrupt incoming missiles' seeking abilities before they hit their mark. Large dummy targets were deployed out into space so Leinad could do some target practice. He used the energy cannons to destroy a few targets and then armed an energy missile. He took aim on a target that was but a few hundred yards away. The resulting blast shook the entire ship. The energy missiles were indeed a force to be reckoned with.

"We should be heading back now," said Elder Traf. "We have been gone for quite a while." No one disagreed. It had been several hours since they had left the atmosphere of Harpatia and the men were ready to get back. There was always something unnerving about being separated from the cold vacuum of death by only metal and glass. They all were a little nervous. This was a very new experience for Leinad. Because he was a level ten magic user and high sorcerer of Harpatia and the King, Leinad was used to having total control of his environment, so it would take a little getting used to before he would feel absolutely confident and comfortable with space travel. Nevertheless he felt good about the days experience and wanted to bring his brother Gressit and the warrior Cassion along with him one day to get their opinions of this technology.

The ship had reentered the Harpatian atmosphere. Guided by Elder Revy, Leinad slowly and gently slowed the craft, angling it downwards towards one of the highest peaks in the Mountains of Harpinia. He flicked a switch on the pilot's control console, and a hatch slid open in the mountainside. Leinad slowly eased the ship through the hatch, and followed the tunnel system back to the hangar bay, where he docked the ship in its berth. With the ship docked safely, Leinad and the Elders went through a post flight checklist to ensure that everything was operating as safely as when they had left. After finishing the checklist, the five men disembarked the craft.

"I think it is time for me to return to our people. Thank you very much for everything you've shown me," Leinad thanked the Elders. After saying his goodbyes to the Council of the Elders, Leinad then left through the main entrance of the Council temple.

He descended the mountain pass and decided he did not want to make the two day journey to the bottom of the mountain. He simply teleported back to where his dragon waited by focusing his energy and intent on where he would like to be. A loud pooping sound erupted as Leinad vanished only to appear a moment later in front of the dragon Monte leaving a blue vapor trail in his wake. Monte jumped back a couple of feet, startled by his master's grand entrance. "Sorry my friend, I did not mean to startle you," said Leinad.

"It is perfectly okay, Master," Monte replied. "Where are we going now, my Lord?"

"Back to the Castle Dakineah, I must meet with Cassion and Gressit at once to discuss my findings with them, so we can further prepare for the upcoming battle," said the well-muscled King.

Leinad then mounted himself on Monte, and, within seconds, they were speeding rapidly along, their speed enhanced by their synergetic magic. A few hours later, they arrived once again at the castle. They set down inside the castle walls towards the rear of the dragon staging area, which was nothing more than a large open field used almost like a parking lot for dragons. Leinad dismounted Monte gratefully. "Thank you, my friend. You may return home for now. I will summon you when I need you. Be ready! Speak to your brothers and sisters, as well, for a war is coming. We want you to be ready for battle. That will be all for now, Monte."

"Yes, my King," replied the dragon as he rubbed his head against Leinad's arm in an act of obedience. Monte then rose back into the air, and soared off towards his cavernous home.

Chapter 8: Getting Ready

Leinad's staff greeted him formally as he strode into the castle, heading resolutely towards the meeting chambers. Amber, his petite Bracelian aide and advisor, scurried to catch up with his long strides. He slowed his pace and glanced down at her. "Amber, please send word for the warrior Cassion and my brother Gressit to return from their reconnaissance missions. I need to meet with them; we have much to discuss."

"Immediately, sire," she nodded.

Leinad stepped into the courtyard. A beautiful area with swimming ponds and artistic landscape, it was his favorite place to unwind. The bushes had been groomed to look like a pride of Dellions. The Dellions were a feline species much like the lions of Earth; only the Dellions were covered in purple fur, and had teeth the size of an elven arm. He took a quick dip in one of the courtyard ponds and enjoyed this moment of peace. The last few weeks had been so busy; it was nice to take a breather. After his swim, Leinad returned to his royal chambers, took a bath, ate a meal, and went to sleep. The next morning he awoke to a knock on his door. "May I help you?"

"Yes, my Lord," Amber answered, her voice muffled by the thick panel. "Your brother and the warrior Cassion have arrived. They are waiting for you in the meeting room, my King."

"Thank you. Please allow me a few minutes to freshen up, and inform them that I will be there shortly," said Leinad.

"Yes, my King," Amber replied.

The meeting chambers were located in the centermost region of the castle, and were decorated with banners displaying the royal crest. Large portraits of the dragons of Harpatia, and antique weapons lined the walls, as well as other pieces of Harpatian history. In many ways, the meeting chambers were quite similar to a museum.

Cassion and Gressit, seated at the large octagon table, rose to greet their King. Leinad waved them back into their chairs. "Good day, my friends, and thank you for coming on such short notice. Gressit, I am anxious to hear about your meeting with the Bracelians." Leinad turned his head to the warrior. "Cassion, I would like to hear of your trip to Nowah as well," said Leinad.

"Our Royal Armies are prepared for battle, brother," said the tall clean shaven elven brother of the King.

"Very good," replied Leinad. "I have much to tell you of what I learned at The Council of the Elders,"

King Leinad seated himself and looked at his brother. "Tell me of the preparations the Bracelians are making."

"Yes my King. I spoke to the leadership and the Bracelian people as well. They are aware of the impending danger and their armories are fully loaded and ready to go. They are well skilled in archery and rifles. They showed me an energy rifle that does a lot of damage," said Gressit. "I even fired one."

"They are amazing weapons indeed," said Leinad.

"The Bracelians also have hundreds of catapults loaded with explosives. They have many weapons to choose from in Bracelia."

"The Bracelians have always been fond of weapons technology and ancient methods of warfare. It does not surprise me that they have a few tricks up their sleeves," said Leinad.

Satisfied with the Bracelians preparedness Leinad then turned to Cassion. "Tell me of your visit with the Nowries. Did you speak to King Roiden?"

"Yes, my King, and I have spoken to his commanders, as well. They are mostly outfitted with heavy swords, spears, and daggers. They have a great many sorcerers, as well. Their cavalry is massive, and their soldiers have Jezelite breast plates and armor, which is virtually indestructible. King Roiden sent me back with three complete sets of their Jezelite armor- one for each of us," said the muscular, fearsome looking warrior.

"When the battle begins, the Nowries will be more than ready, my King. They have scouts patrolling the lands already, to provide protection for the villages in the meantime."

"Excellent news! Once I know exactly what we are up against, I will give the command for you and Gressit to gather all of the armies of Harpatia, and we will then crush anyone who wishes to harm us." Leinad pushed himself up from the table and clasped his hands behind his back.

"Now gentlemen, I will tell you of my interesting visit to the mountains of Harpinia and The Council of the Elders.

"While I was deep within the Mountains of Harpinia, I learned a great deal about the humans of Earth. I found out many things that have been unknown to all of us and I was quite shocked at all that had been kept from me, but we can address that at a later date. The Council of the Elders has had dealings with the humans from Earth for centuries.

"Although we have the ability to teleport, I am not sure that anyone under level ten could even think about interplanetary teleportation, and that is why this next piece of information is so intriguing. The Council of the Elders has a secret hangar bay deep underneath the mountains that contain space craft capable of interplanetary space travel. I knew that the technology for such things existed on Harpatia, but I did not know that anyone had put it to use," said Leinad.

"These spacecraft are completely different from the hover cars we used to drive before we reverted back to the old ways. They can fly at incredible speeds, and they are heavily armed with energy lasers, cannons, and fragmentation weapons. These ships can travel at warp speed across the galaxy; or, such capability has been claimed by the Elders, at least. As information-gatherers in disguise, the Elders have been observing Earth for quite a long time. One of the things I learned is that they are largely focused on warfare, and some of the things I learned about their culture were appalling. The holographic videos I watched lasted for hours, but I do not want to over-saturate you two with everything that I have learned," Leinad explained.

"Feel free to, my King," said the warrior Cassion.

"I agree, we want to learn as much as possible about the enemy," affirmed Gressit.

"Very well, what I took away from the footage I saw was that the humans are an extraordinarily self-serving species that care little for their fellow man. The average man and woman on Earth get over looked. They do not receive medical attention unless they have money or what they call insurance. And even those who do have this insurance are often left with a bill that will take them a lifetime to repay. They have homeless and hungry on an unimaginable scale. Their war tactics involve torture and interrogation in ways that are absolutely horrifying," said Leinad with a concerned look on his face.

One thing is certain; we will have a huge problem on our hands when the humans arrive. I did see images of their military fleets which are largely humanoid, robot looking war machines that are heavily armed with cannons, steel lances, rocket launchers, and large caliber machine guns." Leinad planted his hands on the table and leaned forward. "We will have to utilize our magic and everything else at our disposal to defeat them.

"Within the Harpinian mountain range, there exists a large weapons depot that contains energy rifles and various energy weapons. We are equipped for battle; however, victory will depend entirely on us and our people. We must call upon the School for Combat and Magic Arts immediately. I will send one of my aides to meet with the headmasters. We will need both instructors and students for the upcoming crisis. We must collaborate with them as soon as possible. I am not sure of their exact numbers, but I believe there are a few thousand students with high level magic and combat art abilities."

At that point Leinad motioned for Amber, sending her to the School for Combat and Magic Arts.

"I agree with your decision to send clergy to the School for Combat and Magic Arts," said Cassion.

"I concur," nodded Gressit.

Leinad did not pause. "Moving right along, I must tell you of my visit with the Council of the Elders. Other than being a savage, war happy and self-serving race. There really is not much more to say about the humans. Not all of the humans are bad or evil, but the majority of them seem that way. We will have a large task on our hands when they arrive. Be prepared for anything and everything. We will further assess the situation when it arrives," said the King as he paced the hall.

"We will now await the arrival of the masters of the School for Combat and Magic Arts," said Leinad.

A few hours later two of the Head Masters for the School for Combat and Magic Arts arrived at the Castle Dakineah. They were then escorted to the meeting chambers of King Leinad Seven.

"Welcome my friends. We have much to discuss," said the King.

Master Chew was a tall muscular man with brown hair and dark brown eyes. Master Chew Ruzer was a well-dressed man with no facial hair.

Chew bowed to the King. "Thank you for the kind welcome, my King. Master Dolan and I are happy to assist you with anything that you may need, sire."

The second man, referred to as Master Dolan Rouge, was the co-leader of the School for Combat and Magic Arts. He, just like Master Chew, was a powerful wizard with level ten abilities in fire and wind magic, and a level nine in most of the other magic types. Master Dolan was a rare Bracelian wizard. The Bracelians were not inept to magic, but instead merely disinterested; however, Dolan was one of the few exceptions to the rule. Dolan was a young man, being only a couple of hundred years old in a nation where people could live to be thousands of years old. He was a short, yet handsome, athletic man who was undoubtedly loyal to the King.

"I understand that you are in need of our assistance, my King. What can we do for you, my Lord?"

"I appreciate the two of you making time to meet with us today. I apologize if I have interrupted your teachings in any way, said King Leinad.

"No disruption at all, my King," replied Master Chew.

"I am happy to be here," said Dolan.

"Very well, let us get straight to the business then gentleman. The reason I have called you here today is because I have received insight from the Life Source. There will be an invading force coming to Harpatia soon. A war is going to break out and we will need to defend our planet and our people. We will need you along with all of the teachers, and able students to assist us in battle," said King Leinad.

"Whoa!" said Dolan in a surprised tone.

"I did not realize that this was coming," said Chew.

"This is some very shocking news," replied Dolan.

"I apologize, my friends. I would have informed you sooner but I did not want to disrupt the flow of the school or start any type of panic among the people. We have dispatched many security forces to patrol the various towns and villages in and around our kingdom. There are a few areas that remain unprotected as we have no idea as to when this force may arrive.

"The force will be facing are entirely human. They are not much unlike Bracelians. They are incapable of using magic; however they do possess incredible technology and powerful weapons. They are very ruthless, and we must exercise great caution when dealing with them on any level, especially in combat."

Gressit rose to address the men. "Masters Chew and Dolan, we will need you to form battalions and various other battle groups within your school. You will need to utilize the abilities and gifts of each of your students, as well as your staff. Sort them into different groups based on their abilities."

"For instance, you should pair the elemental mages with each other," Cassion added, standing. "The telekinetic and combat specialists should be grouped together, and you should also form a few special squads with a combination of abilities, as this will be essential to surprise attacks."

"If you have any archers or rifleman put them in a group of their own as well. All of the people with master level aim in the combat arts will be of great use in the upcoming battles," said Leinad.

"How are you so sure of this? None of the other masters have felt anything like this through the Life Source," said Dolan.

"I have seen with my own eyes during my visit with the Life Source," said Leinad

"You visited the Life Source?" said Dolan.

"Yes, I did and it revealed to me what lies ahead.

"This is not an opinion, it is a fact that we need to prepare for. I need you gentleman to assemble your fighting forces swiftly and be ready for my summons," Leinad commanded.

"Yes my King. We understand," replied Master Chew.

"We will assemble the magicians into flights and Master Chew will assemble the combat art sorcerers into their battalions. We will be ready when you call. It should not take more than a day or two to assemble this elite force. We will begin drills at once, my King," said Master Dolan as he and Chew bowed to Leinad.

"Thank you, Masters Chew and Dolan. You may return to your school. I will call upon you soon: be ready," stated Leinad firmly.

* * *

Masters Chew and Dolan called a meeting in the great Assembly Hall to brief the teachers and students on the upcoming situation. The school, located on the outskirts of Dakineah, was a large fortress composed of a series of miniature castles, and surrounded by a great blue stone wall. There were several thousand rooms that served as dormitories for the students, and separate quarters for the instructors. There were also nearly one hundred different training areas.

The school was segregated into three main groups: Magic Arts, Combat Arts, and Telekinetic Arts. Telekinesis was often associated on an equal level with the magic arts. The magic arts taught at the school were Earth, wind, water, and fire. The telekinetic teachings dealt with manipulation of physical objects with mind control such as lifting objects with the power of thought through the magic of the Life Source. Bending objects and manipulating time and space were all parts of the telekinetic teachings. If one had level ten abilities in the telekinetic arts there was not much they could not do. Some of the masters could even teleport. The school for Combat Arts enhanced physical reaction time and combat skills, thus giving the wizard or apprentice super-human strength. Each one of these different elements of magic had ten known levels. Level one being the lowest. Level ten abilities in all three arts would earn you the rank of Master.

King Leinad Seven had been born with an innate ability to perform magic, and he could perform like no other could. In order to be a Grand Master Sorcerer, you had to possess level ten abilities in all three arts... levels which he exceeded. Masters Chew and Dolan also had the honor of being Grand Masters. The Warrior Cassion had only level nine abilities in the magic and telekinetic arts, but he possessed level ten abilities in the combat arts arena. The Warrior Cassion had proven himself in the Royal Olympics for many consecutive years.

Gressit possessed level nine abilities in all of the arts, and was only a stone's throw away from attaining level ten skills in all three arts, but he had not yet tested at the school to earn his level ten commendation.

Masters Chew and Dolan stood at the front of the Great Assembly Hall, watching the students and staff members file in through the wide doors.

Once the last of the twenty five hundred students and teachers had arrived, Masters Chew and Dolan took the stage. Master Chew began his speech.

"Welcome teachers and students alike. We have called you here today to discuss a matter of great importance. Master Dolan and I have just come from a meeting with King Leinad, in which he informed us of a grave situation.

"The King has been in direct communication with the Life Source which has been giving him visions and communicating with him and through him. There is an alien force coming to visit us. We are not sure of their intentions, but in all likelihood they want the Life Source energy we possess. These aliens are believed to be hostile. The people who we will soon meet are called humans. We know little about them; however we know they are a warring race and have a great army. That is why we are here today to discuss this with you. At this point in time I will give center stage to Master Chew," said Master Dolan.

Chew stepped forward and scanned the vast assembly. He observed his young people's promising future, and the imparting wisdom of those who taught them. He took a breath and began, "As Master Dolan has indicated, we feel there will soon be a war on our planet, and we must defend ourselves. Our purpose here today is to recruit a fighting force for the battle sure to come. We will split into three main groups: the magic arts, level six and above; the combat arts; and the telekinetic arts, whose students will be scattered among both the magic and combat art fighting squads. If you have any special skills such as marksmanship, archery, or demolition, please let us know.

"We will be handing out skill assessment sheets to everyone today. This is on a voluntary basis, no one will be forced to fight, but we strongly urge you to join us and help keep Harpatia free. You needn't be a warrior; there are places in support teams as well. We will need medics, supply runners, communications workers, etc. At this point you will be given your paper work. Please fill it out neatly and correctly," said Master Chew with a strong tone of authority.

At that point Chew stopped speaking and allowed the aides to pass out all of the paperwork. The aides handed out about twenty five hundred sign up forms and skill sheets. The process of getting paper and pen in everyone's hand was a lengthy one. Everyone was signing up, both high and low level alike, everyone would fight. About an hour later the aides collected all of the paperwork and again Master Chew took center stage.

"Thank you for signing up, my friends, the training will begin in two days. It will take us a little bit of time to appoint the leaders for our various battle groups. Everyone will answer directly to King Leinad, General Cassion, and High Chieftain Gressit. You will be broken into flights of one hundred men. There will be about twenty five flights. Each group will be assigned different tasks and you will learn more about this in the days to come.

"The training will be vigorous, so be prepared. We have little time to rest, for we do not know when this invading force will reach us and we must be ready to defend our planet and people. I can assure you, no matter what happens our great King will lead us to victory.

"Our King has a great heart and great wisdom. Once the battle begins, we will be called into action, and we must be ready to fight! King Leinad has assembled the Royal Guard, and he currently has them patrolling the lands. Leinad has also sent out the Harpatian Police Force to guard some of the more rural towns.

"General Cassion and High Chieftain Gressit are coordinating with the Bracelians and the Nowries, forming them into battalions as we speak. They are preparing for war, and they will forcefully meet whatever comes our way. As I have said before, we really do not know what to expect. Within the next day or two, Master Dolan and I will process these papers and sort you all into your battle groups.

"We will compose an elite fighting force in a matter of days. We have great confidence in all of you, and we know that you will do well on the battlefield. For those of you with families, go home tonight, and tell your families not to worry about you; but make sure that they are well aware of the danger you are in."

Master Chew then passed the microphone to master Dolan. "This will conclude our meeting for today. You will all be contacted via telepathy."

As the students exited the hall, the teachers stayed to consult with Masters Chew and Dolan. The two masters gave them an in depth perspective on everything that they knew about the coming battle, which in retrospect was very little. Master Dolan told the teachers to go home and get some rest and that they would reassemble tomorrow.

Chapter 9: Aboard *Lancer I*

General Hezekai sat patiently in Meeting Room A, awaiting Lieutenant Colonel Kanak, who had been in direct contact with Central Command on Earth. The colonel entered the room, with a salute to General Hezekai. General Hezekai returned the salute, and with a gesture of his hand, motioned Kanak to a seat.

"General, we are only a few days out from the target planet."

"Excellent!" The general's inner warmonger could not wait to shed blood, though that was a secret he could not share with anyone else. Hezekai understood that the commanders back on Earth, including the Commander-in-Chief, did not want war; they had merely sent him with a small fleet of mechanized vehicles, as a precaution. He also knew the only way he would ever be able to harness this mysterious energy was through the use of force. Hezekai was fully prepared to do whatever needed to be done.

"Thank you for the information, Colonel Kanak, I will brief the commanders at once. We must make them ready," said the General.

"Yes Sir."

"You are dismissed. Have a good day, soldier," said Hezekai.

"And you as well, Sir," Kanak replied respectfully.

General Hezekai made his way to the ship's bridge. Hezekai informed his assistants that they were only a few days' journey from the distant planet. He then ordered all of his commanders to Briefing Room B. Once all of the Commanders were present and accounted for, General Hezekai began.

"At ease, gentlemen. We are only three days away from touching down on our target planet. Colonel Baker… you will set up a reconnaissance team to do an initial sweep of the land. You will need about fifty men for this mission and a sufficient number of mechs, which you can pick from the mech bay. Just make sure that you do not take my personal mech by mistake," said Hezekai.

"Yes sir," replied the Colonel.

"Doctor Styles will accompany you for scientific purposes and data collection. Do not fire unless you are fired upon. I want everyone to be aware, however, they do have the right to defend themselves. Keep in mind there will be no changing course once initial bloodshed has been made. The war will have begun. I would prefer to initiate the combat myself. I want you to contact the leader of this planet and inform them of our needs. I also want you to use the recording devices on the mechs to set up a detailed map system of the planet. We will need a general layout of the lands before we make any rash decisions.

"You and Dr. Styles can do it. I have faith in you both. Obviously we need you to make first contact with these beings," said Hezekai. "Do you have any questions, Colonel Baker?"

"Yes sir. I do have a couple of questions," said Baker.

"Please proceed with them," said Hezekai in irritation.

"Sir, I am a bit unclear about the exact particulars of the mission. If I understand correctly, you want us to provide maps of the planet's inhabited zones, as well as make contact with the leader and try to negotiate a deal on their energy source. I am a bit nervous about going into unknown territory with fifty men and a hand full of mechs."

"That is a chance we will just have to take, Colonel. I chose you to lead this mission because I believe in your abilities as a soldier, and tactician. Just use discretion, and you should be fine. Do not let *anyone* do *anything* rash. Save the decision-making for me. Furthermore, I want you to collect as much data and intelligence as possible. Learn as much as you can about the planet's military, resources, strong points, and weak points, as well. This is not my first rodeo, and I know it is not yours either. I will have Lieutenant Colonel Kanak prepare a written mission plan for you, as well as a soft copy to upload into your mechs," said General Hezekai.

General Hezekai went on to inform him of a few more details of the mission. The General made it very clear that the primary objective was to find a way to harness the energy source and take it back to Earth for scientific scrutiny, and hopefully solve the energy crisis.

"If their leader is not willing to cooperate with us, then we will do it the hard way, we will take the energy by force. With that said does anyone else have any questions?" asked Hezekai.

"No, sir," replied the commanders.

"I guess we will have to just wait and see what happens," Colonel Baker said mockingly.

"That is correct Colonel. Other than that, enjoy the ride for the next few days. Get as much rest and relaxation as you can. Once we land, it will be a whole new ball game." The general made a show of tucking a few papers into his briefcase then handed it to his aide. He glanced up at the quietly waiting personnel as though he had forgotten they were there. The hint of a smirk touched one side of his mouth and then vanished. "Dismissed," he barked at the men as he began to walk off.

* * *

Kelly was exercising on the treadmill in the fitness room aboard *Lancer I*. Exercise was her form of therapy and stress relief, so she had been coming daily since the flight commenced. Lt. Colonel Jake Baker entered about twenty minutes after Dr. Styles had arrived.

"Do you mind if I have a quick word with you, Dr. Styles?" Jake asked.

"Not at all. How are you today, Colonel?"

"I am doing just fine. I wanted to talk to you about our initial mission."

"Ok. Go for it."

"General Hezekai has assigned me to lead a reconnaissance team, and you are on it. We will have around fifty men, and a large group of mechs. I will need your translation and data collection skills. How do you feel about that?"

"That makes me a bit nervous." Kelly pulled the towel from around her neck and wiped the perspiration from her face and neck. "But who would *not* be nervous about meeting an alien species. I know we have a job to do, and I signed up for it, so I guess I am as ready as I will ever be.

"The idea of discovering an everlasting source of energy and being able to harness it so we can save our planet is absolutely fascinating. I look forward to the discoveries we might make," Kelly said as she tied her hair into a ponytail.

"I just want you to be aware of the dangers involved with this. It is very possible we will be walking into a sandstorm. With the general's bloodlust, it may be impossible to avoid war. You did not sign up for that; you did not know you were being led by a lunatic."

"Jake, you do not want to say that too loud."

"True. The General may have hidden microphones in this room, but at the same time I am not concerned about the general's feelings of my opinion on his character. I know how madmen are and I disagree with the way they handle things. That is just the way it is. We will try to do this in a peaceful manner."

Kelly smiled and rewrapped her towel around her neck. "I am looking forward to it. I have all of my tools ready to go. I have all my little canisters in order and I cannot wait to fill them up. I even have several energy harnessing containers. This is huge for me. I have been waiting for an opportunity like this for my entire life. I am not worried about my personal safety. I am more concerned about saving our planet."

"My thoughts exactly. I'm excited about this opportunity, but I fear we're going to get more than we bargained for."

"Well Colonel, I guess our fate will depend on the actions and decisions of General Hezekai. If he goes about this in a civil manner we might not have to see bloodshed."

"I have known General Hezekai for many years, and trust me when I tell you that we are in for a war. I am not looking forward to it... if only we could have used our own resources more sparingly, we would have never had to worry about this. That's all water under the bridge now. We have to deal with the situation at hand."

"I agree with you Colonel. This is going to be a very interesting excursion. I am starting to get tired. I am going to return to my quarters now and get some rest," said Kelly Styles.

"All right Dr. Styles, we need to get rest while we still can. Have a nice sleep. I will see you tomorrow."

"Yes sir!" Kelly gave him a crisp salute and a silly grin. "Good night, Jake."

Jake watched her walk off into the hall, her blond hair swaying with each elegant stride. *Kelly Styles was everyone's dream girl,* or so Jake thought. He promised himself that he would keep her safe.

Chapter 10: Touchdown

They arrived and began orbiting the planet of Harpatia. "This is General Hezekai. I need everyone's attention," said the General's voice over the communication board on both *Lancer I* and *Lancer II*. "We are now orbiting our target planet. We have also noticed another planet off in the distance that may also contain life, but the energy readings on that planet are minimal. The energy readings on our target are off the charts," said Hezekai.

All of the soldiers and support crew stood motionless while Hezekai spoke. Everyone on board the two ships were waiting patiently for touchdown.

"We are conducting visual scans of the planet at this time. We plan to sit down in a rural area. Once landed, we will unload our mechs and equipment and then set up a base camp. We are detecting a large population of life forms and in the large cities we are seeing huge castles, so whoever these people are they may be years behind us in technology.

"I am getting the impression these people are not very advanced, however I do not want to jump to conclusions too soon. The visual readings are good; however we will be dispatching a satellite to gather as much intelligence as possible. By the end of the day we should have a suitable site for our base of operations. Immediately after setting up base camp we will dispatch a reconnaissance team to make first contact and gather information.

"My orders for now are to hang tight. When we land everyone will be required to help set up base camp. We will make plans for further action upon the return of our recon team. This is General Hezekai, at ease and stand by," said Hezekai.

* * *

Upon the completion of the scan the general brought his ship down in what was known to the Harpatians as the Outlands. The Outlands were populated by those who chose not to be part of the kingdom. The humans would meet little resistance in this area; however there were a few hostile creatures in the area such as the Dellions and the Intrepid. The intrepid were a large winged bird like beast with razor sharp teeth and the temperament of a rabies infected wolf. The Intrepid flew in groups of no less than five and the average intrepid was about six foot long with two feet and two winged arms that spanned about a fifteen foot wingspan. They were blue in color and looked a lot like a bat with the face of a wolf. The tail of the Intrepid was about five feet long and had three bright red poisonous spikes that were lethal to most. The Intrepid would definitely attack if it felt threatened.

The Dellions were large lion like creatures that no one wanted to encounter in the wild; however it was possible for the Dellions to be trained. Needless to say, you would not want to encounter one of these beasts if you were unarmed.

General Hezekai gave the order to enter the atmosphere of what they would come to know as Harpatia. The ship's sensor readings were almost at overload upon entering the planet's atmosphere. This was a bit scary for the pilots and engineers, for they knew that when they entered or exited Earth's atmosphere the sensors barely registered at all. The engineers kept quiet about these readings. They did not want the general to know of their incompetence; for they had forgot to send a probe through the planet's atmosphere before entering and that could have been a fatal mistake.

"Hey Riggs, you better shoot out a probe before we land, we don't want everyone to die the moment they set foot on land down there," said a young engineer to his older partner.

"Will do Corporal, we need to make sure that the air is breathable, and that the pressure will not kill us all. Let's keep this oversight between us Smith."

"Absolutely Major Riggs, I don't want General Hezekai to execute us for incompetence."

"Air quality is good, as for the pressure, we will just have to take our chances," said Major Riggs as he perspired heavily in his operations cabin.

"I got a bad feeling about this," replied Smith in a very nervous tone.

Kelly peered out at the topography of this new world through an open viewport in her quarters. She was enthralled by the beauty of the many different landscapes that she was seeing. There were large forests and vast oceans that surrounded what looked to four huge continents. She could not see everything, but what she saw was more than enough to satisfy her curiosity. Kelly began to take notes as she carefully logged down all of the important details of what she was seeing. *This was the pinnacle of her career as an Anthropologist, and it could only get better*, so she thought.

* * *

Lancer I and *Lancer II* landed in a flat area thousands of miles from the large city picked up by the satellite. Immediately after touching down, support staff and soldiers alike started to set up base camp and unload the mechs. This process would take several hours. After the setup of base camp was nearly completed, General Hezekai ordered a few men to set up a medical bay behind the sleeping areas, about fifty yards away.

"Attention squadron, this will be our temporary base camp and headquarters until we make contact and decide the next course of action. I will be sending *Lancer II* back into orbit around the planet. *Lancer II* will serve as our escape vessel should we lose *Lancer I*.

"We will probably be moving ourselves across the sea after the reconnaissance team completes its initial mission. Colonel Baker, I would like to give you the rest of the day to choose twenty to thirty mechs and forty men to escort you on your mission. We will have you sweep this area first and then I will send *Lancer I* to air drop a sea vessel for you, so you can travel discreetly," said General Hezekai.

"Yes sir."

Jake spent the rest of his day putting together his reconnaissance team. He sent two privates to get Dr. Styles. Ten minutes later she arrived at his tent.

"You called, Colonel?"

He smirked playfully at her attempt at humor. "How are you today, Dr. Styles?"

"Not bad. It has been a busy day, unloading everything with the troops. I did not know we had as many mechs on hand as we do. There must be thousands of those things lying around. I hope we do not have to use them."

"Three thousand five hundred to be exact and we have claimed whole continents with the use of half as many. Unfortunately I am pretty sure we will have to use them. General Hezekai is a maniac and he cannot wait to start a war. The man lives for bloodshed and chaos."

"Do not be so rash. How do you know that?" asked Kelly.

"Kelly, I have served under his command for eleven years. I have seen firsthand what he is capable of. He murdered hundreds in the U.S., when the anarchy first started. Nobody is going to punish him for what he has done. Our government needs an enforcer and he is it. I do respect him as a soldier. Hezekai is a very powerful man.

"Anyway, I called you to go over our recon mission. We are going to take about ten RX-99 Tank mechs with aquatic conversion kits, in case we need them. We will have a few of the RXF-10 jet fighter mechs keep an eye on us from above. We will bring twenty RS-777 mechs. I have chosen all of the operators for the mechs. You are in charge of the scientific staff, and along with the other three scientists, will help us in our data collection."

"I cannot wait to get this party started," Kelly said in an excited tone as she did a playful dance.

"You're not excited at all are you?"

"I have my data collection, specimen bags, and recording equipment packed and ready to go. I plan to collect as much data as possible about this new planet. So, when do we leave?"

Jake laughed. "Not anxious, are you? We will leave tomorrow morning at 0800 hours, so get some rest, it will be a long one tomorrow. I will be piloting an RS-777 mech. Stay close to me when we are in the field. I will keep you safe. I promise."

"Thank you Colonel, you are my knight in shining armor."

"Just doing my job, madam," he replied with a mock salute.

* * *

The reconnaissance mission was about to begin. Jake met up with Kelly and her team of scientists. They joined the rest of the crew to gather up their personal mechs, and Kelly hopped in the back of one of the Jeeps. At General Hezekai's order, the team set out on their mission. The group had five Tank mechs and three Jeeps. About an hour into their mission they stumbled onto a village. This is where the initial contact would be made. The village was comprised of small huts.

Upon reaching the village they were greeted by a few Bracelian children. A dark skinned human looking child walked up to Jake Baker. The Colonel made a hand gesture and the mechs came to a halt. There were now about ten children approaching the recon group.

"Wow, what kind of magic is this?" asked a small blonde haired little boy.

Jake was shocked to discover the child was speaking English, but recovered quickly. "Hello young man. How are you?"

"I am good," the human looking child with the unusual bronze skin tone replied.

"Can you introduce us to the leader of your village?"

The kids just stared with their mouths wide open. A couple of minutes later a couple of large green skinned ogre like creatures with purple spikes on their backs approached with swords in hand. Kelly bit down on a terrified scream so it emerged as more of a squeak and was eternally grateful for the team of mechs that surrounded her jeep.

"Halt. Who are you and what are you doing here?" asked the creature in a deep and powerful sounding tone.

Colonel Jake Baker activated the dismount switch inside of his RS-777 mech. The mech lowered to the ground. The chest cavity of the suit opened and he stepped out. This action appeared to alarm the creatures, but they did not raise their swords.

"What are you doing here," the guard demanded.

"Are you Bracelian," asked another guard.

"No I am not. I am a human from the planet Earth," Jake replied.

"Human, Earth?" This obviously confused the guard.

"We do not understand. What are your intentions," asked the second of the creatures as he tapped his fingers on the hilt of his sword.

"We would like to speak to the leader of your village. We have come a long way to learn of your planet and of the energies you possess. We want to learn as much as we can from your people."

"Wait here please," said the guard.

"Stand watch, Crest. I will be right back," said the large green creature as he ran to the village and left his partner behind.

"Wow," Kelly murmured from just behind Jake's shoulder.

"Yeah, I know." The contact they had just made would make history. A couple of minutes later a tall bearded man with pointy ears, blonde hair, and with a full grey beard approached the recon team and addressed Jake.

"Are you the leader of this force?"

Jake acknowledged the man with a nod of his head. "I am the leader of this group, yes. I also have a leader that is waiting for me to contact him with the details of this visit."

"I am called Rouger. I am of Elvin decent. I lead this outland village but our King resides across the ocean. We wish only to live a simple life in peace. What is it that you need? Do you wish to do us harm?" asked the Elven man.

The Elven man's name was Rouger. Rouger was the leader of this village that was deep within the outlands and sovereign of the Harpatian kingdom and separated from it by the ocean. Rouger was a humble man and he did not subscribe to the monarchy of the King, for he had served in the Royal Guard during the Ancient Wars of Segregation. He just wanted to live a life of peace.

"No, we do not wish you any harm. We only seek information."

"If it is information you seek, I may be able to give you some about our planet. You must forgive us. This is the first time we have made contact with an alien species and we are all a bit nervous," said the mystical Elf.

"No forgiveness needed, my friend."

Kelly stepped up beside Jake. "We, too, are experiencing this first contact with a little shock and awe, as well."

The elven man, Rouger, then invited them into his village. He took Colonel Baker, Dr. Styles, and a few of the sergeants over to one of the dwellings to sit down and have a more private discussion. The rest of the M.V.F. waited patiently outside.

While inside Rouger's hut, a small six hundred square foot, cabin like dwelling, Kelly took note of the decorum. There were many works of art hanging on the man's wall that would suggest he was a patriot. There were paintings of a King sitting on his throne, and paintings of some pretty magnificent dragons.

The group was preparing for this discussion by getting paper and pen ready for notes, and starting up recording devices. Meanwhile; outside there were hundreds of curious villagers of various races surrounding the mechs. They were touching, poking, and prodding at the Tank mechs and RS-777's alike. The children were fearless, as they climbed up and sat on the tanks and made conversation with the soldier operators of these giant war machines. The soldiers moved very slowly in an effort to not startle the villagers. General Hezekai had given them all strict orders. It was very clear that if anyone were to engage the enemy it would by his order alone. The operators stood by and made casual conversation with the villagers.

Jake split his attention between their host and the scene beyond the open door. His troops seemed to be handling themselves well.

"This is a very awkward experience for me," Rouger said. "It would seem you have a small army with you today, so I feel compelled to answer a few questions for you."

The man then flicked his fingers and about fifteen candles ignited with flame, startling both Jake and Kelly.

"What did you just do?" asked Kelly.

"I used a bit of my elemental magic to brighten things up a bit in here."

"You people know magic?" replied Kelly in the curious tone of a child.

"Yes, our entire culture is centered on the use of magic. We are able to use magic because the Life Source wants us to. We have the ability to use elemental magic such as Earth, wind, water, and fire. There are a few other abilities that the high level wizards are able to use as well, but I cannot discuss those at this time," said Rouger.

"That is amazing." Jake leaned forward for a better look at one of the candles. "I did not expect anything like this."

"What you just saw was a level one ability. I possess a level nine ability in all of the magic arts; the ability rating system goes up to ten, although I fear I will never surpass my current skill level. If you ever encounter a level ten wizard you should use extreme caution, however they will not attack you unless they are provoked. We are a humble people here on Harpatia," said the Elven wizard.

"We are a group of people who live in what is known as the Outlands, the green skinned creatures that greeted you are called Nowries. The Nowries are great warriors. The people that look like you are called Bracelians, and those of us with pointy ears are of course, are Elves. There are a great number of people that live within the Kingdom of Harpatia and you will no doubt need to talk to them to get most of your answers. I will help as much as I can," said Rouger.

"What is Harpatia?" asked Jake.

"Harpatia is the name of our planet. You are in what is known as the Outlands which is a huge continent of people that want to live independent of the King's rule. It is not that the King is unfair, we just do not subscribe to all of the rules of the monarchy. The monarchy limits the use of our technology and makes the people live by the old ways. We enjoy the use of hover cars and other various technologies, but the kingdom does not allow a new way of life. They would rather travel by stallion then by hover car. So we came out here to be independent. We are not traitors, nor are we enemies to the King. We just want to live our lives the way we want them to be," said Rouger.

"I can understand that. Where is this kingdom of Harpatia?" asked Colonel Baker.

"Once you cross the seas the kingdom will be all around you. The capital city is called Dakineah, and that is where you will need to go if you wish to speak to the King. Dakineah is a huge city. Far outside of it you may find the Aurora sector. You will want to steer clear of that area. The Auroran sector is where the dragons live," said Rouger.

"Dragons, you must be kidding?" Jake's gaze fell upon the paintings hanging on the wall.

"Yes the dragon Legion has been the protector of Harpatia since ancient times. There are some level ten wizards such as the great King Leinad Seven, who have the ability to train and communicate with these creatures. The King is like a father to them and they would gladly die to protect him. Another land of the kingdom known as Bracelia may also be a place of interest to you," Rouger added.

"The Bracelians are not much unlike you except for the fact they have a slightly darker skin color. Few of them practice magic and most of them are involved with building and engineering trades. I do not have too much to say about the land of Bracelia other than the fact that it is a very mystical land. The Blue Forest gives off Life Source energy to all of its inhabitants."

Kelly clutched her pen tighter. "The Blue Forest sounds like a beautiful place; however I am still stuck on the dragons. What else can you tell us about them?"

"There is little more that I can tell you. They are noble beasts with a very deep rooted loyalty to the King. They also have a deep understanding of the magic arts as they are very closely connected with the Life Source," said Rouger.

"This Life Source that you are speaking of, does this give your planet life," she asked as she depressed the recording button on her handheld voice recorder.

"The Life Source is an everlasting source of mystical energy that feeds our planet life and grants us mystical powers. It is revered as a god and is never to be disrespected. Those with level ten abilities in the magic and combat arts are very much in tune with it. As a result of their strong link to the Life Source, they are granted many great powers," said Rouger.

"This is all very fascinating, Mr. Rouger. Can you tell us how we might get to the town of Dakineah in the Kingdom of Harpatia?" Jake asked with a sense of urgency in his tone.

"I do not even know if the King will grant you an audience, but I can tell you that Leinad Seven is a very honorable man with a strong sense of fairness. He believes in honor and loyalty and lives by a very impressive code. He will only do what is in the best interest of his people.

"You will have a heavy burden on your hands, should your commander choose to bring hostilities to the lands. The Harpatian Royal Guard is an elite fighting force that uses both combat and magic arts. I cannot tell you too much about them, for that would be considered treason and treason is punishable by death.

"What I can tell you is this; if you cross the ocean you will come upon a land known as Nowah. There you will be greeted by Nowries that are far fiercer than the ones you met earlier. Tread softly in the land of Nowah, for any mistake you make there will surely be your last. If the Nowries grant you access, you will then be able to travel to the lands of Bracelia.

"You will have to cross the ocean again to reach the land of Bracelia. About a day's journey north and through some treacherous lands you will find Dakineah. The capital city is full of settlements, villages, and shops. Dakineah is heavily protected by the Royal Guard of Harpatia, thus it would not be wise to bring any hostile intentions into that area. As you are not acting aggressively, I believe the King will grant you an audience.

"I can only tell you to head west across the ocean. When you find the land of Nowah you will be greeted by more of the large green creatures with the purple spikes on their backs. The Nowries are fierce in battle. Some of them use magic and some of them do not. They are trained killers, so be careful. The Nowries are loyal to King Roiden who is King to the Nowries; however Roiden and all of his people are also loyal to Leinad Seven, the great King of Harpatia.

"Harpatia is a land of peace and should the Nowries allow you access to their lands you may pass through and once again cross the ocean to the west. Do not attempt to sail around the lands of Nowah, for doing so would bring you a most certain death at sea. There are things that even I do not understand, but hear me now, do not try to bypass Nowah," said Rouger with the strong ring of authority and caution in his tone.

"Thank you very much, Rouger. The information and advice you have given us is greatly appreciated." Jake rose and held out his hand to assist Kelly to her feet. "My superior is watching this conversation via a live camera feed, and I am sure he appreciates your help as well."

Rouger escorted them to the doorway, but paused. "Make sure you request to speak to King Roiden as soon as you land in Nowah. That will ensure you immediate safety. Remember King Leinad has granted Roiden power over the Nowries, but Roiden is loyal to King Leinad, therefore if he seems inclined to do you harm, you may request an audience with Leinad Seven in order to avoid any negative actions from Roiden. The Nowries, Elves, and Bracelians have been at peace for many hundreds of years, so it is unlikely that King Roiden will do anything with you before he consults with the great Leinad Seven," said Rouger.

"Many hundreds of years, no way?" Kelly said in disbelief.

"Yes, Ms. Styles that is correct. The average life span on Harpatia is between three and seven thousand years long, and even longer in some cases. I cannot explain why. I just know that is the life span for the average Harpatian," said Rouger.

"Wow, it is about eighty or ninety on Earth," said Kelly.

"Welcome to Harpatia. This is a wonderful planet full of wonderful things and I hope you are able to discover them all."

"Thank you very much," Kelly replied as she gave the old man a hug.

Rouger blushed and then said, "Head west when you get to the ocean. Keep going until you find land again. Stay on a west heading. When you come upon a large land mass it will be the land of Nowah. Be gentle with the Nowries, for they are a very fierce species. As you can tell, I have a few of the Nowries here in my colony. They make excellent guards. Because they are under my command they will not attack unless I tell them to do so.

"In the land of Nowah they may attack you unexpectedly, but inform your troops not to engage. The Nowries are a force to be reckoned with and you would need many more soldiers than you have right now to stand a chance," said Rouger.

"I appreciate you help. Maybe we will meet again someday, Mr. Rouger," said Colonel Baker.

"Maybe we will indeed. Let us hope it is under peaceful terms."

"There is so much more I wanted to learn from you today," Kelly protested.

"You will have to learn it from someone else, for I feel that I have already said too much. I do not want my actions here today to come under the scrutiny of the King. Any form of information I have given to you could be considered treason, so please keep it confidential," said Rouger.

"You have our word, Mr. Rouger," Kelly assured him.

"May peace be with you."

"And with you as well," Jake answered.

* * *

The M.V.F. expedition then headed west towards the ocean. They were all a bit nervous, but they would not let that get in the way of the task at hand. Upon reaching the cliffs edge of the outlands the M.V.F. recon team gazed down at the ocean. The ocean was blue green in color and as clear as could be. It was truly a beautiful sight for everyone. Unlike the polluted oceans of Earth, this one was full of life. Kelly was astonished by the beauty of this great mass of water.

The crew realized it would probably take several days to reach the land of Nowah. Colonel Baker called in to base camp using his shoulder mounted wireless radio communication device. He requested a small sea vessel be dropped at their location by *Lancer I*. General Hezekai obliged. Within about ten minutes *Lancer I* appeared in front of them slowly descending from the sky. Once the ship was about twenty feet from the ocean a belly hatch opened on the ships underside. A medium sized sea vessel was then slowly lowered into the ocean. The vessel was equipped with a few modified Gatling guns and a couple of missile turrets. This medium destroyer class vessel would be more than sufficient to carry the mechs and the men across the sea.

The vehicles the Colonel had in his possession were equipped with aquatic kits, so it would be no problem getting them onto the sea vessel. Baker did not know what the storms were like here and was concerned about the voyage across the uncharted seas of Harpatia. *Things were going fine now,* so he thought. As far as the crew was concerned, they were on their way to explore a new land. *Lancer I* returned back to base camp after dropping the destroyer into the ocean.

They boarded the vessel and loaded all of the mechs and transport vehicles into the cargo bay. The crew had brought along a jeep and a couple of Hummers to use as needed, but the majority of them got around in their mechs, which were much faster than any truck or car.

Colonel Baker then went to the bridge of the vessel and engaged the thrusters to all speed forward and on a due west heading.

The first day at sea was calm. The crew spent their time marveling at the foreign fish species that swam beside them. There were fish of all shapes, sizes, and colors. They noticed dolphin like creatures, as well as things that looked like overgrown whales. Although there were some similarities between what they were seeing now, compared to the fish of Earth, there were just as may differences.

They did not know exactly what they were seeing and whether or not these fish and sea monsters trailing them were friendly or dangerous, but that did not stop them from enjoying this remarkable experience. At nightfall the majority of the M.V.F.'s crew went to sleep for the night. A few men stayed up for night security detail. One of the experienced operators relieved Colonel Baker, so he could rest. The following morning Jake woke to a large bang as he was thrown out of his bed.

Jake bolted from his cabin, up the companion way and to the rail. An enormous sea creature was ramming the hull. The ship slowed to a crawl so the crew could investigate. The creature looked like a humpback whale but had the mouth of a shark, and large bird like wings. It was ugly, deadly and aggressive—it scared the living daylights out of Jake. Jake was truly frightened. Colonel Baker had never seen a creature like this before and little did he know that this creature was called a Snarvin. A Snarvin was much like a whale and a shark, but far more powerful. The Snarvin was probably an evolutionary version of the dragon, for it did have large wings. The wings of the Snarvin spanned about twenty feet long, but because it was a sea creature it could only fly for a few seconds in the air before gravity returned it home.

Kelly appeared at his side. "What did we hit, what's going on?"

"Take shelter Kelly and be ready for an impact," The Colonel pushed her towards the hatch and safety before sprinting to where the mechs were secured.

He quickly installed the aquatic kit on his RS-777.

Jake punched a combination of buttons on his watch and instantly the mech's chest cavity opened and the mech lowered itself to the floor. Jake entered the small operations chamber entered the required sequence of buttons and closed himself inside of the RS-777. Once manned, the mech was controlled by the movements of its operator. The controls included a joystick, foot pads, thruster throttle levers, and a weapons control unit which could be operated verbally or manually, although most of the mech operators preferred to use the voice option when in combat.

The RS-777 had two arms, two gigantic steel legs, and a titanium armored platinum breastplate. There was a head on the mech which had a human like appearance. The cameras and sensors were located there, giving the operator a three hundred sixty degree view. The control center was actually in the chest cavity of the RS-777 mechs. It took nearly a year of intensive training to become a skilled mech operator.

Jake activated his mech and flew off the ship plunging straight into the water to pursue and engage the creature attacking his vessel. His mech was equipped with all the weapons he could possibly need. Today he was glad to have the retractable lance that was mounted in the wrist area of the mech. He did not want to harm the creature, but it could damage the vessel and kill his entire crew if it was not stopped soon.

He studied the readings on his heads up display and discovered three of the beasts on his sonar. Jake marked all three of the creatures with an infrared beacon and engaged. First he fired the Gatling gun and unloaded about one hundred rounds into the first creature. It bled a purple and red colored blood and died. The next two charged him.

They hit the RS-777's leg with enormous power. Jake felt the metal around his leg start to buckle. He activated his lance and pierced through the whale-like head of the first to reach him. The lone survivor lost interest in the fight and swam away deep into the ocean. At that point Jake activated his thrusters and flew out of the ocean and back to his vessel and docked his RS-777 mech. Jake pushed the release button from inside of the mech and the RS-777 dropped to its knees and opened its chest cavity.

Jake exited the battle craft to the cheers and applause of his crew. "Man that was intense. Those creatures were unbelievable. Without the mech we would have been swimming with Moby Dick today."

"You are my hero," said Kelly as she walked over to Baker's side.

"I am not sure our ship could hold up under that kind of ramming force, but I did not want to take that chance."

"I understand and I thank you." Kelly said as she gave him a giant hug.

Jake examined his mech. "Somebody tell Sgt. Henson to get up here," he ordered.

"Right here, sir," the mechanic called out as he stepped from the crowd.

"One of those monsters got a hold on the RS-777's leg and damaged it a bit. I need you to fix that as soon as possible Sergeant. I think the bite may have weakened the metal."

"Yes Sir," replied Henson.

"By this time tomorrow we should reach dry land and then the real fun will begin," Jake said to Kelly.

"I cannot wait."

The following day Dr. Styles was hard at work making entries in her journal when she overheard someone yelling out that they saw land. Immediately she sat her journal down and rushed out of her quarters. Kelly went topside and sure enough, she could see a beautiful white sand beach and what appeared to be a rainforest in the background. Beyond the forest they could barely see what looked like a village. The crew set a course to anchor near the beach.

Chapter 11: Nowah

The ship dropped anchor about a hundred yards from the beach. The crew flew their RS-777 mechs to shore. The rest of the crew used small transport boats to get to shore. They used the strength of a couple of RS-777 mechs to air lift two dozen of the RX-99 Tank mechs over to the shore as well. Upon reaching the beach the crew disassembled their mech's aquatic kits and made camp on the beach by setting up ten large tents.

The crew set up a mini satellite receiver on the beach, so they could have crystal clear communications. After camp was up the majority of the team continued to head west, as they could see a few townships in the distance. As they continued to walk they passed through a lush and beautiful rainforest. Dr. Styles took many pictures and samples from this forest for research purposes. As the crew came out of the rainforest they could not help but notice a big castle in the distance.

"I hope these folks are friendly," said Kelly as she paced about nervously.

"We will keep you safe Doctor," replied a handsome infantryman.

The recon team was spotted by a Nowrie security force. Within seconds they were completely surrounded by fifty large, green skinned, ogre looking creatures with purple spikes on their back. Baker took quick notice that the creatures were armed with swords, battle axes, and crossbows. There were even a couple of Nowries that looked like they had rifles on their shoulders. All of the weapons were pointed at Colonel Jake Baker's reconnaissance team.

The Colonel spoke through the microphone of his mech, and said, "We come in peace. We mean you no harm."

"Who are you? What sort of magic is this?" said one of the larger Nowries whose features were more pronounced.

This Nowrie was about seven feet tall with huge muscles and vascular green skin. The purple spikes on this one's back had been dyed black. This Nowrie was clearly a leader of some form. The large Nowrie peered up at the Colonel's large RS-777 mech, which stood about ten feet tall and began to speak.

"What are you?" the Nowrie asked while poking the steel leg of the mech with his sword. Instantly the mechs raised their weapons and took aim at the Nowries. "All mech operators stand down, hold your fire, that is an order," said the Colonel.

"Stand ready, attack on my command. Identify yourself and we may let you live," said the large Nowrie.

"I am a human. I am much like your Bracelian friends, although I am not from Harpatia. I come from a distant planet called Earth," said Jake Baker.

"Yes, we have heard about you. Our King has spoken of your impending arrival," said the Nowrie Commander.

"I am going to get out of the machine that I am operating. Please do not be alarmed. I must push a button. This machine will drop to its knees and the chest cavity will open, allowing me to step out. Please do not attack," Said the Colonel while experiencing a cold sweat within his vessel.

"You may exit your vehicle," replied the Nowrie as he lowered his sword.

Jake the pushed the eject button on his console and the large humanoid war machine let out a mechanical noise as it dropped to its knees and opened up at the chest for Jake to step out. Jake noticed that the Nowrie was about twice his size.

"We do not mean you any harm, nor do we wish to receive harm. We only want to speak to your King. I have spoken with a gentleman in the Outlands named Rouger, he was an Elf," said Jake Baker.

"Yes, we have heard of this man. He is a traitor to the Kingdom of Harpatia," said the Nowrie Commander whose name was Goron.

I am not sure of his status, but I can assure you that we do not have any bad intentions, we only came to talk."

"Yes, I am sure that is all that you came for," replied the ferocious looking ogre.

"What are these machines that you possess?"

"They are called mechs. The mechs are part of the M.V.F. which is short for the Mechanized Vehicle Force. The M.V.F. is the main focus of Earth's militaries. We are soldiers, but we do not want war. We seek information about your Life Source and want to see if you can help us to restore life and natural resources on our planet," said Colonel Baker while staring at the large party of monsters that surrounded him.

"Ha, Ha, Ha, if you think that King Leinad Seven will grant any of you access to the Life Source, then you are insane. The Life Source is revered as a god on our planet. Only the divine can make contact with it," said Goron as the other Nowries muttered insults towards the Colonel under their breath.

"Be that as it may, we would like to speak with King Leinad."

"Because you wish to speak to the great King Leinad Seven, you will be allowed to live today, for it is not within my authority to grant or to deny you an audience with our King," replied Goron in a regretful tone.

Dr. Styles was completely engulfed in fear. She did not understand why these Nowries were so hostile, but little did she know she was lucky to be alive. The King had left strict instructions to the Nowries on how to handle a first contact with the humans, should they arrive. Had the King not have left those instructions the whole team would have surely been killed.

Kelly did not like this situation. The Nowries looked like savage beasts to her and she thought that they might attack at any moment, but she was wrong. The Nowries recognized her as a female and the Nowries had a strict code of honor. Part of that code involved never harming a female unless the female meant them harm.

"I do not know if the great King Leinad Seven will grant you an audience, but I will take you to my King, King Roiden of the Nowries. He answers only to King Leinad and to no one else. I hope you know what you are doing, Colonel Baker, for you have placed yourself in unbelievable danger by coming here," said Goron while standing only inches from the Colonel.

"I understand and I appreciate your help. What is your name my friend?" asked Baker as he stared at the enormous Nowrie.

"I am Chieftain Goron of the land of Nowah and I am not your friend."

The Nowries then led the group through the thick forest that surrounded the Castle of Nowah. Hundreds of Nowries surrounded Baker's team as the security force got closer to the Castle of Nowah. Some of the higher ranking Nowries who had already spoken to the King had heard about this alien force that was now in their lands. King Leinad had thoroughly briefed King Roiden on this exact situation, so as a result of their knowledge, the Nowries were not surprised.

The group passed through two large black steel gates. The elite Nowrie Guards would escort them the rest of the way. Goron briefed the Elite Guard unit on the humans.

"Colonel Baker, you may choose two people to join you inside. I cannot permit more than three of you in the Castle at one time," said the Elite Guard.

"I would like to bring Dr. Styles and Sgt. Gates," said Baker.

Sgt. Gates stood about six foot tall with brown eyes and a medium build. He was a handsome man who was married with two kids waiting for him back on Earth. The Sergeant was a humble man who loved his country. Gates was indeed a great soldier and that was why the Colonel chose to bring him inside the Castle with him.

Colonel Baker was fascinated by the Nowries and he took mental notes of everything that he observed while walking through their towns. The architecture was astonishing. Every home looked like a miniature castle. All the colors of the trees and plant life were exotic, there were some colors that baker did not recognize. This truly was the experience of a lifetime for all of the M.V.F. soldiers. There were dog like creatures that the Nowries kept as pets. These were called Darma. The Darma were dog like creatures with a bird like beak and razor sharp teeth. They seemed to be tame. The Darma came in all different shapes and sizes just like the dogs of Earth.

The Elite Guards of Nowah continued to lead Jake, Kelly, and Sgt. Gates into the castle. They searched all three of the M.V.F. personnel for weapons and of course they were unarmed. Although the guards failed to find the pocket utility knife that Kelly kept in back pocket. The Nowries led the team down a great hall of the castle that was inlayed with red jewels and gems. *This was a very nice place*, Kelly thought. The walls were made of blue stone. Little did the humans know that the blue stone was a virtually impenetrable rock. The group continued down the hall at a slow pace. The interior design of the Castle Nowah was just too good to be missed. The group noticed weapons and various artifacts on the wall. They then approached two large crimson doors that had a royal crest on them; the crest was of two shields merging together as to symbolize the peace between the Nowries and the Elves. Kelly was correct in assuming that this was the Royal Crest of King Roiden of Nowah.

The guard knocked on the door and instantly the doors opened. Once inside Jake noticed ten warriors in the room. These warriors were of Elven descent and were in full battle armor and equipped with axes, a shield, and a rifle. These were members of the Royal Guard of Harpatia and they were loyal to King Leinad Seven, but had been sent to aid the Nowries in the event that the humans should arrive.

"I must report to the King at once," said the Elven warrior in a deep and noble tone.

"Go my friend, and god speed," said the other Royal Guard whose gem inlayed battle armor gleamed in the sunlight.

The man then left. When the warrior got outside of the castle he noticed the mechs. It was just as Leinad had foreseen. They were mechanized war machines. Leinad had described them to all of the Royal Guard. *The King was truly a prophet*, the warrior thought.

"Welcome to my castle," said a large and powerful looking Nowrie man who wore a very nice suit of armor that was far more jewel encrusted then any of the suits the humans had seen thus far.

The King of Nowah was far more muscular than any Nowrie that the humans had seen. And the spikes on his back were gold in color. This was by far the most intimidating creature they had met, but he had a smile on his face and seemed very intelligent. King Roiden was in a blue stone armor suit with a jewel encrusted breastplate. He had a large broadsword sheathed on his back and two daggers at his hip. It seemed strange that a King would be so heavily armed in his own home, but little did the humans know that at any time the King of Nowah could be challenged to a duel of swords and the winner of that duel would remain or become the new King. No one had challenged Roiden in many hundreds of years, and there was good reason for that. King Roiden was one of the most battle tested warriors in all of Harpatia. No one knew his age but he was revered as one of the ancients.

"You are an interesting group. I am not used to meeting aliens. How may I help you?" asked King Roiden.

"Thank you for seeing us, great King of Nowah. We seek an audience with King Leinad Seven. We wish to discuss the various uses of the energy source that you possess," said Colonel Jake Baker as he bowed in a show of respect.

"You speak of the Life Source as if it were a toy. Such talk could get you killed in these parts. The Life Source provides life throughout the land. What is it that you want from us?"

"We want your assistance in bringing our planet back to life."

"That is very interesting. The only problem that I can foresee is that we do not know you, you do not know us. Why do you think that I or the great Leinad Seven would be even remotely inclined to help you?" asked the large green skinned Nowrie with golden spikes on his back.

"I do not know, but we would like to see if we could learn from you and you from us. Maybe we could all benefit from this."

"What could we benefit from you? Your Species is a savage race and we want nothing from you except for you to leave our planet and never come back," said King Roiden in a growing tone.

"Well Sir, I too have a leader who I report to and he is a far more savage being than me. I am under strict orders and I must insist to speak to King Leinad Seven," demanded the Colonel.

"I will tell you one thing, Colonel Baker, I am going to have my Elite Guard inspect your vehicles and we will learn as much as possible about them. In return for that I will let you leave Nowah alive. There is a messenger in route to King Leinad as we speak. Should the King be as kind as to grant you an audience, I will provide you with the means to get to him," Declared Roiden as he wiped some sweat from his brow.

"Thank you, King Roiden, I appreciate your kindness."

"I will need you to answer a few questions for me while we wait, and if you answer my questions, I might answer a few of yours," said the King of Nowah.

Jake Baker could not help but be intimidated by this large green creature with golden spikes on his back. King Roiden had the muscles of a horse. This was an uncomfortable situation for Colonel Jake Baker.

"Excuse me King Roiden," said Kelly Styles.

"May I ask a few questions?"

"I am glad that you finally decided to speak. I will be happy to answer the questions of a beautiful lady," said King Roiden as a smiled formed on his chiseled face.

"I am interested to learn of your planet's history. I want to know of the Nowries, Bracelians, and the Elves. Any information that you can share with me would be helpful. Also your magic is also very interesting to me, I would love to learn how to use it," said Kelly in a naïve tone.

"I know a few things about magic. I doubt that I can teach you how to use it; however I will take you to the training area and give you a display," said Roiden.

"That would be great I would love to see a display of your magic," said Kelly as she blushed with excitement.

"A magic show, that is just what I wanted to see today," Jake said mockingly.

"Bowers, come over here," the King shouted.

Bowers was Roiden's main servant and personal guard. Bowers served as an assistant to the King of Nowah. Bowers was a large Nowrie with blue skin. The blue skin was a rare disease that affected skin color in Nowries. The one thing that separated most Nowries from one another were the facial features, in the case of Bowers there was blue skin, he was one of few with the disease.

"Accompany us to the training fields, Bowers," the King ordered.

"Yes my King," replied Bowers.

"I need you to set up some targets for me."

"Yes, my Lord."

Bowers led the foursome down the hallway and through the court yard to the back of the castle where the training fields were. The fields were large open green areas that they used for training. The fields reminded Colonel Baker of the football fields of Earth, for they were lush green in color. A few more Nowries came to the training fields to help and they began setting up targets. The targets were of humanoid statues, dragons, and Dellions. The Dellions were the lions of Harpatia. The Nowries finished setting up the targets and the King looked over to Jake and Kelly.

"Prepare to witness greatness. Stand back and enjoy. I will be using the Combat Arts as well as the elements. These are expert level targets that have been made from the hardest wood on Harpatia, Koa.

Only a fierce warrior could ever think about destroying these targets," said King Roiden of Nowah as he flexed his giant muscles.

"I cannot wait. I am so excited," Kelly said as she paced around in anticipation.

Jake just stood there with an impatient look on his face.

"Watch and be amazed," said Roiden.

Roiden made his way to the training field and looked back at Kelly and smiled. Suddenly King Roiden disappeared, leaving a light blue vapor trail in his wake. The vapor was a sign that teleportation had just occurred. The King reappeared seconds later in front of an Elven target. He struck the target with a vicious right elbow. The statue exploded. The human crowd was shocked. He had used teleportation and a level nine combat arts impact blow. An impact blow was a magic aided strike that only the most highly skilled combat artist could use. Roiden then withdrew his sword and pointed it at the large Dellions target. Streams of fire began spewing violently from his blade to the target. The statue was instantly engulfed in flames.

Roiden then did a very impressive back flip and disappeared in the air and then reappeared behind the dragon target. This time Roiden pointed his sword and lightning spewed out of the blade and into the dragon statue. The target was electrified to a crisp. Roiden extended his left hand and pointed to the electrified dragon. Instantly sheets of ice magic flew from his hand and finger tips. The dragon target was electrified and frozen. Roiden put on a magic aided burst of speed and landed a roundhouse kick to the mid-section of the target shattering it into pieces. Roiden then did another back flip and landed fifteen feet away next to the inflamed Dellions target and sheathed his sword. Using his telekinetic powers, of which he possessed a level nine ability, Roiden lifted the flame engulfed target into the air with a telekinetic gesture of his right hand. He then made a crushing gesture with is left hand and the Dellions target was squashed and broken into little flaming pieces.

Both Kelly Styles and Jake Baker were completely impressed with the power of King Roiden. Baker was sure that this show was not just for their entertainment, but also a warning to the M.V.F. and Baker had to admit that these people were far more powerful than even General Hezekai had imagined. King Roiden had a mastery level in all of the combat and magic arts, but was nowhere near as powerful as King Leinad Seven. It was rare for a Nowrie to possess such high levels of magic, but Roiden was the exception. Roiden came from a very powerful and ancient Nowrie bloodline.

There were only a few targets left on the field now. King Roiden then gestured with both hands in an upward motion and two rocks rose from under the ground and into the statues and smashed them completely. Roiden then drew his sword out and moved it in a circular pattern. A small funnel cloud appeared and swept the debris from all of the destroyed targets into the air and out to the ocean.

"That was an example of our Earth magic."

King Roiden then threw his sword into the air and watched it fall back into its hip side sheath. A blue vapor trail emitted as the Nowrie King teleported off of the fields and next to Dr. Styles.

"Very impressive King Roiden, I do not know what to say," Kelly exclaimed in amazement.

"You would not want to be on the receiving end of any of the things that I have just shown you," Roiden said to Colonel Baker.

"I agree," said Baker with a mock smile on his face.

"How are you able to do such things?" asked Kelly.

"Well my dear that would be a long story. We derive our powers through ourselves and through the Life Source. I cannot tell you too much about our Life Source. The Life Source is a magical being."

"The Life Source is a being?"

"We believe so. It has god like powers. We believe that all life in the universe was created by the Life Source or by whoever created the Life Source. There are some questions that I simply cannot explain," said King Roiden in a sincere tone.

"This has been an absolute treat. Thank you for showing us your magic and for welcoming us to your land," said Kelly as she extended a hand towards Roiden.

Roiden took the lady's hand and said, "You are very welcome young lady. I have a good feeling about you. Those who are savvy in the telekinetic arts have the ability to sense things about people. I sense only good things about you. I can sense no ill will from you. At this point I would like to invite you and Colonel Baker for a meal at the Castle Nowah. We will send some food for your soldiers as well," said Roiden with a tone of concern.

"Yes sir, King Roiden, we appreciate your generosity," the Colonel said with sincerity.

Chapter 12: Breaking News

Meanwhile at the Castle Dakineah, the royal messenger arrives with news of the humans from Earth. It was a typical day for King Leinad Seven. He had been relaxing in his chambers and studying the magic arts, as well as reading through the ancient scripts of Harpatia. The scripts were ancient texts on the history of Harpatia. They contained many secrets about the lands. The scripts also contained ancient spells that only the most powerful wizards could ever cast, such as the protection spell.

The King was trying to hone in on his telekinetic abilities today, as he felt an air of unease circulating in the lands. The King was deep in thought when he suddenly heard a knock at the door. The King closed his texts and put them in a safe place.

"Who is it?"

"It is Royal Messenger Goren, sire."

"You may enter Goren."

The two elven guards that were posted outside of the King's chambers then opened the door to allow Goren entry to speak with the King. Goren then entered.

"My King I come with news from the land of Nowah. The humans of Earth have arrived. There are fifty of them at the Castle Nowah. The leader of their expedition is named Colonel Baker and he is accompanied by a female. They have requested an audience with you. Would you like to grant them permission to see you?" asked the Elven man.

"I appreciate you relaying this message to me, although I knew they were here. I felt them arrive a few days ago. I have been having visions of them for a while. I have seen the female in my visions and I would very much like to meet her. You may grant them permission to come here. You along with twenty of my Royal Guard may escort them to the castle," the King commanded.

"Yes my King," replied Goren as he placed the hood of his black cloak over his head.

"Go now Goren and be fast."

Before Goren left he began to describe the war machines that the humans brought with them, but Leinad interrupted him and simply told Goren that he already knew of these mechs, as the humans called them. Goren acknowledged the King's words and then exited the Royal Chambers and began the journey back to Nowah by way of dragon flight.

About six hours later Goren, accompanied by twenty of the King's Elite Guard, arrived at the Castle of Nowah. Goren spoke to King Roiden and informed him of Leinad's decision. Roiden summoned Dr. Kelly Styles and Colonel Jake Baker to his chambers.

"Take a seat," said King Roiden as the group entered the room. The King's chambers where decorated solely with weapons of all sorts. There was nothing fancy about the room at all. The room gave off a barbaric feeling to Dr. Styles and Colonel Baker.

"Welcome my friends. The messenger Goren has just returned from the Castle Dakineah. The Great Leinad Seven will grant you an audience. Your troops must stay here. The King has sent twenty of his Royal Guard to escort you to the castle. You will be traveling by way of dragon flight. There will be Dragons waiting at the staging area of the castle. You may leave from there at your leisure," said Roiden.

King Roiden, along with the escort from Dakineah, took Colonel Baker and Dr. Styles through the town of Hapunah which was the capital city of Nowah. Located within the castle grounds, Hapunah was a very nice city, full of shops and eateries. Along the way Colonel Baker stopped and reached his troops via his radio C.B. and informed them of what was about to happen. He ordered them to comply with any and all orders of King Roiden while he was gone.

The entire M.V.F. squad was out of their mechs and waiting patiently as some of Roiden's engineers examined the mechs. The King was curious about the technology that was used to create them. Jake Baker knew that General Hezekai would not be happy about the engineers peering at his precious mechs, but it was necessary to complete the mission. After informing his squad about the details the Colonel, accompanied by Kelly Styles, continued to the dragon staging area. Upon their arrival to this grand courtyard, Dr. Styles and Colonel Baker were taken aback by the sight of two dragons that had harnesses on their back with seating for twenty or more.

"These are the King's royal dragons. The big one is named Twinkles. He is owned by the Warrior Cassion. You do not want to meet him on the battlefield, for he is the fiercest warrior in the lands. The smaller one is named Nieko and he belongs to the King's brother, Gressit," said Roiden.

All Kelly and Jake could feel was absolute cold fear, for they had heard of these creatures in fairy tales and seen them in movies, but they had never thought that they would see one in real life.

"It is a high honor that King Leinad sent these dragons to transport you. He could have made you travel by sea. You should arrive to Dakineah within a few hours if the dragons keep a fast pace," said Roiden.

Kelly approached the dragon named Twinkles. She noticed the dragon's beautiful crimson skin and blue tail. Then they looked at Nieko, who was much larger than the female Twinkles, Nieko was about seventy feet long with red scales and a black tail. Although the colored tails looked silly on the dragons, they exuded nothing but power.

"So we just get on their back and strap ourselves into those harnesses?" asked the Colonel in a very nervous tone.

"That is all there is to it my friend. Strap in and enjoy the ride. You will be accompanied by the King's Royal Guard, so you will have nothing to worry about. First time dragon flight can be an exhilarating experience," said Roiden as he let out a loud series of laughs.

Dr. Styles and Colonel Baker took a few minutes to become familiarized with the dragons. The dragons must have been fifty feet long, these creatures were truly amazing. The dragons let out a few mild roars in which King Roiden seemed to understand, for he replied to the dragons. Communication with a dragon was only possible for people that the dragons chose to talk to, and even then you would have to possess some magic in order to comprehend them.

Colonel Baker and Dr. Styles then mounted the dragon Nieko. They strapped into the flight chairs and for all intents and purposes they prepared for takeoff. The dragons leaped into the air simultaneously and began to flap their wings. Within a few minutes the Colonel estimated that they were about ten thousand feet high. At least that was what his altimeter was reading on his watch. Jake and Kelly were amazed by this situation. They were riding on the back of a creature that they thought to be fictional, but it was indeed real.

Kelly wondered if all of the fairy tales of Earth were somehow linked to this place. Kelly wondered how a star map leading to Harpatia was placed inside a secret chamber inside the pyramids of Egypt. She wondered who put it there and why. She hoped that all of her curiosities would be answered one day. Kelly then noticed that after a few minutes of flight that the dragon's wings stopped flapping, but that speed increased.

There was no explanation for the speed of their flight. Kelly concluded that the dragons must have been using some form of magic to keep them airborne and flying. Kelly then looked over to the Elite Guards that accompanied her and saw that they were completely relaxed and decided to follow suit. Kelly relaxed her mind and body and decided to just enjoy the ride. She took in the ocean, the beautiful skin of the dragon, and all of the scenery for a couple of hours. Kelly saw land ahead of them. There were open fields and rainforests and before she knew it, they were flying over snowcapped mountains.

The group passed over the mountains and about twenty minutes later Kelly saw a huge castle in the distance. Kelly knew that this must be the Castle Dakineah and home to King Leinad Seven. The dragons began to descend. The capital city of Harpatia was truly a sight to see. There were streams that flowed through the city and lakes all around. The architecture was like nothing she had ever seen on Earth. There were large octagonal shaped structures and different castle like homes that scattered all over the town.

A few minutes later the dragons were only a hundred or so feet in the air. They flew over the castle walls and landed softly in a large open field, which they would come to know as the dragon staging area. Upon landing, the dragons lowered their bellies to the ground which was a signal for everyone to dismount. The riders dismounted and the guards then instructed Dr. Styles and Colonel Baker to wait, and someone would be along soon to escort them to the King.

Within minutes the humans were greeted by about ten members of the Royal Guard. Their swords were sheathed and the guards had rifles on their backs. Jake Baker took mental notes of what the guards were equipped with. It was an interesting array and he wondered what else the Harpatians might have had at their disposal. Dr. Styles was taking in the bluish color of the stone that was used to build the castle. She had never seen such blue stone before. She noticed that there was gold mortar in between the stone. This was truly a regal castle and it was clear to her that whoever King Leinad Seven was, he was a powerful man with good taste.

The Royal Guard escorted Jake and Kelly through the courtyard. The courtyard was very well kept and lush green in plant life. Kelly stopped along the way to stare deeply at a pond that was glowing bright blue. She had been noticing a lot of bluish glows lately. She seemed to remember flying over what looked like a Blue Forest when she was on the dragon's back. At the time she thought that she was seeing things, but now she knew that it was real. As a scientist Kelly was intrigued by these blue glows. Dr. Styles had a strange feeling that these blue glows were probably related to the energy source that they were seeking. They then entered the Castle Dakineah through a couple of large doors that were engraved with a shield that had the number seven on it with two swords crossing through.

One of the Elite Guard said "Follow me."

Jake and Kelly followed as the rest of the guards left their side. This guard's name was Froth. Froth was an Elven man that stood about six feet tall with brown hair and a slim build. The Elf carried only a sword, which implied that he was a user of magic. The group walked for a while until they were several floors up in the castle. They came upon a pair of golden doors that had an octagon shaped key hole in it. Froth inserted a key into the hole and the doors opened.

Waiting for them inside, they found a tall Elven man with blue-green eyes and a handsome muscular build. The man had black tribal markings on his arms, which Dr. Styles assumed was tattoo art. He was dressed in a dark blue suit and wearing a black cloak. There was a crown of fine jewels resting on the man's head; and at that point, Kelly knew this man was King Leinad Seven of Harpatia. Colonel Baker looked into Leinad's eyes and then back to the floor.

The Colonel was indeed intimidated by the handsome, yet fearsome King of Harpatia.

"Welcome, my strange alien friends. What brings you to my planet?" asked Leinad with a smile on his face.

"We are very pleased to meet you, and we have heard much about you, King Leinad," said Kelly.

"Thank you. I assume you are Dr. Kelly Styles. You are far more attractive than the messenger described. They told me you were gorgeous, but that was clearly an understatement," said King Leinad.

King Leinad Seven had been looking for love his entire life; and from the moment he had laid eyes on Dr. Styles, he knew she was the one. He would not disclose this information to her for a long time, if ever. The King was taken aback by this woman's beauty. Kelly was about five feet six inches tall with blonde hair and blue eyes. She had a beautiful face with an adorable smile. Kelly's athletic build told Leinad that she was an active and sporty type of person, and he liked that.

"Thank you very much, oh great King," said Dr. Styles while blushing bright red.

"You don't have to thank me for such things. Your beauty is unmatched, and it is an honor to have you in my castle. The gentleman standing next to you must be Colonel Jake Baker. Colonel Baker, do you represent the military force of your planet?"

"Yes King Leinad, I am a Colonel in the M.V.F. I am outranked only by General Hezekai. I was sent here by him to establish contact with you."

"That is funny. Why would a General send an underling to meet with me? I would much rather speak to your leader, but I will hear you out for the time being," said King Leinad as he let out a defiant chuckle.

"Thank you for granting us an audience with you, King Leinad. I promise I will not take up too much of your time," said the Colonel in an irritated tone.

Leinad looked at Jake and gestured for him to continue.

"To make a long story short, we are having an energy crisis on Earth. I am afraid that we have exhausted all of our natural resources. We have come here because we found a star map that gave us directions to your planet. We also found writings in a secret tomb room inside of our pyramids in Egypt. These writings spoke of an everlasting renewable energy source. We believe that someone from your planet was once on Earth," said Baker.

Leinad knew that one of the Elders must have left the map for any future Harpatian travelers who might forget the way home. *A sloppy move at best*, he thought.

"I can see why you might think that, Colonel," said the King while maintaining eye contact with the Colonel.

"With the help of Dr. Styles, we were able to decipher the writings; and we are very interested in your energy source."

"You speak of the Life Source. Please continue Colonel Baker."

"The Life Source, or whatever it may be, is of top concern to us. We were led to believe that you may have a great source of renewable energy, and we would like to see if you would be willing to share it with us. We would like to study it and see if we could incorporate it for use on our planet. My mission is to see if you would be willing to help us with our energy crisis. We would like to restore power to our people and end the worldwide conflict on our planet."

"That is an interesting story, Colonel; however, I don't think it will be possible to give you this energy, for the Life Source is more than a source of energy. It is an eternal being, and it would have to choose to help you. It may already be aware of your problems, and my understanding is the Life Source has been on Harpatia since the beginning of time. It is a magical source of energy that provides us with the ability to power our homes and factories for free. We do have some machines as well, although we choose to live by the old ways."

"Why are you telling me all of this?" Baker interrupted.

"Patience, Colonel Baker. There is a point to what I am saying. We prefer to use magic here on Harpatia," said the King as he disappeared and rematerialized a moment later in front of Dr. Styles, startling her.

"That, my friend, was a bit of teleportation magic. I don't wish to show off. I only want you to see the power of the Life Source. The applications of the Life Source are far more than just providing energy. It provides us with our way of life and aides us in all that we do. It is a part of us as much as we are a part of it. There is no way for a human to trap this energy. You are either with it or you are not. The energy of the Life Source is where it wills itself to be. I don't believe that it would will itself to be with you."

"So that's it? Are you telling me we came all of this way for nothing?" asked Colonel Baker in a slightly raised voice.

"You may need to find alternative ways to solve your problems on Earth. As much as I would love to help you, I fear that I can't. The misuse of the Life Source energy would be catastrophic. I wouldn't want to contribute to your planet's demise in that way. I am afraid I must decline your request. You may stay as guests in Harpatia as long as you like. I am sorry that I can't help you."

"King Leinad, I beg you to reconsider. I fear that General Ram Hezekai is going to declare war on you if you don't help us. General Hezekai takes what he wants by force. I don't want war, but once it starts there will be nothing I can do to stop it."

"Are you threatening me, Colonel Baker? Inside of my own castle?"

"No, I am not threatening you. I am only informing you of the intentions of my leaders."

"So what you are saying is that your people prefer to take things by force and by way of warfare. I already knew that long before you ever arrived."

"I guess so," said Baker with a bewildered look on his face.

"This is most unfortunate. I will try to spare your life if I see you on the battlefield, for I think you are a good man. I know that you are only following orders, but I beg you to tell your leader to return to your planet and leave us in peace, for we don't wish war on anyone. However, if any act of war is bestowed upon us, we'll respond with the full force of the Harpatian armies, police force, wizards, and warriors. I fear that if you don't leave, you will be destroyed," said Leinad in a very harsh tone.

"Now it sounds like you are threatening me, King Leinad."

"I am not threatening you, Colonel Baker. I am simply informing you that if your leader, General Ram Hezekai, declares war on us, we'll drive you from this planet."

"We have hundreds of thousands of mechs back on Earth. They will not be able to commit all of them to us here, but they will send more and more until they get what they want," said Baker.

"Be that as it may, Colonel Baker, I stand firm in my decision. I can't give you any Life Source energy. The Life Source is a gift from the gods, and we don't take it lightly. What you propose is an insult to all Harpatians, but I don't expect you to understand that. You may wait here or anywhere in the castle that you wish. I will assign a couple of my Royal Guards to show you around if you like. In the meantime, I would like to get to know Dr. Styles a little better, if that is ok with you," Leinad said in a challenging tone.

"That is fine with me. Please make it brief. We need to be getting back to base camp soon."

"Your wish is my command, Colonel. There are a few things that I would like to share with the good Dr. Styles, things that she might find interesting as a scientist," said Leinad.

"I would be happy to get to know you better and learn some of your customs, King Leinad," said Kelly Styles as she jumped to her feet.

"Just call me Leinad, Kelly."

"Alright then, Leinad. What are we going to do today?"

"I thought that you may be hungry, so I have arranged a nice meal for us at the Royal Dining Hall."

"Oh boy, that makes me nervous. I was never the type that tries new foods. I am very particular about what I eat."

"Well, my dear, you don't have to worry about that. I have done a lot of research on your people and I know what you humans like to eat. I have a lot of foods that are similar to what you have on Earth, and I am sure you will enjoy the meal I have for you today."

"I hope so. As long as it doesn't kill me, I guess I'll be alright."

"I will not let anything kill you, Kelly, so you don't have to worry about that," Leinad said with genuine care in his tone.

King Leinad Seven could not help but feel a strong flood of emotions that engulfed him when Kelly was near. He had never been so attracted to another woman like this before. He had been waiting for this his entire life. Leinad wanted nothing more than for this day to go well. He wanted to tell her that he had a sense they were meant to be together. His magical powers of foresight were giving him the impression that he and Styles were meant to be. Of course, he could not tell her this at the present time, for any human or non-magic user would be overwhelmed by such a claim. Leinad would have to be patient and let time tell him what would become of his relationship with Dr. Kelly Styles.

They arrived at the Royal Dining Hall and were greeted by a few of the King's servants. Kelly noticed the regal design of the dining area. Kelly saw sculptures of the King and beautiful paintings of Harpatia. There was a surplus of artsy decorum in the room. The piece that caught her eyes was a painting of a very large crimson colored dragon that was perched on the castle wall with his wings outstretched. This particular painting was blooming with detail. Kelly noticed that this dragon must have had about a 100-foot wingspan with a body large enough to carry 50 men or more. *The black tail was kind of a funny finish to the giant beast*, Kelly thought.

There were odors of fresh fruit and some kind of chicken dish. These smells reminded her of when she was a child. Her mother used to cook chicken every Friday night and every Sunday there would be fruit. Could Leinad have possibly known this, she wondered? It did not matter if he did or not. The point was that she was having a great time and it had been a while since Kelly was able to just be herself. The whole spectacle was almost more than she could handle. The idea of eating with a King excited her and it was no surprise everything had been laid out in such a noble manner.

As the two sat down at the table, the lights dimmed without warning.

"It has gotten a little dark in here," said Kelly Styles.

"You may have noticed a few hundred candles lying around here," said Leinad in a mischievous tone. There were candles on the wall and on the table as well. Kelly had not noticed them earlier.

"These will take us forever to light."

"Watch this, dear," Leinad said with a smile on his face.

Leinad pointed his fingers in all different directions toward the candles and tiny red flickers began streaming from his fingertips. With the precision of a laser guided missile, the little flickers found the wicks of several hundred candles within a few minutes. The candles were lighting up ten at a time. This was so amazing to Kelly. Leinad was using his fire magic to brighten up the room. The assistants and servants must have spent hours setting all this up for her. Leinad had indeed planned this.

"Watch this!" Leinad said excitedly.

He then disappeared and reappeared in front of the dining table where there were seven remaining candles. Leinad pressed seven of his fingers against the candles, and with no spark they lit up instantly. Kelly was extremely impressed by the show that Leinad had just given her. She had only seen these types of things in the movies, but now she was seeing them in living color. She was indeed developing an attraction to the King. She was amazed by him, but she did not know if that was wise.

"Alright my dear, have a seat. My royal attaché will be presenting our meals very soon."

Leinad then pulled out a diamond and jewel inlayed chair for Kelly to sit in. She got up out of the other chair and sat down in what must have been the King's chair. Leinad pushed the chair in and then took a seat beside her. *This was indeed going well,* Leinad thought. A few minutes later two Bracelian chefs came out to the table with two large covered dishes and sat them down in front of Leinad and Kelly and then walked away. Leinad removed the covers of both plates.

"This is it. I hope you enjoy it," said Leinad as he smiled at Kelly.

Kelly saw two large breasts that looked like chicken, accompanied by what looked like mashed potatoes, and a purple corn looking vegetable.

"So, what are we having tonight?"

"It is wild Intrepid."

The Intrepid were a large bird like creature that were actually quite vicious in the wild, but nevertheless very tasty. The mash was like a potato. It was a large tuberous vegetable called Kwan. The Kwan was very much like a potato in texture and taste. The purple corn like substance was called Moko. Moko was way better than corn, as Kelly would soon find out.

"Feel free to begin, my lady," said Leinad.

Kelly looked at the intrepid and took a bite. The pair then began to eat. Kelly loved the intrepid. It had a very tender texture with a taste that reminded her of the finest chicken on Earth. Leinad knew that humans were fond of chicken and this was the closest thing that he had to it. The intrepid meat was very popular and very rare, for killing an intrepid was a difficult task. The hunters of Harpatia did not enjoy capturing these beasts at all. The intrepid was notorious for putting up a huge fight, and hunters often got injured in the process of taking one of these birds down.

Dr. Styles ate all of her food and enjoyed every bite. She and Leinad had nice conversations during the meal while staring into each other's eyes. Kelly loved the candlelight aspect of the setting, and she was very impressed by King Leinad's chivalry. When the pair finished their meals, King Leinad summoned his staff; and they came in and removed the plates. The chefs gave them a cup of what looked like cappuccino.

"This is much like your coffee on Earth. On Harpatia with call this Froth," said Leinad.

The froth was much like cappuccino, but with a sweeter taste and a chocolate finish. Kelly enjoyed the beverage immensely. Leinad then took her to the courtyard and the pair sat in a swinging chai where they continued their conversation about life. They were indeed getting to know each other better.

"Thank you for the wonderful meal, King Leinad."

"Oh Kelly, just call me Leinad. You don't have to call me King. The meal was my pleasure. Thank you for joining me."

"I hope we can do this again soon."

"I am sure of it. I only fear for your safety in the company of your friends."

"Don't worry about me. I am a tough girl."

"I must worry about you. I care about you. I will be handing out strict orders to all of my commanders that no harm should come to you; and if it does, someone will pay with his life. Please just stay in the rear of the battles and keep yourself unarmed."

"I am scared that war will break out as soon as Jake and I return to General Hezekai," said Kelly as her eyes filled up with liquid.

"I will leave that decision to your General. I would like to invite him here for a discussion before he makes any rash decisions."

"I will let him know. There is so much that I would like to learn about this planet. The culture, species, and plant life are very intriguing to me."

"In time I am sure you will learn everything you wish to know."

"I don't know how long we'll be here, but hopefully I will get another chance to spend time with you. I would like to speak with some of your scientists and historians."

"I will arrange it. The next time you come here, I will grant you total access to my entire staff."

"Thank you very much, Leinad," Kelly said as she gave the King a hug.

"You are very welcome. There is one more thing that I would like to show you tonight. I will take you to the land of Aurora, to the caves of Duguran, which is known as the dragons nesting area."

"Dragons nesting area, that sounds dangerous," Kelly said in a nervous tone.

"The dragons are my best friends, and they already know not to hurt you. I sent a telepathic message to my personal dragon Monte, and I am sure that the entire dragon legion knows that you are a friend. I may have to cast a communication spell on you when we arrive that will enable you to understand their language. This spell will only work for you."

"That would be great Leinad. How far is this place?" asked Kelly.

"Aurora is several hundred miles to the east; however the distance is not a concern for us, for we'll teleport there instantly."

"I can't teleport."

"You will teleport with me," said Leinad.

"I don't know about that. That sounds a little scary," said Kelly with a note of concern in her voice.

"I can promise you that no harm will befall you."

"I will take your word for it. When do we leave?"

Leinad then held Kelly in a tight embrace and closed his eyes. Instantly the two disappeared leaving a cloud of blue smoke in their wake. Kelly felt like she had fallen asleep for a few seconds and then she woke up as she reappeared in the land of Aurora with Leinad. They were in front of the Caves of Duguran.

"I can sense your apprehension, Kelly. Don't fear. I have a telepathic link with all of the dragons. They already know that we are here and I assure you that they will not harm you."

"Well, that is reassuring."

"As it should be. Just try to enjoy yourself. Even if there were a dragon with ill intentions for you, I would sense it immediately and crush him."

"If you have the ability to crush a dragon, General Hezekai will not have a chance against you."

"I am only one man. I can't be everywhere at once. Not all of the warriors and wizards of my planet are as strong as me, but they will be prepared. As sad as it may be, we are ready for war; however we don't wish for it."

"I understand completely, Leinad. I can only hope that Colonel Baker and I can convince General Hezekai not to act."

"I doubt that highly, for I have seen visions of war," Leinad said.

"What do you mean by visions?" Kelly asked.

"I have psychic powers. Just know that I would never invade anyone's privacy, as I am sure that is what you were thinking, although I did not read your mind."

"Sure you did not," Kelly said jokingly.

"We should enter the caves now and begin our adventure with our dragon friends."

Kelly looked up at the large mountains of Aurora and noticed a large dark void in the landscape. She assumed that the void was the entrance to the Caves of Duguran. She was right in her assumption. While staring at the large gaping hole in the mountain, Kelly realized she was about to meet real dragons again, and lots of them. She was very excited.

"Ok, Leinad, let's do it."

"Ask and you shall receive," replied Leinad.

A massive blue vapor trail emitted as the pair teleported to the cavern entrance with their hands joined. They then entered the cavern. It was very dark inside. They could see a few bright blue spherical lights in the distance, but that was it. King Leinad asked her to wait for just a minute so he could shed some light on the situation. He started swirling his arms and hands in a circular motion, and a bright red fire ball began to form in his hands. Then he pushed his hands upward, and the fire ball shot up to the top of the cavern and shattered into 50 or more pieces as it hit the cavern's roof. Instantly, the cavern was illuminated with bright red light.

Dr. Styles was shocked by what she saw next. There were hundreds or maybe even thousands of dragons everywhere. She was deep inside the dragon's lair. One dragon was about 100 feet in length. This one had crimson skin and eyes with a very strong muscular appearance. The dragon dropped from a small nearby cliff and began flying toward them. It landed about five feet away from Kelly and Leinad and let out a roar. This frightened Kelly quite a bit.

"Don't fear, Kelly. Monte says hello," Leinad said. Leinad then raised two of his fingers and a blue light appeared. "I will now make it possible for you to speak to the dragons."

Kelly remembered that Leinad had said something about casting a communication spell on her.

"You are the only human who will receive this gift, and this gift will last forever."

King Leinad pressed his fingers on Kelly's head, and the light disappeared. Kelly looked toward Monte and said. "I guess I am supposed to be able to talk to you now."

"Indeed you can. My name is Monte, and I serve as personal guard and friend to the King. A friend of his is a friend of mine. I am completely at your service, my lady. Welcome to the dragon nesting area. This place is our home, and as the King dragon of Harpatia, I will grant you access and refuge here any time you may need it," said the dragon Monte.

"This is fascinating. Thank you so much for welcoming me into your home, Monte."

"It is my pleasure. If you would like, you and the King can get on my back and I will take you for a tour of my lair."

King Leinad then prepared to mount the dragon Monte. Monte closed his eyes for a moment, and he began to glow bright blue as a harness with two white seats appeared on the great beast's back. It had appeared to Kelly that the dragon had somehow just manifested a harness and mount for them. Was such a manifestation possible? She did not know, nor did she ask. Kelly was beginning to feel like anything was possible on Harpatia.

Leinad stepped to the side of the dragon and offered Kelly a hand.

"I have ridden horses many times back home. I think I can mount this guy by myself."

This woman was as strong and independent as anyone Leinad had ever met, and he loved that about her. While struggling just a bit, Kelly began to climb the rope-like ladder up to Monte's back. She climbed up about fifteen feet and took a seat, only to find that King Leinad was already strapped into chair next to her.

"Hey, you cheated."

"Nonsense," replied Leinad jokingly.

"That was smooth," Kelly retorted.

"Thank you, my dear."

"Where to, master?" asked Monte.

"Take us to the top, to one of the Life Source essences," said Leinad.

The dragon acknowledged his master's request and leaped high into the air and began flapping his wings. In less than a minute, they were on top of a very high cliff that was deep within the cavern. Leinad took Kelly's hand and said, "Take a deep breath."

"Is this really necessary?"

"No, but it is fun."

Leinad closed his eyes and the two vanished from the dragon's back and reappeared on the ground below. Kelly noticed a light blue spherical ball of light. While grasping Leinad's hand, she began to approach the light.

"What is that thing?"

"This thing is what we call a Life Source Essence. It serves as a healing power to the dragons, and to all who commune with it."

"What are we doing here?"

"I would like to formally introduce you to the Life Source. If you don't mind, I would like you to stand within the ball of light. Let it envelop you for a few moments."

"Is it going to hurt?"

"Not at all. It will feel good."

Dr. Styles was clueless to what was about to happen. Little did she know that King Leinad was about to merge her spirit with the Life Source. From that point on, he would always know where she was and if she was ok. This way, he would be able keep an eye on her through the Life Source. There were a few other bonus effects that she could receive from the Life Source energy as well, but she would remain oblivious to all of them for quite some time.

"Stand there for a good minute," Leinad said.

Kelly stood in the light and instantly her eyes rolled into her head and all she could feel was a strong sense of euphoria, joy, and invigoration. She had never felt so happy in her entire life. She felt so energized and so full of life. In all of her days, she had never experienced such feelings. About a minute later, Leinad took Kelly's hand and gently pulled her away from the light.

"That was amazing. What just happened?"

"Nothing, my dear. I just wanted you to feel the love and joy that the Life Source has to offer. The Life Source is a being and not a thing. What you just experienced was simply an essence, a small cluster of the Life Source's energy that sits here in this place. There are several Life Source nexus's on the planet. The healing benefits from these essences are phenomenal," said Leinad.

Leinad was telling her all about the benefits of communing with one of these essences, but he left out the part about her now being able to be tracked through the Life Source. He did not want to offend Kelly; he just wanted to keep her safe. At this point, Leinad could take Kelly directly to the Life Source and ask it to grant her all of the powers that every Harpatian had access to, but that would have to wait for some time. He could not reveal any of this to Kelly, for it would be far too much for her to comprehend. As far as Kelly was concerned, Leinad had just brought her here to see and learn new things.

"I am glad you are having fun, Kelly. Let us get back on Monte and he will take us somewhere else."

"Ok, let's go," replied Dr. Styles.

Leinad and Kelly then mounted the dragon Monte, and Leinad instructed him to continue the grand tour. Monte jumped off of the cliff and began to fly. The caves were getting dark again, so King Leinad pointed his fingers in the air with one hand and with the other hand he drew out a double bladed staff from a storage satchel on Monte's side. Kelly had failed to notice the jewel encrusted weapon earlier. There were three surgically sharp spear heads on each side of the staff and the hilt looked like a treasure trove with all of the fine jewels that it had.

Although he did not need it, Leinad used the staff for summoning magic from time to time. Leinad aimed the staff up high in the caves and instantly large bursts of fire began shooting and spewing all around the cave's upper regions. The light illuminated the entire cavern system. Kelly could now see thousands of dragons clearly. The dragons were mostly just resting. Kelly assumed they were tired from training, or whatever it was that they did during the day. She was amazed as she saw dragons of all shapes, sizes, colors, and features. There were red, yellow, purple, and green dragons. They had some form of biological armor, for their scales looked as solid as stone. The sight of these beasts was one of the most prolific spectacles Kelly had ever been so privileged to see.

Monte continued to fly through the caves until they were several miles in. He then flew toward a very large cave at the top of the cavern system and sat down. With a flick of Leinad's wrist the cave illuminated. Inside was a much smaller female dragon that was purple in color. There were also two six-foot tall baby dragons with blue-green eyes. Leinad informed her that the younglings were three-year-old twins whose names were Zulu and Kai. These were Monte's sons. The female was named Therese, Monte's life mate. Therese was sleeping with the children, but Leinad knew she was aware of all of their presences. She did not move, for she did not want to wake the babies.

"Thank you very much for the tour, Monte. I am afraid we'll need to be getting back to the castle now," said Leinad.

"Do you need a ride, my Lord?" Monte asked.

"No I think that I can take it from here."

"I don't want you to exert yourself, my King."

"Oh Monte, you don't have to worry about me. It is merely child's play to travel a few hundred miles home, probably a level eight ability. I am the great Leinad Seven. I can do anything."

Monte shrugged and said. "It was a pleasure to meet you, Kelly."

"And you as well, Monte. It was very nice to meet you. Thank you for everything."

Kelly then pulled a camera out of her purse and asked Leinad if she could take a picture.

"Ah, this must be your planet's version of an image collector."

"It is called a camera. Can you take a picture of Monte and me? I would like you to be in the picture as well but then we wouldn't have anyone to hold the camera." replied Kelly as she showed the device to Leinad.

"I can fix that problem. Just throw your camera into the air and I will take it from there," said Leinad.

"What?"

"Just trust me. I have not failed you yet."

"Ok. Here you go."

Kelly threw her camera into the air, and it began to float. Leinad told her that he would hold the camera in a telekinetic grasp until she was satisfied with the picture. Kelly showed him how the camera worked. Kelly stood next to Monte and Leinad stood next to her with his staff in one hand and let his free arm wrap around Kelly. Leinad informed Kelly and Monte to smile and on the count of three the camera snapped a picture. Leinad then floated the camera over to Kelly. Kelly was very pleased with the picture.

"Thank you, Leinad."

"You are very welcome, my dear."

Kelly and Leinad then said their goodbyes to Monte.

"Ok, get ready," said Leinad. "Time for another disappearing act it."

Kelly walked up close to Leinad and held him in a tight embrace. Her lips moved toward his, and Leinad leaned forward and kissed her. A fraction of a second later they disappeared and then reappeared inside of the kings chambers with lips locked. As they came out of the kiss, Kelly realized she had just kissed a King.

"That is a kiss that I will treasure for eternity," said Leinad while making eye contact with Kelly.

"I apologize. I don't know what came over me," Kelly said with a bright red blush on her face.

"You don't have to apologize to me. I have waited for over 100 years for a kiss like that; and if you ask me, it was worth the wait."

"You are far too kind. I am just a humble girl from the country who got a degree in anthropology. I am not that important."

"Your humility amazes me Kelly. You are a very beautiful person. You are important to me. I can sense that we should get you back to your group now. I will miss you. Please feel free to come back to the Castle Dakineah and visit me anytime. If you are ever in serious danger, I want you to close your eyes and think of me, call out to me. I promise that I will hear your call, and I will come to you."

"I will do just that," said Kelly.

Kelly was slightly confused about what the King was saying, for these were still the first few days for her on this new planet and she did not understand the full scope of Harpatian magic and all of the ways it could be used. Nevertheless, she accepted his kindness and gave him a hug. King Leinad escorted Kelly back to the area of the castle in which he was sure that Colonel Baker would be waiting. It was very late now, and the King knew they would all need some rest.

Leinad took Kelly to the first floor of the castle. Upon reaching the Royal waiting area the pair saw Jake Baker.

"Colonel Baker, I am sorry to have kept you waiting for so long. I was having so much fun that I seemed to have forgot the time."

"Whatever it takes to make you happy, King Leinad," Jake said in a mocking tone.

"I know you need to return to your troops in the land of Nowah, but I would like to offer you a night's stay here in the castle. I have separate rooms for you both. You will be just down the hall from me. I already have the beds made up for you. We could all meet in the morning for breakfast before you leave."

"That sounds great. Thank you very much King Leinad. Kelly, are you ok with that idea?" asked Baker.

"I am absolutely ok with it. I could use some rest," said Dr. Styles.

"Alright then, follow me."

King Leinad escorted Jake and Kelly to the 20th floor of the castle. The group walked down the hall to a hover lift that took them to the Royal sleeping chambers. Leinad showed them both to their rooms and gave Kelly a sincere smile as he wished her goodnight. The following morning Leinad was the first to rise. He took a shower and then went to Kelly's room and knocked three times.

"Who is it?"

"It is Leinad," the King replied in a gentle tone.

"Oh ok, I am dressed; you can come in," replied Kelly.

Leinad then teleported behind Kelly and tapped her on the shoulder. This startled her.

"You are always scaring me. Why do you do that?"

"I did not mean to scare you, my lady. I prefer making a dramatic entrance."

"I can tell. You do a pretty good job of it as well."

"Thank you Kelly. Are you hungry? I have a nice breakfast prepared for us in the royal dining hall. I would like to send you away with a full stomach," said Leinad.

"That would be great."

"There is just one more thing that I would like to ask you before we go to breakfast," said Leinad.

"Ask away Leinad."

"May I have another kiss?"

Dr. Styles then embraced the King and began to kiss him. After all, how could she deny him? Leinad was probably the best looking man she had ever seen, although she would have to get used to the pointy ears. The two kissed passionately for about a minute sending jolts of electricity through Leinad's body. Once again, Leinad thanked her and told her there was nothing that he enjoyed more than kissing her.

"I hope General Hezekai can see reason and understand that we can't give the Life Source energy to him, but there may be other ways we can help," said Leinad as he held Kelly in a tight embrace.

"I hope so too, Leinad. I don't want anyone to get hurt, especially you."

"Don't worry about me, my dear. I have trained hard all of my life for a moment like this. It will take more than fancy weaponry and machines to hurt me."

"I hope so."

"Perhaps I will come to visit you soon. I will locate you through the Life Source and teleport to you when it is safe. As always, I will inform my entire staff and armies that you have the key to the castle. You may seek refuge here anytime you wish. Just show up, and you will be welcomed. No Bracelian, Nowrie, or Elven man will ever harm you. I will make my intentions very clear throughout the lands. You now have unlimited access to the kingdom of Harpatia. Just keep your distance from the front lines of the battlefield." Leinad said with love in his voice.

"I will do my best, King Leinad."

"That is all I ask; and please, don't call me King. You are my equal. I don't want anything bad to happen to you, and that is why I am so insistent you stay to the rear of any battles."

"Thank you for your concern, Leinad."

"I only want you to be safe."

"You are very humble for a King."

"I take great pleasure in making others happy. Let us go and eat our breakfast," said Leinad.

King Leinad and Kelly styles then went to get Colonel Baker. Leinad knocked on Baker's door and informed him it was time to eat. Although Colonel Baker had just gotten out of bed, he was fully dressed. Baker followed Leinad and Kelly to the dining hall. Dr. Styles, Leinad, and Colonel Baker then entered the dining hall through two large doors. Kelly noticed the lavish layout of golden utensils and a buffet style food line that was full of exotic choices. There were smells of beef and chicken in the air. These aromas ignited a sharp hunger pang in Kelly's stomach.

The group then began making their plates. There was nutrameal, which was much like oatmeal, only much sweeter. They had Waltzer eggs. The Waltzer was a chicken like bird that produced great eggs and meat and was a common breakfast staple on Harpatia. There were all types of unfamiliar fruits and melons. King Leinad assured them they would love the melons, for he had done a wealth of research on human eating habits. There were also several different fish dishes on the buffet line, as well as a wealth of breads and jams. The group also had some juices. The best of the juices was called pog juice, a delicacy made from three different passion fruits. The group then sat down and made small talk as they thoroughly enjoyed their exotic breakfast.

"Well my friends, I guess you must return to your commander now," said Leinad.

"Yes, I'm afraid so," replied Baker.

"Please inform your General that he is more than welcome to come meet with me before he makes any decisions about his next course of action. I am sure there is a peaceful resolution to all of this."

"Thank you very much for breakfast, Leinad," said Kelly.

"You are very welcome. Thank you for your beauty," Leinad replied.

"It was a fine breakfast, King Leinad. Thank you for your hospitality. Are you sure you don't want to reconsider our request?" asked Colonel Baker.

"You are a good man, Colonel Baker. I hope to never meet you on the battlefield; but if I do, I will try to spare your life," Leinad said with a genuine tone of concern.

"Thank you," replied Baker.

"Don't worry, Dr. Styles, I know that you will be safe. I will now summon my personal dragon, Monte, to give you a lift back to Nowah."

"That would be greatly appreciated King Leinad," said Baker.

The group walked outside to the dragon Staging Area. Leinad folded his arms and closed his eyes. A few seconds later the dragon Monte appeared from out of the sky. Kelly wondered how Monte could have arrived so quickly. Monte descended at a fast pace and landed about 20 feet away from the group.

"Hi, Monte, how are you today?" asked Dr. Styles.

The dragon let out a loud roar that startled Colonel Baker, but Kelly heard him say that he was doing just fine. She thought it was great that she could speak with the dragons, but she would tell no one. The two exchanged pleasantries for a moment. All that Colonel Baker could hear was the loud roar of a dragon, and he thought that Kelly was going insane by the way she was talking to it.

Kelly was excited to fly on the dragon again. She was becoming a true fan of the dragons. All of this was still a little strange for Colonel Baker. Kelly then said her goodbyes to King Leinad, and her eyes began to glass over.

"We will meet again very soon, my dear, of this I am sure."

"I look forward to that day."

"Be safe and be smart, Dr. Styles," said the great King Leinad Seven of Harpatia.

"I will, see you soon, I hope," replied Kelly as a tear dropped from her left eye.

"Safe flight, Monte,"

"Yes, my lord," replied the dragon.

Dr. Styles and Colonel Baker then mounted the dragon. Once they were safely belted into their harness chairs, Monte leaped high into the air and began flying. This time, both Kelly and Jake took the time to really see the landscape. They could see mountains way off to the east or was it south? There was no way for them to tell. They noticed all of the beautiful lakes and ponds. Kelly paid special attention to the shiny blue colored rain forest. Leinad had spoken of a magical forest called the Blue Forest. Kelly really wanted to visit that place and believed one day she would. They soon reached the ocean and then began to fly at untold speeds. A few hours later, they reached the land of Nowah.

Upon landing in the capital of Nowah, Hapunah, Dr. Styles and Jake Baker dismounted the dragon. Monte then vanished into the skies above. Colonel Baker then began to prepare a briefing for his troops, after being escorted inside of the castle walls.

Dr. Styles was nervous, for she had developed a secret romance with King Leinad, and she did not want anything bad to happen to him. After a while, Colonel Baker went off to find his troops. Kelly went to speak to King Roiden. Colonel Baker was not looking forward to talking to General Hezekai, who already knew through the emails they had shared, that King Leinad was unwilling to help their cause. Hezekai was very displeased about the fact that King Leinad would not grant him access to the Life Source energy. Dr. Styles was nervous, for she knew war was imminent; and she did not want any harm to befall Leinad Seven.

Kelly had known from the moment she had left Earth that General Hezekai would not take no for an answer. She headed to King Roiden's meeting chambers and awaited his arrival.

"Hello, Kelly. How did your meeting with the great King Leinad Seven turn out?" asked Roiden.

"The meeting went fine. I had a great time. Leinad showed me all around the castle and displayed a lot of magic tricks for me. I even got to take a ride on his dragon."

"Well, I am glad to hear you had fun."

He was being polite, but he could not believe Leinad would take in a human so easily and even let her ride on his dragon. He had always felt King Leinad was too trusting. Roiden suspected that Dr. Styles was nothing more than a clever spy. The King of Nowah would keep his suspicions to himself for now. He knew the enemy was at their gates.

"So, I guess you will be heading back to your leader now," said Roiden as he reached back to scratch one of his golden spikes.

"Yes, and I'm afraid he will declare war on all of Harpatia. I'm not for that in any way."

"If he does, we'll be ready for him. The Nowries were born to fight."

"I just wish there was a peaceful way to resolve this," said Kelly in a somber tone.

"The only thing Leinad and I want is for you people to return home and leave us in peace. I understand that will probably not happen."

"I just wanted to thank you for your kindness. Regardless of what happens, I want you to know that I am a friend to Harpatia; and I wish harm on no one."

"We have already received orders from King Leinad that you are not to be harmed, so you don't have to worry. Even if someone wanted to harm you they will not, for the judgment of Leinad Seven would be fatal for any man who went against his orders. The King may appear to be a warm hearted man, but he is a fierce warrior and yielder of magic," replied Roiden in a tone of surety.

"I agree. He strikes me as a lover and a fighter."

"I have never heard it put that way before, but I guess you must be right. I have to be getting back to my duties now. I will attach a small unit of Nowrie warriors to escort you all to the outer banks of the eastern seaboard, and you can be on your way back to the Outlands. Hopefully, your leader will see the light and return home. These are some very impressive war machines you have. We have been studying them while you were gone and needless to say, we are not in a hurry to go to war with you. However, if we must then we shall," said King Roiden of Nowah.

"Thanks again for your hospitality. It was very nice meeting you, and I hope to see you again."

"If our great King likes you as much as I think he might, I am sure we'll be meeting again. Farewell Kelly, go with the Life Source."

"Goodbye."

Kelly exited the room and made her way back to the courtyard to meet up with Colonel Baker and the rest of the M.V.F. squad to prepare to leave. Jake was gathering up all the troops and issuing some final orders for some of the operators. He had instructed two of his sergeants to head back to the destroyer class vessel and ready the engines. Baker was ready to get this over with. Dr. Styles, along with the M.V.F. and a small escort of ten Nowries, headed back to the beach. It was a fairly long walk to the beach, but Kelly enjoyed it thoroughly. She stopped several times in the rainforest to gather up vegetation and dirt samples for analysis. A few hours later they finally arrived at the beach. The Nowrie escort had not uttered a single word during the journey; and when they arrived at the beach, the lead guard simply nodded his head toward Kelly and left.

Dr. Styles quickly boarded the destroyer and went straight to her quarters. The group then set course for the Outlands. Some of the soldiers played cards with one another, others watched movies in the TV room. The soldiers were enjoying what were probably their last few moments of peace, as they were all very nervous about General Hezekai's upcoming decision. The mission to Harpatia had been a volunteer mission, and it did not take long to fill the 5,000 available seats. Some of the soldiers were having second thoughts, but for the most part they all felt honored to be part of a historical alien encounter, even if they might have to give their lives; and that is what made the M.V.F. a force to be reckoned with.

Kelly went to the exercise room to get in a little run on the treadmill. Baker stayed at the helm of the ship. While he was waiting for Kelly back the Castle Dakineah, Colonel Baker had many conversations through the satellite communication network they had set up when they first arrived. Hezekai told Baker that negotiations were futile, and they should have just attacked the Harpatians to begin with. Baker knew they had lost the element of surprise, and the kingdom of Harpatia would be ready for their next move. Or would they?

Chapter 13: Time for War

Jake Baker knew that General Hezekai was about to change his circumstances for the worse, and he was a bit nervous about all of this. He had taken a liking to the Nowries and even to King Leinad Seven, even though he felt that Leinad was a little on the arrogant side. Baker did not want war, and it did not please him to know he would have to go to war against such a peace loving people. Nevertheless, he knew the time for war was upon him.

About halfway through their return voyage home on the second day, Colonel Baker and his crew noticed a very large whale-like creature off the side of their vessel. Once again, Baker thought *that has to be the third sea monster*; and, indeed, it was. This was the Snarvin that had fled during their last encounter with the beasts. The creature had no doubt returned to avenge his two fallen comrades. It jumped out of the ocean, began to flap its wings, flew directly over the ship. The creature glared down at Jake Baker and let out a loud snarl as it flashed its razor sharp teeth. It did not ram or attack the ship this time; it just followed them. The troops marveled at this beast that had the body of a whale and the face of a shark. The troops called it the "Flying Whale Shark." This creature was truly a strange site. Colonel Baker did not know what to do as the beast was not engaging him, and he was not in a big hurry to engage the beast.

If the beast only wanted to follow them, that would be fine. But if it wanted more, that could be deadly. One of the snipers, a Sgt. Moore, climbed up to the top of the ship's lookout tower and began taking shots at the Snarvin. Baker knew this would be a mistake and ordered Moore to stand down. Moore, however, ignored him. After he put the sixth shot into the Snarvin's belly, Moore lowered his weapon. Immediately after that, the Snarvin jumped out of the ocean and over the ship. Flying directly over the lookout tower, the Snarvin bit off about eight feet of the tower and swallowed Sgt. Moore whole. The beast then returned to the ocean and disappeared. Their radar had been on the tower that was just destroyed, so now it would be impossible to detect any threats from the air. Colonel Baker addressed the entire crew and informed them that Moore's death was a result of disobeying a direct order. He went on to say that no one should ever fire a shot unless they have been ordered to do so.

The M.V.F. still had their sonar and their compass, but their communications receiver and radar was gone. It had presumably been eaten by the giant Snarvin. After mourning the loss of Sgt. Moore, the troops went back to their daily routines. They were a little shaken, but it was not the first time they had lost a comrade to battle; and it would definitely not be the last. The soldiers of the M.V.F. were a hard bunch. They understood there would be casualties, and they could not allow themselves to be phased by that. Sgt. Moore had been careless, and being careless is what got him killed.

The third day of the journey back to the outlands, the soldiers were very close to base camp. They approached the cliff's edge of the Outlands and anchored the ship. *Lancer I* flew overhead and raised them into its hull. The Capital Ship had picked them up on radar about a day ago and had been ordered by General Hezekai to airlift them back to base camp, as the General was very eager to discuss battle plans with Colonel Baker.

***

Back in Nowah, King Roiden had sent a message to King Leinad Seven via courier, who had teleported via the teleportation hubs in Nowah to Dakineah. The message reached Leinad at about midday. Leinad was accompanied by his brother Gressit and the warrior Cassion. The group was so intrigued by the message that they dropped everything they were doing and made the trip to Nowah. Upon their arrival, King Leinad, Gressit, and the warrior Cassion sat down with King Roiden to discuss their plans.

"The reason I asked you here today is because I feel the humans will be back here very soon. I believe Nowah will be their first stop, as Nowah is the gateway to Bracelia, Dakineah, and the rest of the Harpatian kingdom. However, to get to you they will have to get past us first. I know they have a limited supply of jets and several large sea vessels. I don't know much else about their forces. I had my engineers inspect their mechs while they were here, and you can review our findings whenever you like as I have prepared detailed logs for you all to read," said Roiden as he passed out the folders in which the information on the mechs was contained.

"I assume they made the journey to our planet by way of large space vessels. However, I don't think they will risk more than one of their large ships, for they will need a way back home," Roiden exclaimed.

"I have no doubt there will be more of them coming, and I do believe they will attack us very soon. We must hit them, and we must hit them hard. We will defend our homeland with lethal force. The humans must be defeated. There are a few things I will be sharing with you about our defenses, but I don't wish to discuss them at this time.

"Cassion, I want you to stay here and aid the Nowries in battle. Be careful: Harpatia can't afford to lose you," said Leinad as he gave the warrior a light punch to the arm.

"Fear not, great King. It will take a lot more than a human in a machine to destroy me," said Cassion with a smile on his face.

"Just be careful. They have a lot of foreign weaponry, including rocket propelled grenades and missiles. Use your elemental magic to fortify your skin and you should be ok."

"That will definitely help. I will also wear my Jezelite armor. I will be prepared my King. Don't worry yourself over me. We have trained for centuries to prepare for something like this, and I am more than ready for battle."

"Gressit, I will post you in Bracelia. You will aide Santei should they invade Bracelia, and I will make sure you have everything you need in terms of resources. We can't allow them access to our teleportation hubs. I want all of the hubs in the land disassembled by nightfall. We can travel by teleportation anytime we please; everyone else will travel by sea or by way of dragon back. If they want to occupy Dakineah, they will have to earn that right through blood. The kingdom shall not fall," shouted King Leinad Seven in a roaring tone of dominance.

"I agree with you whole heartedly," said Roiden.

"We will put our plans into action immediately. I want you all to know I will be fighting along your side, and I plan to be everywhere when needed. In addition, I will be organizing the School for Combat and Magic Arts. There are many powerful warriors and mages in the school, and their assistance is going to be of great help. Masters Chew and Dolan will be ready. I will not turn my back on any of you. I am in this with you, my brothers."

"And we are with you, brother," replied Gressit feeling somewhat left out.

"Until death becomes me," said The Warrior Cassion.

"And in the afterlife as well," Roiden said with ferocity in his eyes.

"May the Life Source protect us all," said Leinad.

"I think we have a good plan. Cassion, you will be the secret weapon of Harpatia. Strike swiftly my friend," said Leinad.

"I will strike swiftly and accurately, my King. I will serve Nowah as I have served you: wholeheartedly and with honor."

"Gressit, I need you to go to Bracelia now and help them disassemble their teleportation hubs. I must return to Dakineah and dispatch the Harpatian Police Force to patrol all the lands and smaller villages. The people must be protected. At this point, we'll hope they don't slaughter the people of the Outlands. They will be primarily on their own until we can get them all to safety. I will send a message to all of the Outlanders and invite them back to the kingdom to fight along our side.

"I will be leaving now to go and prepare the apprentices and wizards at the school. I will summon you when I need you. We will meet again soon, my friends."

The King bid the men farewell and went on his way. Leinad summoned his dragon and mounted him. Monte leapt into the air and flew back to Dakineah. Once in Dakineah, Leinad planned to visit Masters Chew and Dolan.

***

Upon arriving back at base camp, Colonel Jake Baker and Dr. Kelly Styles went to speak with General Hezekai.

"Welcome back, Colonel Baker. I am glad to see you have returned in one piece, which is good. I have reviewed all your footage and surveillance of the lands. I have also reviewed your conversations with the King. I have no desire to sit and bargain with King Leinad Seven. I think we should attack immediately. I will take *Lancer I* and attack the capital city, and I will drop a few bombs just to make my intentions clear.

"We will then infiltrate the land of Nowah. I will send in battalions by boat and a couple by air. I have informed Lt. Colonel Kanak we'll be needing reinforcements in a month or two, but he informed me we'll need to return to get them. The situation at home has worsened. Both China and Russia are on the verge of attacking us, and they are using most of our resources defending our borders.

"The M.V.F. is building two more Capital Ships that will be even larger and more powerful than the ones we have now. Once completed, we'll be able to transport thousands more mechs to Harpatia and many more troops. Our forces are small right now; however, we'll go back to Earth in a couple of months to regroup, recondition, and rearm. When we return, we'll have tripled our forces. I will be leaving a medium sized battalion here when we leave to hold whatever territories we may have conquered by then," said Hezekai in a maniacal tone.

"Do you think it would be wise to attack their capital city first?" Baker asked.

"I think that it would be just fine. We have to send them a message. I am very curious to see how many innocent lives the King is willing to lose over his precious Life Source. All I want is access to this energy so we can harness or synthesize it and take it back to Earth. That is not an option at this point, so we have to make it an option," said Hezekai with an evil look on his face.

"You can't attack these people, General. They are a peace loving civilization. They don't want war. The King has invited you to come and speak to him, and you should go. There must be something you two could agree on to preserve peace," said Dr. Styles with a strong sense of conviction.

"I will first weaken the King and his army. I will spill their blood until they are ready to cooperate. There is no room for negotiation on this matter. There is a reason we brought an army with us, and that reason was not so we could sit down and bargain. No offense Dr. Styles, but I got the reports on you and the King. And just because you have a crush on Leinad Seven, I will not be merciful. We did not come here to make friends with these people. We came here because they have what we need."

"I can only tell you that King Leinad Seven and his people have amazing powers and you might be getting in a little over your head, General," said Kelly in a mocking tone.

"I don't care about their powers. I am confident we'll be able to conquer them in battle. Our mechs are the most powerful weapons of war in the universe," said Hezekai as he smiled viciously at Dr. Styles.

"I hope you are right, Sir," said Colonel Baker as he stood at attention.

"I love a good fight, and a fight is what we'll give them. The two of you are dismissed. You are to await further orders. I am going to take *Lancer I* to send the mighty Leinad Seven a message." General Hezekai then made his way to *Lancer I*. He took his modified RS-777 with him.

Hezekai's RS-777 mech had been fortified with gold, steel, and titanium metals, and it was fully equipped with every weapon he could ever want. The General's RS-777 series mech had modified Gatling guns, rocket launchers, flame throwers, and few other nifty gadgets on board. The propulsion was the fastest in the fleet, and Hezekai would not let himself be afraid of a self-proclaimed wizard, even if that wizard was the great King Leinad Seven of Harpatia. General Ram Hezekai was arrogant enough to believe he could destroy the King's empire in a matter of weeks; and he felt that if he was able to do so, he could go home with the Life Source energy and fix all of Earth's problems. At the end of the day, all that Ram Hezekai really wanted was to be a hero. But it was that very obsession that made him a villain.

***

Meanwhile, back in Harpatia King Leinad was at the School for Combat and Magic Arts. He was preparing to speak to masters Dolan and Chew.

"Sorry to disturb you today, Masters. The humans have made landfall, and I have made contact with them. I took a personal liking to the female I met, but we can talk that about later over a cup of froth. The human male, Colonel Jake Baker, informed me that they have come to harness the Life Source's energy for use on their planet. As far as I know, the Life Source would have to choose to help them, for harnessing its energy by force would be impossible. But the humans don't care about that. They want what they want, and they want it now. I can't give my blessing for such a thing, so I fear they will wage war on us. War will be upon us soon.

"I don't believe they will take no for an answer. I know you all have been training for a few weeks for this and now is the time I must call upon you. We must dispatch some of the students and teachers to Bracelia and the outer regions of Dakineah. I will need you to send some of your best warriors to Nowah, for I fear that will be the place they attack first.

"I will attach a small detail to the land of Aurora. I feel they will have no luck against the dragons, should they attack in Aurora, so the detail in Aurora should be a small one. I will be calling several hundred of our dragons into service, and more if needed. I just want everyone to be prepared," said the King as he addressed the men.

"We will be ready, my King. We will dispatch our units at once. We will also send and attachment of men to Nowah, as I am sure they could use them," replied Master Chew.

"What about Bracelia?" asked Master Dolan?

"Bracelia is armed with rifles and many other advanced forms of weaponry. They have some very interesting explosive devices, as well as a few good wizards at their disposal. It would probably be a good idea to get a small detail of wizards out to Bracelia as well. I am going to remain at the Castle Dakineah for a while. I will be joining the battle on every front through the use of my teleportation abilities. Once the war starts, I will be observing everything as it happens through meditation; and I will direct troops and resources to you all at the appropriate times. I don't look forward to all of the carnage that is yet to come, but I will be ready," said King Leinad.

***

Back in the Outlands, General Hezekai was preparing for his assault on Dakineah.

"Colonel Baker, on my way to Dakineah I am going to drop you and five hundred mechs in the land of Nowah. I want you to wait for my signal and then attack. We must gain control over the land of Nowah. Once we have control of Nowah, we'll be able to have a centrally located base of operations. And when that happens, we can return home for reinforcements.

"After we conquer Nowah, we'll take Dakineah and all the surrounding lands. Once we destroy the Castle Dakineah and kill King Leinad Seven, his underlings will have no choice but to give us what we have come for," Hezekai laughed and looked at Jake Baker with an evil eye.

"Will you not at least talk to the King first?" asked Colonel Baker.

"There is no room for talk, Colonel, you have made my intentions very clear to the great King Leinad Seven of Harpatia, and he is unwilling to cooperate."

"General, I think you are making a very big mistake, a mistake that is going to get a lot of good people killed. You have not even tried for a diplomatic solution," said Dr. Styles.

"I appreciate your concern, Dr. Styles, but I am not a diplomat. I am a soldier. No offense, Dr. Styles, but your role is to collect scientific data for research and to make discoveries, and so far you have discovered nothing. I don't need you as an adviser.

"Now get everyone ready to board the ship. Dr. Styles, you will be staying here for now. I will send for you when I need you. Colonel Baker I want you to set up base camp and wait for my orders. The rest of the troops will be heading for the beaches of Nowah. Today we'll test the might of the Harpatian kingdom."

***

Leinad was finishing his conversation with masters Chew and Dolan.

"There is one more thing I would like to discuss with you before I leave. I have cast a spell of protection over the Castle Dakineah, as well as the School for Combat and Magic Arts. The spell will keep us safe, but I fear I will only be able to hold the spell for a week or two at which point it will need to be recast. This spell will weaken my powers slightly, but I think I should be just fine. I have foreseen the bombing of our Castle, and that is why I have cast the spell. But I will need your help to cast similar spells in the future; for once I engage in combat, I will not be able to hold the spell for much longer," said Leinad as he paced the floor.

The magic users of Harpatia were able to cast spells; however, when they did cast, their powers would be weakened, for every second of a spell's existence pulled and drained the Life Source energy from its source. Although the energy drained from the spell's caster was a small amount, it still required a constant awareness and attention on some level for it to be maintained. And maintaining a spell of protection could be very draining. There was a difference between using magic and casting a spell. Channeling a bolt of lightning or launching sheets of ice at an opponent in battle are examples of using a magic ability. The wizard simply has the ability to use his elemental magic through his communion with the Life Source. Holding a spell was a much more complicated task, and only the most skilled of masters could even think about using a spell of protection.

"Thank you for casting this spell to protect us, and we'll be more than happy to help you cast the next one," said Master Dolan.

"I concur," said Chew.

If a spell were to be cast by multiple individuals, then it would be all the more powerful. This was called melding. When a group of magic users formed a meld, anything they did would have significant power and strength in terms of magic. For instance, in the ancient Wars of Segregation where the Nowries were trying to take all of Harpatia, there was a group called Ten Meld. Ten Meld consisted of ten warriors and wizards, and they were said to have engulfed an entire battlefield in flames hot enough to melt Bluestone. According to legend, these men were able to do just about anything; and it was through their great efforts that Harpatia was able to be at peace. But now that peace was over.

"We will not let the innocent suffer," said Dolan.

"I appreciate your enthusiasm, masters. I will now return to my Castle. I will be summoning you both soon. Be ready, and may the Life Source protect us all.

Back in the Outlands, General Hezekai was preparing for launch. He had spoken to the leaders on Earth and informed them there was no peaceful option. The Joint Chiefs of Staff, along with the President gave him the go ahead, and that was all that Hezekai needed to start a war. He was a little disappointed he would have to return to Earth midway through the battle to get reinforcements, but he felt a little rest and recuperation would boost the morale of his men. He took in a deep breath and hit the throttles of *Lancer I.*

General Hezekai sat in his pilot's chair of *Lancer I* with a strong sense of anxiety. Although he was a warmonger, he often got nervous before a fight. The general had brought a small force of mechs with him in case something went wrong. Ram Hezekai always had a backup plan.

Lancer I reached the Land of Nowah within a couple of hours. Hezekai had launched a few satellites into orbit around Harpatia when they had initially arrived. The satellites, in conjunction with the onboard computers of *Lancer I*, were able to provide detailed maps of the planet.

Using the satellite cameras, Hezekai was able to get a bird's eye view of the castle grounds. He saw there were heavy concentrations of Nowries surrounding the castle walls but the lands outside the castle walls were not heavily populated. There were many small villages to the west, but for the most part the land was made up of rainforests and beaches. General Hezekai estimated that Nowah was about the size of Australia. Shortly after bypassing the land of Nowah, he began receiving satellite images and ground level views of Dakineah.

Hezekai estimated Dakineah was larger than the continent of the United States of America. The Castle Dakineah was in the city of Dakineah, which incidentally had the same name of the continent Dakineah. There were many towns, provinces, and territories on the Dakineah continent, but the only one General Hezekai cared about was the capital city of Dakineah. The King's entire Royal Guard and Army resided in the capital city, minus whatever number of warriors and wizards already dispatched across the lands. Ram Hezekai knew that if he was able to capture and control Dakineah, he would win the war. What he really wanted was to kill King Leinad Seven, for he knew if he was able to do that, the people would be forced to obey him. Hezekai did not want to conquer Harpatia for personal gain; he just wanted to return to Earth as a hero. He knew that if he was able to solve the energy crisis, he would be the next U.S. President, and with that would come world power.

Lancer I then passed over the land of Bracelia, and Hezekai took note of the giant forest that was blue in color, what he would later come to know as the Blue Forest. All the while, Hezekai was making notes on how he would attack. He knew he would have to conquer the land of Bracelia to have any chance of gaining control of Dakineah. Ram had always been a brilliant tactician, and he was devising battle plans in his head with every breath he took.

Hezekai divided the different lands into sectors, and he would use these sector designations to plot out maps and battle plans. They were getting close to Dakineah now, and he felt a slight sense of fear about what he was doing. A small voice in his head asked him if he was making the right decision. Another voice wondered if taking on a magical race of aliens with domesticated dragons at their disposal was a good idea. Hezekai ignored these fears. He wondered if he was making an intelligent decision, but he did not have time for hesitation. His mission was to harness the Life Source's energy for use on Earth, and Ram Hezekai had never failed while on a mission.

The General reviewed some of the satellite imagery of Bracelia, and he noticed the Bracelian people looked much like humans except for a very distinguished golden brown skin color. Hezekai was intrigued by these Bracelians, and if time permitted he would have loved to stop by and interrogate one of them for a couple of days. But he had a war to win, and he could not allow any curiosities about these aliens to distract him.

Hezekai could not wait to drop a bomb on the Castle Dakineah. He felt that a barrage of explosives might send a better message to King Leinad than Colonel Baker and Dr. Styles were able to communicate. *Lancer I* began its descent into Dakineah; and upon reaching the Castle Dakineah, General Hezekai hovered *Lancer I* in place and ordered his artillery crew to deploy a couple of Stinger missiles that had a huge blast radius and should have been more than sufficient for leveling the castle.

The view from the ground was horrifying. A young elven woman by the name of Sarah was headed to lunch with her sister when she suddenly saw a huge flying ship the size of a small city descending towards her. Sarah took note of the sheer mass of the ship, and she actually thought that the shiny silver metallic color of the ship was pretty. The Capital Ship was probably a million square feet inside. Sarah then saw there were large ports opening up inside of the ship's hull. Large square boxes popped out of these holes, and within a second, two projectile missiles launched from the ship. As the missiles flew toward the castle Sarah was standing outside of, she realized this would be the last thing that she would ever see.

The missiles were accompanied by six 1,000 pound bombs, and they found their targets. They struck the castle walls and gates, and the bombs hit directly in the castle's courtyard and field area. The sensors of *Lancer I* showed an impact on the castle, but no damage had been caused other than some mild grass damage in the courtyard. The castle was still intact. General Hezekai was in disbelief. He quickly pulled up some satellite imagery, and again it showed no damage to the castle. He looked again and again, and he could not believe what he was seeing.

Hezekai ordered Major Alexis to turn the ship around and fly at a low altitude. The ship sounded like a thunderstorm as it approached the castle once again. At this point, a few villagers gathered outside the castle walls to watch. Hezekai launched six more Stinger missiles at the castle. Again there was impact, but there was no damage. From a closer view, Hezekai noticed these impacts were absorbed by a blue glow of energy. This was ridiculous to Hezekai. He could not understand how these missiles could have no effect on the castle. In the wars on Earth, Hezekai had seen these same stinger missiles take out entire villages and towns. How could this be possible, Hezekai wondered?

He ordered the crew of *Lancer I* to fire their gun batteries and laser cannons. Neither the large caliber ordinance nor the energy weapons had any effect on the castle. There seemed to be some kind of a shield that was protecting the castle, and little did General Hezekai know King Leinad Seven had cast a protection spell over the castle. The reason the spell was so powerful was because the Life Source rested underneath the Castle Dakineah; and although not many people knew this, the Life Source would protect the castle under any circumstances. And as long as a spell of protection was cast, the Castle Dakineah would be protected.

The Castle of Dakineah may have been protected, but the villages and townships outside of the walls were not. General Hezekai then decided to double back and create some distance between *Lancer I* and the castle. He dropped two more thousand pound bombs, but this time Hezekai dropped them on the township outside the castle where all the people had come to watch. Ram Hezekai had figured out that whatever was protecting the castle was only protecting the castle. This time the bombs destroyed the entire town and killed thousands of innocents in the process. The crew of *Lancer I* protested loudly, as what the General had just done was a war crime. The crew knew it was illegal to kill unarmed civilians, but Hezekai did not care. He simply ordered them to be quiet. Hezekai stated that for all they knew, those unarmed civilians could all have been magic users in which case his actions would have been legal, but the crew knew better than that.

The soldiers of the M.V.F. were elite, and killing innocent people whether they used magic or not was not justifiable. General Hezekai had lost a lot of respect that day, and he was now a prime target on King Leinad's list. This act would outrage the King, and just like that, the war had begun. General Hezekai ordered *Lancer I* back to the Outlands. King Leinad Seven had felt the impact of all of the bombs that hit the castle's shield, but what he had felt the most was the massive loss of life in the town of Dakineah proper. He knew there would be no more room for negotiations. The time for war was upon him.

Leinad had felt the people of Dakineah proper die; so when news of casualties arrived, it did not surprise him. The entire town was toppled in a matter of seconds. He was outraged by the fact that General Hezekai attacked the innocent. Leinad now knew who he was dealing with and would have no problem killing this man in the future. He did not understand how Hezekai could do such a thing to a people he knew nothing about.

The King immediately summoned his royal advisers and aides and informed his staff the war had begun. He ordered all villagers and townsmen across the lands into hiding. There were many underground protection areas throughout the lands, but the best of them were located inside the Mountains of Harpinia. Most of the villagers would comply with this order. Those who did not seek shelter would be in danger, and all those who were able to fight were urged to enlist in the Harpatian Army at once.

Those with special skills would be enrolled in the School for Combat and Magic Arts. With Gressit in Bracelia and the Warrior Cassion in Nowah, the King felt alone. Leinad knew he would have to go to Nowah, for he was sure this would be the first target for the M.V.F. and the Nowries would definitely need some help. The humans would be looking to set up base camp in a closer region to Dakineah. Leinad knew they would slowly try to take over the planet by taking one region at a time, and he would not let this happen. This would be Leinad's first war as king. He remembered his father, King Albert the Great, who had given his life in the ancient Wars of Segregation so there could be peace.

After the death of Leinad's father, his mother, Queen Diane, became ill and heartbroken and subsequently died from the loss of her love. This left Leinad and Gressit to be raised by the Royal Steward, Wilson. Wilson had been an adviser and friend to Albert the Great, and it was written that should anything ever happen to Albert, Wilson would take care of his sons, Gressit and Leinad.

The Warrior Cassion had been dropped off at the castle walls shortly after the death of the King. Wilson had taken over care of Leinad and Gressit, and out of the kindness of his heart, the Elvin man, Wilson, took in Cassion and raised him with Leinad and Gressit. The three men had been brothers ever since. The fact that Cassion had been an orphan never affected him, for Leinad and Gressit had always treated him like blood.

Upon speaking to his Royal Staff, King Leinad learned the humans had been helped by an Elven man by the name of Rouger. Leinad planned on traveling to the Outlands to speak to Rouger and to give General Hezekai one last warning. Leinad would give Ram Hezekai one final chance to leave to avoid more bloodshed. And if Hezekai did not heed the warning, Leinad would do his best to annihilate the M.V.F. and rid them from his lands.

King Leinad would now begin his secret mission. He informed his staff he would be leaving for a day or two. He did not tell them where he was going, but he assured them there was no need to worry. Leinad summoned his dragon, Monte, late that night and flew to the Outlands. Even at exceptional speeds, the trip took twelve hours. When he arrived in the late afternoon the next day, he sat Monte down near a cave at the Ocean and instructed Monte to wait for him inside the cave so he would be out of sight.

Leinad then made his way to the village in which Rouger was said to have been residing. Leinad was dressed in a hooded cloak with black battle pants on. The cloak would keep him from being recognized. Leinad crept up to the village with his hood raised. No one paid attention to him, for he appeared to be an Elven warrior or drifter. The people of the Outlands were used to seeing new faces in town, and everyone minded their own business in these parts. Leinad made conversation with some of the locals, and it was a Nowrie man that told him where he could find Rouger.

Leinad walked off to secluded area of the village and then teleported inside of Rouger's hut. Rouger looked shocked when he saw this hooded man appear suddenly in his home. The King pulled his hood off of his head.

Rouger looked at the King in a state of shock and said, "King Leinad, what are you doing here?"

"I should ask you the same thing, Rouger. You were once one of my father's greatest warriors and friend," replied Leinad in a sharp tone.

"Sire, I never meant to disappoint you. I needed a break from the kingdom, and I find great peace out here. My moving out here was not meant to defy you."

"Maybe not. But how do you explain your conversation with General Hezekai? You told the humans how to find me, and gave them detailed information about the kingdom. What you have done could be interpreted as treason; and whether you are sovereign of the kingdom or not, treason is punishable by death," Leinad said while keeping constant eye contact with Rouger.

"Please forgive me, my Lord, I was in fear for my life. We live in peace out here. When the humans arrived with their powerful war machines, I felt helpless. They asked for my cooperation, and in return assured the safety of all who dwell in the Outlands."

"Rouger, if I were you I'd gather all my people and return to the kingdom, for it is the only place that will offer you a chance at being safe. Bring them back to my kingdom. It will not be safe for you here anymore. Whatever they have in store for us is not good, and you can rest assured your fate will be the same as ours. To think these war mongers will spare your life is juvenile. They have bad intentions. They have attacked the Castle Dakineah, unsuccessfully, I might add.

"You should put the word out that everyone in the Outlands should return home. Let it be known there will be no repercussions for anyone who returns. I am only interested in the safety of my people. Even though you all left my kingdom, you are still my people. When this is over, you can return back here if you like. Do as I say, Rouger. I am now going to visit the human leader General Hezekai."

"Yes, my King," Replied Rouger as he bowed to Leinad.

Leinad left the village and headed toward the humans' base camp. He wondered how Rouger, one of the ancient Elite Guards of Harpatia, could have been so naïve as to think the humans would actually honor any deal he would make with them. Leinad sat Indian style in the outskirts of Rouger's village to become in tune with the Life Source; and was shown the way to the Base Camp of the M.V.F. He then saw a vision of General Hezekai sleeping on his cot in his large tented quarters with two guards outside listening to music on some kind of portable device. It would be very easy to slip past them, especially if he were to teleport inside of Hezekai's quarters.

Leinad closed his eyes, and in a second he vanished from where he was sitting and reappeared right in front of Hezekai's tent and stared directly into the startled man's eyes. Hezekai experienced a feeling of terror he had not felt since the death of his family. He wanted to kill King Leinad, but he could not move. He was paralyzed.

"I don't mean to disrespect you, as you have disrespected me; so forgive my intrusion. You are in a telekinetic hold right now. Trying to resist it will only weaken you, so please just relax; you will need all of your strength for the next time that we meet.

"My name is King Leinad Seven. I am the ruler of Harpatia. For bombing my city, my castle, and my people, I should kill you where you lay right now," Leinad said as he unsheathed his golden sword and placed it just below Hezekai's throat.

Hezekai was completely helpless as he lay motionless due to the telekinetic hold that Leinad had put him in. He was indeed at the mercy of the King. The guards remained clueless to what was going on inside the tent. Hezekai was in more fear now than he had ever been in his entire life.

"I don't care who you are, or what military power you possess. I will give you two days to leave my planet. If you choose to stay, there will be more repercussions coming your way than you could ever imagine. This will be your only chance to leave here unharmed. I strongly advise you to leave Harpatia and never come back, for if you don't, you will die the next time we meet.

"This is not a threat. This is my promise to you. You will not win this war, but if war is what you want, it is war that I will give you. If I were you, I would go to sleep now, for this spell will not wear off until sunrise. Gather your troops in the morning and leave this place. This will be the last time you see me up close and live to tell about it. Don't be a fool; what you have done thus far has been very foolish. Two days, General, and then I will be coming for you. Two days," Leinad said in growling tone as he removed the tip of his blade from the general's neck and vanished.

Chapter 14: The Beginning of the End

Leinad closed his eyes, vanished, and teleported back to the edge of the Outlands to retrieve Monte. He greeted the beast and informed him it was time to go back home. Monte begged Leinad to let him go and unleash his wrath on the humans, and possibly even eat a few; but Leinad told him there would be a time and place for that, and now was not the time. He told Monte he gave the humans two days to leave. Monte wanted to kill those responsible for the bombing in Dakineah, and rightfully so, for Monte was an elite protector of Harpatia. Leinad assured him the people who fell in the bombing would not be allowed to die in vain: they would be avenged. He then mounted Monte and headed back to Dakineah.

General Hezekai was not able to sleep that night, and he was furious about what had happened. *He pondered to himself that if King Leinad was able to subdue him so easily, then perhaps he would prove to be much harder to kill than he had originally thought.* The next morning when the sun rose, Hezekai screamed out in rage and told his commanders what had happened. He ordered a large portion of his troops to the land of Nowah to take it by force and set up a new base camp.

Hezekai needed to set up a central command so he could seize Dakineah. He checked in with Central Command on Earth to get a status report on the reinforcements and instructed the Joint Chiefs of Staff he would need to fit as many mechs as possible onto *Lancer III* once it was ready. The Chiefs informed him the super Capital Ship would be able to carry tens of thousands of mechs and personnel. Lt. Colonel Kanak told Hezekai not to worry, and assured him the new and improved versions of the RS-777 mechs would be more apt to resist the elemental magic the Harpatians possessed. The new mechs would be better armored and much more agile for combat. Kanak told Hezekai they were working on a couple of different prototype designs that would be very helpful to their cause.

The leaders on Earth reminded Hezekai they would need him to return to help organize the efforts of the M.V.F.'s mission to Harpatia. They told him to bring half of his personnel back for a little rest and recuperation. Lt. Colonel Kanak informed Hezekai the new ship would be ready in about two months; and since the journey home could take about a month, Hezekai knew he would need to head back to Earth in about a month's time. He also knew that if he was going to return to Earth with half his men, he would need to conquer and secure the land of Nowah soon. If he could do that, he would feel safe leaving his men with Colonel Baker for a couple of months to maintain their base of operations.

Hezekai knew he would have to leave all the mechs on Harpatia to defend whatever territory they may have conquered by that time. He was furious over this decision, for he did not want to return to Earth. He did not need a break, but he knew he was the best man for the reinforcement mission to Harpatia. Hezekai briefed Colonel Baker on the plan and prepared for his next step.

The M.V.F. began to move their personnel and mechs across the sea by way of boat and air ship. They would drop about 1,000 men and mechs on the shores of Nowah to begin the fight. *Lancer I* would arrive at the beaches in a matter of hours to do a quick air drop, but it would take a few days for the boats to get there. The only reason they did not send the entire force by air was because they did not know if Harpatia had any viable air defenses, but they would soon find out.

General Hezekai dispatched 200 jet mechs to fly in groups of ten while bombing the beaches of Nowah. This way they could bomb the beaches and the surrounding rainforests around the clock, thus ensuring an empty beach to unload on when the boats and other personnel of the M.V.F. arrived. They bombed the entire shoreline of Nowah and quite a bit of the rainforest as well. They tried to bomb the castle of Nowah, but the bombs had little effect. Hezekai decided there must have been some sort of shield on this castle as well. Although there was some visible damage to the castle, it was not significant enough to devote more resources to at this time. Hezekai focused on the surrounding villages instead, and he was successful. The M.V.F. killed several hundred villagers in a matter of minutes.

The Nowries were able to get most of the villagers to safety within the castle walls, and many of the others fled to nearby valleys and an underground cavern system. The warrior Cassion mounted his dragon, Nieko, and flew to the bombing area to confront the Jet mechs. The dragon Nieko unleashed his powerful fire breath onto the squad of jets and was able to incapacitate a few of them, as they fell to the ground in flames. Some of the pilots managed to eject, but were quickly killed when they landed. About 40 more dragons appeared on the scene shortly thereafter to aid in the air defense campaign. The air battle had begun. Cassion cast a spell of protection over himself and his dragon, thus making them both very hard to kill as the bullets of the fighter mechs simply bounced off of Nieko's skin upon impact. The spell would not last forever, but it would do for now.

A jet mech flew up behind the dragon Nieko and launched a missile that struck the dragon's backside. The missile took Nieko by surprise and he passed out from the impact. The two began falling from the sky and Cassion shouted at Nieko, telling him to wake up. The dragon opened his eyes and immediately began to fly upward at remarkable speeds. The dragon honed in on the RXF-10 fighter. The fighter unleashed a barrage of cannon fire on the dragon, but it had little effect. The dragon was slightly beaten, but was not out of the fight. Nieko intercepted the jet in mid-flight and slashed the right wing off with his talons. The mech began to fall toward the ground, and the RXF-10 jet exploded upon impact.

Cassion and Nieko were tired at this point, and they decided to head back to the Castle Nowah for some rest. The rest of the Nowrie warriors remained at the battlefield along with the dragon legion. They were successful at keeping the M.V.F at bay. The bombing raid had only lasted a day, as General Hezekai called off the raid that night. He decided not to waste any more resources until they could gain more ground. Hezekai was hard at work thinking about a new strategy for the taking of Nowah.

Ram knew the dragons must have a weak spot, and he needed to find an effective way to neutralize them. Meanwhile back at the Castle Nowah, Cassion was in conference with King Roiden.

"I have sent a dragon scout team over the ocean, and what they found is disturbing. The scouts have reported there are many ships on the way to Nowah. A couple of the dragons tried to attack the ships and were shot with some form of plasma laser. Those hit by the lasers were injured. Although dragon skin is virtually impenetrable and equipped with Jezelite armor as well, the lasers scorched their skin, and were said to have made them dizzy. One of the riders even lost an arm. The battle for Nowah is getting bloodier by the minute, and it has only just begun," said King Roiden.

"Indeed it is," replied Cassion as he bowed to Roiden.

"Cassion, I am going to send you along with a battalion of warriors back to the beach. Rest up tonight, and you can leave in the morning. I can't thank you enough for all your help."

"It is my pleasure, Roiden. We will rid ourselves of these pests; it is only a matter of time. I will kill as many as I can."

The next day, Cassion marched the Nowries back to the edge of the rainforest near the beach. They set up camp in the rainforest and waited. Shortly thereafter the ships began to dock. The dragon legion tried to keep the ships at bay, but the ships' powerful laser cannons were actually able to keep the dragons at bay. The ships unloaded about 2,000 mechs and ground troops, and they began battering the rainforest with heavy fire. Cassion and the Nowries found cover and were able to stay in one piece. Cassion knew they would have to make their move soon, and he willed his sword to a ten foot length and yelled out the command to charge.

The battalion of several thousand Nowries raided the beach, and Cassion was on the front lines with them. There was heavy cannon fire, and many Nowries fell; but they eventually penetrated the ranks of the humans. The Nowries used hand to hand combat; and once they were close enough, the M.V.F. foot soldiers did not stand a chance. The soldiers were able to get some shots off here and there, but the water was painted red with their blood as the Nowries unleashed with their swords and battleaxes. Cassion began teleporting mech to mech, and slashed several of the tanks into pieces. The RS-777s tried to shoot him down, only to find his skin was hard as rock, bluestone to be exact, as he had evoked a spell of Earth magic to solidify his skin. He was not invincible, but he was heavily protected. An RS-777 flanked him as it flew up to his side and stabbed at him with its lance. This blow grazed his ribcage and drew first blood.

The warrior Cassion instantly spun on the mech and slashed upward at the mech, cutting the right arm off completely. The mech responded with a close range rocket propelled grenade. The RPG knocked both Cassion and the mech back. Cassion was now slightly battered, as the blast was enough to wear his Earth spell off completely. He still had his Jezelite armor, and he would not let a desperate attack like that get the best of him. Cassion was surprised to see that the soldier would risk his own life by launching an RPG at its own feet. He then teleported directly in front of the mech and began slashing at it. The mech slashed back and barely missed Cassion's head.

The warrior stepped out of the way and counter attacked with a left to right slash that took the mech's head off. It was still very nimble on its feet, as it had a camera system with a 360 degree view so it could still see. The mech's head was simply a display, for the true visuals were shown on a Heads Up Display. The HUD was a bit fuzzy inside of the mech; and just as the picture was coming back to life, everything went dark for the operator for Cassion had slashed completely through the RS-777. A shower of sparks emitted as the machine crumbled to the ground.

A few seconds later Cassion found himself surrounded by a half dozen more of the humanoid mechs. He put on an impressive display as he teleported behind, in front, and on the sides of the mechs. Cassion moved at the speed of light; as he sliced the arms off of one mech, he would send a blast of lightning magic through the next one, sending it sparking to the ground. *Five mechs left*, he thought to himself. Cassion jumped, did a front flip, and kicked at the mech's leg and it fell back. He hit the remaining mechs with a strong telekinetic push and sent them flying back as well; he then drew up his sword and willed it to a katana blade. He chased after the downed mech he had kicked a moment ago, and slashed the legs clean off of it. The mech emitted a shower of sparks, and the warrior hit it with a strong blast of ice magic. A single white stream of ice emitted from Cassion's blade and froze the downed mech in place. Four mechs left.

Cassion saw four rockets out of the corner of his eye, and they were coming straight at him. A spray of blue particles filled the air as he teleported about 20 feet away, and the rockets slammed right into the four mechs that previously had him in the crossfire. With the remaining four mechs destroyed by their own rockets, Cassion continued down the battlefield. He noticed a lot of the Nowries had fallen and fell back to help them and ordered them to retreat to the rainforest. Immediately after giving the order, the dragon legion swooped into combat. Some of the dragons crushed the mechs with their claws, and others simply doused the M.V.F. with fire breath that was hot enough to boil the operator inside.

Suddenly a rogue RS-777 mech came down at them from high above in the sky. The mech slammed its lance through the heart of the dragon known as Kirby. The dragon Kirby vanished as it dissipated into blue light crystals. Apparently when a dragon died, it simply rejoined the Life Source. Kirby was a great warrior, but he was gone now. The Nowries had taken a beating that day. Upon learning about the dragon's death, Colonel Baker ordered a cease fire for the rest of the day. The Nowries followed suit. The Nowries fell back to the Castle Nowah for some rest.

Central Nowah was home to the Castle Nowah. The main city, Hapunah, was one of the largest territories in the land of Nowah. The M.V.F. knew if they could conquer the capital city, they would control Nowah. Cassion met with King Roiden that night to discuss the first major battle with him. Roiden was upset to hear they had lost a dragon and several hundred Nowrie warriors. He knew there would be causalities, and he also knew there would be many more to come. Cassion informed him how he was able to eliminate the mechs he fought. He told King Roiden the mechs were susceptible to elemental magic, lightning being the most effective in short circuiting the mechs, and fire being a way to overwhelm the operators inside. He also said he was able to slice through the mechs' joint areas rather easily.

The Jezelite forged weapons of Harpatia were some of the sharpest weapons in the galaxy, and Roiden could not wait to slice through one of these mechs with his own sword. He had received a large shipment of energy rifles from the Council of the Elders a few days before the battle, but he had not issued the rifles to his men yet. He would do so soon. The next day the warrior Cassion, along with a battalion of 2,000 Nowries, headed back to the beach to assist those who had stayed to hold the forest. When they reached the beach, they noticed the humans had set up gun batteries all along the beach. Apparently, they had worked through the night to fortify their position. There were more ships coming into the beach, and they were dropping off more and more mechs and personnel.

The Nowries took their positions on the edge of the forest and readied their own cannons and catapults. By mid-day, the battle was raging on. Cassion knew he needed to find a way to neutralize the jet mechs and gun batteries. He did not want to lose the air battle, for he knew this battle would ultimately be won or lost in the air. He decided to deploy 200 dragons to fight the RXF-10 jet mechs, a force to be reckoned with.

This time the dragons used fire, ice, and lightning magic. They used fire breath in conjunction with lightning magic to disrupt the jets. The dragons discharged lightning from their eyes and fire from their mouths. This served as a double whammy to the RXF-10 mechs. By early afternoon, the dragons had destroyed 40 jet mechs and 30 tank mechs. The Harpatians had the upper hand on this day, and the battle raged on.

Although Cassion was able to keep the M.V.F. at bay that day, he knew the battle was far from over. He wanted to destroy the gun batteries and retake the beach, so he gathered up some elite fighters and walked a few miles down shore where he then told them of his plan. They would swim up behind the M.V.F. on the beach and hit them hard. Cassion brought only magic users with him for this mission. He planned to use his telekinetic magic to crush the gun batteries. Once that was done, he could issue the command to charge. The group would then jump into the water and begin swimming. Cassion was the first to jump off of the 20-foot cliff into the ocean, and the others followed. The warrior Cassion lived by a strict code: If you fear, you hesitate. If you hesitate, you die.

The group began a slow-paced swim until they were close enough to be spotted. Cassion instructed his team to take in a deep breath of air and use their magic to hold it, for they would be swimming underwater from this point on. The group rode on an invisible current to get to the shore. Cassion sent a telekinetic message to the Nowrie commanders in the forest instructing them to charge and create a distraction. The Nowries felt this was going to be a suicide mission for Cassion, but for Cassion it was just another day.

The great warrior sprang out of the water with lightning quick speed and teleported next to one of the gun batteries, of which there were about ten. With a downward slash of his Jezelite bonded blade, Cassion slashed the gun battery in half. His blade was about seven feet long now. No one knew how or why Cassion had the ability to shift the shape his sword. After seeing the ease with which his sword had cut through the large gun emplacement, Cassion threw his sword about 20 feet away; and with the assistance of his magic, the sword tore through four more gun batteries. One after the other the guns fell to the ground in pieces.

Cassion then noticed an RS-777 mech heading straight toward him. He willed his sword back to him right at the point that the RS was in front of him, and his katana sliced straight through the war machine's leg sending the mech to the ground. Cassion then summoned a blast of fire magic that he deployed through the tip of his sword, and instantly the mech was engulfed in flames. Cassion was now confident that he could take out the remaining gun batteries with ease. The rest of his men were battling the troops by the sea in an effort to buy him more time to complete the mission. The group had surprised the M.V.F., and in doing so was able to kill quite a few of them.

Cassion then noticed two more RS-777 mechs coming at him, and at the same time he also saw all five of the large gun batteries were now pointed at him. He watched the human commander order his men to fire, and at the last second Cassion teleported away. The five football sized projectiles slammed into the two mechs that were behind him, and they were completely incapacitated by the blow.

He saw a look of horror in the face of the commander when he reappeared in front of him. Cassion winked and unsheathed his sword, and with a lateral strike ended the commander's life. He focused his attention on the remaining gun operators, and with a single telekinetic attack, he heard five loud snaps as he watched the five men fall to the ground with broken necks. The warrior Cassion then lifted all five of the gun batteries in the air telekinetically and threw the mechs about 30 yards out into the ocean, and the guns sank to the bottom of the sea.

Upon the completion of his mission, he looked back to the beach and noticed most of Nowries who had accompanied him were dead, but there were a few Elite Guardsmen still alive. Cassion saw about five RS-777 mechs lying motionless on the ground, at which point he praised the men for fighting so valiantly, and then ordered them back into the ocean. It would not be long until the next fleet of ships arrived, and he did not want to be around when they did. The men then swam away; but just before Cassion was about to jump in the water, he noticed a large number of Nowrie warriors being overrun further up the beach.

Cassion put on a barrage of teleportation, going from mech to mech slicing them in to two or more pieces with every attack. Slashing, slicing, kicking, and punching, Cassion was able to take out 20 large mechs. He had destroyed five tank mechs and about fifteen RS-777s in less than two minutes. He took a laser burn to his left arm as he noticed the foot soldiers were now firing straight at him. The blast had grazed him; it was just a flesh wound. Cassion then engaged in hand to hand combat with the soldiers. The humans did not have a chance against Cassion. He killed 50 of them in fewer than five minutes.

After being hit by the laser, Cassion evoked a spell of Earth magic that coated his skin with rock. Although he could not hold the spell for long, he would be impenetrable for as long as he could hold it, which would be about five minutes. He was getting tired now, for the use of such powerful magic would make anyone tired regardless of their skill level. Cassion noticed the air battle was still raging on, and he teleported to the nearest dragon in the sky. The rider was startled at first, but quickly recognized his General, Cassion of Dakineah. Cassion looked at the man and said, "It is ok, my friend. I am very tired. I need you to take me to the center of the rainforest, so I can get some rest."

"Yes, Sir," the Nowrie replied, and he took Cassion to a secluded spot in the forest and hovered about 30 feet above. Cassion thanked the man and then teleported to the rainforest below to take shelter under a large Banian tree which was almost identical to the Banyan trees of Earth. With branches thick enough to hold a house and a trunk wide enough to house a small family, Cassion felt safe closing his eyes under this large beast of a tree. He took a 30-minute nap to regain his senses, and then started back to the beach.

When he returned to the edge of the forest, he informed the Nowrie commander, Jester, that the gun batteries were down and ordered him to charge. Jester was one of King Roiden's elite warriors, and a General who was second in command of the Tokechi, the elite warriors of the Nowrie guard. The lead General of the Tokechi was Jester. General Jester stood seven feet tall with a muscular build. He had a large scar that started on his forehead and went all the way down to his navel. He had been mortally wounded in the ancient Wars of Segregation but had been saved by the members of Ten Meld. Jester had literally been cut in half by an elven warrior. The healing of Jester was in the history books as one of the most prolific uses of magic ever. Jester ordered the Tokechi to charge, and so began another day of battle.

Back in Dakineah, a messenger had arrived to the Castle to inform Leinad that Roiden would soon need reinforcements. Leinad was surprised by this request because it had come only one day after the fighting in Nowah had started. This was not a good sign. The messenger stated the humans' air attack had severely weakened their defenses; they had lost thousands in one day. Leinad also learned King Roiden had deployed 50 ships on a secret mission to flank the M.V.F., but the ships were destroyed in a matter of minutes once they were out to sea. They had been bombed by a very large air ship according to a few surviving Tokechi elite that had somehow managed to make it back to shore and safety.

Leinad immediately dispatched a legion of 500 dragons to Nowah. Their mission would be to protect the Nowries from air attacks and to take out tank mechs as well. Roiden had also requested security protection for the outer villages of Nowah, for he had been receiving reports that RS-777 mechs were killing villagers across the land. Leinad was outraged to learn Hezekai was killing innocents again; and as a result of his outrage, he dispatched several thousand of his Elite Guard out to the outer villages of Nowah. He ordered his reinforcements to Nowah immediately for he knew if the Nowries lost the beach, they could lose the battle. The beach was so close to the castle, only ten miles away to be exact.

In addition to the legion of dragons, Leinad sent 10,000 more of his Elite Guard to join the battle. King Leinad was staying close to Dakineah, for he did not know when Hezekai would make his next move. Neither Leinad nor any of the people on Harpatia had ever dealt with an enemy such as the M.V.F.; and as a result, they did not know how to go about the war. There was no right or wrong way to fight the humans. Leinad knew he would learn how to defeat the mech army through observation and battle. He would figure out a strategy for ridding Harpatia of these barbarians; and when the time was right, he would cut the head off of the snake.

***

General Hezekai and Colonel Jake Baker were back in the Outlands putting together a plan for the next attack on Nowah.

"Colonel Baker, I want you to lead a team of 500 RS-777 mechs to the outer cities of Nowah. Take control of the cities and set up camp. I want you to wait for my order; and when the time is right I will have you converge on the Castle of Nowah. I may or may not need you. Nevertheless, I want you in the area. I have a plan for the siege of Nowah, and I will inform you of my plan when you need to know," said Hezekai who was dressed in full battle attire.

"Yes, sir," replied Baker as he saluted the general.

Colonel Baker then left the tent and went to rendezvous with the battalion of mechs. They would be air dropped deep in the outer regions of Nowah, where they would begin their mission. Baker knew the Nowries were so busy trying to keep the beaches of Nowah that they would overlook any attack on the smaller villages and cities. He also knew that if everyone played their cards right, the M.V.F. would soon control Nowah.

Back at the beaches of Nowah, the battle raged on. The Nowries charged into battle both on foot and dragon back. While riding his dragon Nieko, Cassion began spraying the jet mechs with flurries of lightning magic and was able to destroy a few of the jets right off the bat. Nieko followed suit by tail whipping and blasting the RXF-10s with intense fire breath. Leinad's legion of dragons had arrived within a few hours after they had been dispatched. The King's decision to send the more dragons in to help had been a good one. The ratio was about five to one, with the dragons heavily outnumbering the jets now. The air battle would soon be over.

Back on the ground, King Roiden was engaged in battle with an RS-777 mech. The mech fired its Gatling gun in a barrage against Roiden, but Roiden's Jezelite armor along with the use of his magic was more than enough to keep him from being harmed by the bullets. Roiden drew his shiny silver Jezelite bonded broadsword and sliced the Gatling gun off the mech's shoulder mount. The RS-777 then thrust its lance straight at Roiden's head, but the King of Nowah parried the blow. Roiden threw a magic aided kick at the mech's knee and rocked the metallic war machine upon impact. The mech then initiated the thrusters on his foot and back jet packs and began flying around Roiden in circles. Roiden felt a flare of pain in his chest as the mech landed a straight right handed punch on him. The blow sent him flying back into some thorny bushes on the beach. He was dazed, but by no means out of the fight. The King of Nowah then unleashed a powerful level nine blast of lightning from his sword and into the RS-777.

Showers of sparks emitted from the knee and other joint areas. Roiden followed up with a downward left to right slash that took off the mech's head and left arm. He then pushed his blade through the mechs chest, and this fight was over; but he continued to fight alongside his Nowrie army.

The M.V.F. continued to drop troops and mechs at the beach, but they were smothered the second they got off of their ships. The Tokechi and the dragon legion were dealing powerful blows upon the M.V.F.'s sea vessels as they came to shore and many of them did not make it. The Nowrie's rifles had little effect on the RS-777 mechs. However, their swords were able to slice clean through the mechs' steel frames. There was something about the Jezelite metal that was allowing the warriors to slice and dice these mechs. Maybe it had something to do with the fact that Jezelite was 100 times stronger than steel and 20 times sharper than a surgically sharpened blade on Earth.

The battle boiled on with intense heat. About 30 miles from the beaches, *Lancer I* dropped several hundred mechs in a small town area of Nowah. The dragons had spotted *Lancer I* and had followed it to the city of Dakur, a small province in the flatlands of southern Nowah. The town was made up of small huts, and the Nowries of Dakur were mostly farmers who had enjoyed a peaceful life until the humans arrived.

The M.V.F. squad was led by Colonel Jake Baker who initiated his jet packs and flew directly into the village. The mechs began firing some sort of energy weapon on the Nowries, and the plasma bolts stunned the villagers. The Nowries began to fight back with all of their hearts. Baker and his crew then used their rockets and Gatling guns on the Nowries. The ground battle was almost over, but the air battle had just begun. The 200 or more dragons that had followed them into Dakur were engaged in a blazing air battle. So far the jet mechs, with the assistance of the flying RS-777 mechs, were keeping the dragons at bay. Baker knew if they took Dakur, they would be in a perfect position to storm the Castle Nowah upon Hezekai's orders.

***

At the Castle Dakineah, King Leinad entered a chaos meditation which would enable him to see the battles being fought through the eyes of his men. This form of meditation was accessible only to the most powerful of wizards. The battle on the beach was going well for the Harpatians. The warrior Cassion, along with the aid of King Roiden, delivered heavy amounts of damage to the mechs. Leinad could also see the battle of Dakur, and he could feel the presence of Colonel Jake Baker.

The King saw the dragons doing a fine job of keeping the mechs busy in the battle for Dakur. He noticed that battle was more organized, for Leinad saw a heavy resupply chain in the rear of the battlefield. Colonel Baker and his troops were getting in and doing as much damage as they could. They would use up their ammo, and then go and rearm in the rear. *What an excellent strategy indeed*, he thought.

Leinad knew the Nowries, the students from the School for Combat and Magic Arts, as well as the Elite Guard who were fighting in the battle for Dakur were unaware of the Colonel's strategy; thus they would need some help. He would have helped his men, and he would have to go now. A blue vapor trail emitted as Leinad teleported to the rooftop of the Castle Dakineah, which looked like a large helipad. Once there, he summoned his dragon Monte. It was a nice day; the skies were blue and the temperature mild. He teleported to Monte's back and said, "My friend, we must teleport to Dakur, for we don't have much time."

"Yes Master," replied the dragon, as he closed his crimson eyes and summoned his own teleportation magic.

It was rare for a dragon to teleport, and Monte was one of the few that could. It was just a little trick his master had taught him a few years back. A giant blue vapor trail emitted as they disappeared. Colonel Baker did not believe his own eyes when he saw a huge dragon suddenly appear on the battlefield, and his heart sunk deep into his chest when the scanners on his mech revealed that the man on the dragon's back was King Leinad Seven of Harpatia.

Monte wasted no time, he immediately began overwhelming the RS-777s and RX-99 tanks with his fire breath, and following up the attacks with a bone crushing tail whip. As Monte pounded and trampled over the mechs on the ground, Leinad was busy using his lightning and telekinesis on the other nearby mechs. The pair was able to destroy more than twenty mechs in less than five minutes. Monte then took flight to the rear of the Harpatian line where there were many satchels filled with explosives. The Elite Guard was planning a large air drop, and Leinad knew exactly where the bombs were, for he had seen them in his chaos meditation. Monte grabbed a few satchels with his mouth and began flying toward the supply line.

Leinad and Monte were met by a few RS-777 mechs on the way. Leinad summoned his level ten lightning and unleashed it on the mechs, and the mechs imploded from the blast of electricity and simply fell to the ground. They were then attacked by the fast flying RXF-10 jet fighters. Leinad sent a huge blast of ice magic into the jets. The last thing the pilots ever saw was a tall muscular man on the back of a huge dragon, with his sword raised, as sheets of ice came at them from the tip of Leinad's golden blade. The fuel inside the jets instantly froze upon contact with the ice magic, thus sending them to the ground. Some of the pilots managed to escape, but most of them found their ejection controls and equipment were frozen stiff.

Leinad spotted another jet mech that was quickly approaching him from the left. He used his ice magic once again. As the jet mech became frozen, Leinad decided to hit the mech with a blast of fire magic as well. The icy hot reaction caused the jet fighter mech to shatter into pieces. Leinad was learning how to defeat these war machines, and that made him very happy. The extreme temperature of the elemental magic was just too much for the RXF-10 jets to handle.

"Keep up the good work, Monte," said the King as he gave the large beast a pat on the neck.

Monte took out another ten jets before reaching the rear of the battlefield. He had been hit in the chest by a few plasma lasers the jets were firing at him, but the lasers only left a few minor scratches as his skin was nearly impenetrable. Dragon skin was very tough indeed, but they also wore a Jezelite mesh body suit. Therefore, the art of killing a dragon was a hard one to master, but they were vulnerable at the throat and eyes. Plasma lasers made most dragons dizzy, but Monte was not an ordinary dragon.

Although getting shot by plasma lasers was painful for Monte, he felt quite safe. He had several leather satchels filled with explosives, and they were approaching the rear supply lines. Once the supply chain was visible, Leinad used his fire magic to light the fuses on the explosives, and Monte then dropped one of the satchels over the target. Twenty bombs came out of the satchel; and with lit fuses, they all found their targets. Monte then dropped the other bomb-filled satchel over the remaining contents in the supply chain, and again the bombs found their targets. There was then a massive set of secondary explosions. The supply line went up in flames as the munitions stores detonated. The supply line was destroyed and the secondary explosions had destroyed the surrounding gun batteries.

All that remained now were a couple hundred RS-777 mechs and a handful of ground troops. At this point, the soldiers and villagers charged the remaining human soldiers and mechs with intent to kill. Leinad knew it would only be a matter of time until they would regain control of Dakur. Leinad chose random targets to attack on the battlefield. One by one, he and Monte swooped down on the RS-777 mechs smashing, freezing, and blazing them up in flames. Leinad moved gracefully through the battle: he was so fluid, it looked like a choreographed battle scene as he and Monte just strode through with minimal effort.

All of a sudden, an RS-777 mech came up from behind and took the dragon by surprise. It poured showers of purple energy bolts into Monte, and these bolts were piercing his skin. Monte turned around; and when he did, Leinad saw a shiny silver mech that stood about fifteen feet high with a humanoid figure. The knee and elbow joints of this mech were heavily armored and equipped with pointed daggers that were about two feet in length. The chest of this giant war machine was gold and silver which told Leinad there was someone important inside. The mech had two huge arms and shoulder mounted plasma guns. Leinad knew at that point this was the mech of Colonel Jake Baker.

Baker recognized Leinad as well, but things had changed now. The battle for Harpatia had begun, and Baker knew that he would have to kill or be killed. Leinad circled Monte around Baker's mech, but Baker was too quick. Baker spun and drew out his lance and struck Monte's leg so hard it drew blood. His mech was a high powered machine indeed. Leinad did not understand how the Colonel's mech had thrust its lance so hard it pierced Mont's skin, and he did not care. Monte spun and tail whipped Colonel Baker's mech and sent him flying ten feet back. The mech landed hard on its back, and instinctively, Colonel Baker issued a neural command through the control band on his head. Instantly, the jet packs ignited on his back and thrust him up to a standing position. Baker's mech was very strong and agile. He engaged his foot and leg thrusters as well, and began flying straight toward Leinad.

Monte took in a deep breath as Baker's mech approached. Then Monte unleashed his fire breath onto Colonel Baker and he was caught in the blaze for a few seconds. Using his lightning fast reflexes, Baker was able to escape; but in the few seconds that he was in the fire, he experienced severe heat that caused his skin to burn. Baker engaged the mech's cooling system to keep him from being broiled alive. The RS-777 mechs had been outfitted with internal cooling systems years ago so they would be able to aide in fighting large scale forest fires on Earth. Baker laughed at the coincidence.

He turned around, but this time he did not see Leinad on the back of Monte. This confused him and made him hesitate, and it was in that hesitation that Colonel Baker almost met his fate. Leinad had teleported off Monte and behind Baker; and with a magic-aided burst of speed, Leinad summoned a stream of lightning magic from his staff and into Baker's mech. Showers of sparks emitted from its joint regions, and it froze in place. Leinad slashed off the head and the right arm of Baker's mech. He then levitated six large boulders up in the air; and with the use of his telekinetic and Earth magic at the same time, the King of Harpatia sent the giant rocks slamming into the chest plate of Baker's mech. The rocks shattered upon impact, and the mech fell to the ground with a roaring bang.

Leinad knew that Baker was dazed at this point. He closed his eyes and saw the Colonel was badly bruised and beaten. Seeing the inside of the mech through Baker's eyes, Leinad saw the red ejection button; and with a gesture of his right hand, he telekinetically depressed the button. Though the mech was half crumbled and beaten, the chest cavity opened to expose the defeated Colonel. Jake Baker was exhausted from the fight. Every muscle in his body hurt. Blood was dripping out of his nose—it must have been broken, no doubt being slammed around inside of a war machine could be dangerous. Leinad had not even broken a sweat.

Leinad looked into the injured eyes of the Colonel and said, "Colonel Baker, as I have told you before, I believe you are a good man. I know you are just following orders. You are a great tactician; and had I not have come here today; I know you surely would have won this battle."

Meanwhile, the rest of Baker's troops were annihilated on the battlefield as the dragons slashed, tail whipped, and engulfed them in flames. The mechs began to retreat; and in doing so, they left their commander, Colonel Jake Baker, solely at the mercy of the King. Jake's muscles twitched in pain from exhaustion, and his eyes burned as he looked into the gaze of Leinad Seven.

"As I have told you before, Colonel, I will spare your life on the battlefield if I can; and today I shall. Had you been met by my brother, or God forbid the warrior Cassion, you would surely have been killed."

Leinad pulled out a golden cloth from his tunic pocket and handed it to Baker and said, "Wear this cloth around your head, and my armies will know I have spared your life. I don't know if I will be able to grant you this courtesy the next time we meet. I urge you to overthrow your commander and leave. Tell your superiors there is nothing of value to them here on Harpatia, and don't come back."

"You should kill me now Leinad, for I don't think I would have done the same for you today," said Baker as tears streamed down his bloody face.

"Yes I know, but I am merciful; and that is part of what makes me a great King. We are not savages, and I think you know that. This is a battle you can't win. I only wish General Hezekai could understand my logic. Go now Colonel Baker, and pray we don't meet again. And Jake, may the Life Source protect you," said Leinad as he helped the Colonel to his feet.

Baker looked deep into the eyes of Leinad, and could not help but feel a sense of kinship. Baker thanked Leinad for sparing his life and went on his way. After securing the battle of Dakur, Leinad took Monte and returned home to Dakineah.

Chapter 15: The Taking of Nowah

As the battle for the beaches of Nowah continued, the warrior Cassion was surprised to see the mechs in the rear of the battle using large Mechanical shovels to dig deep holes in the ground, deep enough to fit both mech and humans alike. They were digging hundreds of holes in the ground, but why? The humans had sent a large attack force forward in an effort to secure the rear of the battlefield, and the rear was indeed secure.

The digging continued. Cassion began to worry when he noticed an object flying straight toward him and his men. It was a missile; and although it struck about 50 yards from Cassion, he was knocked down by the blast. The missile killed 55 of his men, and that made him very angry. Another missile came toward him, but he teleported 200 yards away just in the nick of time. He reappeared and was thrown 20 feet, for the blast had caught him for a millisecond right before he vanished. He got up, saw his body was intact, and moved back toward the rear of the battle.

Cassion wondered how a missile attack could have happened, as the dragons were supposed to be warding off the air campaign. He summoned all of the Life Source energy he could muster, and he teleported once again. This time he reappeared in the middle of the battlefield. He slashed several mechs into pieces with his sword which was now a bright silver glow about five feet in length. The sword seemed to change its shape according to Cassion's mood. The warrior was using all of his powers now, as he moved swiftly from one mech to the next. He was then surrounded by three of the RS-777 mechs which attacked at once. The first one used its Gatling gun in an attempt to shoot the warrior down, but Cassion simply teleported behind the mech and summoned a blast of ice magic that instantly froze it in place. He grabbed the next mech in a telekinetic hold and threw it at the frozen mech. The frozen mech shattered. The warrior then teleported behind the mech he had just thrown.

Cassion noticed the third mech was retreating, and he let it go. Still held by the telekinetic grasp, the second mech could not move. Cassion summoned more of his elemental magic, and his right hand began to glow bright red. The mech became engulfed in flames when Cassion touched it. The warrior then thrust his sword through the mech, pulled it out, and walked away. He teleported back to the rear of the battle, as this type of magic usage was very exhausting for anyone. Even a level ten combat artist such as warrior Cassion needed rest after summoning so much magic in such a short time. The teleportation magic was by far the most draining of all, and he had been using teleportation in association with his combat arts all morning.

Cassion felt like he was wearing bluestone boots when he reappeared in the rear of the battlefield, for he was now getting very tired. His heavy eyes then noticed two more RS-777 mechs, and he vowed to ignore his pain and fatigue. The mechs began firing energy bolts at him which he dodged almost effortlessly. However, they pushed the warrior back a few feet as a couple energy bolts struck his Jezelite chest plate. The lasers did not penetrate the armor, but he could feel the burn as the heat transferred from the Jezelite metal onto his chest feeling like someone had just poured hot wax all over it. This angered the warrior, and he summoned a burst of Earth magic; and rocks began to rise. Large rocks rose up from the ground and formed a shield around him.

The mechs then flew 100 yards away and launched two small rocket propelled grenades at the warrior. The stone shield fell back to the ground upon impact. Cassion was unharmed. The mech operators began wondering if this guy could be killed. He then pulled his sword from the invisible sheath at his side which now took its original form of a katana. He willed the blade to six feet long and leapt forward at the mechs slashing in a low to high motion. The mech pulled out its lance and blocked the blow. Cassion's blade managed to cut halfway through the lance as it blocked his attack. It should have cut all of the way through. Cassion forgot about the other mech for a second. It had flown away, and he thought it was fleeing as the others had fled before. He was wrong. Cassion felt a strong pain in his back as something struck him from behind. He felt his bones crack as he flew forward and down to the rocky ground beneath him.

Had Cassion not used a magical burst of speed to roll with the punch of the mech, his spine would have surely fractured. Cassion, though in much pain, quickly came out of the roll and got back to his feet. He teleported behind the mech that had surprised him and with a lateral slice he quickly put it to rest, and then telekinetically threw the pieces of it into the ocean. The warrior was now raging with anger as he looked toward the last mech. He dashed toward his other attacker and jumped high into the air and landed on top of the mech, wrapping his legs around the head of the mech, he then twisted his body downwards and flipped the mech to the ground. He then unleashed a barrage of punches to the mech's chest which dazed the operator inside. Grabbing his katana with his bloodied hands, he willed it to about four feet in size and thrust it through the mech's chest cavity. Cassion stood up and was relieved that he had defeated his attackers.

When he looked back toward the rear of the beach, Cassion saw all the mechs and soldiers were retreating, or so it seemed. Had they won this battle while he was occupied? Then he noticed all the mechs and personnel were getting inside of the holes they had dug earlier. As the M.V.F. crawled down into their holes, they pulled large steel covers over their heads and locked them into place. It all began to make sense to Cassion. As he saw the Capital Ship, *Lancer I*, his eyes widened; and he knew they were in trouble.

The Capital Ship must have been a million square feet in size, Cassion thought; *and this large floating city was coming straight for them all.* He was horrified, for he now knew what was going to happen. The ship had the body of an octagon with the head of a triangle. Several hundred large square hatches began to open on the ship's hull and revealed large missile and gun batteries. Then some large doors on the underbelly opened, and out came a spindle that was loaded with bombs. Cassion felt stupid. He should have ordered a full retreat when he noticed the holes that were being dug earlier. It was too late now. They would have to weather the storm, he thought.

Laser fire began riddling the Nowries. Large caliber gun fire pounded the ground and everything on it. Cassion screamed for his men to retreat. The Capital Ship also began to target the castle of Nowah. They were sending missiles and large caliber ordinance straight at the castle. There was a lot of resistance at first, but Cassion knew that whatever type of protection spells were in place over the castle Nowah would not last long, for the strength of Leinad Seven's magic would be largely focused on protecting Dakineah. The Harpatian ground troops were running and screaming in horror. There were thousands of panicked men running from the beaches. Nowries, Bracelians, and Elven men alike were dropping by the hundreds.

Some of the Nowries made it to nearby caves; those were the smart ones. Cassion knew this ship was simply distracting them by attacking the beach, and he felt the Capital Ship was saving its rage for the castle Nowah. There was nothing more he could do here except die, so he teleported back to Roiden's castle. He quickly found the King of Nowah, who was standing under the shaking castle walls, shouting out orders for his men to get as many people as they could into the underground shelters. There was a large cavernous area under the castle Nowah that had been used as a safe haven throughout the history of the Nowries. Those who could make it there would be safe.

"Roiden, we must go now. I fear we have lost Nowah. The spell of protection you have cast will not last much longer. Our only safe haven will be in Dakineah," said the warrior Cassion with a tone of deep regret and sadness.

"What are you talking about? The spell is working just fine. I will not abandon my people."

"All our forces on the beach and in the rainforest are about to be annihilated. If you had seen what I just saw you would know we must go now. The sheer size and strength of this ship attacking us is beyond belief. If we stay here, we die. Come with me Roiden, and you will live to fight another day. They have missiles and bombs, and they are about to unleash them all on this castle. We must go now. As the General of the Harpatian armies I feel it is my duty to keep you, Roiden, King of Nowah, alive.

"I am sure many Nowries will survive. Let me remind you there are hundreds of thousands of Nowries in Dakineah, and they will need their King to lead them in the many coming battles. We need to regroup and come up with a new strategy to defeat these humans once and for all," said Cassion as he stared into the eyes of the Nowrie King.

As Cassion spoke, the walls of the castle began to shake violently and the masonry was starting to give in. Small pieces of stone began falling all around them. Roiden saw fragments of bluestone as they fell to the floor. He wondered how this could have been possible, for the bluestone of Harpatia was one of the most solid substances in all of the land. *Whatever types of weapons the humans were using must have been very powerful, Roiden* thought.

Hezekai was enjoying the view from the cockpit and bridge of *Lancer I.* The cameras fitted all over the ship's exterior were more than ample for getting an up close and personal view of the carnage he was unleashing on the Harpatians. He switched from one camera to the next as he watched the destruction take place. It was like a video game for him. He simply targeted something or someone, and then watched it die or be destroyed. *This was a beautiful sight to see,* Hezekai thought. He had all but annihilated the forces on the beach.

The twenty or thirty 1,000-pound Mark-88 bombs were more than ample for the killing all the ground troops. Half the foliage in the rainforest had been destroyed as well. The only problem was the general knew he had a very limited supply of munitions, and he was using over half of what he had on the land of Nowah today. Hezekai thought, *if they would have waited a little bit longer and came to Harpatia with four or more Capital Ships, they would have conquered the land in a matter of days.*

Hezekai was dropping everything he had on the Nowries and was about to send a wave of 1,000 stinger missiles into the Castle of Nowah. He knew King Leinad had made a mistake by fighting in the battle of Dakur. Hezekai felt Colonel Baker had done an excellent job in distracting the King and was lucky to have been spared by the King's mercy. If given the chance, Hezekai would never show Leinad that type of mercy. He would soon have total control over the continent of Nowah. The general knew once he secured the city of Hapunah, he would have control over all of Nowah.

Hezekai had personally targeted 50 dragons with his large laser cannons. He was able to drop all of them to the ground, for the power of the ship's mounted laser turrets was more than they could handle. He was okay with the fact that he was using most of his munitions on the Nowries, for he knew he would be returning to Earth soon to regroup and rearm. *Lancer I* was loaded with most of the weaponry, and *Lancer II* was loaded with most of the food, clothing, and tech. Most of the repair work that was done on the mechs took place on *Lancer II*.

"Time to kill them all," said Hezekai in an excited tone as he flipped a button on his control display which opened thousands of small missile ports, each holding five missiles. He entered the firing codes into the digital display on his cockpit's HUD and fired on the Castle of Nowah. Loud booms sounded off inside of the castle walls, and whole sections began to fall apart as the missiles struck home. If not for the spell of protection that had been cast, the castle would have been reduced to burning ash. Another boom hit, and people were dying in the hundreds.

Roiden ordered as many people as he could get to go to the teleportation hub within the castle to transfer to the castle Dakineah. Cassion and Roiden made their way to the teleportation hubs along with several hundred of the King's people. Once everyone one was inside the teleportation ring, Roiden entered the codes for Dakineah; and they all vanished just in time to keep from being destroyed. The teleportation hubs were large circular areas where the people would stand; and once a destination code was inputted, the large silver metallic ring would hover down from the ceiling and around the travelers. And by some sort of magic combined with ancient technology, the travelers would simply vanish and reappear at the chosen destination. That was how people without magical abilities would teleport. The secrets of this technology were stored and protected deep within the Mountains of Harpinia by the Council of the Elders.

Roiden, Cassion, and several hundred the Nowries made it safely to Dakineah. King Roiden had dispatched 40 of his elite Tokechi warriors to aid the civilian Nowries who had taken shelter in the underground tunnels beneath the castle. The humans would not be able to find them, for they were completely unaware of the underground tunnels. The Tokechi would wait until they received the proper signal from their King, and then they would retake their castle.

The humans would no doubt be occupying the castle of Nowah, but not for long. The Tokechi had a plan for this. They had plenty of food and supplies, enough to last six months or more. The Tokechi would train the civilian Nowries to be warriors, and when the time was right they would have their revenge. The only entrance to the tunnels was from a secret chamber hidden within the throne of Roiden; and even if the humans found the door, they would never be able to open it as it was protected by a magical spell that only a wizard could unlock. The Nowries were safe for now.

Jester, the leader of the Tokechi, was the most fearsome of all of the Nowrie warriors. He was Roiden's best friend and general of the Nowrie army; and he possessed a high level 8 in the combat arts and a strong level 7 in the magic arts. Roiden and Jester were several thousand years old, and they had fought alongside each other in the Ancient Wars of Segregation.

Jester had no doubts about retaking the castle; but right now they would just have to wait. He dispatched several messengers throughout the land of Nowah to warn the others and instructed them to go into hiding until the time was right. It was very unfortunate to have the lost the land of Nowah the way they did, but the Nowries would be back, of that Jester was sure.

Back in Dakineah, King Leinad greeted Cassion and company with arms wide open.

"My friends, I did not expect so many of you; but you are all welcome. I am glad I left the teleportation hubs here in the courtyard active. Tell me what has happened today," said Leinad.

The warrior Cassion began to describe how Nowah was lost to the humans. "The bombs fell out of the sky like a rainstorm of hot metal. There were so many explosions and so much death. We could not handle the sheer volume of explosives they unleashed upon us. I wanted to send those bombs back at them, but we did not have nearly as many masters of the arts present for a task like that.

"Many lives were lost my King, and I am afraid we have the lost the castle of Nowah as well. I was able to get Roiden and several thousand of his people to safety. For that I am very grateful. I know the majority his people were able to make to the underground shelters of Nowah. Roiden has a group of Tokechi with the survivors, and they are waiting for a signal to attack. Roiden has assured me that they have plenty of resources, enough to keep them both well-armed and well nourished," said Cassion in a very fatigued and strained tone.

"Leinad, I have lost my land and my home today. So long as I breathe, I will get it back. When the time is right we'll retake Nowah. We must come up with a plan," Roiden said in a tone of rage as he paced the floor like a caged lion.

"We do have a plan. I am sending many Bracelian engineers to the Mountains of Harpinia. They will meet with the Council of the Elders. I am also sending several hundred wizards, warriors, and apprentices to meet with the council as well. Some of our greatest technology and secrets lie within the Council of the Elders.

"I will now share with you all a great secret of which I have been aware for a very short time. Deep within the Mountains of Harpinia there is a secret hangar bay. In this hangar, we have space craft of our own. I call these craft Equalizers, and they are fully outfitted with an elaborate weapons array as well as a very impressive propulsion system. I will also be sending you and Roiden up to the council soon so you can learn to pilot them. This will be our secret weapon, and we'll not use it until the time is right."

"How could we have never known such a thing, my King?" asked Cassion.

"Now is not the time for asking how or why. We will unleash these ships on the enemy when the time is right. I have had visions of a larger force invading our lands. The humans will be leaving soon, and for how long, I am not sure. But I know they will be going home to regroup and rearm. The important thing to remember is they will no doubt return with a modified and improved war machine that will be more capable of fighting us. We must develop plans to exterminate them swiftly upon their return.

"I have seen all this in my dreams at night. The Life Source is granting me small views of the future so we can be ready for their final attack. I have full confidence in our ability to drive these humans away from our lands. Also, I have a secret order of Elite Guard on a quest to capture many of these mechs for the purpose of study. I am confident the Council will devise a powerful weapon to help us destroy the M.V.F. It will just take a little bit of time, my friends.

"We are already working to develop a weapon to immobilize these mechs permanently. Until then, we must defend our lands from these monsters," said King Leinad.

King Roiden looked at Leinad with his eyes glazed over. A tear rolled down the cheek of the great warrior Roiden as he said, "I put my faith in you, Leinad. I know you will lead us to victory."

"Yes I will, and I promise you Roiden, great King of Nowah, you will get you land back; and you will return home soon. Have patience, my friend; and don't blame yourself for what happened in Nowah. We are facing a new enemy, and we were completely unaware of the full scope of their technology and weapons until a couple of days ago. We will learn something new about our enemy every day, and we'll use all the knowledge we gain about them against them. They shall fall; but until such a time comes, we must prepare for the battles to come," said Leinad.

"I fear they will be heading for Bracelia next," Cassion interrupted.

"Good. We will let them have Nowah for now. We will unleash an entire legion of dragons on them when they arrive in Nowah. Also, we'll meld together in meditation to create a most powerful spell of protection on the Castle Bracelia. Furthermore, we must not cluster our forces together in one spot, for that would make a bomb attack way too easy for them. We will spread out and take them out with strategy, as opposed to brute force.

"We will take them out one at a time if need be, but we'll out-strategize them this time. Roiden, I am sending you and Cassion to Bracelia with a legion of 3,000 dragons and 10,000 warriors and Elite Guard members. I will also dispatch 500 of the most talented students from the School for Combat and Magic Arts. Bracelia will not fall," said King Leinad Seven as he paced around in his shiny blue and silver colored Jezelite armor.

Chapter 16: The First Battle for Bracelia

The next day, Leinad sat with his advisors to discuss strategies. He was surprised by a knock at the door; it was his brother Gressit.

"Brother, I have come with great news," said Gressit with a smile on his face.

"What is it, Gressit?" asked Leinad in a tone of curiosity.

"The humans sent a small reconnaissance group to Bracelia to scout out the lands. When we found them, they were in the process of developing maps of Bracelia. I used my lightning magic to defeat them, and no lives were lost. It was a tough fight but the Bracelian army helped me capture one of the mechs. The operator is in our jail. I thought you could take the mech and its operator to the Council so they could get a better understanding of how to defeat them. I am sure the Elders would love to analyze the mech and interrogate the prisoner," said Gressit.

"Well done, brother. You may have just helped us in the effort to win the war. Thank you very much Gressit, you have done very well."

"You are welcome, brother," Gressit replied as he gave his brother a big hug.

"I have dispatched both Roiden and Cassion to the land of Bracelia to aid and assist Santei. The land of Nowah has fallen into M.V.F. hands."

"What?" Gressit replied with a shocked expression on his face.

"Yes. Unfortunately, the humans released thousands of bombs and missiles on the Castle of Nowah. There were not enough dragons or a warriors present to defeat them, and Roiden's protection spell was not strong enough to protect the castle. They were simply overrun. It is very disappointing to me as well."

I will go to the Mountains of Harpinia to deliver the prisoner and his mech to the Elders. In the meantime, you should return to Bracelia and help fight for I am sure the humans will arrive there soon. Between you, Cassion, Roiden, and Santei, you should be able to cast a strong enough spell of protection on the castle. We will not let Bracelia fall, and we'll certainly not let Dakineah fall," said Leinad as he pounded his fist on the table.

The men all nodded in agreement as Leinad said, "I have had visions of these humans returning home soon. In that time, we'll regroup as well. We will storm Nowah after the humans leave, and we'll retake the castle. When they come back, they will be forced to fight once again on all three fronts; and we will defeat them on all three fronts. We have been lucky so far, as we have only had to fight them on one front at a time.

"I have no doubt when they come back they will have enough soldiers and mechs to fight us on all fronts. But that is ok, for we'll defeat them and drive them from our lands. For the time being, they are still here. We will send warriors to Nowah to keep the pressure on the humans and to let them know that we are coming. Wilson will be in charge of Dakineah while I am gone."

Wilson was the closest thing to a father that Leinad, Gressit, and Cassion had. He was a strong level ten magic user; and although Wilson was one of the ancients, he was still a fierce warrior.

"Alright my friends, I am going to leave for the Mountains of Harpinia now," said King Leinad with a look of anxiety on his face.

"Ok, brother," replied Gressit with a smile on his face.

"May the Life Source protect us all! This meeting is concluded," said the King.

The men finished exchanging handshakes and hugs and parted ways. King Leinad went to the courtyard and summoned the dragon Monte. He had a few of his servants' tie the mech to a Harness on Monte's back. Leinad had the human sit next to him, and they prepared for takeoff. He anchored the man in his seat with a telekinetic restraint to ensure he would not fall off of dragon during flight. First time dragon riders were prone to fainting, and in some cases they would fall to their death. The soldier's name was Lt. Smith.

"Well, Lieutenant Smith, we'll be flying for a couple of hours. We may as well get to know each other. As you are aware, we are in a time of war. That is no secret to any of us. When we get to our destination you will need to be very honest to the men I am going to introduce you to. If you help us, we'll offer you refuge here in Harpatia. I don't see a ring on your finger. Are you a single man?" asked Leinad.

"Yes, sir. I am single. I have no family," replied Lt. Smith.

"Then you staying here to avoid charges of treason should not be a problem for you, and it will not be a problem for me. Be honest with the Elders," said Leinad as he used his telekinesis to pour soothing thoughts of reassurance into the mind of Lt. Smith. Only the most skilled of wizards could use the mind influence techniques that Leinad had just employed.

"Ok, anything you want, sir; just please don't kill me," replied Smith as his entire body was trembling in fear.

Lt. Smith was a coward of sorts. He was a fierce warrior when inside a mech as he was an expert operator. However, he felt nothing but fear when he was outside the safety the armored war machine had offered him for so long. Smith had played video games his entire life and was a fun loving man at heart. When he was in his senior year of college, he had heard of the M.V.F.'s officer training program, and he could not resist. All he really ever wanted was to play with a big toy. Smith was not cut out for war, nor did he enjoy killing. He was just stuck, and now he had a way out. He was lucky to be alive, for he had engaged in combat with Gressit. Fortunately for him, his life was spared.

"Lt. Smith, all I can tell you is that we never wanted this war. We knew you were coming, and we offered your leader a peaceful retreat, but your General is convinced he will take what we have, and I will not let that happen. If there was a way to help your kind, we would. I can't trust men like General Hezekai to use such a power for good. Do you understand Lt. Smith?" asked Leinad as the two men soared through the air on Monte's back.

"Yes, sir."

"Just call me Leinad."

"Yes sir, Leinad," Smith nervously replied.

Lt. Smith was a disciplined soldier, and he would have a hard time calling any man of rank by his first name, especially the King of Harpatia. A couple hours later, they arrived at the Mountains of Harpinia. Upon their arrival at the Council of the Elders, Leinad knocked at the door in the mountain that bared the Royal Crest of Seven. The door opened, and Leinad was greeted by Elder Rom.

"What have you brought us today, great King?" asked Rom.

"We captured this man on the battlefield, and I have brought him here to teach you all about the inner workings of this mech. I thought you may be able to engineer some interesting weapons for the non-magic using warriors of Harpatia. In return for his help, I have offered Lt. Smith refuge here in Harpatia. I will guarantee this man's safety and Harpatian citizenship as long as he cooperates with you," said Leinad as he stared deeply at Lt. Smith who was shaking badly from fear.

"That will do just fine. Come on in, son," Rom said to the terrified Smith.

Leinad brought the mech inside the mountains with the use of his telekinesis, and floated it down to the Hangar Bay. After dropping off the mech and speaking with the Elders, Leinad felt Lt. Smith would be just fine. The Elders told Leinad to come back in a couple of weeks to see what new weapons they had created. Leinad said his goodbyes to the Elders and left. On his way out, he was stopped by the Nowrie Elder Revy. The large green man with purple spikes on his back looked Leinad in the eye and said, "Safe travels, my friend and my King. We all think you are doing a fine job with the humans. Keep up the good work."

"Thank you, my old friend, and may the Life Source protect us all," Leinad replied with a strong sense of pride as he exited the Council Chamber.

Upon leaving from the Council of the Elders, Leinad summoned Monte who was only a short distance away up the mountain. Monte appeared within seconds and asked Leinad where they would be going next. Leinad informed him they were to head for Bracelia because he needed to meet with his Generals. Monte jumped high in the air and flew off. Leinad needed to get with Cassion, Gressit, Santei, and Roiden to meld up a strong spell of protection for the Castle of Bracelia so the Bracelians would not receive the same fate as the Nowries.

Several hours, later Leinad landed at the Castle of Bracelia. He caught up with his two brothers, and the three of them went to meet with Santei and Roiden in the meeting chambers of the Castle Bracelia. Leinad walked through the doors of the meeting chambers and was greeted with exceptional cheer by both Santei and Roiden. The two kings were very insecure right now, but seeing Leinad made them feel better, it made them feel safe. That was the effect Leinad had on most people he encountered. Regardless of their race, people perceived Leinad as a great protector, a powerful wizard, and a glorious King.

"Welcome, my King," said Santei who was dressed in full battle armor.

"It is great to see you, Leinad," said Roiden who was looking quite fierce that day.

"And you as well my friends. We have much to discuss," said Leinad as he gestured for the men to take a seat.

"Thank you for sending Gressit, Roiden, and the warrior Cassion. I feel they will all be of great help, my lord," said the medium sized and stocky King Santei of Bracelia.

"I do believe we have a significant advantage this time. Because we are surrounded by the Blue Forest on all sides, we'll not have to fear any large scale ground attack for the plant life of the Blue Forest will protect us for a while. We will have to focus on the air battles. We can't give them the edge this time. As you all know, the plants are able to discern hostiles from friends. We will set up ambushes throughout the Blue Forest.

"We will set up battalions of warriors and wizards alike at different points in the forest, and I will dispatch several thousand dragons to protect them from airstrikes. I have already dispatched several thousand of my Elite Guard to help protect the Blue Forest. We will not let them take Bracelia," said Leinad with a bright blue glow in his eyes.

The men sat and discussed more details throughout the night, and they all agreed that Leinad's tactics were sound.

"I would like to meld our magic tonight so we may cast an unbreakable spell of protection over the Castle of Bracelia. The only way the humans would be able to take the castle is by a ground attack, and I just can't see that happening. We will crush all who oppose us.

"There is one more thing I think you should all know. I took the captured human, Lt. Smith, to the Council of the Elders; and they are hard at work trying to create a more efficient weapon to defeat them. I have offered the human a safe haven here in our lands in exchange for his help, and I will make similar offers to the other humans at a later date. Killing the enemy is not always the only way to defeat them. Sometimes you must embrace your enemy, and in some cases your enemy will become your friend. I will return to the Council soon," Leinad said.

"I can't wait to see what they come up with," said Santei.

"Thank you for providing a safe haven for my people, Leinad. I am embarrassed by what has happened to me and my land," said Roiden as red blush came over his green face.

"Don't be embarrassed, Roiden. We are learning more and more about our enemy each day. As you know, they have a lot of interesting weaponry; and we were simply caught off guard at Nowah. I should have sent more men, but I did not anticipate an attack such as the one you received. I have learned from our mistake of underestimating the humans, and I know we'll all be better prepared for the enemy in the future," replied Leinad in a compassionate tone.

"I am also aware of the capabilities of the humans. Using our lightning magic is one of the best ways I have found to defeat the mechs. We now know the energy from our lightning magic causes the mechs to short circuit. I have also found the metals used in the armoring of the mechs to be vulnerable to our Jezelite blades. So we know we can shock them. We also know we can overheat them, and we know we can pierce through these war machines. I feel that is all that we need to know to defeat them," said the warrior Cassion as he paced the floor of the meeting chamber in his golden and regal looking Jezelite garb.

"Thank you for your insight, Cassion. I will make a mental note of that. I am now going to return home to Dakineah. When I arrive home, I will dispatch a large unit of my Elite Guard to help fight here in Bracelia. Santei, I want you to reopen your teleportation hubs to Dakineah. I will have my men teleport through the hubs immediately," Leinad commanded.

The group then said their goodbyes. Cassion and Roiden remained with Santei, and Leinad took Monte back to Dakineah where he assembled his Royal Elite Guard. He briefed his commanders on the tactics they would need to use against the humans. Then he ushered his men to the teleportation hubs in the courtyard and sent them to Bracelia. Leinad had several hundred thousand warriors at his disposal, but he was keeping them in reserve and on call for he knew the biggest battles were yet to be fought. He was a very smart tactician, for his adopted father and caretaker, Wilson, had taught him the many secrets of the art of war. Leinad sent his Elite Guard over to Bracelia; and after a couple of days, the M.V.F. arrived at Bracelia by way of air and sea.

Bracelia was a mystical land with a lot of beautiful coastline. The Bracelians fished, surfed, swam and kayaked. They were adventurists and intellectuals. The land of Bracelia contained many beautiful rainforests were full of exotic wildlife. At the edge of the first rainforest of Bracelia came the beginning of the Blue Forest Territory which spanned for much of the continent. This forest held a mystical bright blue glow, for all of the foliage within it was bright blue in color. The reason for the distinct color was obvious: this place was directly linked to the mystical Life Source.

The view of the Blue Forest at night was remarkable, for you could see a bright turquoise/blue glow from miles away. There were The Blue Forest held many inexplicable mysteries within its boundaries, but the most epic of all was the Ponds of Rejuvenation. Only a handful of people knew how to get to them, for the ponds were regarded as sacred grounds. In the Ancient Wars of Segregation, the Bracelians brought their injured and mortally wounded to these ponds because it was said they could heal any wound. Only a few routes lead to the ponds, but they were heavily guarded and booby trapped. No outsiders would ever make it to the ponds alive. Very few Harpatians had ever been to the ponds, and those who had kept it a secret. No one wanted the Ponds of Rejuvenation to become a tourist attraction.

Leinad and his men had unlimited access to these ponds, and he visited them frequently to swim and have fun. Anyone who swam or bathed in these ponds when not injured would simply get a strong feeling of rejuvenation throughout their body. The ponds were said to be the life blood of the Life Source. The Blue Forest was the only forest of its kind in all of Harpatia, and Harpatia was a big planet. Although many areas of the land were scarcely populated, the kingdom was centered on three of the four main continents: Bracelia, Nowah, and Dakineah. The Outlands was the fourth continent, and it was inhabited by those who wished to live outside the kingdom.

During the Ancient Wars of Segregation, the Bracelian warriors covered their bodies in bright blue paint to blend in with the Blue Forest perfectly. They usually attacked at night. Seasoned Bracelian warriors could move through the forest like ghosts, thus making them a most formidable opponent in combat. The Blue Forest was home to thousands of plant and animal species, and they all seemed able to communicate telepathically through the Life Source. Many venomous plants thrived within the Blue Forest, but they would not attack or harm any Bracelian, Elf, or Nowrie at this time as the Wars of Segregation were over and the people were as one.

The live forest would grant all Harpatians safe access through its lands, but the humans would not have such an easy time should they try to pass through this elegant, yet deadly land. In peacetime, the Elves were primarily in Dakineah and the Nowries usually stayed in Nowah; but the Bracelians would go wherever their hearts desired. However all that had changed now, for they all would have to work together as one if they were going to drive the humans from their lands. It was being said that Rouger would lead the sovereign movement back to the kingdom to aide in the fight, but that was just rumor at this point.

Everything had changed now, and Rouger was indeed on his way to Dakineah with thousands of warriors to aid in the battle, with even more peace-loving people who desperately needed a safe haven. Rouger left the Outlands with his people on boats left in the middle of the night to avoid detection. He was not sure what General Hezekai would do if he knew they were leaving for the kingdom, and he did not want to find out. To avoid the humans of the M.V.F., the Outlanders sailed around the long way to Dakineah. They were spotted by a couple of vessels that belonged to the humans; but they were not attacked, for the humans were concentrating on Bracelia now and had no time to waste.

Meanwhile, back in Bracelia the humans began dropping off their forces on the Bracelian shoreline. The Bracelians did not offer a fight at the shores; they simply allowed the humans to gather. A couple of rouge snipers took a few random shots here and there, but the strategy of the King was to attack them in the forest. The goal was to get them in the Blue Forest, for it was a far more treacherous area. Leinad and Santei had entered into a deep battle meditation a day before in an effort to commune with the living forest and inform it the enemy was coming. The Harpatians would be aided by the forest, and they would have an overwhelming force of dragons to assist in the air battles.

Upon receiving word the humans were landing on the shores of Bracelia, King Leinad dispatched his brother, Gressit, the warrior Cassion, and King Roiden of Nowah to aid in the battles. The three would take up various positions in the Blue Forest and simply wait for the humans to arrive.

Back at the shores of Bracelia, Colonel Baker and his mech battalion commanders began discussing battle plans with General Hezekai.

"Colonel Baker, I am not going to bring *Lancer I* to the Castle of Bracelia, for I am sure they will have countermeasures in place for us now. We will soon have to return to Earth to rearm and regroup. We can't risk the Capital Ship. We have control of Nowah, and we'll try to take Bracelia before we return home. I want you to take your mechs though the forest. We will need to win a ground battle here to ensure victory. I will send a jet mech division to Bracelia to provide air support and to carve a path for our tank mechs which we need to get within firing range of the castle.

"We will take out as many of the enemy as possible from the air and engage their dragons in the air; so you will have to deal with only their ground troops. We have installed a super high-powered thrusting lance on most of the RS-777 mechs. Use it wisely. I will remain here in Nowah. Fight hard, soldier," said General Hezekai as he slapped the Colonel on the shoulder.

"Yes, Sir. I will keep you updated as the battle continues," replied Baker as he maintained his military bearing.

Colonel Baker and his men entered the initial rainforests of Bracelia. They encountered some light resistance by a few stubborn warriors who did not want to wait for them to reach the Blue Forest. Those Bracelians perished quickly. Some of the RS-777 mechs were equipped with large chainsaws used for path clearing in the rainforest. The M.V.F. battalion, which consisted of several thousand troops and mechs alike, made it through the rainforest and to the edge of the Blue Forest Territory. All they could see was a bright blue glowing forest that seemed to stretch for hundreds of miles in every direction, and indeed it did. The mechs attempted to cut the trees in the Blue Forest with their oversized chainsaws, but the blades simply bounced off. Some of the blades even broke on contact with these blue trees. It seemed the wood in the Blue Forest was far stronger than any of the other trees they had come into contact with on Harpatia. Colonel Baker ordered some of the mechs to fire missiles at the trees, and upon impact, the trees shattered into pieces. Baker now knew that it would take a lot more high explosives than he had to cut a path through this forest.

The tanks would remain in the rear for now, and the mission for Bracelia was going to be a hard one. The tank mechs were of little use thus far, but they had taken out a few dragons in the battle for Nowah. Air support was their number one weapon now. Colonel Baker knew that when Hezekai returned home from Earth he would bring a new and improved force of mechs with him; and that excited him, for he knew they would need their mechs equipped with better shields and weapons if they were to conquer this planet and take home the Life Source energy. They needed mechs able to withstand the lightning magic of the Harpatians.

General Hezekai had told Lieutenant Colonel Kanak of the Joint Chiefs of Staff all about the fire, ice, and lightning magic. Kanak was hard at work getting things done for Hezekai. He was directing the building of a new Super Capital Ship that would hold five times more mechs, troops, and supplies than *Lancer I* or 2. He was also getting his military engineers to create better cooling and heating systems for the mechs so they would be better able to defend themselves against the Harpatian wizards.

Kanak even assured Hezekai he would have a number of pleasant surprises for him and his men upon their return, but he told Hezekai he would have to wait to see them. This created great suspense for Hezekai. He could not wait to see all of the new "toys" waiting for him. Kanak was equipping the RS-777s with titanium and gold bonded swords. He figured since the Harpatians liked sword play so much, why not oblige them.

Baker began to lead his men through the Blue Forest. The ground shook as the large mechs stomped through the forest, and the vibrations of their march could be felt by the enemy beyond. Baker headed toward the castle, probably a week's journey by foot. Upon nightfall, he noticed the bright blue glow of the forest had intensified. The men could perceive about ten different hues of blue in the glow; and they also noticed the tree life had seemingly come alive, for some of the plants were swaying in a way that made the soldiers feel like they were being watched. And indeed they were.

Baker felt this bright glow would be helpful to them for they could now see everything clearly, but what he had forgotten was that the enemy could too. The men were physically exhausted from walking all day. Also, the mech operators were mentally and physically fatigued as well, for being hooked up to a neural band all day was enough to drain even the most seasoned of operators. The mechs had two control options, the first being the manual controls consisting of various buttons, levers, and foot pedals; but no one ever used the manual controls, for the neural bands were far more convenient. The second option was the neural bands which were made of two halo shaped discs worn over the forehead like a crown. Once connection with the brain was made, the operator would have a type of telepathic control over the mech, thus making it almost effortless to control. The reaction time with the bands was much faster, and that was why the operators preferred the bands over the manual controls.

Baker announced to his troops they would be taking rest soon. The majority of the troops were intimidated by the Blue Forest, for it was a very foreign and strange place. The men had never seen a glowing forest before. They soon stopped in a small area of the forest that looked harmless enough, and Baker told everyone to get some sleep. Most of the men could not sleep, for they either missed their families or were scared senseless. The ones who did sleep did so with one eye open, which was probably a good decision. In the middle of the night, around 0200 hours, Colonel Baker heard screams from five of his men. When he looked over to see what was happening, he was shocked to see large blue glowing, thorn covered vines wrapped around his men. The vines were choking the life out of his men. Then, just as some of the troops went over to help the men, they were dropped to the ground by a shower of flying darts that came out from the tree with the vines. The men died upon contact with these darts.

The poisonous darts had just killed thirty of Baker's men within seconds. *The forest was attacking them,* Baker thought. Panic started to set in among the troops. Baker then knew that this mission was going to get ugly. They had not encountered any of the Harpatian wizards or warriors yet, and they were already losing men. They were on foreign soil, in a foreign forest that glowed, and the trees were attacking them. The men were in a state of shock and disbelief. Baker launched a few of his rocket propelled grenades at the tree that was attacking them. The grenades were effective: while they did not kill the tree or even damage it, the blast was enough to make the tree let go of the five men that it held with its vines.

Baker knew the trees could not be chopped down, but they could be shot down by high explosives. He did not want to waste all of his high explosives on the tree life; and now he was angry and frustrated. He ordered the men to put on full body armor mesh which would protect them from any future flying tree dart attacks. He ordered all mech operators to stay in their mechs. Baker once again issued the order of sleep to his men. He told them all to remain calm, and insisted on them getting at least a few hours of sleep, without which they would be as good as dead. He knew they were holding a double edged sword. If they slept, the forest could kill them; but if they did not, the warriors of Harpatia would have an easy time with killing them. Baker set up men to patrol and watch over the grounds. The crew would sleep in shifts.

While walking through the Blue Forest a few hours later, Gressit came upon a squadron of the M.V.F. spread out over the length of a mile or so. He contacted both Cassion and Roiden telepathically and informed them on the situation. Gressit would be the one to draw first blood, and he could not wait. He had waited patiently for the commanders of the M.V.F. to also fall asleep with the rest of the men. After he was sure that the commanders were asleep, he knew it was time to make his move.

Gressit noticed there were several guards pulling night watch. He would kill them first. As he crept into the camp of the M.V.F. like a snake, he moved slowly and accurately through the forest with superb stealth. He came upon a middle aged man wearing a Sergeant's lapel and looking through some form of scope. Apparently the man was looking through an infrared scope to search for any enemy who may be hiding. Suddenly the man saw a bright red glow in his scope, and by the time he realized that it was not one of his own, it was too late.

Gressit unsheathed a golden dagger form his hip and slashed the man's throat, killing him silently to avoid being seen or heard by anyone else. He moved up and down the mile long stretch of the camp, taking out both guards and commanders alike. He knew the insignia of a commander, for the Nowries had killed and interrogated many at the Battle of Nowah.

Upon eliminating all of the guards, Gressit contacted his Elite Guard telepathically and ordered them to attack. The Elite Guard was also accompanied by many strong warriors and magic from the School for Combat and Magic Arts. They charged into the M.V.F.'s campsite and thrust their swords into the tents of the sleeping men killing many of them in the process. This attack lasted about twenty minutes, and they managed to kill over 100 men for a sleeping human was not a hard target to kill at all. Some of the men actually made it to their RS-777 mechs; but it was too late, for the wizards from the School for Combat and Magic Arts were waiting for them. Several Nowrie wizards had come from the school, and they simply waited for the men to get in their mechs; and when they did, the Nowries used their Combat Arts magic to thrust their swords through the steel chest plate of the mechs to impale their operators. The Nowries had a special interest in the war, and they would show no mercy to the humans who had killed so many of their people in the Battle for Nowah.

After destroying a large section of the M.V.F.'s camp, Gressit and his men retreated back into the depths of the Blue Forest where they would wait and attack again. The Harpatians were employing a stick and move strategy. Gressit and the other Harpatian Commanders who were in the battle knew the Blue Forest like the back of their hand. The humans had made a huge mistake by coming to fight them in their own backyard, and the Harpatians would make them pay for that mistake.

King Roiden was a few miles east of Gressit, and he was staging a surprise attack on a platoon of mechs. Roiden and his battalion of men attacked the mech squadron from behind. There were hundreds of mechs and men, but there were thousands of Harpatian warriors and wizards alike. The three races of Harpatians were fluidly fighting as one, and it was beautiful.

Roiden growled and leapt out from behind a bush and lunged forward at a group of mechs. The King of Nowah fought with a level of ferocity unheard of to most. Using his large golden sword, he slashed and cleaved at the mechs taking them down one at a time. In conjunction with his superior sword and magic arts skills, Roiden tore the mechs in half, slicing them into pieces with little or no effort at all. The King was raging and out for revenge.

Roiden laughed to himself silently each time he got a kill on the battlefield, for he knew that the scenery had changed; and the humans were now engaged in a close quarter battle with him. And no one in their right mind would ever want to be in a close combat situation with a Nowrie, for even a Nowrie with no magic powers at all was still strong enough to rip your arms right off your body and beat you with them. The Bracelian warriors and wizards were dressed in their full blue camouflage war paint, and they attacked slowly, stealthily, and with excellent precision. King Roiden continued his attack, and several miles down the forest the warrior Cassion followed suit.

Cassion sprung into battle as the soldiers awoke in surprised horror and struggled to get into their mechs. He was outraged by what happened in Nowah, and he was ready to shed some human blood. Cassion noticed the men who had made it into their mechs had put on some kind of head band right before the chest cavity closed around them. He also saw that after the men had put their head bands on, they then pushed a small red button which seemed to close the chest plate and operator compartment of the mech. He was intrigued by this.

Cassion then cut down one of the running mech operators just as he made to his mech. He then sat down in the chest cavity of the kneeling mech and placed the headband over his head. He pushed the red button and the chest cavity closed around him. Instantly a heads up display screen appeared.

Cassion was now inside a fully upright and operational mech. The words on the HUD read: "Begin thought control process." Cassion thought *this could not be much unlike telekinesis or telepathy,* so he began to control the mech with his mind. When he thought left, the mech walked left. He was catching on very fast. Cassion saw many buttons and hand controls and experimented with the mech for about ten minutes. He thought forward and began moving forward. He had noticed he had a shoulder mounted Gatling gun on the right, and a shoulder mounted rocket launcher on the left. He then saw the mech had a lance that was tucked into its forearm. Cassion willed the lance to his grip and began swinging it around like a staff. At this point, he had full control of the mech; and he was very excited. He sent out a wave of messages through his telekinesis to inform his men he was operating a mech.

Cassion slashed the lance from the top left eye and down to the right leg. This would make him recognizable to his allies. In the next instant, he saw three RS-777 mechs coming his way; and heard a voice from inside one of the mech's say, "What are you doing, Sergeant?"

He had a moment of wild thought, and then heard the voice say, is this sergeant Smith

"Sergeant Smith is dead," Cassion replied through the mech's loud speaker as he targeted the RS777's knees and sawed it to the ground in a haze of bullet fire. Cassion was amazed by the ease with which he had just taken out the mech. In the next millisecond, he visualized two rockets slamming the other two mechs and blowing them into pieces. The mechs that had approached him did not have their shields engaged; so when the rockets hit them, they were blown into pieces. He had just taken out three mechs in less than thirty seconds.

Cassion made his mech spring forward as he thrust his lance through the chest plate of the damaged mech that was struggling to get back to its feet. *Three mechs down. This is great*, Cassion thought. As he made his way through the camp, he killed all those who were dumb enough to still be asleep with his machine gun and occasionally with a rocket propelled grenade. He was able to take out the RS-777 mechs with ease, as if he had been a mech operator for years. Within 30 minutes, Cassion killed 100 soldiers and destroyed 30 mechs as well.

At this point, the warrior noticed his ammunition levels were at zero. He had not paid attention to his ammo stores, but his HUD was telling him he had fired 5,000 rounds; and the machine gun heading was blinking red. There was a green light by the rocket ammo indicator display that showed him that he had one RPG left. He then visualized his jet packs igniting and began to fly.

Cassion flew to the rear of the forest where the HUD's radar was telling him a resupply line was available. He saw a couple of low ranking privates and said, "I need to rearm at once." These supply men had not gotten the word there was a rogue mech wandering about, so the men rearmed him and wished him good luck. He took notice at how the men had rearmed him and then killed the ten soldiers who were in the supply area.

Cassion took his mech back to the area of combat that King Roiden was in and saw Roiden was engaged in battle with two RS-777 mechs and was doing just fine. Cassion contacted Roiden through the Life Source and told him he was in the mech with the large scar on its face and body. Roiden then saw Cassion out of the corner of his eye and shouted, "You always were the crazy one." Then Cassion flew his mech straight up about 25 feet and dive bombed the first mech attacking Roiden. He impaled the mech with a straight blow to its chest from his lance, and at the same time he unleashed machine gun fire on the other mech. With the other mech staggered from the machine gun fire, Cassion summoned his magical katana, willed to a large size that would fit the mech's gauntlet, and sliced the second mech in half.

"A little bit of this, and a little bit of that, just another day on the battlefield for me," Cassion said through the loudspeaker of his mech.

"Thanks for your help," replied Roiden as he gave Cassion a wink.

The two mechs lay on the ground in a heap of twisted metal and blood. The warrior's mood was that of absolute joy. There was nothing else on the whole planet that could make him happier than fighting for a noble cause. He had trained his whole life for something that he thought would never come; but now it was here, war was here, and he loved it. Roiden, on the other hand was an ancient, and he had fought in the Ancient Wars of Segregation. He had enjoyed centuries of peace, and he did not want more war; but now that war was here, he was ready to bring out the old savage killer that lurked deep within him. The humans truly had no idea what they had gotten themselves into, but they did not care. They just wanted to get their Life Source energy, and they would not leave the Harpatians alone until they got it.

"I am going to fly a couple miles down range to check up on Gressit," said Cassion.

"Happy hunting," replied Roiden.

Cassion contacted Gressit through his mind, and Gressit informed him of his position. When they were together, they went to meet up with Roiden for they had received news that King Leinad was at the Castle Bracelia. Leinad had decided it was time to significantly weaken the humans' position in the Blue Forest and had brought an entire battalion of his elite guard with him, about 20,000 men to be exact. Cassion, Gressit, and Roiden decided they would return to the Castle Bracelia to meet up with King Leinad Seven. When they arrived, Leinad was discussing battle plans with Santei in the castle's meeting chambers.

"Welcome, brothers," said Leinad as they walked into the room.

"We have received news the humans will take a large part of their forces back to Earth to rearm and regroup. We learned of this from a captured M.V.F. soldier we interrogated. The humans will return with a renewed force within a few months, and Leinad and I are discussing our future plans of action," said Santei.

Cassion, Gressit, and Roiden took their places at the octagonal table, and the men began to discuss their battle plans.

"We will mount a large offensive strike against the humans tomorrow; and with any luck, we should be able to crush them and drive them away from Bracelia. I will be coming with you tomorrow," said Leinad who was dressed in a gold embossed Jezelite armor suit.

"Sounds like fun," Gressit replied jokingly.

"I can't wait," replied Cassion.

"I will enjoy spilling human blood with you all," replied the tall green skinned Nowrie with purple spikes on his back.

"Roiden, when the humans leave, I will have you lead a task force to retake the Castle of Nowah; and you shall regain your lands, my great king," Leinad said.

"I appreciate that Leinad, and I look forward to that day."

"It will be upon us soon. But for now, we must plan for tomorrow's attack," replied Leinad in a serious tone.

After a long day of waging war against the Harpatians in the Blue Forest, Jake Baker was tired. It had seemed the Harpatians were done fighting for the day, and Baker hoped there would be no more surprise attacks during the night again. He had lost about a quarter of his forces during the battle on this day. Nearly all of the M.V.F.'s air missions were thwarted by the dragon legion that was stationed in Bracelia.

Colonel Baker opened up a communications channel to General Hezekai, who was back at the Castle of Nowah. Hezekai began to bark orders at the Colonel almost immediately as he was planning a large scale attack for the next morning.

After being briefed by the General, Baker shut his eyes and began sleep, only to wake up an hour later in a cold sweat and a sharp stinging pain in his right ankle. Upon gazing down at his feet, the Colonel noticed a large blue vine wrapped around his foot. Baker unsheathed a large combat knife from his hip and was able to cut himself free from the vine after a few minutes of struggle. He then began to scan his surroundings; and when he did, he noticed that many of his soldiers had also been entangled by these blue vines. Some of the soldiers had been choked to death by the vines and others were still fighting to get free. At this point, all available personnel were hard at work trying to free their comrades. *The forest was indeed alive*, Baker thought.

Earlier that same day, some of the soldiers had encountered lion-like creatures, and some had reported sightings of large flying predators looking like pterodactyls; and those were indeed the Intrepids and Dellions of Harpatia. Now they had to fight nature as well as the Harpatians, and Baker knew it would take a lot more mechs, men, and heavy ordnance than they had if they were going to penetrate these forests. A successful air campaign would be useless if they could not reach the castle walls on foot. The majority of the M.V.F.'s forces were on the ground. The RS-777 mechs could fly, but if they did so for long periods of time they would risk a power failure, and that was any mech operator's worst nightmare. The RS-777's that did try to fly to the Castle of Bracelia were quickly intercepted by the dragon legion, and once a dragon had you in its grip, you were as good as dead.

General Hezekai had issued a no fly order to the mech operators in an attempt to save resources. The no fly order meant the mechs were not allowed to fly for long distances. Although the M.V.F. had been in Harpatia for only a short while, their mechs were starting to lose power at a rapid pace. The Capital Ships contained only about a hundred or so charging stations, and charge time had to be limited to one hour per mech per charge to ensure they would not drain too much of the ship's power reserves. The Capital Ships operated on a combination of fuel, solar, and battery power. The M.V.F. was forced to use their power reserves very sparingly.

After a while, Baker's squad was finally able to free themselves from the maniacal vines of the living trees in the Blue Forest. He counted 20 dead and 35 injured. Most of the men who had been stung by the vines were developing cold like symptoms; but ironically, Baker felt just fine. After assisting in the tagging and bagging of his fallen brothers, Baker closed his eyes, and returned to his little spot in the woods in an attempt to get some sleep. He knew the next day would be very challenging and exhausting.

Hezekai's plan was to stage a strong offensive against the Harpatians and gain control of the Castle of Bracelia. He was debating whether or not he should use his Capital Ship, Lancer; but he was unsure if that would be a good idea or not. The Harpatians would surely have some new countermeasures in place after what had happened to them in Nowah, and the General was sure they would be expecting another visit from his warship. Hezekai wanted to capture Bracelia as he had captured Nowah, but little did he know this time the Harpatians would be ready for him.

The next day Baker woke up early. He was exhausted, for he had only had a couple of hours of sleep the night before. His whole body ached as if someone had thrown him down a flight of stairs. Every step he took was a battle, but somehow he found the inner strength to move on. Baker made contact with General Hezekai through a com channel, and the General issued the order to attack at once. The M.V.F air dropped 1,500 RS-777 mechs along with 20,000 ground troops at various locations within the forest.

All the mechs were equipped with heavy weapons, especially the RX-99 tank mechs escorting the ground forces which were equipped with 20-foot long barrels with the circumference of a basketball. These tanks could pack a punch, and the soldiers did not mind walking behind them. General Hezekai brought in *Lancer I* and cut a large path through the forest that would lead them in the direction of the Castle Bracelia. Even with the use of ultra-high explosives, it took Hezekai several hours to cut a path for his men.

Upon the completion of the path, the M.V.F. began to make their way through the Blue Forest. The tanks and RS-777 mechs made it about midway through the trail when they were met by the Harpatian Royal Guard, the elite members of the School for Combat and Magic Arts, and many other surprise guests. The sudden appearance of the Harpatian warriors took the entire M.V.F. by surprise.

King Leinad looked at his brother Gressit and said, "Brother today is the day for you to shine as the Chieftain of the Harpatian armies. You will solidify yourself as an elite warrior, as we all will. I want you to take 5,000 men into the forest and engage the humans in battle keeping them as far from the castle as possible. I will also dispatch 200 dragons to provide you with air support.

"Roiden, you will go with the Nowries to a different section of the forest, and your task will be simple: kill as many as you can.

"Thank you, Leinad. I like that idea," replied Roiden.

"I thought you would. Santei and I will take a battalion of the Royal Guard along with half the elite members from the School for Combat and Magic Arts, and we'll engage the Capital Ship. Cassion, your job is to engage the tank mechs and destroy them. Gressit will help you with this. You may take the remainder of the members of the School for Combat and Magic Arts and as many of the Royal Guardsmen as you see fit. All my other commanders have already received their orders and are heading into the Blue Forest as we speak.

"Good luck to all of you, and may the Life Source protect us all," said Leinad in a tone of love and respect.

The men nodded in agreement and set out to their respective areas of the battlefield. King Leinad summoned the dragon Monte and flew off with the rest of his men toward the Capital Ship. Once airborne, the Harpatians became engaged by several RS-777 mechs. A fierce air battle had begun as the students from the school along with masters Chew and Dolan were engaged by several hundred RS and jet mechs alike. The students and their teachers began to cast lightning, fire, and ice magic at the pursuing mechs.

Most of the students from the School for Combat and Magic Arts had never seen battle before, and as a result of their inexperience they quickly perished. Masters Chew and Dolan were dropping the mechs like flies as they flew through the air battle with relative ease. Leinad headed straight toward the Capital Ship, accompanied by several hundred of his Elite Guard dragon riders. When he finally reached the Capital Ship, he decided to cast a powerful spell of protection upon his men and himself; and that spell would act as armor against some of the ship's attacks, but not all.

Massive amounts of heavy gun and laser fire came at the Harpatians as they approached the ship. They bobbed and weaved as best they could to avoid taking damage. One hundred dragons were able to land on the Capital Ship taking General Hezekai by total surprise. The General made sure his shields were up at full strength and continued to pound the rainforest.

King Leinad dismounted Monte; and as he walked along the ship, he ordered Monte to do his worst. Monte slashed at the ship and exhaled large breaths of fire upon it. He also unleashed some very powerful lightning magic through his eyes and onto the hull of the ship. Despite his efforts, the dragon was only able to inflict small amounts of damage to the ship. The rest of the dragon legion had followed suit.

Leinad knew he would have to damage the Capital Ship from within. This would be a very risky move for the King to make, for he was unfamiliar with the ship's interior. He closed his eyes and teleported inside; and when he reappeared, he was surrounded by several mechs and quite a few men. He guessed he must have teleported right into a trap.

Leinad then began to dodge massive amounts of gun fire as he made his way through the ship. He noticed many computer control consoles as he looked around; but he did not have the time to take in all of his surroundings for he was using the majority of his focus to deflect the gun fire that would have surely killed anyone else. Leinad had created some sort of kinetic barrier around his body that was able to deflect the projectiles coming at him. The King then decided to send out a wave of lightning magic; and with a gesture of his hand, large currents of white hot electricity began pouring from his fingers and into the computer consoles.

Leinad watched the consoles explode. He could feel General Hezekai's hatred through the Life Source, and he began to run in the direction of the General's presence. Leinad was growing tired, for he was using a massive amount of his energy to teleport and run around, all the while trying to maintain his protection barrier. The King knew he had to move fast, for even he would eventually grow tired from this massive exertion of astonishing magic usage. He was able to kill dozens of men with his lightning magic and he could now smell the scent of victory at hand.

When Leinad came upon a set of sealed doors, he used his magic to see behind them; and what he saw was disturbing: a large walkway of undetermined length protected by a laser field. He knew if he came into contact with any of these lasers, he would be vaporized.

The King decided that teleporting through this area would be too dangerous. He knew if he tried to traverse the hallway there would be a good chance that he would get cut in to pieces. At this point, he did not know what to do. He turned around and prepared himself to engage in combat with the mechs and soldiers pursuing him.

Leinad let out a burst of lightning magic from his gem encrusted dual bladed staff that instantly dropped the foot soldiers coming after him. He then summoned up a powerful blast of ice magic and channeled it from his staff into the mechs surrounding him. Upon impact with the ice magic, the mechs froze in place. The King of Harpatia wasted no time as he quickly sliced the frozen mechs into pieces.

Leinad twirled his staff in a circular motion to deflect an incoming laser blast from one of the mechs he had not seen earlier. In conjunction with his spell of protection and the strength of his Jezelite armor, Leinad was able to remain unharmed by the M.V.F. He then turned toward one of the mechs just as it fired a missile at him and teleported behind it. A blue vapor trail emitted as he reappeared behind the mech, his staff was safely attached to a harness on his back. He quickly unsheathed his golden sword and impaled the mech and its operator. The missile meant for Leinad made impact a second later on the ship's interior, and it's blast sent Leinad flying backwards as a piece of shrapnel hit him in the leg. He immediately entered a healing trance; and he knew that if he was going to remove the shrapnel from his left leg, he would have to leave the ship and go somewhere he could concentrate.

"What in the heck is going on down there? Stop firing in the ship you morons," said Hezekai in an enraged tone through the ship's speakers.

Leinad teleported directly to Monte's back and flew away from the ship. He found a safe spot in the Blue Forest where he would be able to heal himself. The bleeding was severe at this point, so he could not afford to waste any time. The rest of the warriors that had accompanied him to the ship had fallen back as well; and as they were leaving, they noticed the Capital Ship had turned around and was slowly—as if injured or damaged—flying away.

"I can't believe this! How was this man able to enter our ship?" demanded General Hezekai.

"Sir, we have multiple fires onboard; and we have fire crews working on them as we speak. Several systems are down, and shields are only at thirty percent," said Captain Hunter.

Captain Hunter was the head pilot of *Lancer I*, and he reported only to General Hezekai. Hunter was a thin man with blond hair and one of the M.V.F.'s star pilots.

"Well, now we know that the King is able to teleport through our shields and into our ship. We will have to figure out a way to stop that from happening when we return to Earth. We must return home soon, for we can't afford to lose *Lancer I* just yet. Get those fires put out and get us out of here, Captain," the General commanded.

"Yes, Sir!" replied Hunter.

"We are going to have to change our strategy."

Hezekai flew back across the sea to the Castle Nowah. He did not need to be present at the battle, for three-fourths of his forces were there; and he was sure Colonel Baker could get the job done. Although he would never admit it, Hezekai was very frightened by the fact that Leinad Seven was so powerful that he could teleport into a ship that was protected by energy shields. He wondered how he could ever stop such a powerful man. And then he thought to himself, *he will be stopped when I have cut off his head.*

Leinad decided to bypass the Blue Forest and return to the Castle of Bracelia. Once at the castle, he removed the shrapnel from his leg through the power of the Life Source. After a painful healing session, Leinad decided to rest for the remainder of the day. He located his brother by way of meditation and saw that Gressit was fighting fiercely in the Blue Forest. It had not taken long for Gressit to find a battalion of mechs within the Blue Forest. Roiden was a couple of miles down forest fighting hard against the mechs.

Gressit had been waiting for this day his entire life. Today was the day for him to prove himself to his brother. He had always felt he had lived in the shadow of the great Leinad Seven, but today would be the day for Gressit to shine. And for that he was grateful. He had always been known as the King's brother, but today he would earn the title that Leinad had given him. Today he would truly be the Chieftain of the Harpatian Armies. He approached a squadron of mechs and leaped directly into battle as he unleashed a barrage of lightning magic directly into the mechs. Five of the RS-777 mechs immediately short circuited and fell to the ground in a shower of sparks. The other mechs were firing some medium caliber bullets at him, but the munitions were no match for his Jezelite armor.

Gressit showed no fear as he slashed and kicked at the enemy mechs. His elite guard followed his lead, as he was followed by thousands of elite warriors. The Harpatian Royal Guard along with many prominent members of the School for Combat and Magic Arts were hard at work assisting in battle. Masters Chew and Dolan were fighting alongside Gressit today as well. Chew and Dolan were now heavily engaged in combat deep within the Blue Forest. By mid-day Gressit had dropped at least 50 mechs, and then he saw a particularly shiny silver mech. He sensed the operator of the attractive mech was none other than Colonel Jake Baker.

Gressit rushed Baker with ferocity; and as he did, he swung at the Colonel's mech with all of the strength he could muster. His sword barely missed the head of Baker's mech. Colonel Baker launched a rocket at Gressit, so he teleported about ten yards behind Colonel Baker as he dodged the RPG attack. Baker was astonished by his skills and thought his brother had taught him well. Gressit lunged at Colonel Baker and unleashed a barrage of lightning magic on Baker's RS-777 which had little effect if any at all. Baker's mech had been outfitted with a far more effective shielding system than the rest of his men, and it was that shielding that kept him alive for the moment. Baker then drew a large mech-sized sword from the hip slot of his mech. Colonel Baker had just gotten the sword upgrade a couple of days earlier when he was at base camp in Nowah. The M.V.F. would be decommissioning the lances and re-outfitting all of their RS mechs with swords instead of lances, but this would take some time to complete.

Baker swung his oversized broadsword at Gressit's body in an attempt to cut the man in half. Gressit quickly blocked the attack with his own broadsword; and it was only by the power of the Life Source that he was able to deflect the blow, for the power of Baker's mech was equal to the might of 20 men. After blocking the blow, Gressit threw a magic-aided kick to the mid-section of the mech which knocked it back a few feet. Baker replied with a straight right punch that landed to Gressit's face and knocked him back about ten feet.

The Elven Chieftain was dazed, but he was not out of the fight. Gressit decided to try a new strategy, for hand-to-hand combat against this war machine was not boding well for him. He used his telekinesis to levitate a nearby boulder in the air; and with a gesture of his hand, he sent it flying straight at Colonel Baker. The rock struck the chest plate of the mech. and Baker fell back several paces staggering to regain its balance. Instantly, Gressit sent a sheet of ice magic into the mech which froze it into place.

Gressit was shocked when the ice began to melt almost instantly and the mech broke free from it. Colonel Baker did indeed have a superior mech—far more powerful than the ones that he had come into contact with before. While stuck in the ice magic, Colonel Baker had initiated the mech's external heating mechanism which was another new modification that had been added to only a few of the mechs. The heating mechanisms were comprised of super-heated coils within the mech's exoskeleton; and when activated, they would do exactly what they were designed to do which was defend against ice magic. Many engineers were aboard *Lancer II*, and they were constantly coming up with ways to make their war machines more effective against this magical race of beings they had encountered.

Baker charged forward toward Gressit and slashed at him with his mech sword. The attack grazed Gressit's right arm, but it did not pierce through his Jezelite armor. Gressit spun on the mech and again hit it with a blast of ice magic. This time the mech froze into place and did not instantly heat up the ice. Apparently the mech's heating systems had not cooled down and recharged yet, and Gressit took full advantage of this. Gressit came down with a powerful left to right slash which sliced the right leg of the mech clean off. Sparks began to fly, as Gressit held his sword in a high stance as he went in for the kill. Gressit swung his sword down at the Colonel's mech in an attempt to finish his opponent when suddenly, from out of nowhere, he was broadsided by one of Baker's men. The RS mech rammed into Gressit with amazing force and knocked him to the ground. Gressit was about half conscious when he looked up. He saw the mech draw out his lance and thrust it straight at his chest; and he teleported out of the way just in time to avoid being killed.

Gressit stood up and noticed another RS-777 mech had arrived; and as it did, the other mech that had nearly killed him went to help the Colonel. The two RS-777 mechs picked up the Colonel's half frozen mech by the arms and flew off into the distance. Colonel Baker would get away again, but that was ok. There would be plenty of time to kill Baker.

Just as Gressit was about to leave the area, another RS-777 mech landed in front of him, and Gressit wasted no time as he instantly froze the mech into place with a strong level nine burst of ice magic. When he noticed the ice was beginning to melt, he unleashed a strong level ten shower of lightning magic into the mech. The combination of melting ice and lightning magic overloaded the mech's capacitors, and showers of sparks emitted violently throughout its joint areas. Gressit lunged forward, jumped, back flipped, and landed behind the mech. He then issued a reverse sword thrust into the mech's back and impaled the operator.

Gressit had gotten his first good kill, and he was deeply satisfied. He continued to move swiftly through the battlefield engaging the M.V.F. with ferocity. Meanwhile, a little bit deeper into the forest, King Roiden was hard at work in the skies defending against the jet mechs. He flew through the skies of Bracelia on his dragon, Arkon, who was an elite member of the Harpatian dragon Legion and a great friend of the dragon Monte. He was a medium size dragon with pale green skin and a quick and nimble predator on the battlefront. Arkon had formidable fire breath and very strong lightning magic that he was able to channel through his eyes. Arkon and Monte were ancient dragons. No one really knew the true age of the ancients, but they had a good idea they were several thousand years old. In ancient times, the Harpatians did not catalog the ages of their dragons. Monte and Arkon had been around a long time, and they planned on keeping it that way.

Roiden was engaged in a fierce air battle with the RXF-10 jet mechs. His objective for the day was to kill as many of the enemy as possible; and after his discussion with the warrior Cassion, he decided it was best to stay in the skies to keep the jets at bay to save their warriors on the ground from an air attack, for the bombs and missiles of the M.V.F. had been the biggest advantage that the humans had thus far. Roiden planned to end that advantage.

The warrior Cassion was hard at work deep within the Blue Forest devising a strategy to destroy the several hundred tank mechs that were making their way through the Blue Forest and toward the Castle Bracelia. The warrior was confident the tanks would never make it to the castle. And even if they did, he doubted they would be able to inflict any damage for King Leinad, Cassion, Gressit, Roiden, and Santei had joined together in a meld to cast a very strong spell of protection on the Castle Bracelia. The melding they had performed was reminiscent of the ancient group of Ten Meld, and the spell they had cast could not easily be broken. The Harpatians had learned a lot on the day that Nowah fell, and they would not make the same mistakes twice.

A few of the jet mechs did make it to the castle; and when they did, they launched several bombs and missiles at the castle walls. Their attacks had no effect for the spell of protection simply absorbed the energy of the bombs and used that same energy to strengthen the existing spell.

Roiden was flying through the air battle with ease; and with the aid of his dragon Arkon he was able to drop many of the jets mechs out of the sky. The lightning magic the dragon was sending into the jets was far too much for them to handle, it fried all of the jets to a crisp. The telekinetic bond of Roiden and Arkon allowed them to move as one. If Roiden thought it, Arkon did it.

Roiden thought that the air battle was won, for after a few hours of fighting he could no longer see any jets in the sky. He was just about to start celebrating when suddenly, out of the corner of his eye, he saw 70 jet mechs pop out from the skies above. The jets wasted no time as their surprise attack killed three dragons within the first 20 seconds. The dragon legion had been caught off guard, but they were not out of the fight. The jets were firing energy missiles; and when these missiles hit a dragon that was not wearing armor, the dragon simply fell from the sky. Most of the dragons within the legion were not protected by a spell, for the majority of the dragon riders were more warrior than magician.

Those who had the heavy Jezelite armor were still stunned by the missiles and some were even killed. Only a spell of protection from a most powerful wizard would be effective against the munitions and weaponry of the M.V.F. for the technology that the humans possessed was very powerful. The humans learned the eye and throat areas of the dragons were vulnerable. Once the jet mechs got a target lock on the throat or eyes, there would be little that an unarmored dragon could do to protect itself. But the majority of the dragons did wear armor. Only the older and more stubborn dragons had refused for they claimed it made them slower and less nimble in the air. The dragons that did have a skilled magic arts user on their back were the lucky ones, for they had little to no fear. A dragon could take a lot of pounding from cannon fire; but as tough as their scaly hides were, their skin would break eventually. They were by no means invincible.

Roiden glanced up to see three jets were in hot pursuit of him; and through the Life Source, he felt a strong sense of danger. Although he was flying at untold speeds, he knew he could not evade all of the attacks that came at him, for a 50-foot long dragon was a very big target. Roiden took some cannon fire in the shoulder of his dragon. He quickly checked Arkon's armor plating; and much to his relief, he saw the munitions did not pierce the armor. Jezelite was a very strong metal, but it was not completely impervious; and sometimes if the pilot got a lucky shot on one of the weak sections of welding, the Jezelite would break.

Roiden bucked and twisted in the air in an effort to evade the jet mech cannon fire until Arkon took a missile blast on his right flank. The impact stunned the dragon for a few seconds, and he began to plummet toward the ground. Roiden hit Arkon with a jolt of lightning magic in his shoulder in an effort to wake him. The trick worked—Arkon quickly regained his senses and steadied himself in the air. The dragon quickly entered into a healing trance; and with the aid of Roiden, he was able to feel no pain from the blast that had almost sent him to his death.

Arkon spun on the jet mech, doing a 180° turn in the air. He was now on a collision course with the jet fighter mech. He raised up his talons and lifted himself into the air slightly; and as he passed just inches away from the jet's hull, he slashed the mech in half. It exploded upon impact, but the spell of protection that Roiden had cast upon himself and his dragon was strong enough to keep them both from feeling the effects of the mid-air explosion. Roiden and Arkon were instantly engaged by two more jet mechs unleashing a barrage of cannon fire at them. Arkon then began a vertical climb so high into the atmosphere that the pursuing mechs started to form ice crystals on their hulls causing their engines to sputter and almost stall. The jets backed off. Roiden informed Arkon he was having difficulty breathing. The air pressure would have surely killed Roiden if he was not a magic arts user, for the only thing that was keeping him alive at these altitudes was his magic.

Arkon dove back down toward the jets, and Roiden unsheathed his sword and sliced the left wing off of one of them sending it crashing into the ground in a blaze of glory. Arkon then did a corkscrew maneuver and went into a 360° flip that landed him behind the last pursuing jet. He then put on a burst of speed and flew directly above the jet. Roiden anchored his feet into the dragon, ordered him to fly upside down, and looked at the pilot and winked at him. He was not sure if the pilot saw his taunt or not, but he quickly thrust his blade through the cockpit of the jet and impaled the pilot, thus sending the jet crashing into a group of five RS-777 mechs that were standing in the forest below. All of the men were killed.

Roiden continued to fly through the air battle, assisting his warriors whenever he was needed. The dragon riders of the royal guard were the best in the land and had trained their whole lives for air battle. They had trained against other dragons to prepare for a possible civil war or an invasion from a neighboring planet, so they were prepared. Fighting a jet mech was a bit different than fighting a dragon, but they made do with the training they had.

By the end of the day, Roiden managed to push most of the jet mechs out of the way. The Royal Guard had taken out several hundred of them that day. Roiden did not know how many jets the humans had left; and he did not care for if more came, more would die. He knew many more would come after the humans went home to regroup, but there was always hope that maybe the humans would never return once they left.

Roiden flew back to the Castle Bracelia after he was satisfied there would be no more air reinforcements coming on that day. The King of Nowah left 500 dragon riders in the sky to patrol for the rest of the night. As tempting as it was to send the dragons down to the ground battle to assist, Roiden knew he could not do that; for if they dropped their guard for even a second in the air, they could face an overwhelming air attack on their ground warriors. The role of the dragons was to provide air support at this time—nothing else. The dragons would fly in teams of 20 and patrol in shifts, each taking a rest break whenever needed.

The air battle had been a success for Roiden, and he returned to the castle to take rest. Deep within the Blue Forest, the warrior Cassion was waiting for total darkness to set in when he would use the blue glow of the forest to his advantage. The warrior was wearing turquoise-blue war paint all over his body. Tonight he would make an even bigger name for himself.

The RX-99 tank mechs had managed to make it about three-quarters of the way through the Blue Forest, and several hundred of them were within range of the Castle Bracelia. The tanks opened fire with their heavy cannons, and the mech operators were astonished as they looked at the satellite imagery of their assault. They saw the large caliber, high-explosive rounds hitting the castle, but there was simply a slight blue glow as the projectiles and explosives seemed to be absorbed by some strange energy. Leinad, Santei, Roiden, and Gressit just laughed at the attack. The King had decided to wait until morning to press the next big offensive against the humans.

The warrior Cassion was blending in perfectly with the forest and was about 20 yards away from the tank battalion. He was accompanied by a small group of warriors on the ground and a few dragons flying above him just in case. The tanks spotted the dragons above and started to take pot shots at them. This was the distraction he needed, and he issued the command to attack. The warriors rushed the tanks and began the attack. Cassion withdrew his sword from its invisible sheath at his side and willed it to about six feet in length. He then teleported beside the first tank in a line of many and sliced the tracks right off of it. Just as he started to think this was going to be easy, he encountered several RS-777 mechs.

The mechs took aim at the warrior Cassion and fired a barrage of bullets and missiles at him. Cassion fell back from the tanks to avoid being hit by the ordnance, but he was confident he would have all the RX-99 tank mechs destroyed by the end of the night. The warrior then engaged in combat with three of the RS-777 mechs; and just as he did, he saw the three mechs get plucked off of the ground and into the air. The dragons had swooped into the battle to help him. His own dragon, Nieko, was there as well. Nieko grabbed one of the mechs with is talons and crushed it into the hard ground. There were now five dragons on the ground keeping the RS-777's busy so Cassion could continue to slice and dice the tanks.

The tank mech operators were surrounded and confused. Their orders had been to fire upon the castle of Bracelia, but now they had to fire at the dragons; and those that did would not live to tell about it for the dragons on the ground had heavy Jezelite body armoring specifically designed for ground combat, and the tank fire had little effect on it.

Cassion issued a telepathic command to the dragons, and one by one they began to swoop down from the sky and pluck the tanks up off of the ground. The dragons flew off and dropped them into the ocean where they would sink to the bottom. At a certain depth, the tanks would crush in on the operators, for the pressure at 10,000 feet below sea level was far more than they could handle. Some of the dragons flew the tanks 10,000 feet up in the air and simply dropped them from the sky; and when they hit the ground, the explosion looked like a lightshow.

The battle raged on for several hours. The M.V.F. was in a state of confusion for they had heard news of the attack on the tank battalions and had sent a large portion of their men to go and help in the fight. At this point, Gressit flew into combat on his dragon Twinkles. He located a squadron of men within the forest and flew down to them. Upon reaching the ground troops, Twinkles unleashed a powerful blast of her fire breath that killed many of the troops. Gressit was accompanied by a legion of 100 or more dragons, and they engaged the enemy with ferocity. Many of the dragons remained in the air, for there were many RXF-10 jet fighter mechs that were attacking them from above. The battle was raging on into the night.

Gressit dismounted his dragon and plunged himself into battle. He took on both soldier and mech alike. He felt enraged that the humans had come here and upset his way of life, and he would make them pay for their infractions with their lives. Gressit engaged in hand-to-hand combat with the enemy as they came at him three, four, and five at a time. He created a wall of scrap metal and bodies all around him as he continued to fight; and he ordered the Elite Guard to charge, for they had been patiently awaiting his command from within the forest. The Elite Guardsmen rushed in and began to overwhelm the mechs with the use of their elemental magic.

The battle was progressing wonderfully, Gressit thought. He then noticed that a small platoon of 20 mechs and fifteen M.V.F. soldiers hiding in the woods toward the rear of the battle. He rushed toward the platoon and disabled the mechs with his lightning magic in record time. And as the mechs fell to the ground in sparks, he moved in to impale them. The ground troops only got off a few shots before he teleported behind them and used his ice magic to freeze the men in place. He then approached a tent he saw a few meters away sensing a fearful presence inside it. He used his telekinesis to rip the roof off of the tent and raised his broadsword up in a high offensive stance. He was about to deliver the killing blow, but when he looked down at the person inside of the tent, he was shocked.

Gressit saw a medium-sized female with long blond hair and an athletic build. The woman had her arms raised as she begged him not to kill her. Gressit saw a faint blue glow in the woman's eyes. This was the woman his brother had told him so much about, the woman that his brother was infatuated with.

"Dr. Kelly Styles, I presume? I am Gressit, brother to King Leinad Seven, and Chieftain of the Harpatian armies. Don't fear, for I will not hurt you," said Gressit as he sheathed his sword back to his hip and extended a hand to the woman.

"Thank you for not killing me," said Kelly Styles as she trembled in fear.

"You don't have to thank me for such a thing. What are you doing so close to the battle?"

"When they told me they were coming to the Blue Forest, I got very excited. As a scientist, I could not pass up the opportunity to explore such a mystical place, and General Hezekai granted me access. I knew I might be putting myself in harm's way, but Leinad told me to stay to the rear of the battlefield whenever possible. I thought I would be safe here."

"It is not safe for you here, Dr. Styles; but I feel you will be protected."

Gressit knew in the back of his mind that Leinad must have somehow merged Kelly's soul with the Life Source. He could also sense Dr. Styles had a very powerful spell of protection upon her, a spell that could have only been cast by his brother. Gressit was not really sure of what he was supposed to do at this point, but he knew he had to go back to the battle and assist Cassion.

"Dr. Styles, stay in the rear and hide. I will send a telepathic message to my warriors that you are out here and that you are not to be harmed. I will also inform my brother of our encounter. Be safe."

Gressit heard some voices from behind him. The voices told Dr. Styles to get down and take cover. Two M.V.F. soldiers fired at Gressit from behind with their M-16 rifles. One of the bullets grazed Gressit's right arm, and he yelled out in pain and spun toward the soldiers. He then teleported behind the two soldiers and issued a series of up and down slashes with his sword, and the soldiers fell dead to the ground. He then continued to move up the battlefield. His wound healed almost instantly, for he was a powerful healer in his own right.

Gressit made his way through the forest and back to the warrior Cassion; and as he did, he sent a telepathic message to all of the wizards and warriors on the field of battle. He informed them that Dr. Kelly Styles was present in the Blue Forest and that she was not to be harmed. Most of the men were already aware of Kelly Styles' protected status, for King Leinad Seven had been very clear in his orders to Guardsmen of Harpatia that Kelly was not to be harmed. The warriors of Harpatia had mixed emotions about this. They did not understand why their King would grant immunity to one of the enemy, but Leinad did not see Dr. Styles as an enemy; and therefore she was not. Any man who challenged the command of the great King Leinad Seven would surely meet his death.

Gressit then contacted his brother through the Life Source and informed him that he had met Kelly Styles in the forest. Leinad simply told him that he already knew that and he was constantly aware of her location. But he did thank his brother kindly for the information. Gressit met up with Cassion about an hour later. Only a few hours of darkness remained now.

"How is it going, Gressit?" asked Cassion.

"Good my friend. Are you about ready to take care of the rest of these tanks?"

"Yes, I am. Roiden left a short while ago to help in the air battle. The dragon legion was here earlier; and with their help, I was able to destroy many of these tanks, but there are many more to be destroyed.

"The tanks are vulnerable to blade attacks and lightning magic. The dragons had to leave to fight in the air battle; but Masters Chew and Dolan are here now, and they have explosives with them. The explosives have a slide trigger in the center and can be detonated by telepathically moving the slide from left to right.

"You and I, along with Chew and Dolan, must plant these explosives on the tanks. We will cast a spell of protection on ourselves before we rush in," said the warrior Cassion.

"Ok, so we plant the explosives, retreat, and then detonate. That sounds easy enough," replied Gressit.

"We will move on to the ground forces after we defeat the mechs," said Cassion in a tone of confidence.

"Sounds like a plan," said Master Dolan from behind a tree in the distance.

"Indeed it does," said a deep voice from behind as Master Chew popped out his head.

Cassion issued a command for the Elite Guard to attack. The guardsmen engaged the RS-777 mechs that had been called in as reinforcements after the dragons left. The guardsmen would be the distraction, and Cassion and company would take care of the rest. Cassion looked at Gressit and winked.

"There are roughly 200 tanks here. I will get the first 50. Dolan will take out the next 50, then Chew, then you. Let's finish this!" said Cassion.

Cassion then teleported and reappeared in front of the mechs. He was moving fast as he placed his explosive packs in the tracks of the tanks. The other three men followed suit as they teleported to their designated areas, and one by one they planted their explosives. Some of the men placed only one explosive, some of them place two or more on the tracks. Some of the tanks tried to turn and shoot on them; but the mechs had no shot, for the men were in too close. Cassion was on is 40th mech when he noticed a man climb out of the top hatch and mount the machine gun that was affixed to the tank's exterior. Before the M.V.F. soldier had a chance to pull the trigger, Cassion emitted a strong blast of lightning magic from his fingertips and shocked the man to death. The warrior continued with his mission, and soon he would be done with his 50 mechs.

Gressit was on his 20th tank mech when he was suddenly caught up in crossfire as two of the tank mech machine gunners took aim at him and started firing. Gressit was lucky, for the gunners were very nervous and as a result they missed. In the process of missing their target, the M.V.F. soldiers gave Gressit and few extra seconds to react, and that was all he would need. He did a high backflip into the air, a magic-aided parry that allowed him to keep from being hit by machine gun fire; and the slight spell of protection he had cast upon himself was apparently affecting the enemy's concentration. As a few of the bullets ricocheted off his Jezelite armor, Gressit looked toward one of the men firing at him and noticed a slight blue vapor trail behind the man. Suddenly the warrior Cassion appeared behind the man and snapped his neck. Cassion then immediately grasped the machine gun after kicking the dead soldier to the ground. The warrior gunned down the other man who was shooting at Gressit.

"Place your explosives, Gressit," Cassion said in a serious tone.

"Thank you for your help, brother. I will place the explosives now," replied Gressit.

Cassion moved down the line of tanks Gressit was working, and he swiftly killed all those who dared to pop out of their hatches. Gressit finished placing his explosives just as Chew and Dolan were finishing. The M.V.F. had informed the rest of their battalion of what was happening. The tank crew had a pretty good idea of what was going on, and they could only hope their tanks' armor would protect them from the impending blast. Orders had been issued to stay in the tanks, for exiting them would surely have been an act of suicide.

Cassion and Gressit met up with Chew and Dolan. Cassion told the men to follow him. The men dodged large cannon fire attacks as they ran quickly back into the forest. The men had to teleport a few times, but they did manage to escape the tanks unharmed, for the trees of the Blue Forest protected them. The trees did take damage as they formed a canopy over the men.

"Alright, my friends. Let us merge with the Life Source in a deep meditation. We must visualize the detonators and slide them over with our telekinesis. The men then telekinetically slid the electrified Jezelite ball up to the explosive in the charge.

"If you can believe it, you can achieve it," said the warrior Cassion.

The four men successfully triggered their explosives and heard a series of deafening booms as the charges detonated. The tanks were left in a scrap of twisted metal, some looking like they had melted while others had simply been blown into pieces. There was one thing that the tank operators had in common: they were all dead. A few seconds later the secondary explosions began to sound off with ear shattering loudness. Shrapnel flew everywhere as the ordnance inside of the tanks started to explode. It did not take long for the secondary explosions to come to an end. At this point Cassion and the rest of his crew were satisfied that all of the M.V.F. tanks were disabled, and all of the operators were dead.

As the men walked away, they felt an overwhelming sense of accomplishment. Then, upon Cassion's request, Gressit summoned his dragon Twinkles and went to assist Roiden in the air battle. Masters Chew and Dolan decided to aid the warrior Cassion in the ground battle, for they were all determined to push the humans away from Bracelia. Gressit wasted no time—he quickly engaged in battle with the RXF-10 Jet mechs pursuing the first jet mech he encountered with Twinkles. The jet mech began evasive maneuvers in an effort to outrun its attacker, but Gressit put on a strong burst of magical speed which allowed him to get very close to it—so close, in fact, that he could feel the heat from the jet's afterburners as it warmed his face. He then commanded Twinkles to send a blast of ice breath into the mech. Twinkles took in a deep breath, and through the power of the Life Source he exhaled a strong burst of ice magic that instantly froze the jet in place.

The jet mech fell to the ground, and it exploded with ferocity. Gressit then noticed Roiden was being tailed by two jet mechs about 300 yards to the east. He flew over to Roiden and anchored his feet into the side of his dragon as it flew upside down with Gressit hanging on with his feet alone. When Gressit and Twinkles crossed paths with the first mech pursuing Roiden, he unsheathed his sword and ran it through the cockpit and along the body of the jet. The mech fell to the ground in two pieces as Gressit sawed it in half.

The other pursuing mech broke off from Roiden and began to pursue Gressit. The RXF-10 launched a couple of stinger missiles at Gressit, but he simply grasped the missiles with his telekinesis and sent them flying back toward the jet mech that had fired them. The missiles found their new target, and the mech exploded into hundreds of fiery pieces. Roiden was very impressed by Gressit's valor. He caught up with Gressit and thanked him with smile and a wink accompanied by two thumbs up. Gressit winked back and told him it had been his pleasure, for he was sure Roiden would have done the same for him.

Gressit and Roiden flew side by side as they engaged many jet mechs throughout the day. The two men received a lot of resistance, and at times their dragons took a pounding; but they managed to survive the day. More than 100 dragons were injured that day, and five were even killed. By mid-afternoon, and with the aid of several thousand dragon riders, the Harpatians were able to destroy the majority of the M.V.F.'s air battalion. Very few jet mechs were left now, and the air battle for Bracelia was won. Upon completion of the air mission, the dragon legion returned to the Castle Bracelia leaving a small attachment of dragons to patrol the skies.

Upon arriving at the Castle Bracelia, Gressit was greeted by his brother, Leinad.

"Hi brother, how are you? I have been monitoring your progress through the Life Source, and you have indeed fought very well. I am extremely proud of you," Leinad said as he gave Gressit a big hug.

"Thank you, Leinad," replied Gressit.

"I want you to stay and rest for the remainder of the day. You deserve it. Santei and I are confident in Cassion's ability to defeat the rest of the ground troops in the forest, for he has 10,000 warriors with him in the Blue Forest, both Elite Guardsmen and students from the School for Combat and Magic Arts.

"I recently had a telekinetic chat with Cassion, and he has informed me the humans are making their final push right now. I will be monitoring the battle through the Life Source until it is over," said Leinad.

"Very well, brother. My men and I will take rest," replied Gressit as he gave his brother a firm hand shake.

"You have secured a place in the history books my brother. Take rest and I will meet with you later," said Leinad as he went back into the Castle to discuss further battle plans with Santei.

***

Deep within the Blue Forest about 20 miles south of the Castle Bracelia, the warrior Cassion made his final push through the Blue Forest. Upon stumbling on a large battalion of mechs, he ordered his men to attack. Cassion believed this would be a very fierce battle. Lead by Masters Chew and Dolan, the Harpatian wizards and warriors attacked the humans with all their might. Cassion knew one of the sides would be completely annihilated by the end of the day, and he was confident his side would be the one left standing.

Running through the Blue Forest with astonishing speed, Cassion was followed by Masters Chew and Dolan, who were struggling to keep up with him. He had hidden his stolen mech in a safe place within the forest a day earlier, and he would return to it at the appropriate time.

"All right, boys, I hope you are ready for blood," said the warrior Cassion as he continued to dash through the forest.

He disabled and killed many mechs and humans that day. The humans were being overrun by the Harpatians, and all was going well until from out of nowhere a small group of RS-777 mechs appeared behind them. The mechs began firing showers of bullets and missiles at Cassion and his men. Master Chew was hit in the leg by a large caliber bullet, and he screamed out in pain. Chew was badly injured. Cassion ordered Chew to teleport to a safe place within the forest to tend to his wound. The warrior assured him they would come find him after they finished off their attackers.

Cassion and Dolan engaged the mechs. Lunging forward and raising his katana, Cassion willed the blade to about eight feet in length and proceeded to engage in combat. He quickly sliced through and impaled the first two mechs. As he spun around to face the next mech, he took a piece of shrapnel in the right leg. Apparently, the mech had fired an RPG at him and missed horribly; and lucky for him, he had only gotten a small piece of metal in his leg instead of being blown to bits.

Cassion was bleeding, but he paid the wound no mind. He was confident his Jezelite armor and the spell of protection he had cast upon himself earlier would keep him safe. It was just a coincidence and a little bit of bad luck the shrapnel had found his leg. It had to pass in between a gap in his armor that was less than an inch wide to be able to get to his leg; and, unfortunately, it had. The warrior continued to fight as he watched Dolan take out two more of the mechs with a strong blast of lightning magic. Cassion followed suit, as he sliced the left leg off one of the mechs and simultaneously held the wounded mech in a telekinetic grasp as he engulfed it in flames with a strong burst of fire magic that streamed from his free hand. The warrior then threw the white hot metallic fireball at another mech that was shooting at him. That mech exploded upon impact, thus killing both operators.

There were six mechs left. Cassion then noticed a distinctively shiny silver mech that had a huge plating of armor on it, and he realized this mech belonged to none other than Colonel Jake Baker himself. Baker had apparently received a quick repair for the missing leg his mech had suffered in his fight against Gressit. Cassion rushed Colonel Baker and swung his katana toward the leg of his mech as his armor was being pounded by bullets. Cassion missed the leg and quickly teleported behind one of the mechs that was thrusting its lance at Master Dolan. Upon regeneration, Cassion impaled the operator that was harassing Dolan. Master Dolan quickly rebounded and pursued the remaining mechs.

Cassion put on a barrage of teleportation attacks as he sliced the leg off one mech and impaled the next. He then willed a burst of lightning magic through the tip of his blade and into the head of another mech. The mech fell to the ground instantly. Having electrified the mech and its operator, Cassion continued to dodge the shots and lance strikes of the three remaining mechs as he continued his fight. One of the mechs unleashed a barrage of gun fire at Dolan. As Cassion wore a full armor suit equipped with a Jezelite helmet, he teleported in front of the attack and shielded Dolan from the barrage of bullets as he used himself as a Harpatian shield.

The warrior Cassion engaged in sword play with the next mech as it tried to strike him in the head with its lance. The lance ricocheted off of the warrior's helmet as he grasped the mech with a telekinetic hold and began to electrify it. The mech emitted a huge shower of sparks and fell to the ground. At that moment, Cassion felt a piercing blow to his lower back and saw the tip of the mech's spear was protruding through his stomach. The warrior had been wounded badly. Instantly he spun and sliced the leg off of his attacker. The mech that impaled him was the mech of Colonel Jake Baker. Cassion quickly pulled the spear out from his torso; and as he did, he began to bleed profusely.

The warrior kept fighting as he bled from his torso. Master Dolan came from out of the woods and tackled Baker's mech to the ground, which was an easy task considering the mech was missing its right leg. However, it then took hold of Dolan's right arm and crushed it. Dolan used his telekinetic magic to break the mech's grasp on his arm and mounted the mech and tried to hold it to the ground with his legs. As Dolan continued to fight the mech, he suffered a piercing lance blow to his already broken arm. Colonel Baker would not give up easily. Dolan fell back away from the mech as he screamed out in pain. The mech with the missing leg was on one knee as it began to fire a barrage of gun fire at the warrior Cassion. Cassion used his telekinesis to send a missile that the mech had fired at him back at the mech. Baker's mech had great shielding, for the missile blast did not harm it very much at all.

Cassion was bleeding heavily and was starting to feel dizzy. The warrior placed his sword in the ground and grasped the mech in a desperate, but very powerful telekinetic hold. Cassion did not know how long he would be able to keep up this type of exertion before he would pass out, but he was determined to find out. With a clench of the warrior's fist, the mech's armor began to buckle. Once Baker had decided that he was about to be crushed to death, he pushed a blue button inside of the mech. The mech's chest cavity opened at once to reveal a battered Jake Baker.

Colonel Baker stepped out of his mech with a couple of broken bones. He was lucky to be alive at all, for a few more seconds within the warrior's telekinetic grasp would have been the end of him. Cassion ordered the Colonel to surrender as he released the now crushed mech from his grasp.

"Please don't kill me. I can give you valuable information about my people," replied Baker in a cowardly attempt to save his own skin.

Cassion noticed a flashing red light within the crushed mech that Baker had just exited, and he instantly recognized the flash as a distress signal. He knew he would have little time before the M.V.F.'s reinforcements would arrive. Just as Baker was kneeling down to surrender, he pulled a 9 mm handgun from his side and unloaded the clip into Cassion. A couple of his bullets had found a way through the small gaps in Cassion's armor as they hit him in the chest. The warrior grunted and just smiled. Upon being shot, the warrior summoned his sword to his side; and although being mortally wounded, Cassion teleported directly behind Colonel Baker and sliced his right arm clean off from his shoulder. Baker began screaming like a wild animal as his blood rushed out of his shoulder socket.

Cassion raised his sword and was about to decapitate Colonel Baker when he was kicked hard from the side by a fast flying RS-777 mech. He was knocked five feet back and into a tree. The warrior laid by the tree in a half conscious state. The mech approached Cassion and raised its arm up to prepare for a killing strike, but was interrupted by an angry M.V.F. Commander.

"You fool! I will have you shot if you don't get over to me right now. Take me to a medical bay at once. Don't worry about that idiot. He is going to bleed to death anyway," said Baker in an enraged tone.

The rescuing mech was quickly joined by another RS-777, and they made their way to the mortally wounded Colonel. The mechs lifted the Colonel off of the ground and held him sideways. As the mechs began to get a blood red paint job, they initiated their jet packs; and they quickly flew their Colonel to the nearest medical bay. Cassion teleported away from the battle scene after the Colonel left. Once the warrior was in safe spot in the woods, he would summon his dragon Nieko. The warrior met up with Masters Chew and Dolan, who were badly injured as well. Cassion summoned his dragon, and when Nieko arrived the men mounted him quickly.

Once the men were safely aboard the dragon's back, Cassion commanded his beast to take him to the Ponds of Rejuvenation. Nieko obeyed and flew at high speeds to the ponds. Masters Chew and Dolan would be ok, but Cassion did not know if he would be so lucky, for he did not know how close the bullets had come to his heart; and he did not want to think about it. The warrior's chest was engulfed in fiery pain, and he was just about to pass out from blood loss as the dragon landed at the Ponds of Rejuvenation. The men quickly got off the dragon and into the ponds. Nieko assisted Cassion to the water as he lifted the warrior by his armor with his teeth and placed him neck deep into the pond. The men spent the next five hours soaking in the ponds. After just a couple of hours, Cassion noticed the bullets come out of his chest. His wounds were healing as new skin formed around his stab and bullet wounds alike. A few hours later, the men began to feel very tired, especially Cassion; but they were going to live, and for that they were extremely grateful.

After healing, Cassion mounted the dragon Nieko with Masters Chew and Dolan. The men flew back across the forest to the Castle Bracelia and were greeted by King Leinad and King Santei of Bracelia upon landing.

"I thought you were dead, Cassion. I felt your presence diminish in the Life Source. I am glad you are well. You must rest, my friend," said Leinad in a concerned tone.

"I must not rest, my King. There is still a battle to be fought in the forest, and my men need me," replied Cassion. The warrior did not want to leave his men out there without him.

"You are a very noble warrior, my good friend. But I must command you to rest for three days. Santei and I will take care of the rest of the men in the forest. The battle is almost won; and thanks to your efforts, I am sure it will soon be over."

"I respect your command, my King. I will take rest for three days; and when I am recovered, I would like to help Roiden take back his lands."

"You will have your wish, Cassion."

King Leinad then helped the warrior Cassion to one of the sleeping chambers in Santei's castle. Cassion collapsed on the way in to the room, but Leinad caught him in a telekinetic grasp just as his head was about to hit the bluestone floor. Leinad levitated the man six feet in the air and gently lowered the floating man onto the bed. He then tucked a large red blanket over the noble warrior and patted his head gently. The King then left the room so Cassion could sleep.

Leinad made his way back down to the meeting chambers within the castle. Upon entering the large, well-decorated room, Leinad noticed Masters Chew and Dolan were sleeping in the chairs at the table where they had been waiting for him.

"Masters, wake up! The two of you deserve a break as well. This table is no place to rest for a couple of sentinels such as you. You both need to rest to regain your strength and with that strength you will be able to fight again," said Leinad to the two heroes.

"Yes, my King. Thank you for the recognition," replied Chew.

"I agree with you, Leinad. We could definitely use some rest," replied the well-built bearded Dolan who looked like he had fallen down a flight of stairs.

"The grit of the warrior Cassion is immeasurable. I can't believe he wanted to go back out and fight after almost being killed," said Master Chew.

"That is why Cassion is my most valuable warrior. I will not allow him to get himself killed, for Harpatia needs him. You men did a fine job and you will be rewarded for your service. Now go and rest. There will be plenty of time for discussion later," said Leinad in a genuine tone of concern.

Masters Chew and Dolan went off to their respective sleeping quarters. As Dolan walked off, he passed a sheet of rolled parchment to Leinad. On the paper was a complete battle update. Leinad learned of all that had happened to the men while they were out in the forest. Dolan liked to keep records of everything, and King Leinad admired him for that. It takes a special kind of man to find time to make a journal entry in the midst of battle. King Leinad began to walk back toward Santei's royal meeting chambers and was shockingly surprised when he felt an overwhelming sense of danger through the Life Source. The King was sensing that Dr. Kelly Styles was in danger.

***

The two M.V.F. Sergeants had gotten Colonel Baker back to the medical bay the M.V.F. had established within the Castle Nowah and was greeted by General Hezekai who ordered his physicians to begin work on the Colonel's arm immediately. The doctors had their TX-9 medical mech cauterize the wound immediately. The mech superheated a long round piece of metal with a torch and placed it on Baker's wound. The Colonel passed out from the pain, but he would live.

The TX-9 medical mech was comparable in design to the RX-777 mech, for it had a humanoid body that was perhaps even better protected than the RS models, for the role of the TX-9 was often a role of quick extraction of the wounded from the battlefield. The M.V.F. had been keeping their TX-9s in the rear, for they were extremely valuable to the General. He had once been saved by a TX-9, and because of that he had a special interest in the safety of those mechs and their operators who were mainly physicians, not soldiers.

Baker's right arm had been sliced clean off his shoulder, and Jake would have to return to Earth to get a cybernetic prosthetic replacement. The Colonel could only think about getting his new robotic arm and coming back to Harpatia to kill the warrior Cassion. He wanted to make the warrior suffer for taking his arm. General Hezekai entered the Colonel's room a few hours later to check up on him.

"Colonel Baker, what the hell happened out there?" asked Hezekai who was dressed in full battle attire.

"That bastard warrior Cassion cut off my arm."

"I have heard much of this Cassion. It will indeed be a pleasure to kill him. That man needs to be stopped," replied the General.

"The pleasure of killing him will be mine if he is not already dead. I shot him a few times after I impaled him with my lance, but somehow he kept coming."

"We are losing the battle in the forest. I am going to fly over there to see if I can help. We need to keep as many of our men alive as possible to hold down the Castle Nowah while we are gone."

"Yes sir, General," said the battered Colonel Baker as he slowly fell off into a deep sleep.

General Hezekai went to the mech docking bay they had established at the castle's courtyard which was formerly known as the dragon staging area to the Nowries. Hezekai entered his shiny golden metallic RS-777 mech which had been heavily modified in the days since landing on Harpatia. He informed the ten standing guard in the mech bay he would be flying out to the Blue Forest to assist in the battle. The General depressed the red button within the chest cavity of his mech, and it closed over him as the mech stood up. Hezekai engaged his rear jet packs and flew off into the skies above the Harpatian seas which were known as the Seas of the Life Source.

***

King Leinad Seven and Santei were both very concerned for Dr. Kelly Styles as they mounted the dragon Monte. The men flew off to find her. Leinad and Santei landed within a mile of the battlefield location in which Kelly was believed to have been. Leinad dismounted Monte and instructed Santei to shadow him in the forest just in case he was needed. He dispatched Monte back to the skies to patrol with the rest of the legion, but there was no activity to be found for the legion had all but destroyed the M.V.F.'s Air Force of RXF-10 jet mechs. Leinad saw a vast amount of wreckage from downed jet mechs on the forest floor. All that remained in the forest was a small force of ground troops and mechs.

Leinad made his way through the forest stealthily, as he used his magic to make himself virtually invisible to the enemy. He walked right past several M.V.F. ground troops as he made his way to Dr. Styles. He continued to slither through the forest like a Harpatian King snake, the most deadly snakes in all of the lands, for their blue skinned color was enough to blend in perfectly with the surrounding blue forest. It was said that if one was lucky enough to ever see one of these snakes , it would probably be the last thing they ever saw for the venom of the Harpatian King snake was ten times more lethal than any snake of Earth. The King snakes were very intelligent and ate only grass and bugs, and for the most part they were non-aggressive. Only a few men in all the lands had ever been able to tame them, and many more men that had died in the process.

When Leinad reached the rear of the forest where the battle was brewing more intensely, he saw Dr. Kelly Styles. Kelly was curled up behind a tree that was receiving heavy bullet fire. She was caught in crossfire from her own people who either did not know or did not care she was there. Leinad was unsure of what he should do. If he rushed in to save her she could be shot dead as a traitor; but if he did not, she could be killed by friendly fire. Leinad had a brief moment of indecision until he saw a bright golden metallic mech land beside her. The features of this mech were so distinct he knew it must have belonged to General Hezekai. The mech had a regal looking face plate, and thick armor plating that was much stronger in appearance than any of the mechs he had seen in the past. The shiny gold color of the mech gave it a noble appearance. Leinad could see large caliber turrets mounted on its shoulders along with a rocket launcher, and a large gold and silver mech sword that was sheathed on its back. *This was a serious piece of equipment,* Leinad thought.

General Hezekai approached Dr. Styles, and the bullet fire that was spraying in her direction quickly ceased.

"Why are you cowering behind this tree?" said Hezekai through the loudspeaker of his mech.

"Because your idiot soldiers are shooting at me," replied Kelly in a defiant tone.

"They are not shooting at you. They are shooting at the Harpatians behind you."

"The people behind us are innocent villagers who are trying to migrate to safety. This is a senseless slaughter."

"No one is innocent in war. Why do you show sympathy for these people? You should be shot as a traitor," replied the General from within his mech.

"You are a barbaric mad man. Someone should relieve you of duty," replied Dr. Styles in a defiant tone.

Leinad then noticed that the General's mech was lowering to its knees, and as it did the chest plates separated and the General stepped out of his mech and said, "You dare call me a mad man."

"I'm sorry. I did not mean it," replied Kelly with an expression of fear on her face.

Hezekai withdrew his 9mm pistol from his hip side holster and told her that he was getting tired of her insolence.

"I am tired of you, too, you jerk," replied Kelly as she spat toward the General's face.

The General then raised his gun in the air and backhanded Kelly in the face with its butt end, thus rendering the woman unconscious. Leinad was shocked by what he had just seen, but more so, he was angry. He decided now was the time to act. The King of Harpatia let out a loud enraged war cry as he leapt out from behind the tree and toward the General. As Leinad bolted from the bushes, Hezekai made eye contact with him and emptied his entire gun clip into Leinad's chest, but Leinad's full Jezelite armor chest plate deflected all of the shots. Leinad drew close to Hezekai and head butted him in the jaw. The blow broke the General's jaw and knocked him back several feet.

Hezekai stood up and was greeted by a side kick from Leinad that broke his ribs in several pieces. The kick was followed by a straight right handed punch which shattered Hezekai's nose. The general cried out in pain to his men who were close by.

"Kill this man," Hezekai shouted.

A couple of RS-777 mechs flew over to Hezekai. The mechs did not fire at Leinad, for the General would be at risk if they did.

"Striking the lady was your last mistake, General," said Leinad as he as clenched his fists using a telekinetic crush technique.

Leinad heard a series of cracking noises as the telekinetic blow began to crush the body of Ram Hezekai. The General fell to the ground in a screaming state of panic and said, "He just broke all of my bones! Quick, hurry, kill him, and get the Doctor."

Leinad saw 20 mechs fly into his position, and the King stepped far away from the General. The mechs formed a protective circular barrier around Hezekai. One of the mechs placed Hezekai in his golden mech and depressed the blue button, and once the broken General was safely locked inside of his mech, the rescuing soldiers placed a large silver magnetic cable onto the General's mech. The rescuer then attached the cable to his mech and instantly both of the mechs' jetpacks ignited. All 20 of the mechs then flew off with the injured General. The soldiers had seemingly forgotten about Leinad while they were saving their commander.

In the time it took for the RS-777 mechs to form a shield around Hezekai and fly him off to safety, Leinad had quickly run to Kelly's side and lifted her off of the ground.

"You are with me now, and you will be safe," said the Harpatian King as he closed his eyes and teleported both himself and Kelly to a safe location within the Blue Forest.

Leinad then summoned his dragon Monte. The dragon arrived with Santei on his back. Santei noticed the battered woman with Leinad. He cringed at the sight of blood on such a beautiful woman's face.

"Oh my, what has happened to this little lady?" asked Santei.

"That barbaric human General pistol whipped her. I crushed the General's body using my magic."

"Is he dead?" Santei asked.

"He is not dead, but he will be wishing he was for the next few weeks. He will have a very painful trip home. I am going to take the lady to your castle to receive care and take some rest."

"I will have my personal physicians attend to her. I will remain here for a moment to run a clean sweep through the forest with the rest of the Royal Guard. We will eliminate the rest of the M.V.F. that remain in our forest," said Santei.

"The battle for Bracelia will be won today. I have faith in you, Santei," said Leinad as he securely harnessed Kelly Styles onto the back of Monte.

Leinad was greeted by Gressit and Roiden upon reaching the Castle Bracelia.

"By the power of the Life Source, what happened to that woman? I told her to stay away from the battle," said Gressit.

"She had no choice, brother. She was caught up in crossfire. Her General was going to kill her. I had to intervene."

"Very well, brother," replied Gressit.

"You are a merciful King," said Roiden.

"I must take her to receive medical care. Santei is finishing up our business on the battlefield. He should be returning to us later tonight," said the great King of Harpatia.

After speaking with his friends, Leinad took Kelly to a place of rest where she was treated for her injuries. Upon waking, she was still quite dazed from the pistol whipping she had received but recognized Leinad's face and called out his name. He assured her that she was safe now.

"You are with us now, and you will be safe. I am going to place my hands over your head and help you enter a state of recovery. I will wake you in a few days," said Leinad in a loving way.

"Uh, ok," replied Dr. Styles in a confused and exhausted tone.

Leinad then placed his hands over Kelly's head. As a blue glow emitted from the King's hands, the young Doctor fell asleep. Leinad had a lot of training in the healing Arts; and as a result, he was able to enter Kelly into a healing trance with relative ease. Once Kelly was asleep, Leinad carried her to her sleeping chambers which were directly across the hall from his. The King gently placed the girl onto the bed and tucked her in with a purple gem inlayed blanket. After laying Kelly down to rest, Leinad returned to his brother.

"The battle for Bracelia has been won, brother. The humans and their mechs are retreating. They were seen boarding a Capital Ship off the coast of Bracelia. Those who did not leave are being slaughtered in the forest as we speak," said Gressit to Leinad.

"That is very good news, brother. The humans are probably going home to gather more forces. We have not seen anything yet, for the Life Source has shown me visions of the M.V.F. returning to our planet in greater numbers. We must be prepared for their return.

"Gressit, I have gathered information from various sources, and they all claim it will take several months for the humans to return once they have left. We will use this time to relax and to prepare our men for the final battle. We will convene with the Elders and see what type of technologies they have come up with in the past weeks, for I know they have been working on many new weapons for us," said Leinad.

The men spent the rest of the night talking and drinking wine. Leinad and his friends began to set new plans in motion.

***

When General Hezekai arrived at the medical bay screaming in pain, the medics quickly sedated him. While under mild sedation, General Hezekai got on the communications line with Lt. Colonel Kanak, who was back on Earth. Kanak assured the men they would receive the finest medical care available upon their return, and he informed Hezekai he would receive a steel and titanium bone infusion that would have him up and running in no time. Kanak also promised Jake Baker that he would receive an excellent cybernetic arm replacement, and Baker vowed to use that replacement to snap the neck of the warrior Cassion, the man who had mauled him.

Hezekai was relieved, and could not wait to get home. He issued the order to return to Earth, and Captain Hunter saw to the organization of the return mission. The M.V.F. brought *Lancer II* down from orbit to reinforce their troops at the Castle Nowah. After *Lancer II* unloaded 200 more mechs and men, the M.V.F. leaders dispatched the ship back into orbit. The M.V.F. was about 1,500 men strong at the Castle Nowah, and Hezekai felt confident they would be able to hold their position for a few months. But little did he know the Harpatians were just waiting for the M.V.F. to leave.

Lancer II was ordered to use its long range weapons if needed; but they were to remain in orbit, for risking *Lancer II* was not an option. The ship would be the only way home for the men if anything went wrong upon the return of Hezekai and the reinforcements. Hezekai was looking forward to briefing the Joint Chiefs of Staff who were very intrigued by the newly discovered Life Source energy. The M.V.F. would be returning home with gifts, as they had captured and subdued a couple of Harpatian magic users. These prisoners would no doubt be interrogated, poked, and prodded upon their arrival to Earth.

The Joint Chiefs of Staff had gotten very excited the first time General Hezekai told them how the homes of Harpatia were powered wirelessly through a mysterious and magical energy. The M.V.F. wanted the Life Source energy not only for the purpose of solving their energy crisis, but to further their weapons technology as well. If the M.V.F. could find a way to power their war machines wirelessly with an unlimited stream of energy they would be able to crush their foes overnight—or so they thought.

As far as the Joint Chiefs of Staff were concerned, the mission to Harpatia was a complete success. The M.V.F. had only lost a few thousand men and about $200,000,000 dollars in mechs. They were far more upset about their financial losses than the loss of life of their men. The mission for the Harpatian Life Source energy was about money, and the USA would sacrifice as many soldiers as necessary to get what they wanted. The M.V.F. knew that once they had control of the Life Source energy they would have control of the world's energy, and with that would come total world domination. Of course, the scientists of Earth were under the impression that if they were able to harness this awesome energy the M.V.F. would provide it to the world for free. So for the scientists this was a mission for world peace.

This had been a good scouting mission. The powers that be would deploy their new super Capital Ship *Lancer III* back out to Harpatia fully loaded with 100,000 men and mechs. The new plan was the same as the old plan. They would simply overrun and kill as many Harpatians as possible until which point the King of Harpatia would freely give them their precious Life Source energy. There had been strict orders in place for the safety of the King. No one was to kill Leinad Seven until he gave them what they wanted; but Hezekai listened to no one, and when he returned to Harpatia his primary goal would be to kill Leinad Seven. Hezekai had a world of envy for the powerful King of Harpatia, and with that envy there was hatred.

The M.V.F. did not really have an interest in Harpatia. They simply wanted what the Harpatians had, and they were willing to do whatever it took to get it. They would probably leave and never come back if they ever got their hands on the Life Source energy, for their interests were solely on their own planet; but Leinad knew better. The King felt the humans would be like a parasite to Harpatia, and it was in that belief Leinad found his will to defeat them. The King knew the only way to be rid of the humans would be to kill them all upon their return.

All of the necessary troops and personnel had been loaded onto *Lancer I* by the end of the day. Colonel Baker and General Hezekai lay in the medical bay in beds right next to one another. The men would have plenty of time to talk about their future plans during the long journey back home. Although both Baker and Hezekai were in great pain, the men somehow found the strength to stay awake and discuss their plans for the taking of Harpatia. By the end of the day, *Lancer I* was ready for launch.

Captain Hunter engaged his thrusters and activated is QTL drives. Once the quicker-than-light-speed drives were engaged, the Captain quickly shot *Lancer I* into space. And without a second thought, they entered the crew of Lacer I into a QTL flight path back home. The month-long flight home went smoothly day in and day out. The M.V.F. soldiers spent their days playing sports like ping pong and games of chess. Some of the soldiers used their time to communicate with family through the internet, which even from light years away only had a two-hour delay. Some of the men asked about Kelly, but were quickly told that her information was now classified. Colonel Baker and General Hezekai spent most of their time sleeping and trying to recover from their serious injuries, although compared to some of the other men they saw in the medical bay their injuries were minor. The Colonel and the General had exhausted themselves of all communication, for they had spent their first two weeks on the ship discussing their plans for revenge. They simply had nothing more to say about the matter. When the men were not sleeping or receiving treatment, they would watch old war movies to keep themselves entertained. After a little more than a month, *Lancer I* had reached Earth. The men were finally home.

Chapter 17: Intermission

Although they traveled at speeds faster than the speed of light, it took the M.V.F. about a month to get back to Earth. Many of the soldiers of the M.V.F. were just kids between the ages of 18 and 21. Most of them had been very excited to go to Harpatia, but now they were terrified of returning.

The morale of the M.V.F. had dropped significantly throughout the battles for Harpatia. The soldiers were greatly relieved at the idea of returning home, and some of them would not return to Harpatia for they would rather do jail time then go back and fight an Ogre that could shoot flames from the tip of his sword or fingers. Colonel Baker was well aware of the morale of his men, and he would try to improve it in the near future as soon as he was able. General Hezekai did not care about the morale for he would rather shoot a coward dead than console him.

When Colonel Baker and General Hezekai were not sleeping, they spent their days discussing their future plans of battle. All that Hezekai could think about was conquering Harpatia, and killing King Leinad Seven and his friends. Hezekai was extremely bitter after having his bones crushed by Leinad Seven, and he vowed to get revenge for the humiliation that had been cast upon him. The Colonel was also enraged by the fact that he was now missing his right arm. Baker could not wait to meet the Warrior Cassion again, for he had now sworn a blood oath to the man and would not rest until the warrior was dead. Baker had always been a mild mannered and professional soldier. He had never really had the blood lust that was so deeply engraved in the General; but after all he had seen and done in recent weeks, he was quickly becoming a stone cold killer.

The M.V.F. docked at an old retired NASA station that was located outside of Houston, Texas. They had to be discreet upon their return, for the mission to Harpatia was top secret. The M.V.F. did not want their enemies in China or Russia to find out what they were doing; for if they did they would then have competition for the Life Source energy, and they did not want that. The ultimate goal of the M.V.F. was to harness this Life Source energy and create new and improved weapons sufficient enough for them to crush all their powerful foreign enemies such as China and Russia. Once they had achieved world power, they would then solve the energy crisis. The plan of the M.V.F. was simple: they would defeat their enemies, both foreign and domestic, and then ration out energy to the world; and once again everyone one would have electricity, jobs, and money in the bank. Everything always went back to money at the end of the day, and the powers that be would have it no other way. When the energy crisis began about 50 years earlier, the United States of America was the first victim. The power grid for the entire US had blinked out completely almost overnight, thus leaving hundreds of millions without power. Eventually the gasoline that was available to the public was diminished, which crippled the trucking industry and destroyed the ability for cities and towns to receive goods. That is when the anarchy broke out in the US.

The government kept all the available resources to itself and barely gave the people enough power and resources to keep them alive. At that point, the American economy was crippled, and the value of the U.S. dollar fell so low that it could not even be used to repay debt anymore. At that point, China began to attack the U.S. and their friends—Russia in particular—followed suit. The Chinese had given the U.S. plenty of opportunities to make a deal for repayment, but the US arrogantly declined. The Americans were somewhat fortunate they had the most dominant military mech program on the planet, and it was through that program the M.V.F. was able to keep both China and Russian at their borders. The M.V.F. was using most of their resources to keep from being invaded. After a few years, they were able to get a hold on the anarchy that was taking place; and they established work programs for the people who wanted to work. The M.V.F. began distributing food and goods to the people through air drops. Over time, the government had been able to keep the anarchy to a minimum by posting military guards in every city. The rules were very simple: either you follow the instructions of the M.V.F. and adhere to the curfew laws, or you would be shot. This was how the people of the U.S. had to live for now.

Once the M.V.F. had successfully docked at the NASA station, they were picked up by large cargo jets and flown to Washington for debriefing. Within a week, Colonel Jake Baker had received a fully functional cybernetic arm that was 20 times stronger than his old arm, and he loved it. Baker had requested a few cybernetic implants for his legs and other arm, and he received them. Baker was now far stronger and faster than ever and had lightning fast reflexes.

In the same period of time, General Ram Hezekai had received some serious bone infusion surgeries that were still experimental; but the titanium infusion with his bones was a success. Hezekai received a few cybernetic joint replacements throughout his entire body, for the cartilage of his joints had been vastly diminished by the crushing magical grasp that Leinad had placed him in. At this point Hezekai was about one-fourth robot though he did remain human; and the one human emotion that defined him was his rage, and that was enough to keep him going. The development of *Lancer III* was very close to completion. Hezekai spent the next few days with the Joint Chiefs of Staff discussing new strategies for the taking of Harpatia.

Hezekai was informed by the Joint Chiefs that Lt. Colonel Kanak would be accompanying him back to Harpatia. Kanak was a man of Polynesian descent who stood about five feet nine inches tall with a thin muscular build, dark skin, and a handsome face devoid of any beard or mustache. He was an ex special forces combat operator who had seen many years of battle before he was elected to the Joint Chiefs of Staff as a consultant. He had served under General Hezekai on a few special assignments over the years, and Hezekai was pleased to have him on the team.

Upon the completion of Super Capital Ship one month later, the M.V.F. began moving tens of thousands of newly upgraded RS-777 mechs onto the ship. They loaded *Lancer III* to capacity with 100,000 mechs and men. *Lancer I* was also loaded with both RS-777 mechs and the TX-9 medical mechs. They also loaded several hundred tank and jet mechs as well, both of which had received a few upgrades.

The TX-9s were now programmed and outfitted to perform surgeries on the battlefield. The medical mechs had an oversized pistol that was concealed within their legs, as well as a mech sword that was concealed within their back's armor. The TX-9 operators were under strict orders not to use their weapons, for their primary objectives were to save lives; and if too many of them were seen attacking, they would then be useless. The new medical mechs were painted in bright white hues that had large red crosses on the back that said "Non-Combatant Medical Aide."

General Hezekai, along with the Joint Chiefs of Staff, had called a meeting at the newly remodeled White House to discuss the final plans for the taking of Harpatia.

***

A few days after the humans left, King Leinad got together with the well-rested Dr. Styles along with the warrior Cassion, Gressit, King Roiden of Nowah, King Santei of Bracelia, and Masters Chew and Dolan. They would all be going to the Mountains of Harpinia to get an update from the Elders concerning the new and experimental weaponry they had been engineering. The group set off to the Council of the Elders by way of dragon. Upon their arrival, they noticed thousands of refugees were being sheltered and cared for within the confines of the Council.

Once inside, Leinad's group was escorted to the lower levels of the council where the Elders, along with many of the brightest Bracelian engineers, were hard at work developing new ways to combat the humans. Leinad and his company were greeted by Elder Traf, who then led them to a room in which the other elders were seated and waiting. The group then began discussing the findings the elders had made.

"Welcome, Leinad. It is good to see you all are still alive," said Elder Rom.

"It is good to be here," replied Leinad.

"I see you have brought a few friends with you, and even a human friend," said Elder Rom.

"Gentlemen, it is my pleasure to introduce you to Dr. Kelly Styles. I have granted her citizenship on our planet for as long as she wishes to stay."

"You could not have chosen a more beautiful woman to bestow such an honor upon," said the Nowrie Elder, Revy.

"Tell me about," said Gressit.

"I agree," replied Cassion.

"Shall we get down to business then?" Rom said as he escorted the group to an even lower level of the mountains where the hangar bays were located.

The Bracelian engineers were hard at work down in the hangar bay. When the group entered the first bay, they noticed there were thousands of cylindrical football sized devices that were being assembled by a large group of Bracelians who were working on an enormous assembly line.

"As you can see, we have set up this assembly line. These devices you see are not bombs. They are EMPs: electromagnetic pulse emitters. These devices are equipped with a drill head on the top and a small rocket pack on the bottom. They are designed to be buried within the ground until the sliding detonator has been activated within them, at which point the drill and rocket pack will engage simultaneously. Once engaged, the EMPs will dig themselves out of the ground and fly up to a random altitude ranging from ten feet to 20,000 feet above sea level.

"The devices have a sliding metal detonator that can only be triggered telekinetically; but once it is triggered, it will send a signal to the next one down the line triggering a domino effect that will detonate them all at once. You must be sure you want to detonate all of them when you do decide to trigger one of them; for once the process is initiated, it can't be stopped.

"You must designate one man to do this. Once the wireless message is sent to the remaining devices, the EMPs will detonate and release a strong electromagnetic pulse throughout the lands. We have evidence this pulse will render all of their machines inoperable, so use this at the right time and you will find victory. We will be planting hundreds of thousands of the devices about three or four feet within the ground throughout the lands," said Elder Traf.

"We will put these devices in every nook and cranny in every town. Each device will emit a pulse that will span for several miles in every direction. They will hover in the air until all of them have been launched and are at their predetermined altitude. Remember: these devices have been programmed with a hive-like mind, so know that they can't be detonated one at time," said Elder Rom as the old man paced the floor.

"They are to be used as a last resort effort. We don't want to detonate these devices prematurely. We don't know if such a large scale detonation of these EMPs will have any bad effects on our people, but we have seen a few cases of nausea among our own wizards upon being exposed to these blasts. Some have claimed feelings of lightheadedness, and some have actually fainted.

"We also run the risk of some of our own Life Source power plants becoming inoperable, but the bottom line is we just don't know exactly what the ramifications of the blasts will be. So we really would rather not use these if we don't have to. I can guarantee any of the technology we possess here will be rendered useless upon the detonations of these pulse emitters," said Revy.

"We will be sending thousands of engineers and work crews throughout the lands in the coming weeks to plant these devices. We will show you these items up close and teach you how to set them into action. They must be activated by your command alone, Leinad, and we have set spells in place to ensure it is so," said Elder Rom.

"Very well, Elder Rom. May we see a demonstration now?" asked King Leinad Seven.

"Absolutely, my King. The demonstration will begin soon. We have several captured enemy mechs in fine working order which were delivered by an elven man named Rouger. I believe you may know him."

"Rouger is here?"

"Yes. He brought his people back by way of boat, and many of them died at sea at the hand of the M.V.F. But Rouger has seen the error of his ways, and he wishes to rejoin the kingdom as a warrior to the King."

"That is good news. I will speak to him later."

"You are going to love this, my King."

"I am sure of it," replied Leinad.

The Elders escorted the King and his group to a seating area that sat outside of a testing bay where a fully operational RS-777 mech stood. The group took their seats and peered through the thick glass windows of the testing bay and waited patiently for the demonstration to begin. The Elders gave the command for the mech's operator to activate its systems and the mech began moving around. Elder Rom closed his eyes and visualized the small slide within the EMP, and made it move. The device then rocketed out of the hole it had been placed in and hovered five feet in the air for about ten seconds. The cylindrical shaped device then detonated, and the entire room shook from the blast.

The glass walls of the room did not break, for the glass on Harpatia was synthesized with Jezelite materials making it virtually indestructible. Upon detonation of the EMP, the mech fell to the ground and was rendered offline and powerless. The operator would probably be trapped inside of it for a short while until the Elders could pry him out, for they would not use magic in this experiment. The operator remained unharmed, and Leinad liked this fact especially. If the King could render the mechs useless and keep the soldiers alive, he might have a chance of being perceived as merciful among the human soldiers which he felt would give him an edge.

Leinad was well aware that if they were able to strategically place these devices at the right places and detonate them at the right time, he would not only win the battle but he would drastically reduce the amount of bloodshed on the battlefield. Furthermore, he could give the soldiers of the M.V.F. a choice to either resign their commissions as M.V.F. servants and join in the Harpatian cause or die. Although it was not the most desirable choice, it was more of a choice than the M.V.F. had ever allowed them to make. King Leinad Seven was about freedom and equality. He allowed his men to be with their families when they were not training or in battle. Every warrior of the Harpatian royal guard was a free man who had the option to leave at any time, and without reprisal; and that is what made the King's men such a devastating force to be reckoned with on the battlefield. The warriors of Harpatia loved their King, for they had whatever he had. He gave them everything, and they would be more than happy to fight and die for him.

After the electromagnetic test was over, Leinad, Santei, Kelly, Roiden, Cassion, Gressit, Chew, and Dolan joined the Elders for a meal. The group enjoyed a wide variety of exotic foods such as baked Snarvin, intrepid eggs, and kwon along with many fruits and vegetables. After lunch, Leinad and his group sat down with the Elders and discussed the exact locations where they would like to plant the EMP devices. The Elders were very confident they could manufacture tens of thousands of these devices within a matter of weeks. Soon they would have yet another secret weapon waiting for the M.V.F. should they return.

The plan was to scatter the devices throughout the lands. The Elders would facilitate the production and installation of these devices during the next couple of weeks. After discussing the plans for their defense, Leinad sent Roiden with the warrior Cassion back to the land of Nowah with a large company of Elite Guardsmen. Leinad would see to the implementation of the EMP devices upon the retaking of Nowah.

Leinad and his group went back to the Castle Dakineah after the meeting with the Elders had come to an end. The next day, the King awoke by the side of Dr. Styles. They were just about to take a bath, but they were interrupted by a knock at the door. When Leinad answered, it was his royal aid, Amber, who informed Leinad a guest that was waiting for him downstairs.

Amber escorted Leinad to his royal meeting chamber; and along the way she informed him the man waiting for him had not identified himself, but he was an older gentleman of elven descent. Leinad knew right then the mystery man had to be Rouger. Upon entering the meeting chamber, Leinad saw he was correct.

"I heard you were back in town, my old friend."

"Yes I am indeed, and I wish to serve under you as I served under your father, King Albert the Great," said the tall skinny elven man with the very long and grey beard.

"Are you ever going to shave that horrid thing from your face?" Leinad said jokingly.

"For you I will, my King."

"Ah, you once again acknowledge me as your King. I don't wish for you to shave your beard, Rouger. I only think it looks silly."

"My lord, I would never say a word about the tribal tattoos that cover your arms from elbow to wrist, so please leave my beard alone," replied Rouger in a half serious and humorous tone.

"As you know may know, I have given my word that any and all defectors could return to the kingdom at any time and without repercussions, and I will honor my word. I only pray that when this is over you will remain in the kingdom. You are a valuable asset when you are not busy being sovereign."

"Indeed I shall my King. I appreciate your forgiveness of my abandonment."

"You did not abandon me, Rouger. You simply wanted a sovereign life, and I don't hold that against you. I am sure there are some duties I have bestowed upon our people that have caused resentment, although I don't know what they would be. At any rate, we'll not waste any time on regrets. I want you to report to the elite guard. I will give you the rank of commander.

"You are to meet up with Gressit for some training immediately, for after all of these years your magic and swordsmanship must be a bit rusty. Also, I want us to meet again and see if we can set up a new version of the old Ten Meld, for I fear we'll need it. Tell my brother of my wishes, and ask him to find Cassion, Roiden, and Santei and bring them to me when they are all available. We must set up an active meld."

"Yes my lord. By the way, I have kept up with my magic arts more than you may think, but I could use a refresher in swordplay. It has also been a while since I rode my dragon. I assume my dragon, Roman, is still waiting for me at the caves of Duguran. I will train with Gressit, and then I will get the men together to forge a new meld.

"Once again I would like to apologize for my desertion. I swear my allegiance to you from now and until the day I die," said Rouger.

"You are forgiven, my good man. Now go and meet up with Gressit, for you have much work to do with little time to spare. The humans will soon be returning. There will be a period of games at the castle courtyard. Be sure to bring yourself to the games, my friend. They will be fun for all. Now go, my friend, and begin your training," said the King as he gave Rouger a hard pat on the back.

Rouger left to find Gressit in the courtyard. The two men met; and after a brief exchange, they began their training. King Leinad met up with Kelly that afternoon and spent the remainder of the day giving her the grand tour of the castle, for she had not seen all of the ins and outs of it yet. After the tour was complete, the two ate dinner and enjoyed a romantic candlelit setting while sharing intimate conversation with one another. Leinad took Kelly back to his royal chambers, and the two stayed up half the night bonding and caressing one another.

The following day, Leinad woke up with an abundance of energy and was excited to spend time Kelly hiking in the forest. Meanwhile, somewhere in Nowah, Cassion and King Roiden were hiding within the rainforests of Nowah discussing their plans for the retaking of Roiden's land. After coming to an agreement with Cassion about how the battle was going to play out, King Roiden ordered the elite guard to land on the beach with their dragons. Roiden and Cassion had neutralized the small security detail posted there when they landed, and as far as they knew no warnings had been sent. After the elite Royal Guardsmen had landed, they slowly made their way through the forest. Once they reached the end of the forest and the Castle of Nowah was in sight, King Roiden closed his eyes and sent a telepathic message to Jester, the leader of the Tokechi.

Jester had been waiting for weeks for the order to attack, and Roiden told him that now was the time to attack. He made his way to one of the many secret hatchways leading back into the castle. With their General and Colonel being absent, injured, and on their way back to Earth, Captain Nave Delsion, who was left in charge, was relaxing within the castle walls. Nave's guard was down, for he did not think that the Harpatians would be coming back to Nowah for a while, but of course he was wrong. Captain Delsion was a vicious man and close friend to General Hezekai. He stood five feet two inches tall with bright blonde hair and a chubby build.

In the weeks since the taking of Nowah, Captain Nave Delsion spent his time torturing the captured Nowries or berating and humiliating his men. He was known to use public humiliation and bullying tactics to get what he wanted from his men throughout the years. No one really respected the short pathetic man, but they did have a healthy fear of him. Today would be the day that karma would come knocking at his door.

Roiden issued the command to charge the castle Nowah. He then sent a telepathic command to Jester, the leader of the Tokechi, and Goron, who was the second in command. Jester and Goron, along with 100 other Tokechi warriors entered the castle after kicking out a few of the false floorboard hatchways they had been hiding beneath for some time now. The Nowries wanted blood on this day, and it was blood they would have. They sprung out of the holes, and Jester was the first to reach the floor level. Upon entering, Jester was greeted by a barrage of machine gun fire from a small group of human soldiers; but fortunately for him, he was still wearing his Jezelite armor. And unfortunately for the humans, they were not inside their mechs.

Jester leaped forward toward the M.V.F. soldiers firing at him. He paid no attention to the bullets ricocheting off of his armor as he unsheathed his sword and swung it in a left to right side slash. He followed with an up and down strike, thus cleaving the arms off one soldier and cutting the other soldiers in half. Jester continued to make his way through the castle with his men following closely behind him. He took 30 men to the upper floors of the castle while Goron and his men ran a sweep of the lower halls. The floors of both the upper and lower halls of the castle were slowly but surely beginning to be painted in blood. The Nowries came across many M.V.F. soldiers on the lower levels who offered a fight, but Goron swiftly killed all the humans who came at him and his men in a very savage and barbaric nature. Goron and his men were using their magic to enhance their strength, and with that strength they were literally dismembering their enemies with their bare hands.

Meanwhile, on the upper levels of the castle Nowah, Jester was busy freeing some of the Nowries who had been enslaved by the humans. Once freed, they began to fight against the humans in hand to hand combat. Some of the Nowries fell, but most would live to fight again. Jester came upon another group of M.V.F. soldiers hiding in one of the castle rooms. Just as the first soldier took aim at Jester there was a large snapping noise as Jester had snapped the man's neck with a slight turning gesture of his right hand.

Jester was a high level eight telekinetic arts user. The rest of the Tokechi who had accompanied him began shooting magical bursts of lightning from the tips of their blades and into the M.V.F. soldiers. The soldiers died quickly and with great pain. Without their mechs, the M.V.F. soldiers were completely out-matched for not only did the Nowries possess some of the best sword fighting skills on the planet, some of them were extremely adept in the magic arts as well.

Most of the soldiers inside the castle were dead now. Jester had wanted to do this a week ago, but he had been under orders from King Roiden to stand by, for Roiden feared that if the humans were able to get in their mechs, the Tokechi as well as all of the innocent women and children would have been in great danger.

Cassion, Roiden, and their squad of warriors had penetrated the castle walls and were now fighting intensely. After setting the last M.V.F. trooper ablaze, Jester began to work his way to the lower levels of the castle. He stumbled over dead human soldiers as he made his way down to the ground floors of the castle. Apparently Goron had wasted no time in exterminating the human soldiers. Jester guessed any of the remaining soldiers who were not dead must have fled into the courtyard to get their mechs and make their final stand. He was right. Goron was already fighting in the courtyard alongside King Roiden when Jester got there. The battle with the mechs was pressing on with intense heat.

The warrior Cassion found himself surrounded by three modified mechs equipped with large heavy broadswords. The warrior put on a barrage of teleportation attacks, as it was all he could do to try and dodge the swords and gunfire of the large RS-777 mechs. The warrior bobbed and weaved out of their way, and just as a mech raised its broadsword and was about to try to decapitate him, Cassion noticed a flying Nowrie. The Nowrie had used a magic aided jumping technique to propel himself at the mech that was attacking Cassion landing on the mech's back. Goron then thrust his sword through the back of the mech, thus impaling the operator within.

Goron's attack had given Cassion the few precious moments he had needed to regain his balance. He grasped the other two RS-777 mechs pursuing him in telekinetic hold and slammed them together. The impact dazed the mechs and made them hesitate. Cassion rushed the mechs and kicked one of them a few feet back. He then issued a large stream of lightning magic at the mech through his katana. The mech was fried and inoperable within seconds. Goron had found a weak point in the other mech's armor and had disabled it while it had become distracted by Cassion's lightning magic.

Cassion then went to aid Roiden who was sharply engaged in combat with a handful of mech's 30 yards away. Ten RS-777 mechs surrounded Roiden, but that was not a concern for the Nowrie King, for he was aided by 50 Tokechi warriors. While Roiden used his strong level nine lightning magic to subdue the mechs, the Tokechi quickly swarmed the mechs and either impaled or dismembered them with their magic aided strength. The Tokechi specialized in the combat arts; and with a self-imposed brute strength spell in place, they easily possessed the strength of ten or more Nowries. So ripping the mechs limb from limb was not a problem.

An hour into the battle, all of the M.V.F. troops within the castle walls had been slaughtered including Nave Delsion who had been brutally decapitated by a member of the Tokechi. Delsion had been found hiding like a coward in one of the King's wardrobe rooms. After finishing the bloody battle, the King of Nowah commanded his men to run a clean sweep through Hapunah, the capital of Nowah, and all surrounding areas. Their orders were very clear: patrol the lands and kill all remaining M.V.F. forces whether they wanted to surrender or not. Roiden was not merciful like the King of Harpatia, and he would not take any prisoners. The Nowrie King felt the humans owed him a blood debt, and he would have his blood.

Once Roiden had regained his castle, he started making himself at home again. While he was relaxing at his castle, Jester and Goron were leading thousands of his men through the forests of Nowah, killing humans they came in contact with along the way. Many of the humans were disarmed and holding white flags while begging for their lives, but begging a Nowrie for anything was a waste of time for they were barbaric savages in times of war, and their orders had been clear: kill all humans in their lands. And so they did in a very cruel fashion.

After a couple of days, the Nowries had completed their objective; and they spent the next few days burying their dead, for they believed everyone killed in battle deserved a proper burial. A couple hundred M.V.F. soldiers did survive and had been seen flying across the ocean in their mechs, presumably to the Outlands. Many of them died by way of drowning for due to the intensity of the battles that they had fought in the past weeks; their mechs' batteries were almost completely drained of power. The mechs that were completely drained of power simply powered off in mid-air, thus sending their operators plummeting into the ocean in a two ton sinking metal casket.

The Outlands were largely abandoned by now, so the humans would be safe there for a while. Once the Nowries had finished burying the dead, they went back to their castle and began training for the humans' inevitable return. Roiden was a very busy man now. He was reforming his empire and reorganizing his tactics all the while maintaining constant contact with King Leinad Seven. The implementation of the EMP devices in the lands of Nowah began about a week after Roiden had retaken his lands.

Roiden sent a large team of Nowries to escort the Bracelian workers installing the EMPs to the Outlands. When they arrived, they were not offered a fight, for the humans seen flying around there were nowhere to be found.

Back in Dakineah, King Leinad Seven had received his first shipment of EMP devices. Leinad had his men working around the clock to install the EMPs throughout the lands. Santei was also hard at work with all of his men installing the devices throughout Bracelia. The installation would take a couple of weeks to complete.

***

Early one morning, the King of Harpatia had taken Kelly through the cavernous tunnels leading to the Life Source. Once they arrived at the Life Source, Leinad placed Kelly in front of giant blue sphere, took a seat beside her, and began a meditation that would allow him to communicate with the Life Source. Once he and the Life Source were communed, he indicated he would like the Life Source to merge completely with the soul of Dr. Styles. The god like entity indulged him.

Kelly stared at the huge bright blue sphere, and as she did all she could feel was bliss. She found herself fully engulfed within the Life Source in a matter of minutes. The Life Source had embraced her, and she now had access to its energy. Kelly passed out from the intensity of the whole experience. Leinad caught her before she could hit the ground and carried her back to the castle without the aid of magic. When Kelly woke up, she saw Leinad sitting in the same weird cross-legged position he had been in before. As soon as Kelly opened her eyes, Leinad opened his and said, "You are truly one of us now my dear; and if you so choose, I will begin training you in the magic arts."

"I don't understand," Kelly said with a look of confusion on her face.

"You have a strong spirit. You may now learn the ways of the magic arts."

"I can't begin to describe the sensations and feelings that engulfed me while I was within the Life Source."

"I know exactly what you mean, Kelly. I, too, have been in communion with the Life Source. I am happy the Life Source chose to embrace you," said Leinad as he unfolded his legs and began to stand up and offered Kelly a hand.

He informed Kelly they had much to do, and told her to follow him. The two lovers made their way to the castle's dining area where they sat down to enjoy a satisfying meal of baked Snarvin, steamed kwon, and Moko. Upon finishing, Leinad took Kelly to the courtyard and began to teach Kelly the ways of the magic arts. He set up several wood piles loaded with parchment and twigs and told Kelly to close her eyes and concentrate on one of the fire piles. He said to visualize a spark at the base of the wood pile and visualize that spark becoming a flame. He then told her to visualize moving that flame to the other two fire piles; and much to Leinad's surprise, the three wood piles ignited.

"Well done! You may open your eyes now," Leinad said in a tone of excitement.

Kelly looked at the fire piles with amazement as she saw that she had manifested fire magic upon all three of them. She had made fire, and she was now a level one fire user. Kelly continued training for the next week, and by the end of that week Leinad had managed to get her skills up to a level three in the fire arts. At the end of seventh day of Kelly's training, Leinad presented her with a shiny dark purple metallic short sword that was about three feet in length. He then taught her how to shoot flames from the tip of the sword.

Kelly kissed Leinad after he told her the sword he had bestowed upon her had belonged to his grandmother. He informed Kelly the sword had secret powers of protection, and that as long as she kept it by her side she would be safe. Kelly was now able to shoot white hot flames about ten feet in length. Over the course of the next couple weeks, Kelly got up to a strong level five in both fire and ice magic as her skills continued to grow on a daily basis.

Kelly began to fall deeply in love with the King during her training, and the two were growing closer to one another with each passing day. Leinad woke Kelly up early one morning and told her they must go to the Council of the Elders, for there was something she must see. They took in all of the scenery while flying upon Monte's back, and some of what they saw while in the air was disturbing. As they flew over the Blue Forest, Leinad and Kelly noticed thousands of disabled mechs on the forest's floor. The once beautiful Blue Forest now looked like a scrap yard in some areas. Leinad knew the cleanup would take a while, but he postponed any efforts for the time being for he wanted the humans to see what they would be getting themselves back into upon their return. He knew seeing their own mechs in millions of pieces would rip the morale from the M.V.F., and that could only help the Harpatians in the battles to come.

Upon reaching the Council of the Elders, Leinad reintroduced Kelly to all of the Elders. The Elders gave Kelly a warm hug-filled greeting at the door. Elder Traf had embraced her for what Leinad felt was a bit too long as the King had jokingly told him to unhand his woman. Traf blushed as he stepped away from Kelly. Leinad took her to a lift that transported them about a mile below sea level, or so it seemed to Kelly. She asked him where he was taking her, and he told her it was a surprise. After the lift came to a stop, the Elders escorted them through a series of tunnels until they reached a large Jezelite door that read "Hangar Bay 1." Elder Rom waived his hand, and the large mechanical door rose up with astonishing speed.

The group saw a large blue spherical ship upon entering the room that had multiple gun emplacements along with several missile and bomb port holes. Leinad had not seen this ship before and rightfully so, for it had just been custom made for him a week ago. A large emblem on both sides of the ship read "The King's Sword" and multiple decals on every side of the ship were of the Royal Crest of Seven. It consisted of two swords passing through shield with the number seven in the middle wrapped by a blue dragon. Elder Traf told Leinad to enter a specific four-digit code on the side of the vessel where a small keypad had been installed. Leinad entered the code and an entrance ramp lowered down from the ship.

Leinad began walking up the ramp and instructed Kelly to follow him. She hesitated for a brief moment, but then began ascending the catwalk into the ship and noticed the laser and gun emplacements that were scattered around the hull. She was a bit overwhelmed by the enormity of the ship. Upon entering the ship, Leinad noticed three chairs mounted into the floor of the cockpit: one for the pilot, one for the co-pilot, and one for the navigator. Hundreds of buttons clustered on the main control board, all of which were labeled. Two control yokes were equipped with red triggers and blue buttons. The triggers would be used to fire the laser cannons, and the buttons would be used to launch missiles or drop bombs. The rear of the ship contained crew quarters that would comfortably sleep five people as well as a small room for bathing.

This Equalizer had been custom made for Leinad, and he was very happy with it.

"Wow! I would have never guessed you had such technologies on this planet," said Kelly in genuine disbelief.

"We have many technologies here in Harpatia, but we choose not to use them for the most part as we prefer a simple life. However, in the case of our wireless power systems we use for all of our homes and businesses, we find the technology is of great value," replied Leinad.

He informed Kelly they would be using the ships against the humans upon their return and went on to describe the ship's features. He showed her the energy missiles and bombs displaying a bright yellow glow in the munitions room, and had no doubt been constructed from the Life Source energy they possessed. The ships had been designed by the Council of the Elders with the help of many brilliant Bracelian engineers. He made Kelly aware of everything she needed to know.

Leinad went on to tell Kelly he had not been aware of the ships' existence until a few months ago. She was shocked by that admission, but he assured her that he trusted the council to inform him of what he needed to know when he needed to know it. He looked at Traf and told him there would be no more secrets between them, and Traf gave him a knowing smile. The Council of the Elders had been built upon a foundation of secrets, and Leinad knew there were many things going on in the temple of the Elders he was not aware of. But he did not let that bother him for he had more important things to worry about.

The King launched the ship with Kelly in the navigator's seat and Traf in the co-pilot's chair. He made his way through the tunnels and up toward the peak of the mountain. Before exiting the mountain, Elder Traf informed Leinad the humans had a Capital Ship orbiting on one side of the planet, and they would have to fly around to the other side if they were to remain unseen. The Elders had sent a jamming signal to the Capital Ship a few weeks prior, so they would not have to fear being picked up by a scanner. *The Equalizer*s were equipped with a stealth mode, but the stealth was still experimental and there was no way to be sure it would even work. So flying in for a close look at the Capital Ship was out of the question for one equalizer would be no match for a human Capital Ship; however, 100 Equalizers would probably blow the Capital Ship out of the sky.

Traf assured Dr. Styles everything would be fine. Leinad then entered Harpatia's orbit, deployed many targets out into space, and used his forward and aft cannons to destroy the targets. The ship had also brought up several medium-sized wooden targets that had been carved into the shapes of the RS-777 mechs. Leinad told Kelly it was now her turn to do some shooting. She smiled and told him it would be her honor to do so. He instructed her to place the crosshairs on the target of her choice, and she depressed a blue button on the control yoke deploying an energy missile. The missile struck its target a few seconds later and shattered it into thousands of tiny pieces.

Leinad then had Kelly fly a half mile above the next target and deploy an energy bomb. The bomb used its guidance systems and found its target. The explosion was so intense it shook their spacecraft from a half mile away. This frightened Kelly a bit, but Leinad gave her a reassuring hug and told her everything was ok. Leinad, Kelly and Traf continued to fly around for the next few hours. Leinad had now mastered the art of piloting *the equalizer*. Kelly was also fairly comfortable with the ship as well. Traf informed Leinad they had been training hundreds of Bracelian and Nowrie alike to pilot these ships, and when the time arrived, they would be ready to launch an offensive.

Leinad felt confident they would crush the humans upon their return. He wanted to drop an energy bomb on *Lancer II*, but he knew better than to try that for he did not want to get himself or his new found love interest vaporized on that day. After several hours of flying, King Leinad Seven decided it was time to go back to the hangar bay that lied deep within the Mountains of Harpinia. They re-entered the Harpatian atmosphere; and upon reaching the peak of the mountain, Leinad handed the controls over to Kelly. She depressed a blue button on the dashboard per Elder Traf's direction, and she saw the peak of the mountain fold back as a large mechanical hatch began to slide back revealing the entrance tunnels. Kelly moved the ship forward at a very slow pace and weaved her way clumsily through the tunnels, scraping the Jezelite reinforced walls a couple of times along the way. It took her 20 minutes to make her way to the hangar bay, but she made it. Kelly docked the ship successfully and lowered the exit ramp.

Leinad congratulated Kelly on her newly found piloting skills and took her back to Dakineah by way of dragon back after bidding farewell to the Elders. Leinad and Kelly dismounted Monte after arriving at the dragon staging area within the castle walls. The pair spent the rest of the evening with one another and enjoyed various romantic activities. Just before they went to bed, Leinad dropped to a knee and took Kelly's hand.

"I love you Kelly," said Leinad with very large smile on his face.

"I think I love you too," replied Kelly joyfully as a single tear fell from her eye and ran down her cheek.

"I know it may seem like it is a bit too soon," said Leinad.

Kelly put her finger over Leinad's lips in an effort to silence him. She then kissed Leinad and told him you can't put a timetable on destiny. The two embraced passionately and let themselves fall into the moment. The following morning Leinad woke up and went to see his brother Gressit and his old friend Rouger in the courtyard. He was surprised at Rouger's speed with a sword, for by Harpatian standards he was an ancient—or for lack of a better term, an old man. Rouger was able to carry his own weight, and at times he even gained advantage of Gressit. The two men fought at a frantic pace with their wooden training swords.

Leinad approached the two men and interrupted them as he said, "My friends, today we'll travel to Nowah to talk with King Roiden and the warrior Cassion as well. We will stop in Bracelia along the way to pick up Santei.

"Masters Chew and Dolan will be there as well. The purpose of this journey is to set up our own version of the ancient Ten Meld. Ours will be called the Seven Meld, for we shall have seven members," instructed the King of Harpatia.

After concluding his meeting with Gressit and Rouger, King Leinad Seven took the men to the dragon staging area where he had arranged a reunion for Rouger with his old personal dragon, Roman. The dragon Roman was a fierce battle seasoned beast of the same bloodline as the dragon Monte. Rouger was pleasantly surprised to see his old friend. Rouger and Roman exchanged a brief telepathic conversation, and then it was back to business as usual. The great thing about having your own personal dragon was the dragon remained loyal to you regardless of the amount of lost time between you. Although they had been separated for years, it had seemed like only a few days to both Rouger and his dragon. The dragon truly was man's best friend.

Gressit mounted his dragon, Twinkles, and Leinad mounted Monte. The men then flew to Bracelia where they then met up with Santei, King of Bracelia, who rode with Leinad on the way to Nowah. They men landed in Nowah the next day and were a little tired from flying through the night. The group had been greeted with food and drink as they met with Roiden, and they felt better after eating breakfast. The group had been joined by Masters Chew and Dolan, who had been there waiting for Leinad for several days, at the dinner table.

Roiden had settled back into his castle nicely and had been successful in retaking his lands. He had spared no one and had shown no mercy while retaking his lands, as thousands of M.V.F. personnel had been brutally slaughtered; but that was the way of the Nowries. Roiden was sure a few stragglers remained within the forest; but that did not bother him for he knew that if the Intrepids did not get them, the Dellions surely would.

No human could survive the Harpatian wilderness, of this Roiden was sure. Many large game beasts lurked within the forests, and they would attack a human whether they were provoked or not. Once Leinad and his group had landed and staged their dragons, they went to meet with Roiden at the Castle of Nowah and were escorted to Roiden's meeting chambers. The purpose of the meeting was to discuss the creation of a new meld, a meld that would come to be called the Seven Meld.

The men sat at the table all day and listened attentively to Rouger as he told them of his experiences of the ancient Ten Meld. He gave them a step-by-step tutorial on how to meld their magic with one another and spoke of Albert the Great and how he was able to focus his magic with other wizards and create extraordinary results. The men began to iron out all the details of the Seven Meld. They chose Leinad Seven to be the leader of the meld, and then handed out ranks and responsibilities throughout the rest of the group.

After receiving a thorough explanation of the art of melding, King Leinad and his group went out to the courtyard within the Castle walls and sat in an Indian style position. The men kept their backs straight and their eyes closed as they began their meditation. Roiden had his servants set up a few targets within the courtyard, some of which were made of bluestone and others out of Jezelite or Banian wood. The wooden targets had been carved in the shapes of the M.V.F.'s tank mechs. Rouger began to speak as he instructed the men to focus on the wooden targets. The men were instructed to visualize the wooden target in their minds, and as they did the wooden target began to float up and hover about five feet in the air.

"We will bestow the power of the meld to our King, Leinad Seven," said Rouger in a serious tone.

King Leinad then stood up and opened his eyes to see his body was glowing bright blue. Leinad pointed his dual bladed staff at the target and unleashed an unbelievably huge blast of fire magic which hit the target and reduced it to ash within a few seconds. The blast was larger than anything Leinad had ever seen cast in the magic arts. Rouger congratulated the men and told them to take in a deep breath and amplify their powers. The men did so as they continued to focus on the King, and Leinad began to glow in an even brighter hue of blue than before.

"Leinad, I want you to use your telekinesis on the large piece of bluestone over there," said Rouger as he pointed to the large boulder that had been placed in the courtyard.

Leinad then focused on the boulder and said, "Shatter bluestone?"

"Yes, my King. All is possible within the realm of melding," replied Rouger.

The rest of the men were instructed to open their eyes and keep their concentration on the King. Leinad approached the boulder and felt invigorated as he drew closer. Rouger instructed Leinad to destroy the boulder whenever he was ready. The King of Harpatia felt more powerful than ever before as he reached out and clenched his fist. The large boulder shattered into thousands of pieces and simply crumbled to the ground. The King had crushed a fifty foot boulder that was made of bluestone. The men were amazed.

"Anything is possible when melding. This was but a small display. Through the power of the Life Source, we can accomplish many great things. The powers of the meld will grow much stronger as you continue to train your focus through meditation. May the Life Source guide us to a swift victory against the humans," said Rouger in a passionate tone.

The men cheered and laughed as they were completely dumbfounded by what they had just witnessed.

"This has been a very impressive lesson. This meld will be a most useful weapon in the future," Leinad said to Rouger.

Leinad then instructed Gressit, Cassion, Chew, Dolan, Roiden, Santei, and Rouger to await his summons. Although eight men were in the meld, Leinad chose to call the meld Seven Meld, for Rouger's involvement in the meld was temporary. Rouger's job was to train the men in the art of melding; and once they were trained, he would move on to more important duties within the kingdom of Harpatia.

"I will summon you all when you are needed for melding. I want you all to practice every night, as I will do the same. I look forward to melding again with you all," Leinad said.

The men sat around for a few hours and talked about various things then disbanded. Roiden returned to Nowah. Leinad, Gressit, Cassion, Masters Chew and Dolan, and Rouger mounted their dragons and returned to Dakineah. Santei went back to Bracelia. Leinad instructed the men to enjoy some free time and told them he would be setting up a series of celebrations and games in honor of their recent victory against the humans.

Leinad met up with Kelly upon returning home to the Castle of Dakineah and spent the rest of the day with her. They enjoyed a romantic walk through the townships of Dakineah where they were greeted by thousands of villagers. After touring the surrounding townships, Leinad and Kelly returned to the castle where an elaborate meal had been set up for them in the Royal Dining Hall. After thoroughly enjoying their dinner together, the two went to the King's chambers and began to talk.

Kelly looked to Leinad and said, "I have checked my calendar, and I wanted to tell you that a very important holiday for me is coming up soon, and I was wondering if we could celebrate it."

"Of course we can. Tell me of this holiday."

Kelly went on to tell Leinad of Jesus Christ and the celebration of Christmas. Leinad told her that he was planning a celebration along with many games. Leinad told her that they would set up the games on December 25th, followed by a gift exchange in recognition of the Earth holiday of Christmas. Kelly was elated and very thankful.

The next day Leinad met with his advisors to set up the various games and celebrations. There would be many combat games such as wrestling, archery, and magic casting competitions. Kelly had informed Leinad her favorite game was disc golf a few days prior while they were in the courtyard of the Castle Dakineah. In disc golf, the humans used a series of plastic discs with the goal of getting it into a small metal basket with two layers. The game was played just like the regular golf of Earth, and most of the holes, as they called them, were anywhere from 200 to 1,000 feet or more in length with various trees or other obstacles in the way. After giving Leinad a thorough explanation of the game, the King had his engineers' construct an 18-hole disc golf course; and through the use of magic they were able to manufacture several hundred discs, each of which had its own unique label on the top.

Leinad had successfully installed the disc golf course within a half a day's time. There would be a special disc golf tournament in which Kelly would participate where the use of magic would be prohibited. The winner would receive a purse of jewels, and the King was sure the winner would probably be Kelly; for although his people were fast learners, none of them had ever played disc golf before.

Leinad and Kelly spent the rest of the day playing disc golf at their new course which had been named "The Kelly Styles Disc Golf Course." Leinad had a special sign erected near the first hole of the course. The sign was in honor of his newly found love. The following day, the Christmas gift exchange and the Harpatian games—including the new game, disc golf—had begun. On December 25th, according to the human calendar, the festivities and celebrations had begun. The combat art games had begun early that morning, and by mid-day Cassion had won gold medals in the wrestling games after defeating Gressit in a very close match by way of submission due to a triangle leg choke.

The warrior Cassion had also taken first place against King Roiden of Nowah in the archery competition. It had been a very close competition, but Cassion's combat arts skills were unrivaled throughout the lands, and the people loved him for that. The crowds roared as Cassion made his way through the various combat games. By mid-day the disc golf tournament had begun. There had been 100 competitors in the beginning of the tournament, but within a few hours there were only three left: Dr. Styles, King Leinad Seven, and Gressit. Gressit and Leinad were naturals at the game, averaging 300 feet per throw, but Kelly had the kind of finesse and accuracy in disc golf that took years to develop. She ended up winning the disc golf tournament later that day, and she was awarded the large purse of gems. The crowd favored Kelly as they watched her nail the chains of the basket with ferocity. The Harpatians had indeed taken a liking to disc golf and they would incorporate it into their lives accordingly. By nightfall the great feast had begun, and after the feast the Harpatians had a gift exchange in recognition of the Christmas holiday. Kelly had received a most interesting gift from Leinad.

***

A few weeks prior, the humans had loaded their new super Capital Ship, *Lancer III*, to capacity with the newly upgraded mech they would use to conquer the lands and gain the Life Source energy. The humans only stayed on Earth for a couple of weeks. The soldiers had celebrated the Christmas holiday a few weeks early with their families, for they knew that once the repairs were completed on *Lancer I* and the final tests were run on *Lancer III*, they would be going back to Harpatia.

With both Capital Ships having been loaded to the brim with mechs, personnel, and weapons, the M.V.F. would be returning to Harpatia with over 100,000 mechs and men. The newly remodeled RS-777 mechs had been equipped with a futuristic and stylish broadsword that had been forged in steel of the highest quality. In addition to being outfitted with the mech sword, the RS-777s had also been uploaded with a sword fighting program, an auto fight program that could be engaged with a push of a button. There were many new upgrades on the RS-777 mechs, and the soldiers could not wait to try them out on the Harpatians.

Hezekai learned that Russia and China, their two biggest enemies, had formed an alliance and were trying to breach the borders of the U.S. China and Russia had conquered all of Mexico and the surrounding areas, as well as Canada. They were creating a stronghold and preparing to invade the U.S., but the M.V.F. had countermeasures in place. The major battles were taking place at Texas, Arizona, California, and Wisconsin borders. Some of the enemies did make it through the borders, but they did not last long for the humans had completed the construction of several super Capital Ships and had deployed them at various strategic locations throughout the lands. The super Capital Ships destroyed the opposition with ease as they entered the borders of America.

The President of the United States of America and the Joint Chiefs of Staff had engaged in talks with the leaders of both Russia and China; but they did not get very far for Russia wanted to dominate and control the US, and China would back their play. The Russians wanted the reserve natural resources the Americans possessed. There had always been a power struggle amongst these three world super powers. The Americans had assured the Russians and the Chinese they were working on a solution that could provide power for everyone, but they would not share the details of the operation with them.

The US wanted nothing more than to provide power to the world for that would give them world dominance, thus the reason for the mission to Harpatia. If the US could control the world's energy supply, they would control the world's money; and that was the goal in a nutshell. The M.V.F. knew that if they could harness the Life Source energy on Harpatia they would be able to broker a worldwide peace deal for once Russia and China signed a treaty with them, the rest of the world would follow suit. The US wanted to get back to doing what it did best—making money and buying things.

The super Capital Ships *Lancer III* and *Lancer I* had left a few weeks prior and were in route to Harpatia. Hezekai knew it was only a matter of time until they arrived back at the mysterious planet that he so wanted to conquer.

***

After the Christmas gift exchange and the long day of games, festivities, and celebrations, King Leinad Seven went back to the Castle Dakineah with Dr. Styles. They took a long walk through the courtyard and spent the rest of the night in the King's dimly candlelit chambers. The two engaged in a series of romantic exchanges with one another throughout the night before going to sleep.

King Leinad awoke from a deep sleep in the middle of the night covered in sweat and very nervous for he had an extremely disturbing vision while he was sleeping. He had seen a giant human spacecraft descend upon his city and unleash a horrifying level of destruction upon the city. Leinad had also seen swarms of mechs and M.V.F. personnel invading his lands once again.

The King rushed out of his chambers and summoned all of his commanders to come to the castle for an urgent meeting at once. It did not take long for everyone to arrive for those who were outside Dakineah used the newly reactivated teleportation hubs. Now that all the commanders were present including Cassion, Gressit, Roiden, Santei, and Rouger, Leinad could begin his meeting.

"I fear the humans will be back sooner than we originally thought. Roiden, I want you to set up your warrior battalions along the beaches of Nowah and throughout the forests. Santei, you need to make your people ready as well. I will deploy my entire dragon legion as well as the Elite Guard throughout our three main lands.

"Gressit, my most loyal brother, I want you to go with Santei and help defend Bracelia. Rouger, you will go with King Roiden to help defend Nowah. Cassion, I would like you to go with Roiden as well for I fear Nowah will be hit hard. Masters Chew and Dolan will remain here in Dakineah for I need them to organize the members of the School for Combat and Magic Arts and make them ready for battle.

"I need all of you to evacuate all your noncombatant citizens to the Mountains of Harpinia and other safe house areas throughout the lands. The people must be kept safe at all costs. I command you all to do this at once. Harpatia will not fall. I have received word that the installation of the EMP devices has been completed.

"I want you all to stay in constant telepathic communication with me. Furthermore, I want you to brief all of the men about our Equalizers, and inform them not to attack our own ships. I had the Elders send out letters to all of you weeks ago regarding *the Equalizers*, so I assume everyone is up to speed on that topic," said Leinad as he addressed his commanders.

"We are all aware of the technology that lurks within the mountains of Harpinia, my King. We will be happy to give you updates on the battles as they happen," replied the warrior Cassion.

"We will wait for the humans to bring the majority of their forces to the ground, and at the right moment I will trigger the EMPs. Now go and assemble your commands, make your men ready, and evacuate your people. The worst part of this war is about to arrive. We have little time, my friends," said Leinad in a serious tone.

The group acknowledged their King and disbanded. Before leaving, Gressit gave his brother a warm hug and asked if he could meditate with the Life Source in the tunnels. The King returned his brother's hug and escorted him to the fake bookshelf in his chambers, opened it, and gave his brother permission to enter.

After Gressit had illuminated the tunnel systems leading to the Life Source, King Leinad Seven went to the castle's library to plan a new strategy for defeating the humans. The Bracelians would focus their archers and rifleman around the castle walls for the castle was protected by the spell. The Harpatian elite guard would set up catapults and cannons along the hillsides nearby. The men knew their castles would be safe from bombardment, but outside of the castle walls there would be no protection for anyone from any missile or bomb attacks.

Rouger dispatched 500 dragons to patrol the skies upon reaching Nowah, and the rest of the territories and provinces did the same. The dragon legion was in the air ready for battle, and they would patrol the skies 24 hours a day flying in three 8-hour shifts. The common people of Harpatia had been evacuated to various underground shelters and safe houses throughout the lands. Seeing thousands of dragons in the air was a tremendous sight—an intimidating one at that—for the warriors of Harpatia knew if King Leinad Seven had deemed the releasing of the entire dragon legion necessary, there must have been a very large enemy force en route.

In Dakineah proper, the King dispatched several hundred thousand warriors of the elite guard to patrol the various cities and provinces throughout the region including the Blue Forest, the Aurora province, and the mountains of Harpinia. The King's orders were simple: be ready to fight and be ready to die; and his men would be happy to do both in defense of their great planet. Leinad told Kelly to go to the Life Source and hide within the tunnels once the battle began. He assured her no one would find her there. He also informed Kelly he would have to be present on the battlefield. Kelly embraced Leinad as the two had grown deeply in love since they had first met and she did not want to see Leinad get hurt or killed. She was now recognized as the King's maiden; and as far as the people of Harpatia was concerned, she was the future queen. Leinad was exhausted after a long day of planning; and after eating his dinner with his beloved Kelly Styles, Leinad tried to get some sleep.

Chapter 18: M.V.M. Mech vs. Magic/the Battle for Harpatia

The following morning, Gressit woke to loud boom noises echoing throughout Bracelia. He wasted no time as he put on his Jezelite armor suit and helmet, sheathed his broadsword at his hip side, and reported to Santei who informed Gressit the archers and rifleman stood ready at the castle walls. The elite guard was already engaged in battle on the ground, and the dragon legion was fully engaged in battle against *Lancer I* which was hovering over Bracelia. Gressit made his way to his dragon Twinkles and flew into the battle against *Lancer I.*

Back in Nowah, the same type of situation was unfolding; only instead of having to fight a Capital Ship, the Nowries saw many battleships off the coast of Nowah and those ships were sending large amounts of cannon fire at the Nowries on the beach. It did not take long for the M.V.F. to land their large transport boats on the beaches of Nowah. With the battle ships pounding the beaches and tree lines of the forest, the M.V.F. had easy access to the beach where they were unloading both tank and RS-777 mechs alike.

Roiden had not slept very well the night before as he was very anxious to get back to the shedding of human blood. Cassion had guessed the M.V.F. would arrive during the middle of the night, and he guessed right. The warrior Cassion made his way to the beaches of Nowah. He and Roiden had become good friends; and although the King had wanted him to remain in Dakineah, Cassion insisted on returning to Nowah.

A similar series of events were taking place in Dakineah as well, but on a much larger scale. King Leinad Seven woke up that day and saw a very large shadow had been cast over his castle. But the funny thing was that there were no clouds in sight. Leinad knew exactly what he had to do. He opened the door that lead to the Life Source and illuminated the tunnels for Kelly. He told her to go and hide, and she did. She took the purple sword Leinad had given her for Christmas along with a small backpack of food and supplies. The two kissed and Leinad told Kelly he loved her and he would come back for her. Kelly began to cry and made her way through the tunnels toward the Life Source.

Leinad went to the upper section of his castle and walked out on the balcony. He saw what must have been a mile long ship with a triangular nose just hovering in the air where he could see thousands of little port holes on the ship's hull that would without a doubt be used for launching missiles and other nasty forms of weaponry. This was indeed the Super Capital Ship Leinad had seen in his visions. It was unleashing a barrage of missile strikes on Dakineah proper and quickly reducing the town to rubble, but for some reason *Lancer III* was not firing on the Castle Dakineah. The M.V.F. must have known there would be a spell of protection in place. The majority of the Harpatian noncombatant citizens had been evacuated, but those who had chosen to stay and fight would all be dead by the end of the day. King Leinad then dispatched his dragon in the air, and so the battle for Harpatia had begun.

Back in the land of Nowah, King Roiden and the warrior Cassion were engaged in battle against the RS-777 mechs. This time Roiden had hundreds of thousands of Elite Guard; and although the new mechs had been upgraded, they were still no match for the wizards with level 8 or higher magic art abilities. The battle raged on. Many would die on this day.

Lancer I was pounding the forest floor and all the surrounding villages of Bracelia. The missiles fired at the castle Bracelia had little or no effect at all. The Bracelians sent a massive amount of cannon fire at the Capital Ship, but their explosives barely scratched the ship. Gressit landed atop *Lancer I* and had begun to dig his sword into the ship's hull. He was causing some damage, and he was not the only one. He had been escorted by hundreds of warriors and wizards who had all flown and landed on the ship as well.

Gressit was engaged in battle with several RS-777 mechs, and he was winning. He pointed his sword at one of the mechs, and the mech turned into stone. This was a form of Earth magic Gressit had been practicing for a while. After shattering the petrified mech, Gressit used his lightning magic to destroy the next one. The last RS-777 mech Gressit fought had gotten off a lucky punch to his head which had nearly knocked him out. But as Gressit was falling to the ground, he saw the RS-777 mech become crushed within the claws of a mighty dragon. The dragon Twinkles impaled the operator within the mech and tossed it aside like a rag doll.

The Dragons of Harpatia were hard at work crushing, tail whipping, and engulfing the enemy in horrific blazes of fire breath. With the help of their dragons, Gressit and their men were able to deal more damage to the ship as they used their magic to rip some of the ship's gun turrets completely off the hull. The warriors on the ship's hull were lucky for they did not have to worry about the jet mechs firing at them. The RXF-10 jet mech fighter pilots had all received the order to not fire upon the combatants who had boarded the exterior of the ship for risk of damage was too great. Gressit noticed a large porthole had opened 20 feet away from him, and a tall thin man dressed in M.V.F. fatigues and carrying two large briefcases arose out of the hole. He set the briefcases on the ground and depressed a button on each of them. The briefcases transformed into a metal exoskeleton which Gressit thought must have been some form of armor.

The tall thin man, who was none other than Lt. Colonel Kanak, then stepped into the metal exoskeleton that had just assembled itself. He then began to advance toward Gressit at a very fast pace. Kanak's suit had large magnets in the feet which allowed him to stick himself onto the hull of *Lancer I*. Gressit did not know what to expect from this man who he had never seen before. He pointed his sword in the direction of the man and issued a bolt of electricity at him, but the lightning had no effect. What type of armor was this? Kanak withdrew a long steel sword of his own, pointed it at Gressit, and depressed a button on the side as two thin electrified lines with a three prong hook in the end shot out at Gressit.

Gressit deflected the first shock line with his sword, but the second one hit him in the leg. A surge of painful electricity flowed through Gressit's body, and it was all he could do to stay conscious. The attack nearly paralyzed him, but in a last ditch effort he managed to grip the electrode and rip it from his flesh. Lt. Colonel Kanak smiled. "You are a tough guy. I see that I am going to have to do this the hard way."

"Bring it on," replied Gressit with a smile on his face.

Kanak rushed Gressit and began swinging his sword in a violent left to right attack grazing Gressit's left shoulder in an attempt to decapitate him. Gressit began to bleed from his arm and was shocked by the quickness of this man. The Exo suit Kanak wore allowed him to move as fast as a common combat arts user. *The humans had indeed made some upgrades,* Gressit thought. The next series of blows Kanak sent Gressit came at him about twice as fast as before. Kanak issued a kick toward the chest of his opponent, but Gressit blocked it and threw a counter right handed punch straight at Kanak's head. The blow pained Gressit's hand as it landed, for hitting hard steel was just the type of thing no man wanted to do.

Kanak then faked a blow to Gressit's head and thrust his sword down at his right leg. Gressit blocked the attack with his own sword and swung at the Kanak's head. The blow landed and Gressit's sword became stuck in Kanak's head armor. Kanak then kicked Gressit in the chest and sent him flying a few feet back. A couple of the elite guard warriors approached them and were about to intervene. "No...Stay back. This is my fight," Gressit commanded.

The two warriors acknowledged their Chieftain's command and returned to the battle that was raging on all around them. There were many RS-777 mechs on the ship's hull, and they were fairing quite well against the dragon riders atop the ship. Lt. Colonel Kanak had given a similar order before he engaged in combat with Gressit. Kanak said any man who intervened in his fight would be shot for treason. Gressit popped back to his feet and unleashed a strong level nine blast of ice magic that should have frozen the Lt. Colonel in place, but it did not. Kanak's suit began to glow bright red almost immediately after Gressit issued the attack. Kanak then pulled Gressit's sword from his headpiece and took it in his left hand while he held the other in his right.

Kanak attacked Gressit in a high arched dual bladed stance. As Kanak swung the two swords in an attempt to decapitate Gressit, he was shocked as saw the two blades fly from his hands and bury themselves in the ship's hull. Gressit had used his telekinesis to rip the swords from Kanak's grasp. Kanak then issued a three hit combo to Gressit's face. The punches landed and were followed by a roundhouse kick to the jaw that sent Gressit rolling across the deck of the ship. Gressit almost rolled right off of the ship, but he anchored himself with his telekinesis at the last second. He was becoming very frustrated.

"I want to see you block this. This ends now," said Gressit as he summoned up a strong level nine storm of lightning magic.

Gressit unleashed the lightning and sent it straight into Kanak's robotic armor suit. The Lt. Colonel's Exo suit began to glow blue as tiny holes opened up all around it. Kanak's suit was somehow able to harness the lightning magic, and the electricity was flowing in a circular pattern around his body. He walked forward as his suit continued to pulsate with blue electrical currents. Kanak reached forward, grabbed Gressit by both shoulders, and redistributed all the electrical current Gressit sent at him back to Gressit. Kanak held Gressit in the air for a good 20 seconds, shocking him almost to death. Once the electricity had run its course, Kanak threw Gressit to the ground unconscious.

Kanak retrieved a pair of stun cuffs that had been developed by the engineers of the M.V.F. After testing the cuffs on a few of their Harpatian captors, the M.V.F. concluded that if the cuffs sent electrified pulses through the arms of the person wearing them, that person would be incapable of using magic. The cuffs were designed with a state-of-the-art brainwave sensor system; and any time the brain activity spiked to a level that indicated magic usage, the cuffs would stun the magic user rendering his magic abilities useless. Kanak placed the stun cuffs on Gressit's wrists and decided to take him as a prisoner as opposed to killing him. Gressit's dragon Twinkles suddenly appeared from above and swooped down toward Gressit who was now on Kanak's shoulder; but just as it did, it was knocked back by heavy turret fire from five of the rear emplacements.

Twinkles fell to the ground in a half unconscious state. The dragon was very fortunate, for he landed in a small lake which cushioned his fall considerably. He was injured, but he would live. Kanak carried Gressit into *Lancer I* and loaded him into the copilot's seat in one of the jet mech bays. Kanak ordered the ship's pilot to take Gressit to *Lancer II* and place him in an electrified holding cell. He went on to instruct the pilot to make sure Gressit was placed in an electrified harness to keep him from using his magic. His final order was to have Gressit put into a medically induced coma if he gave them any trouble.

The pilot acknowledged the orders and powered up his RXF-10 jet mech. He flew out of the hangar bay and made it to *Lancer II* in 30 minutes. Once the pilot safely docked within *Lancer II*, he powered down his mech. The M.V.F. doctors received Gressit and relieved him of his personal belongings and put them in a storage locker. The humans found many small daggers, a large broadsword, and one amulet that held a bright blue glow within it. The M.V.F. paid no mind to the amulet or any of Gressit's possessions as they placed them into item bags and stowed them away.

The M.V.F. then took Gressit to the electrified holding cell area that had been specifically designed for the imprisonment of Harpatian magic users. They strapped Gressit into the electrified harnesses so he would not be able to use his magic. Gressit awoke a short while later and was shocked when he realized he could not use his magic. He was helpless.

"I sense a great disturbance within the Life Source. I fear that my brother is in grave danger. We must find him," Leinad said to Masters Chew and Dolan.

"We will mount our dragons at once, sire. We will find him," replied Master Chew.

"Please hurry, my friends. I fear he has little time," replied the King while fidgeting around nervously.

Leinad sent out a telekinetic message to his commanders. He commanded them to find his brother at once. He was in a mild state of panic for this was the first time he could not sense his brother's location through the Life Source.

Back in Bracelia, *Lancer I* continued to pound the Blue Forest with missile strikes and heavy cannon fire. The battle raged on in Bracelia as fleets of RS-777 mechs rushed the Harpatians in the forest. Santei was losing his advantage and was in need of help.

In the land of Nowah, the warrior Cassion was busy killing as many M.V.F. troops, mechs, and personnel as possible. The warrior had taken up post at the edge of the forest. The Harpatians were taking a heavy pounding by the fleet of 20 or more battleships that were offshore sending heavy ordnance at them.

"Cassion, stay here and assist the Nowries. I will go for a swim and see what I can do about those pesky battleships," said Rouger with a smile on his face.

"It is good to have you back, Rouger," replied Cassion.

Rouger stealthily made his way through the woods toward the ocean. He encountered a few mechs and swiftly destroyed them with a level ten burst of lightning magic that even the newly upgraded RS-777 mechs could not withstand. After killing everything that came his way, Rouger made it to the top of a high cliff and leapt head first into the ocean. He summoned a high level ten burst of water magic as he reappeared out of the water in the form of a half-mile wide typhoon. Rouger made his way through the ocean as a giant tornado made of water, and it was now very clear to those on the beach who had doubted him that he was a force to be reckoned with.

Rouger moved through the ocean with ferocity as he headed toward the first battleship. He slammed the giant ship head on and sliced it in half with the sheer force of the attack. The ship quickly began to sink. The next two battleships turned their cannons away from the beach and took aim at the giant spinning wall of water coming at them. Of course, the cannon fire had no effect on Rouger for the projectiles were stopped instantly by the giant mass of water. Rouger then dipped the typhoon back into the water and once again rose out of the water, but this time he was in the form of a 100-foot high tidal wave. Rouger slammed the wave onto the deck of the next battle ship, cracking it into two pieces.

After destroying the third ship, Rouger focused even harder on his magic and formed a 200-foot tall, half-mile wide wall of water that swallowed the fourth ship whole as its wave crashed over the vessel. The ship simply did not resurface. It was as if it had been eaten by the giant wave. Rouger rose up once again as a giant typhoon of water. He continued to move down the line of battleships; and within a couple hours, Rouger had managed to single-handedly destroy the entire M.V.F. fleet of ships in the ocean. Thousands of lives had been lost at the hand of one man who General Hezekai believed to be old, feeble and weak. There was now a large underwater graveyard that would serve as a monument to the Harpatians in the future.

Rouger's attack on the battleships had given the Nowries a sizeable advantage on the beaches. Jester and Goron were hard at battle against the RXF-10 jet mechs in the air. One of the jet mechs had issued a three-pronged missile strike on Goron and his dragon. The blast blew both the mighty Goron and his dragon into oblivion. After being hit by three very powerful missiles, Goron fell from his dragon and plummeted about 1,000 feet down to the ground where death was waiting for him. Jester had been unable to help his best friend Goron, and now Goron was dead. Jester was infuriated. He put on a burst of speed with his dragon and caught up with the jet mech that had killed Goron. Jester leapt onto the jet's hull, ripped his claws into the cockpit, tore the pilot from his seat, and threw him out of the jet to his death. After killing the pilot, Jester jumped off the jet mech and back onto his dragon that was flying by his side. Jester had his dragon, Ford, return him to the battlefield where he would seek vengeance for his friend's death.

King Roiden was engaged in battle with several RS-777 mechs. The Tokechi Elite were engaged in battle with thousands of mechs on the beaches and in the forests. The warrior Cassion was hard at work destroying the RX-99 Tank mechs on the beach. It took the warrior only a couple of hours to destroy all of the tanks. Cassion used powerful combinations of lightning, fire, and ice magic on the tanks. He experienced a case of déjà vu as he took out the mechs. The tanks never stood a chance against him. Roiden was engaged in a sword fighting contest with two of the RS-777 mechs. The newly upgraded mechs had been outfitted with large mech swords. The mech swords were six feet long by two feet wide. The RS-777s had been programmed with extensive sword combat training, and were now quite a challenge to even the most skilled swordsman in the lands.

Roiden was impressed with the human's technology. He continued to fight and was surprised when one of the mechs had managed to parry one of his attacks and knock his sword from his hands. Roiden was then kicked in the back from behind by the other RS-777. He was on the ground in a dazed state from the kick he had just absorbed. The mechs came in to issue the killing strike to the defenseless King of Nowah. Roiden was shocked as the two mechs froze in place just as they were raising their swords and about to reign down their final blows on him. He seized the opportunity and shattered them into pieces with his sword.

"I am back and here to serve, King Roiden. These humans are nothing compared to the Nowrie Elite I encountered in the Ancient Wars of Segregation," said the skinny old bearded Elf.

"I agree, brother. Let us remind them of whom they have come to fight," replied Rouger as blood dripped from his mouth.

Rouger and Roiden moved through the battlefield as one and killed many of the M.V.F. as they did. The warrior Cassion went to aid the elite guard against the RS-777 battalions on the beaches of Nowah which numbered in the thousands, and he fought hard as the battle raged on throughout the night. After defeating several hundred RS-777 mechs, Cassion went back to the Castle Nowah to get a few hours of sleep. The following day, Roiden met up with Cassion and informed him they were keeping the humans at bay.

"Santei is being pounded by *Lancer I* in Bracelia. There has been word that Colonel Jake Baker is present in the Blue Forest of Bracelia. Santei is in trouble. Colonel Baker has been pounding the Blue Forest throughout the night with his Capital Ship, and he is believed to be on foot within the forest as we speak. Cassion, I feel that you are needed in Bracelia," said the King of Nowah.

"I will go at once, and I will stop Colonel Baker once and for all. May the Life Source protect us all," replied the warrior Cassion as he made his way to the courtyard still under protection by the spell the meld had cast.

Cassion mounted the dragon Nieko and made his way to Bracelia arriving a few hours later. Once there, he established telekinetic contact with Leinad who was busy fighting outside the Castle Dakineah. Leinad had told Cassion he would soon release *the Equalizer*s against *Lancer I* and *Lancer II*. Cassion knew he had to help the Bracelians hold off the humans for only a little while longer. He located Santei through the Life Source and saw that he was heavily engaged in battle with the M.V.F.

Cassion dismounted Nieko and told him to go hide in the Blue Forest. Nieko wanted to stay and fight, but he obeyed his master. After locating Santei, Cassion made his way through the Blue Forest. There were hundreds, or perhaps even thousands of RS-777 mechs in the forest. Cassion noticed many tank mechs as well, and the air battle raged on in the skies above as the dragon legion was hard at work fighting off the RXF-10 jet mechs. Cannon fire erupted on the ground all around him as *Lancer I* was firing at the forest floor with extremely hostile intentions.

Cassion was amazed by the humans' barbaric nature as he continued to make his way through the forest. He killed and destroyed all the mechs that attacked him along the way. The warrior used his now level ten fire magic to incinerate the mechs that opposed him. Cassion had leveled up from a level nine warrior to a level ten in the months since the humans had first arrived. Two of the RS-777 mechs managed to get a couple of shots off at Cassion, but the Gatlin Gun fire simply ricocheted off of his armor. One of the bullets even bounced off of his headpiece.

Cassion grasped the two mechs firing at him with his telekinesis and slammed them into the ground. The warrior then approached the main battlefield within the Blue Forest. Upon reaching the main battle, Cassion noticed Santei was engaged in hand to hand combat with a bright silver RS-777 mech. The mech was equipped with an enormous sword. Cassion made his way to Santei; and he sliced, punched, froze, and crushed all that got in his way.

"I will kill you now," said Santei to his attacker in the distinctively shiny silver RS-777 mech.

Santei unleashed a powerful blast of lightning into the mech. The mech absorbed most of the blast, but not all. Small showers of sparks began to emit from its left shoulder joint. The mech countered as it slashed downward at Santei with its sword. The attack hit Santei's chest plate and was followed by a barrage of heavy machine gun fire. Some of the bullets actually pierced Santei's blue armor and entered into his body. He was knocked down by the assault, but he got back to his feet very quickly and made one last desperate move. Santei extended his right hand and clenched his fist. He then motioned to the right, and the Gatlin Gun tore away from the mech's shoulder.

As Cassion got closer to the fight, he knew the mech fighting against Santei was none other than Colonel Jake Baker himself for he could feel the Colonel's presence within the Life Source. Colonel Baker withdrew his mech sword from its sheath on his back and began to slash and hack at the injured King of Bracelia. Santei was able to block much of the Colonel's attack with his own sword while using his magic to enhance his own strength. Cassion struggled to fight through the haze of mechs on the battlefield. He could have teleported, but he did not have a wide enough opening to reappear in. Cassion did not want to teleport into a mech sword, so he made his way to Santei on foot.

King Leinad Seven had fought through the night and was getting tired. He had sensed both Santei and Gressit were in trouble, and it was at that moment he ordered the release of *the Equalizers*. At some point during the middle of the night, Dr. Styles had managed to get the Life Source to enable her to teleport to the Mountains of Harpinia. Once she arrived there, she sought out the Council of the Elders immediately. She told the Elders Leinad had sent her to aid in the air battle. The Elders did not bother to consult with Leinad on this matter, for they did not want to insult Kelly's integrity.

After convincing Elder Rom she was there at the order of the King, the Elders gave her a room to sleep in for the night. The next day, the Elders escorted Kelly to *the equalizer* that was marked as "The King's Sword." After Leinad had ordered the release of *the Equalizer*s, the Elders, along with the several hundred Bracelian, Elven, and Nowrie pilots they had trained, entered their ships and prepared for battle. The pilots had been trained well over the last few months and were ready for battle. After running the preflight checklist, the fleet of Equalizers left the Mountains of Harpinia and headed toward their various targets.

***

General Hezekai was growing impatient as he continued to pilot *Lancer III*. He wanted desperately to be in the fight on the ground, and he would soon have his chance. Hezekai continued the bombing and shelling raid on Dakineah, but he was suddenly distracted when his radar picked up several hundred unidentified bogies. Hezekai was shocked upon seeing the foreign aircraft. Before he could even react, *Lancer III* was rocked by an energy missile and bomb attack. The Super Capital Ship took on some damage, but for the most part the shields held. An intense air battle had just begun in the skies of Dakineah. The dragon legion backed off from *Lancer III* and allowed *the Equalizer*s to go to work.

Lancer I was swarmed by 100 Equalizers an hour later. The Harpatian space vessels began pounding *Lancer I* with heavy laser fire and energy missile attacks. It took on heavy damage from the attacks, for its shields were not as strong as *Lancer III*'s. *Lancer I* focused all its munitions on *the Equalizer*s; and many of the ships did fall, but not all. With *Lancer I* distracted, Cassion now had a clear path to Santei. Cassion teleported over to Santei, but he was too late. The warrior had arrived just as Santei was being impaled by Colonel Jake Baker.

The warrior Cassion let out a very intimidating war cry as he lifted his katana from his side and willed it to about five feet in length. The warrior's blade glowed bright blue as it slashed down at the mech sword that had impaled Santei. The mech sword broke in half upon impact. Cassion followed up the attack with a thrusting straight kick that knocked Baker's mech a few feet back. He then grasped the mech in a telekinetic hold, but he was interrupted when he noticed three miniature rockets coming his way. The warrior teleported out of the way just in time. Cassion reappeared behind Colonel Baker's mech only to notice the three rockets that he had just dodged had hit and killed King Santei of Bracelia.

Cassion's heart began to race as a raging sense of hatred for the Colonel overwhelmed him. He took his katana and slashed the right leg of the mech clean off. The warrior then grasped Baker and his mech in a crushing telekinetic hold and slammed him on the ground; and with an extension of his arm, the warrior threw the Colonel's mech through one of the nearby trees in the Blue Forest. The Colonel was no match for the warrior Cassion. As he approached the downed mech and grew closer, Baker saw his sword transform into a smaller three-foot serrated short sword. Cassion walked up to Baker, who was trapped within the downed mech and thrust his sword into the mech's chest cavity, thus impaling Colonel Baker.

The warrior withdrew his sword from the mech in a twisting motion. Cassion then ripped the armor from the mech and Baker crawled out onto the ground. To the warrior's surprise, Baker got to his feet very quickly and punched him in the head. The blow had felt much harder than any human should have been able to issue. Cassion fell back a few feet and was a bit dazed. The warrior looked at Colonel Jake Baker and said "You will die for what you have done today."

"You will soon bleed out and become food for the Dellions," said Cassion in a tone of hatred.

"Not likely as I have been given implants. And I am sure the nanotechnology within me is working hard to heal my wounds as we speak," replied Baker in a mocking tone.

Colonel Baker then rushed Cassion and grabbed him by the throat. The warrior felt a strong crushing sensation in his throat. Cassion quickly spun and brought his sword up and over as he severed Baker's wrist from his arm. Sparks emitted from the man's wrist, and Baker let out a pathetic cry.

"Is this how you have planned to kill me? Do you think your technology can kill me, a few weak implants? Your mechs can't stop me; nothing you humans possess can stop me," said Cassion as he kicked the Colonel to the ground.

The Colonel was now screaming in pain as Cassion took him by the throat, lifted him into the air, and again impaled him. Blood sprayed violently as Cassion threw Baker to the ground. The Colonel began to cough as he choked on a pool of his own blood. The warrior looked at him and said "I am done with you. May you bleed out and die like the filth you are."

The warrior turned his back and began to walk away in a show of total disrespect. The Colonel reached for his communications device with his one good hand, and ordered all available RS-777 mechs to form a shield around him, and they did so in record time. Two of the mechs that came were medical mechs; and although they managed to slow the blood loss the Colonel was experiencing, they could not stop it entirely. The Colonel was flown to the nearest jet mech and taken to *Lancer II* where he arrived safely. After cauterizing the Colonel's wounds, the doctors began to administer a blood transfusion. The Colonel then slipped into a coma. The Doctors did not think he was going to make it; in fact, they gave him a five percent chance of living. Jake Baker would probably be dead soon.

The warrior Cassion continued to fight in the battle for Bracelia. As he made his way through the battlefield, he noticed *Lancer I* was being defeated as medium-sized explosions were going off all around the ship's hull. *The Equalizer*s were doing their job. With *Lancer I* in a damaged state, the Bracelians quickly gained the advantage on the battlefield.

Leinad had been in constant telepathic communication with Elder Rom since *the equalizer* attacks on the humans had begun. He had been stunned when he found out that Dr. Styles had somehow made her way to the Mountains of Harpinia; and he wondered how she had been able to convince the Life Source to help her for there was no doubt in his mind that it had teleported her to the Elders' location.

After learning that Kelly was inside his personal ship, "The King's Sword," Leinad ordered *the Equalizer*s to fall back to the Mountains of Harpinia which had initially been part of the plan anyway. *Lancer I* had been heavily damaged and was about to fall at any moment, and *Lancer III* had no doubt heard about it for it had broken from its attack on Dakineah to pursue the fleeing ships headed back to their base in the mountains. *Lancer III* followed the ships and fired upon them as it did. *The Equalizer*s deployed their countermeasures and remained unharmed by the missile attacks the Super Capital Ship sent at them.

Their high speed maneuvering was far superior to *Lancer III*'s attacks. Hezekai was shocked the Harpatians had such technology. After a couple hours of flight, the ships reached the Mountains of Harpinia. King Leinad Seven was in constant telepathic contact with the Council of the Elders, as well as the warrior Cassion, and King Roiden. Leinad was very upset that his good friend Santei had been killed. He had been in contact with everyone except Gressit which told him that his brother was either dead or unconscious. He informed all his commanders the EMP attack would commence shortly, and everyone should be prepared for the final attack on the humans.

Leinad knew he would have to go to the Mountains of Harpinia immediately to defend them against the Super Capital Ship. *Lancer III* was in hot pursuit of *the Equalizer*s, and someone was going to have to take that Capital Ship down. Leinad summoned Cassion, Chew, Dolan, Roiden, and Rouger to the Mountains of Harpinia. Without the help of Gressit, the group would become known as the Six Meld. Leinad felt excited today, for today was the day he would be able to use his melding magic and, hopefully, end the war. He was ready to die for his people. The King felt that the battle for Harpatia would soon be decided.

King Roiden left Jester, the Nowrie leader of the Tokechi Elite, in charge of the battle for Nowah. Roiden then mounted his dragon and began his journey to Harpinia. He would have to get within a few hours range of the mountains before he teleported there, for his teleportation magic was not the best. Cassion was the first to arrive at the Mountains of Harpinia, and he took a seat on the peak of the mountain which stood 20,000 feet high. The air was very cold and thin up there, but the warrior could breathe just fine. Before they left for the mountains, Masters Chew and Dolan appointed a few high level Magic Arts teachers to command the warriors of the School for Combat and Magic Arts in Dakineah. Their instructions were very clear: kill as many as you can, and do not let Dakineah fall.

Rouger wasted no time as he made his way to the Mountains of Harpinia melding location. He was able to teleport the several thousand miles from Nowah to Harpinia, a skill requiring level ten abilities in the telekinetic arts. Rouger was indeed a most valuable asset to the Kingdom of Harpatia. Only a few men on the planet of Harpatia could perform such awesome feats of magic, and those men were all about to convene in the same place to meld their magic into something so powerful, so prolific, that it would not soon be forgotten.

It took *Lancer III* a couple of hours to arrive at the Mountains of Harpinia. The ship began firing erratically at *the Equalizer*s entering the mountain though a large hole near the peak, but the laser fire could not affect that region for the meld had cast a strong spell of protection atop the mountain's peak. The Super Capital Ship then targeted a bright blue equalizer that was marked as "The King's Sword." That was the ship that Kelly was in. *Lancer III* unloaded a barrage of laser and cannon fire into the ship, and "The King's Sword" was rocked but not damaged too badly. Kelly kept the ship moving forward. Elder Rom then initiated a corkscrew flying pattern in an effort to dodge the heavy cannon fire that was coming straight at them. A buzzer then began to hiss loudly within the cockpit of "The King's Sword". That was the missile lock warning. Kelly immediately deployed most of the flechette they had left out of the hatch. The flechette had done its job, for they were still alive; but upon impact with the flechette, the ship did take damage, heavy damage.

The rear engine compartment of "The King's Sword" took a direct hit. The engine room had taken on a lot of damage, and the ship was going down. Loud ringing sounds erupted throughout the ship's cockpit. Through the expertise and flying skills of Elders Traf and Rom, "The King's Sword" was able to make a smooth landing at the base of the mountains; but they were still being fired upon. Kelly, Rom, and Traf found themselves surrounded by a group of five RS-777 mechs upon exiting their ship. Elders Revy and Tone, who had been watching from a heavy cannon emplacement about halfway up the mountains, began firing at the RS-777 mechs that had surrounded their friends.

Revy ordered a large group of Elite Guardsmen to go fight the M.V.F. fleets forming at the base of the mountains in the large open fields. Elder Revy made his way to the base of the mountains in an effort to aid his friends. He had used his telekinetic magic to smooth out the landing of "The King's Sword" upon its descent; and little did Rom and Traf know that if it was not for Revy's magic, they would have been dead. Revy teleported to the crash site where Kelly, Traf, and Rom were being attacked by the RS-777 mechs; and upon arriving to help, he noticed a bright purple glow coming from the hip side of Dr. Kelly Styles. The purple short sword that Leinad had gifted her during the games was glowing with intensity.

"Now might be a good time to unsheathe your sword, Kelly," said Elder Rom.

"I think you are right," replied Dr. Styles as she unsheathed her majestic purple sword.

An RS-777 mech came in to attack Kelly just as she withdrew her sword from its sheath. The purple sword raised itself up and blocked a sword attack from the mech with ease. The mech sword that had attacked Kelly crumbled into pieces and fell to the ground upon impact with Kelly's ancient sword. Kelly stepped toward the mech, and as she did her sword continued to glow. The RS-777 mech took aim at her, and then suddenly turned to stone. The ancient sword of Maryanne had the power of 20 wizards or more. No one was quite sure of all the sword's abilities, but they were sure the Sword of Maryanne would keep its wielder safe.

In the next instant, Kelly and the Elders were attacked by rocket fire. The missiles reached within 50 feet of their location and detonated against a giant purple shield. The sword of Maryanne was doing what it did best, protecting its owner. Kelly was indeed in possession of a most valuable weapon. The sword of Maryanne has been said to have been cast from the same materials as the warrior Cassion's magical blade. There were very few enchanted blades in the land of Harpatia, and Kelly did not realize how lucky she truly was to have the purple sword. She continued to make her way up the mountainside with the Elders as bullets and missiles alike all seemed to bounce off the invisible shield cast by her sword. A couple RS-777 mechs then flew up and landed 20 feet away from Kelly. She thought the mechs were much closer as she spun and slashed her sword into the thin air behind her, and was surprised when she saw the two mechs that were quite far away from her slice directly in half. Leinad had promised her the purple sword would keep her safe, and so far his promise had been kept.

Kelly continued to traverse the mountain. Most of the mech operators began to back away from Kelly and the Elders for they had seen what her magical blade had done to their comrades, and they did not wish to fall victim to the same fate. *Lancer III* was busy pounding the mountains with heavy ordnance until its pilot, General Ram Hezekai, was distracted by a very large crimson dragon that flew right past his viewport. Hezekai noted the man on the back of the large dragon was King Leinad Seven. Leinad had used a level ten telekinetic spell in conjunction with the magic of his dragon Monte that had allowed the two to teleport from Dakineah to the Mountains of Harpinia. Rouger was close behind. The warrior Cassion was waiting atop the peak of the mountains in a crossed legged position and in deep meditation. The rest of the dragon legion arrived shortly thereafter and began to engage in battle with *Lancer III*. *The Equalizer*s that had been trapped outside the mountain were now able to return safely to their docking bays.

The dragon legion of Harpatia blasted the super Capital Ship with fire and ice breath alike, and the Capital Ship answered in kind with heavy turret fire. Many dragons began to fall from the sky as they were quickly overwhelmed by the sheer quantity of laser, bullet, and missile fire coming at them.

"We will kill them all today," said Hezekai to Captain Hunter as he shot down members of the dragon legion.

"Yes, Sir," replied Hunter.

Hezekai showed no mercy as he continued to unleash the wrath of his Capital Ship. Leinad flew up in the air and had Monte drop him off atop *Lancer III*'s hull. He thrust his dual bladed gem encrusted staff into the ship's hull and began running along the roof. The staff was causing some damage to the shields of *Lancer III*. The ship was firing at Leinad, but for some reason everything the gunners were sending at the King was missing. It was as if he could not be hit. Leinad was one with the Life Source today, and the Life Source was indeed protecting him through the meld. The meld of Rouger, Roiden, Cassion, Chew, and Dolan was now complete. The men were all sitting in a row atop the mountain and focusing deeply on their King.

General Hezekai knew that now was the time to fight, and he was eager to kill Leinad. He passed over the control of *Lancer III* to Captain Hunter and told him to provide support fire.

"I am going to kill a King today. Tell everyone not to interfere. Leinad Seven will die by my hand alone. You are free to do whatever you see fit if I fall," said Hezekai as he left the cockpit and made his way to his prototype RS-777 mech.

The General's mech had been forged by the hardest metals on Earth. It stood ten feet high with a color of bright gold and blue accents. The face plate was that of a lion. The mech was equipped with a large caliber machine gun, several mini rocket launchers, a large mech sword, and a mech hand gun hidden within the leg. Hezekai punched in a code on the side of the wall after he entered his mech. A large porthole opened in the rear of the docking bay that he was in. Hezekai took in a deep breath and engaged his jet packs. The General flew out into the open air of Harpatia.

At this point, thousands of mechs were on the ground as well as in the air. The battle for Harpatia raged on. The Meld continued to focus on Leinad as he saw a large golden mech flying straight for him. As Hezekai approached Leinad, he unleashed a barrage of machine gun fire at him. Most of the bullets bounced off the King's Jezelite armor, and the rest missed completely. Leinad pointed his staff at Hezekai and sent a stream of lightning into his mech as the General flew past him. Leinad then jumped off of the Capital Ship and fell 50 feet onto Monte's back.

He was now in hot pursuit of the General. The lightning attack had not phased Hezekai's mech at all. Monte flew toward Hezekai and was stunned by a massive amount of laser fire. Monte's left flank had been badly scored by a massive laser turret blast. Captain Hunter had gone against Hezekai's orders when he targeted the beast, but he knew his General needed his help.

Monte was badly injured and was headed to the ground. Leinad stayed on Monte's back until he was 100 feet from the ground, at which point he teleported himself to the ground and quickly used his telekinesis to cushion Monte's fall. The King grasped the 100 foot long dragon in a gentle telekinetic hold and slowed his fall almost to a halt. The dragon hit the ground hard and was bleeding badly, but Leinad had saved his life with his split second decision to cushion his fall. Dragon's blood was a rare site to see, and Leinad did not like it at all.

Monte was half conscious as Hezekai came in for the kill, flying toward the wounded dragon at full speed. Leinad teleported in front of Hezekai just as the General was swinging his mech sword toward Monte's throat, and the King's staff caught the blow. The sword was now stuck in the staff. Leinad then kicked Hezekai's mech as he pulled his staff free from the mech sword. Hezekai landed on the ground ten feet away from where Leinad had landed. Hezekai then withdrew his mech sized revolver from its hidden leg holster and fired six shots at Leinad. One of the jet mech caliber bullets grazed Leinad's ribcage slightly wounding him.

King Leinad Seven then grasped Hezekai's mech in a telekinetic hold; and with an extension of his arm, he slammed Hezekai into the mountainside. Hezekai rushed Leinad and said, "This time I will kill you, and then I will take your precious Life Source energy back to Earth and save my people. Your people will be my slaves."

"I will never let that happen," replied Leinad as he braced for impact.

Hezekai issued a three pronged attack with his mech sword as he slashed at the King. Leinad pivoted in a defensive 360° turn and spun his staff around in circles, blocking the General's attacks. The King of Harpatia then brought his staff down across the General's right knee joint. The blow landed and ignited sparks within the prototype's knee. Leinad followed up his attack with a kick to the mech's chest. After kicking it, Leinad sent a magic aided punch into the mech's face and sent it flying back ten feet. The meld was doing its job, and Leinad was growing stronger. Hezekai got back to his feet quickly and began firing at Leinad with both his hip side revolver and his large shoulder mounted turret. Hundreds of rounds ricocheted off of Leinad's armor, but the impact from the turret fire dazed him.

Leinad then teleported behind Hezekai and pointed his staff at him. He picked Hezekai up in a tornado of wind magic and sent him spiraling into the mountainside once again. The mech hit the bluestone hard and fell to the ground. Ram Hezekai felt like he had just been hit by a train, but he stood right back up. This time he engaged his rocket thrusters to full blast and began flying circles around Leinad, shooting at him as he did. Hezekai continued to fly around the King and poured turret fire at him from his shoulder mounted machine gun. Leinad extended his awareness to the large shoulder mounted turret and grasped it in a telekinetic hold. He clenched his fist and tore the gun off from the shoulder of Hezekai's mech.

Leinad sent the turret to the ground in a crushed heap of metal. Hezekai was getting frustrated as he flew up to Leinad and threw a punch at him. Leinad stuck his staff into the ground in front of him, and the general's strike impacted the staff, but did not move it. Leinad stepped back and unsheathed his golden broadsword from his back. General Hezekai continued to rush King Leinad Seven as he withdrew his mech sword and swung it down hard toward Leinad's chest. Leinad quickly teleported out of the way and reappeared directly behind General Hezekai and sliced the right leg clean off his mech. In the next instant, Hezekai spun and slashed his sword so hard against Leinad's chest plate that it actually cracked the Jezelite armor.

Hezekai engaged his jet packs in order to stabilize his mech, and then hit Leinad in the face. The blow knocked the great King of Harpatia a few feet back. Leinad teleported once again and appeared on the right flank of the General. Leinad swung his sword to decapitate the mech, but Hezekai blocked the attack with his own sword. Hezekai grabbed Leinad with his left arm, clutching his throat. He then pointed his right arm at Leinad's stomach and deployed the hidden lance from the mech's arm. The lance fired out of the mech's arm with tremendous force as it impaled Leinad through the stomach. Hezekai then threw the King to the ground and ran a quick diagnostic to assess his mech's damage.

The four foot long lance had gone through the torso of the King. The King let out a loud cry as he took hold of the lance. His hands started to glow bright red as he melted the tip off the lance in a strong usage of his fire magic. Leinad then melted the tip off of the back as well. Leinad pushed the lance out of his body as he once again let out a cry of extreme pain. He was able to telekinetically pull the spear from his body, but he was badly injured and bleeding.

Leinad touched the blade of his golden broadsword, and it instantly began to glow red hot. He touched the blade to the rear opening of the wound and the wound sealed itself shut. He let out a pained yelp. The King then touched his blade to the entrance of the wound, and the opening sealed itself shut as well. Leinad had successfully cauterized his wound; and though he was still bleeding a little, he would not bleed to death.

After healing himself in a matter of seconds, Leinad walked up to General Hezekai whose mech was now lying on the ground, missing a leg, and emitting a shower of sparks from its severed joint. Leinad raised his sword up in a high stance and stared at the General. Hezekai made one last desperate attack as he swung his sword straight out at Leinad. Leinad used his combat arts magic in association with the power of the meld and spun on the attack with lightning fast quickness. Leinad ripped the mech sword from Hezekai's grasp in the middle of his spin and brought the General's own sword down upon the mech's arm, thus slicing the right arm of the mech off completely.

Leinad back flipped over Hezekai's mech and impaled the General as he thrust his sword in a reverse strike that pierced through both the mech and its operator. The King then grasped the General's beaten prototype mech in a strong telekinetic hold and clenched his fist. The mech began to fold in, and once again, all of the bones in Hezekai's body began to break. Hezekai was now crippled and bleeding badly. The metal infusions he had received back on Earth were not as strong as he thought they would be. He was beaten. General Hezekai issued one last command to Captain Hunter from inside his mech. Leinad then saw 50 jet mechs drop from the sky. The RXF-10 jet mechs began to pour heavy cannon fire toward Leinad. Some of the bullets even hit Hezekai's mech.

Leinad managed to evade the cannon fire as he quickly teleported out of the way of the ordnance. The mechs began to fly low to the ground as they continued in toward the General. A large caliber jet mech round grazed Leinad's right leg causing a small cut. Had that shot been a couple inches more to the right, it would not have been deflected by the Jezelite armor; and the King would have surely lost his leg. Leinad quickly cauterized the wound on his leg just as he had done earlier when he had sealed up his impaled torso. He then teleported out of the way; and when he reappeared, he noticed his entire body was suddenly glowing bright blue. The magic of the meld was starting to take effect on him. The King felt invigorated as his body was embraced by the amplified Life Source energy.

The jets continued to press forward. In the next instant, Leinad received a series of telepathic pleas. Jester was urging him to release the EMP devices. Leinad informed him the time was coming very soon and asked him to make sure everyone was ready. He then noticed a large round metal anchor being lowered from one of the jet mechs. The anchor was held by a chain. The large round sphere was a magnet, and it lifted Hezekai's mech from the ground and attached itself to him. The jet reeled in Hezekai's mech with its anchor; and just like that, the General was gone. The jet mech took Hezekai to *Lancer III* and loaded him into an escape pod within the super Capital Ship. Two doctors accompanied the General. The crew punched in the coordinates for *Lancer II*, which was in orbit, and the pod jettisoned out into space. The doctors began to cut the mech from Hezekai's body with torches, and what was revealed behind the mech was shocking, even to the wartime doctors.

Hezekai's face was badly disfigured and his body was broken and contorted. The doctors worked hard to stabilize him, but they did not know if Hezekai would live or die. Once their pod reached *Lancer II* and was pulled in to a docking bay, the doctors got Hezekai onto a medical cart and wheeled him to the operating room in the medical bay. They then induced General Ram Hezekai into a coma. Hezekai was now lying beside Colonel Jake Baker who was also in a medically induced coma. Had the men been awake, they would have surely experienced a strong sense of déjà vu.

Back at the battlefield at the Mountains of Harpinia, Leinad teleported up to the mountainside where Dr. Styles was climbing with the Elders and helped the group get safely inside the mountain. Leinad teleported down to the base of the mountain after helping his friends get to safety. The King of Harpatia looked up to *Lancer III* and used his magic to amplify his voice so everyone in the area would be able to hear him and said, "Is this all you have for me? Is this all?"

Captain Hunter heard the King's taunt loud and clear from within the cockpit of *Lancer III*. He stared at Leinad through his heads up display and marveled at the bright blue glow that surrounded the Elven King of Harpatia. Captain Hunter unleashed hundreds of missiles toward King Leinad and the surrounding mountains as well as Leinad braced for impact. The missiles impacted the mountain and created a large rockslide. King Leinad continued to glow bright blue as he waived the missiles directed at him out of the way with his telekinesis. He closed his eyes and located one of the EMP devices and used his telekinesis to trigger the sliding detonator within, thus initiating a domino effect throughout the lands as hundreds of thousands of EMPs rocketed out of the ground and up to their random altitudes.

It only took a few minutes for the several hundred thousand EMPs to fully deploy throughout the lands. Back in Bracelia, the crew of *Lancer I* saw thousands of these small spherical devices floating in the air all around them. The crew began firing at the devices, but it was too late. The devices detonated in the next instant and emitted a devastating electromagnetic pulse throughout Bracelia, Dakineah, Nowah, the Outlands, Harpinia, and all the other territories of Harpatia. *Lancer I* powered down upon the detonation of the EMP devices and began to fall from the sky. Lt. Colonel Kanak began to panic as his ship fell toward the ground. He tried to initiate his thrusters, but none of his systems would respond.

Lancer I plummeted to the ground from several thousand feet up and exploded violently upon impact killing all of the men on board. The Bracelians along with the Harpatian Elite Guard swept the battlefields after *Lancer I* fell, but *Lancer I* was not the only thing that fell from the sky. All the jet mechs fell from the skies to their deaths as well following the EMP attack. The RS-777 mechs stood frozen and inoperable on the ground. Tens of thousands of mech operators were now helplessly trapped in their powerless mechs. None of the wizards were hurt from the pulse. Some of the warriors experienced mild headaches from the pulse, but that was the extent of it.

There were now hundreds of thousands of inoperable mechs throughout the lands of Harpatia. The jet mechs had all crashed to the ground, the tank mechs were frozen and inoperable, and the RS-777 mechs were now useless. The Harpatians in the Blue Forest would make quick work of the humans as they swept through the battlefields. The Nowries would take no prisoners as they moved to clean up their lands. The M.V.F. had been defeated. The Nowries frothed at the mouth when they saw the mechs fall from the sky. Jester ordered the Tokechi to attack all of the downed mechs. The operators were stuck in their mechs and were about to meet a horrible fate.

Back in Harpinia, *Lancer III* had powered off completely for a few seconds; but it did retain a few thrusters as it fell to the ground. The Super Capital Ship hit the ground hard, and explosions went off at various points around the enormous ship which was now grounded. King Leinad Seven continued to glow bright blue as he watched the situation unfold. The Elite Guard and the dragon legions began cleaning up the battlefield until they noticed a massive amount of dust and debris flying up from under *Lancer III*. The ship had been outfitted with emergency generators, and the thrusters engaged. *Lancer III* began to rise back up into the air. This was not good.

Lancer III began pouring cannon fire at the Elite Guard. Captain Hunter was furious as he began to shoot down and kill as many Harpatian warriors as possible. He had no idea that the Harpatians possessed such technology. He received word from *Lancer I*'s automated messaging system that the ship had been destroyed along with all of those who were onboard. Hunter knew his comrades were trapped in their mechs and probably being slaughtered. He knew he was the only hope for the men now, and he prepared to make his final move.

Lancer III hovered up to 2,000 feet in the air. Hunter let the ship hover in place as he ordered his artillery crew to send everything they had at the mountains. He depressed every weapons button that he could find and targeted Leinad with several missile locks. Hunter directed the majority of his Laser cannons and missiles at the bright blue glow on the ground, which was indeed King Leinad Seven. Leinad took a few hits from the laser cannons, but he was not hurt, for the meld magic was very strong. The King pushed forward as he extended his hands toward the super Capital Ship and sent a supercharged blast of lightning into *Lancer III*. The Captain's control board sparked as the ship became electrified by Leinad's attack. Captain Hunter depressed a red button on the control board of his firing console and a countdown began. When it reached zero, hundreds of missiles would begin flying toward King Leinad Seven.

Leinad zeroed in on Captain Hunter using his magic arts to enhance his sight. Leinad saw the Captain through the viewport of *Lancer III* and could hear him as well.

"We are about to unleash everything we have on this man, Lt. Ringo. I will assign the ship to you shortly after I launch the rest of our missiles at King Leinad Seven. Should anything happen to me, you will be in charge of the ship."

"Yes, Sir," replied the young 30-year-old man.

After zeroing in on Hunter, King Leinad plucked his dual bladed, gem encrusted staff from the ground. He superheated the staff, spun in a 360° turn, and launched the staff through the air. It flew through the air like a missile, glowing bright red as it did. The staff speared through the viewport of the ship and went into and through the chest of Captain Hunter knocking him from his pilot's seat. Hunter fell to the floor of *Lancer III* and stared at the large spear like object that had pierced his chest. He just smiled as he let out his last breath, for he was in complete awe of what had just happened.

The countdown had ended and the missiles were en route to their target. Twenty missiles hit the ground in front of Leinad. He was launched into the air spinning in a corkscrew pattern. A few pieces of shrapnel hit the King in the chest through his armor, but he continued to spiral through the air. There was now an enormous rockslide coming down at him at a very fast pace. Leinad began to glow in an even brighter blue as he spun through the air for the meld had intensified their focus on him when they saw the last missile launch out at him. He was somewhat dazed by being blasted high up into the air, but he had the presence of mind to save himself. It was as if time had slowed down to a crawl as he summoned a prolific combination of wind and Earth magic.

Leinad used his magic like a vacuum as he pulled the rockslide into him. The giant boulders and rocks from the rockslide were now swirling around him in a cyclone of wind magic. He pulled all of the rocks and shrapnel into his body; and when he was finished, Leinad stood 300 feet high as a huge rock creature. He had used the magic of the meld through the Life Source to create a type of super magic. The King should have been dead from the missile attack or crushed by the rockslide, but somehow he had managed to slow time down to almost a halt and use his deadly surroundings as an ally.

The rock creature had the facial features of Leinad with an enormously large frame that was made from the Bluestone of the Mountains of Harpinia. The Earth shook violently as King Leinad Seven walked toward *Lancer III* as a giant rock creature. He extended his right hand toward the ship and issued a devastating blast of lightning magic into the super Capital Ship. A series of explosions began to erupt from all around the ship. *Lancer III* was now badly damaged. Lt. Ringo ordered the artillery crew to fire everything they had left at the giant rock creature. Waves of laser fire began to slam into the rock creature as small portions of rock began to chip away from its body.

Lt. Ringo sent out a message to all the gunners on board. He told them to initiate the "Hail Mary" which simply meant to fire everything at the target and pray that it works. Thousands of missiles began to plow into the rock creature. The rock Leinad was knocked several feet back by the blasts, but he kept walking toward *Lancer III*. A small portion of the creature's leg had been blown off, but he just kept going. The giant rock creature Leinad then extended his hands and sent a huge, perhaps half-mile wide blast of fire magic into the super Capital Ship. The ship began to glow red hot as it continued to fire at Leinad. The wave of fire magic had taken out half of the ship's remaining thrusters. *Lancer III* was now struggling to hold its place in the air as it began weaving back and forth and tried to steady itself.

The rock creature then paused as the tens of thousands of boulders that comprised the creature began to disassemble and fly around Leinad in circles. The King now stood in the center of a giant rock tornado shield that *Lancer III*'s attacks could not penetrate. Leinad stood on the ground and was bleeding from some of his previous wounds, but he did not let the pain distract him. His blue glow intensified once again as he extended his palms downward and began to levitate into the air. The King rose up to the middle of the rocky whirlwind and hovered in place. In the next instant, Leinad extended both his arms toward *Lancer III*. Thousands of the boulders swirling around the King began to fly toward the super Capital Ship at ridiculous speeds. This would be King Leinad's final attack.

Leinad was using a super wind, Earth, and fire magic ability as the boulders he sent at *Lancer III* became superheated. The glowing red hot boulders exploded violently as they hit *Lancer III*'s hull. Within a matter of 30 seconds, all the boulders and rocks that had made up the body of the super rock creature made impact with *Lancer III*. The super Capital Ship exploded into thousands of pieces as the last series of superheated boulders hit the ship dead center. *Lancer III* fell to the ground in thousands of pieces of fiery twisted metal. The warriors of the King's Elite Guard began to cheer loudly for they knew the battle for Harpatia had just been won.

The Elite Guard ran through the lands of Harpatia to collect prisoners and eliminate any remaining hostiles, a process that would take several weeks to complete. King Leinad Seven collapsed to the ground and was bleeding heavily; but before any of the members of the meld had a chance to help their King, Leinad was picked up by Monte. Though badly injured, he found the strength to lift the King gently onto his back using his own telekinetic magic to anchor him. King Leinad Seven was heavily injured by the impaling he had endured earlier as well as by the many missile blasts he had absorbed during his manifestation of the rock creature.

Monte began to fly through the sky with the King on his back. The meld noticed Monte was flying with Leinad and quickly determined they were heading for the Ponds of Rejuvenation. Rouger knew the pair would never make it on their own, so he quickly directed the meld's focus to the dragon. A bright blue glow enveloped both Monte and Leinad. The dragon and his rider disappeared, leaving behind a blue vapor trail. Monte was shocked when he reappeared about a mile away from the Ponds of Rejuvenation. Leinad, who was in a half conscious state, had determined the meld must have teleported them to Bracelia, and he was very grateful for that.

Monte grew dizzy as he got closer to the ponds. Leinad could barely see anything when Monte finally passed out for the King was barely clutching to his own life. The two began to fall from the sky. Monte and Leinad crashed into the Ponds of Rejuvenation and began to sink until something grabbed them and quickly returned them to the surface. The Life Source had intervened and brought them back. The two then floated over to a shallow area of the pond. Monte lay half immersed and totally unconscious in the beautiful pond. Leinad rolled off the dragon's back and fell toward the water. Just as he was about to fall in, his staff harness caught onto one of Monte's scales leaving him neck deep in the water. The King then passed out.

In the hours after the fall of *Lancer III*, the majority of the M.V.F. forces were either killed or taken prisoner. The Nowries, however, took no prisoners. Most of the humans were trapped within their mechs and offered no fight at all upon being freed. Those who did make it back to *Lancer II* considered themselves lucky. *Lancer II* had sent a couple of transport ships to retrieve as many mechs and personnel as they could. The transport ships did not fire on the Harpatians; and as a result, they were allowed to gather their injured. The Captain of *Lancer II* quickly decided it was time to go home for as soon as they had finished recovering some of their men, the Captain engaged his light drives and began the journey back to Earth.

Leinad and Monte had become completely engulfed by a bright blue and purple glow as the Life Source energy of the Ponds of Rejuvenation began healing their wounds. Leinad regained his consciousness a couple hours later and swam to the shore where he sat half immersed in the pond. He looked down toward his torso and noticed the giant gash from the impalement was gone. The ponds were doing their job. Monte's large gash on his side was also now almost completely healed. Leinad then engaged in telepathic conversation with Monte for a while. The warrior Cassion, Rouger, Roiden, Chew, Dolan, the Council, and Dr. Kelly Styles arrived at the Ponds of Rejuvenation around sunset.

Kelly ran to Leinad and jumped into the water. Kelly embraced Leinad in a tight hug and said, "I thought you were dead."

"Oh, not so rough my dear. I am still very sore. You should have known I wouldn't die on you. I love you," said Leinad to Kelly.

"I love you, too."

Leinad looked to his men and said, "Thank you all for coming. Has anyone heard from Gressit?" Leinad asked.

"Not yet, my King. But we'll find him," replied the warrior Cassion.

"Kelly, Harpatia has needed a queen for a while. Are you up to the task?" asked Leinad.

"Are you asking me to marry you?"

"Yes I am, my love" replied Leinad as he took Kelly's hand on bended knee.

"I do, I do, I do," replied Kelly as tears began to stream down her beautiful cheeks.

The group remained at the ponds for a couple more hours. Once Leinad could walk again, they made their way to a nearby teleportation hub and returned to the Castle Dakineah. They had not encountered any hostiles as they made their way through the forest. The King was greeted by a row of thousands of Elite Guardsmen upon his return to Dakineah. The warriors formed a hall like column as they raised their swords to create a royal entrance for their King. Leinad dismissed the meld and told them to take rest for they would have much to discuss the following morning.

Leinad was a little groggy and quite sore when he awoke the next day. He looked at Kelly and said, "I will announce our engagement to the kingdom today."

"That makes me very happy, Leinad. But before we do, I think you should go to your royal meeting chambers. Cassion has been waiting for you there all morning," replied Kelly as she passed a small note to the King that had been slid under his door in the middle of the night.

King Leinad examined the note with an intense gaze. It had come from a Bracelian warrior and stated several warriors had witnessed Gressit being taken captive by the humans. Leinad now knew his brother had been captured and probably taken to Earth. He was devastated, but he did not lose hope. He simply told himself he would rescue his brother when the time was right. He felt confident Gressit would survive until he could save him.

Leinad made his way to the meeting chambers but was surprised when no one was there. He looked on the table and saw a message that told him Cassion was waiting in the courtyard. He walked down a flight of stairs and out the main door and marveled at what a beautiful sunny day it was as he made his way to the garden area of the courtyard. Cassion was sitting on a large stone with his sword resting on his knee when Leinad arrived.

"Good day, Leinad," said the warrior Cassion.

"Good day, my friend. They took Gressit."

"Yes, I am aware my King. I spoke to the Elders this morning and they are working on a new way to transport us to Earth as we speak. It may take a little time, but we'll rescue Gressit," replied Cassion.

"Indeed we will, my friend. I know the humans' journey back to Earth will take them well over a month. We will have a plan in place for rescuing my brother by then. In the meantime, Harpatia needs a new Queen, and Bracelia will need a new King. Cassion, kneel before me."

"Yes, my King," replied the warrior as he took a knee.

Leinad placed his sword upon the warrior's head and said, "I hereby dub thee Cassion, King of Bracelia. Now rise up as a King," Leinad said as he extended his hand to his lifelong friend.

"Thank you, Leinad," said the warrior as a single tear fell from his eye.

"Thank you for your loyalty to Harpatia. Making you a King is an honor and a privilege. My friend, something tells me the Life Source has many more adventures in store for us."

"I will be ready when you call for me," said Cassion.

"I know you will, my friend."

To be continued…

Made in the USA
Charleston, SC
15 February 2012